HAWK

A Castle Sin Novel

Book Two

A Dark Suspense Novel

By

Linzi Basset

HAWK - CASTLE SIN #2
Copyright © 2019 Linzi Basset
Edited by: Kristen Breanne
Proofreaders: Marie Vayer, Melanie Marnell, Kemberlee Snelling,
Charlotte Strickland
Published: Linzi Basset & Cover Design: Sweet 15 Designs
ISBN: 9781695547155

Contents

Linzi Basset

Author's Note

Dear Reader,

Castle Sin is a dark suspense series.

Castle Sin
Seven dungeons
Seven Masters
Seven times the kink.

An exclusive BDSM club offering memberships only to selected Dominants. Submissives and slaves were available for every taste.

Personally, trained by each of the Castle Masters.

In HAWK, book 2, we meet Hawk Sinclair, the powerful Training Master, and the woman he chose as his sub, Savannah Thorne.

9

A tale of love, lust and lies.

"Well, did the cat catch your tongue or am I supposed to hazard a guess?"

She craved his Mastery.
Caught in a web of deceit and lies, Savannah Thorne was the game piece in a demented criminal's game. Desperate to save that which was most precious to her, she was left no choice but to entrench herself in the training program at Castle Sin ... the willing prey in the claws of the powerful Training Master.

"Make no mistake, Savannah, no matter where we are, I'll always Dominate you, don't ever forget that."

He craved her body.
Hawk Sinclair wanted her from the day she set foot on the island, but when she blatantly broke one of Castle Sin's rules, he realized she couldn't be for him despite the fact it seemed a call for help. Yet, his nature as a caring Dom compelled him to give in to her unspoken desperation to escape the emotional demons that chased her.

Amid their throes of unbound lust and the struggle to keep everyone at Castle Sin safe from Savannah's past, Hawk became her safe place, and she became his home.

Now that the Hawk had caught his prey, could he convince her to stay?

Or would her dark secrets send him spreading his wings,

To soar high into the sky,

Lost to her forever?

Editor's Note:
Hawk tugs at your heartstrings and other ... ganglia
...
One moment, you're hot and bothered and hoping for her release—or your own—the next your ovaries want to burst as a completely new concept is thrown into the mix, and then you want to murder a sonofa-gun who would dare to treat another human being that way. This story will have you smiling and gritting your teeth, crying, and swooning and all in more ways than you're used to.
Soon, your heart, too, will be pumping chocolate at the words, "Ack! Ack! Up!"

I trust you will enjoy this story as much as I did in creating it.

Warm regards,
Linzi Basset

Chapter One

"Let me go, you big bully! This ishn't Castle Sin and you have no right to ... hic ... order me around on the Mainlan'."

Savannah Thorne struggled against the hard hand locked around her elbow. She looked up as the Goliath of a man suddenly stopped and she stumbled into his chest. Her attempt at an immediate retreat was stemmed as he yanked her closer. His nostrils flared, and for the first time since she'd arrived at Castle Sin on the private island— The Seven Keys in Key West—she feared this man.

Hawk Sinclair, aka Rothman as he was known as an actor, was one of the owners of the exclusive BDSM club and training facility for submissives. He never showed his emotions, much like the rest of his six cousins who were part owners in the club. To see him this furious shocked her ... to almost sobriety ... but not quite.

"I said to lemme go," she tried again but with a lot less vehemence and more wariness.

"For as long as you're a trainee at Castle Sin you remain my responsibility. You *will* follow our rules, sub ST, especially insofar as your own safety is concerned. Or is that what this is? An attempt to get kicked out of the program and off the island?"

"I have a name and sinche we're not on the island, ushe it!" she snapped—albeit ineffectively as her slurred speech doused her irritation. The hard glint in his eyes warned her it might not have been clever to throw caution to the wind.

"You're so fucking drunk; I doubt you even remember your own name. What the hell is the matter with you?"

Hawk had never been this close to losing his temper. It tampered with his restraint because he always had the utmost control over his emotions. Then he'd walked into the bar and saw the beautiful blonde woman completely sloshed. It brought back memories he'd locked away in the deepest compartment of his brain—ones that had been forbidden to ever surface. That she could reach that deep inside his mind, infuriated him.

"Shay it. I wanna hear you shay it ... jush once."

He pressed his face close to hers and sneered, "I don't accommodate drunks. We're leaving and—"

"Shavannah, my name ish ... hic ... Shavannah! Say it, damn you," she bleated and slammed her fists against his chest.

"Is there a problem, missy?" The lanky bartender approached with another drink.

Hawk's arms wrapped around her and held her against his chest in a strong protective cocoon. The Dom instinct was to protect and care for his sub—or trainee in her case. The power in his body and the rhythmic beat of his heart was the conduit that made Savannah lose the tenuous hold she had over her frayed emotions. The sobs started from deep within her soul as she burst into tears.

"She had too much to drink, which, if you were a responsible bartender, would've noticed long ago and refused to serve her more fucking booze."

"Looky here, Mister, who do you think ... hey! Let go!" the man cried, his eyes wide as Hawk fisted his shirt at the front of his chest and yanked him closer without letting go of the crying woman.

"I'm the man who's about to beat the shit out of you if you don't fetch this lady's purse." Hawk shoved him away with a disgusted snort. "Now, before I lose my temper," he snapped when the man stood like a statue, staring at him in fear.

"Relax, Mister, I'm going," he said and quickly went to grab Savannah's large shopper bag from the booth where she'd been sitting most of the day drinking.

"Has she eaten anything at all?" Hawk glared at the offending bartender who continued to loiter, barring his way.

"Not that I can remember. Hey, you can't just leave, what about the bill?"

Hawk had earned the nickname in college from one of his professors because, like his totem animal, the Hawk, he always observed before acting. He studied each situation thoroughly before making any rash decisions and he approached life with skilled precision. He was no fool and didn't hesitate to take the lead in situations. This time, he struggled to free himself from the mental block that rose as a protective barrier when he found Savannah as drunk as a skunk.

He turned on the bartender like his bird totem, swift, decisively, as he swept down onto his prey.

The barkeep retreated hastily.

"You run a cash per order only bar, shithead. I've been here numerous times myself, so don't insult my intelligence. I'm not going to tell you to get out of my way again."

He began to walk, grunting irritably when Savannah stumbled as he dragged her along, still crying pitifully. He picked her up and shouldered his way past the man like he was nothing more than an irritating barfly.

"I'm s-sorry. I didn't mean to—" Savannah hiccupped as he cut her short.

"I suggest you just shut the fuck up. My patience is hanging on a thin thread as it is." His cold gaze cut into her with razor sharp warning. "Don't test me, trainee. At this moment, all I want is silence. Say one more word and I'll dump you in the goddamned ocean." He snorted as his eyes trailed over her disheveled hair. "And I won't even blink if you drown in your drunken stupor." Hawk made no effort to hide the disgust from his voice.

It had been at his insistence that the employed submissives and trainees were limited to one drink at the members' dungeons per night and one glass of wine at dinner. His cousins had all agreed. They ran a tight ship; the training was grueling, and they didn't have the time or the patience to babysit drunk or tipsy women. In the eight years since they'd opened Castle Sin, this was the first time one of the women had become completely intoxicated. It didn't even matter that it wasn't on the island.

He jumped effortlessly into the speedboat waiting at the marina of the Margaritaville Key West Resort on Key West. Danton Hill—the senior of the training Doms at Castle Sin and the Security Director of the island—shook his head as he watched Hawk sit Savannah down in the backseat and strap her in.

"Let's go, Danton. I need to get back to my training session." He pushed a plastic bucket into Savannah's hands. "If you wanna barf, make sure you do it in there," he growled before he took a seat in the front next to Danton and blithely ignored her.

His jaw turned rigid as he listened to the sounds of vomiting before they were even halfway to The Seven Keys Island, owned by his cousin as well as his best friend, Stone Sinclair. Hawk and his five cousins combined, owned forty-five percent to Stone's fifty-five of Castle Sin, but Stone was the sole owner of the island. He was also the Master Dom and the ruler of all the dungeons in the castle, the seven training dungeons, and three member dungeons, aptly named, The King's Dungeon, The Dungeon of Sin, and The Royal Dungeon.

He refused to turn around and assist her. Her pitiful sobs penetrated and took him back ten years.

"Goddammit, Vee, again? What's your excuse this time?"

Hawk stared at his wife with growing anger. She had just come out of rehab two months ago. This time he'd believed her when she'd promised it was the last time. She claimed she'd realized she was destroying their lives, their happiness. He'd been over the moon. They'd been married for five years, and it had been anything but moonlight and roses. She'd hidden her drinking habits from him while they were dating. During the year Vee and Hawk had

19

lived together prior to the wedding, he'd missed it due to his rigorous work schedule, juggling to fulfill the contract with Marvel Studios. Eight years earlier, he and his cousins were drawn into acting in the blockbuster series, Space Riders on a whim. Also, he and Stone had started the company, Be Secure Enterprises, at that time.

When he'd returned from shooting a movie a year into their marriage, he'd come to a shocking realization. His wife was an alcoholic. He'd done his best to help her, to guide her, and be there for her through her first rehab stint. It had been a waste of time. She'd begun to drink two weeks after returning home. So, it continued every year; she gave in to his urgings and tried to stop.

"You doan unnershand, baby," she wailed in a drunken voice, rocking back and forth in their modern home in Beverly Hills. A home he'd paid millions for because it was the one she wanted … and he hated. He would've preferred to live in the hills of Santa Monica, but it was too far away from the hustle and bustle of stardom for her. Vee thrived on it and lived the life of a spoiled, rich man's wife.

"No, Vee, I don't, so why don't you explain it to me?" Hawk stood watching her, rooted to the spot in

the arch leading into the grand open room. He hated the stench of imbibing, especially on a woman. The fact that this was his wife, made it twice as hard to swallow.

"I'm shorry I dis-shappointed you. I tried, I did, babe! Pleashe believe me."

She looked at him with her big Bambi eyes but this time he was unmoved. He'd reached the end of his tether. He couldn't continue like this, constantly worrying, wondering when she was going to do something stupid in a drunken state, babysitting her when she was too drunk to help herself. Intimacy in their marriage had become a chore because if she wasn't drunk, she was lethargic. The past three months had been different. He'd begun to hope … until now.

This was it. He'd had enough.

"Itsh like a drug, Hawk!" She pleaded as she realized he hadn't moved, that he stared at her with an impassive expression. "I can't stop."

"No, Vee, you don't want to stop, that's the difference. Becoming a drug addict is a choice a person makes the first time they give in to it. You can stop but you refuse to admit how big your problem is. It's always one more with you. One more drink,

21

Hawk, just one more chance, Hawk. How many one mores are there going to be before you drink yourself to death?"

Her eyes widened as she shook her head. "I'll never go that far. I know when to sht ... hic ... shtop."

"No, you don't. Look at yourself. Jesus, Vee! Is this what a woman looks like who knows when to stop?"

"But thishh ... hic ... ish the lass time," she said, struggling to her feet. She stumbled toward him.

Hawk was hard pressed not to step back when the liquor fumes filled his nostrils. He reached out and placed his hand on her shoulder, keeping her at a distance.

"Why should I believe you? What makes this time so different? You've been in rehab six times over the past four years. It hasn't helped. What's going to make you stop now?"

She attempted a smile, but it was more a lopsided grimace as she was overcome with hiccups. Hawk cursed; he shouldered her out of the way and strode to the bar. He returned with bottled water and shoved it into her hands.

"Drink this."

Her lips pulled into a disgusting sneer but one look at the anger swirling in his eyes, she conceded and took a few small sips.

"Well? I'm waiting," Hawk snapped impatiently. All he wanted to do was leave. To pack his bags and go. He'd had enough.

"I went to the doctor thish morning," she said, wringing her hands. She blinked at him with growing fear. Another attempt at a smile as she reached out to touch his chest. He remained aloof. "I'm pregnant, babe. We're gonna have a … hic … baby."

Hawk felt the punch of fury explode inside him. What should've filled him with unbound joy, delivered in a drunken stupor, made him see red.

"You're pregnant? And this is how you react? By getting sloshed? Do you even fucking know what it could do to a baby? Do you even fucking care?"

"I know and I'm sh-orry! It wash jush so … overwhelming … I needed … I had to—"

"Had to celebrate by getting drunk. Congratulations! You just potentially caused permanent harm to our child!"

"You're mean," she began to sob. "You doan even try to unnershtand."

Hawk didn't attempt to stop her when she stumbled to the front door and ran outside into the night. He was too disappointed, too tired to care. He should be shouting with joy at the prospect of becoming a father but all he could think of was that she'd never be a good mother. He finally realized she'd never quit drinking. The fact that something this joyous moved her to grab the bottle instead of staying steadfast, realizing the responsibility that came with a child, was the only proof he needed.

His body turned to stone for a brief moment when the sound of screeching tires and a scream echoed through the front door. He tore outside and ran out to the street. Vee lay in a crumpled, bloodied broken bundle in the middle of the street. Her sightless eyes looked up at the stars.

His world crashed around him as he stared at her mangled body, tears running down his cheeks. In one blind moment of rage, he'd pushed her over the edge.

He caused her death.

Hers and the life of his unborn child.

"Hold on, sub ST, we're almost there."

Danton's gruff voice yanked Hawk back to the present and Savannah's pitiful crying behind him. He cursed, kicked off his shoes and ripped off his shirt.

"Hawk! Hey, what the fuck, man!"

Danton's voice drifted across the ocean as Hawk's body hit the water with a perfectly executed dive off the speeding boat. Since the accident, the ocean was the one place where he could find solace, a little release when he felt the darkness cloud his mind with memories that tried to escape his mind. With the guilt that had been hounding him for the past ten years.

He pushed his arms faster, cutting through the water like a motorized fan, his body was tight as a coiled spring. His chest burned but he didn't let up, he forced himself to move forward at a speed that drowned all thoughts, all sorrow and pain from his mind.

Everything he'd managed to keep suppressed for the past five years had burst to the surface—all because he saw the first woman since Vee who had managed to set fire to his veins, as drunk as a skunk.

Struggling to breathe, Hawk clawed his way onward until he reached The Seven Keys Island and stumbled from the surf. He fell onto his back, trying to catch his breath.

He had finally believed he was ready to move on. He smirked.

"Not with Savannah Thorne, I'm not."

Hawk had no intention of ever becoming involved with another alcoholic. No matter how he lusted after her.

All Savannah wanted to do at that moment was to crawl into a dark cave and hide for the rest of her life. She had never felt this miserable and drunk.

Good lord! What was I thinking?

She moaned as the boat hit another wave and her stomach heaved for the umpteenth time. Bile rose in her throat, and she leaned forward, hurling into the bucket that bore witness to the many times she'd already vomited in the short time they'd been at sea.

The sob tore through her chest without forethought and then the dam burst ... again. She couldn't stop the tears and she didn't bother to try. Through watery eyes, she watched a tense Hawk jump up, kick off his shoes, and yank his shirt over his head. All in what appeared to be one smooth move, he dove into the ocean.

"Oh god!" she cried in apprehension. Danton's hoarse cry echoed in her ears as she leaned over the side, frantically searching for Hawk's body. She sighed in relief when he surfaced a short distance from the boat and started to swim in the direction of the island, which in her estimation was still miles in the distance. His movements were confident as his hands cut into the water with what she had no doubt was fury.

She cringed at the memory of the look on his face when he'd seen her slumped in the booth at the bar with a glass of whiskey in her hands. It wasn't the kind of expression she'd wanted to entice from him, not from Master Hawk and most assuredly not from the man, Hawk Sinclair.

"He's very angry at me, isn't he?" she said in a small voice. Danton didn't respond, and she leaned back with a sigh. Maybe it was a good thing he didn't hear the question. She'd already made a big enough fool of herself once today.

"Anger is putting it mildly, little one. I've known Hawk for eight years and I've never seen him like this."

Oh, that's just great. I've managed to wake up the demon in him.

"I'm sorry. It was a stupid thing to do," she said as he docked the boat at the recently rebuilt marina at The Seven Keys Island. It had been damaged by a missile that exploded a couple of yards into the sea. She looked back over the ocean. Her bottom lip suffered the worry as she searched for Hawk. The black speck in the distance coming closer set her mind at ease.

"I'm not the one you should apologize to and yes, it was." Danton secured the boat and held out his hand. "Come, let's get you inside. You need a hot bath and loads of coffee." His gaze lifted to the man rapidly approaching. "You need to get sober and quickly."

"Shouldn't you go back and fetch him? He's still miles out and must be dead tired by now." The trip from the mainland and the fresh sea air had done wonders to sober her up. She took his hand

and carefully got off the boat. She might feel better, but her body was still suffering from the shock of all the liquor she'd forced down her throat.

Danton barked a short laugh. "I value my life too much, little one. No, he needs to vent and that's how he does it." He took her arm and assisted her up the winding pathway toward Castle Sin.

"What do you mean I need to get sober quickly?" she asked as his earlier words registered.

Danton slanted a sideways look at her. "You don't honestly believe there won't be repercussions for you leaving the island with one of our members without telling anyone, did you? Besides that, you know the rule about liquor for as long as you're a trainee or an employee at Castle Sin." He shook his head. "I'm afraid you're in for more than a lecture from Master Hawk, little one. You'll appear before all of them, and you better be prepared for the possibility of being kicked off the island."

Savannah stumbled alongside Danton, her heart missing a beat as she listened to him. She initially came to the island because she'd been blackmailed into it by her ruthless and corrupt boss at the FBI, Decker Cooper.

She was just relieved to know he was now behind bars but with it came a devastating problem that had crippled Savannah's strength. Her uncharacteristic imbibing came after Decker Cooper had made it clear over the phone that morning that he wasn't done with her and refused to divulge the information she was desperate for.

She didn't want to leave Castle Sin, not since she'd realized how Hawk Sinclair affected her. He was the first man who made her heart beat faster, who was the reason she could dream again at night.

Of love, happiness, and a life without threats and ugliness.

Decker Cooper had shattered all those dreams … again, for the second time in her life.

Chapter Two

"She was completely inebriated, Stone. As drunk as a skunk. We have the rule about drinking alcohol for a reason, and Castle Sin isn't a fucking rehab center! If that's why she decided to remain after that bastard boss of hers was caught, then she can swim back to the mainland for all I care."

Stone silently studied his cousin. They were born a few days apart and because of that grew up as close as brothers. He had been the one to keep Hawk from falling into a well of despair and guilt after Vee had died. More than anyone, Stone knew why he'd insisted on the law about alcohol at Castle Sin.

"That's just it, Hawk, I believe you do care, more than you're willing to admit."

Stone ignored the snort of denial Hawk released. He glanced at Shane, the oldest of the cousins, who had also joined them for the discussion about Savannah's fall from grace.

"I've seen how you watch her during training sessions and you're always close to her in the members' dungeons. You can't deny that your interest in her is more than that of a trainee," Stone said firmly.

"I look out for all of them. I'm the Master in charge of the training academy and it's my responsibility to ensure they're treated well and that they don't fuck up with paid members around."

The fact that Hawk cursed so much was another sign of his anger. Of all the cousins, he hardly ever did. It was refreshing in a way to see the usually stoic man lose a little of his stiffness.

"Let's backtrack for one second." Shane glanced between the two men. "Savannah has been on the island for four months, is that correct?"

"Yes," Hawk said shortly.

"And in the entire four months, she's never been tipsy, let alone drunk." Shane frowned as he searched his mind. "For that matter, I think she's one of the few women who doesn't have wine at dinner."

"That could only be because she prefers hard liquor. She was drinking whiskey when I arrived at the bar." Hawk straightened in the chair. "Four months mean shit in an alcoholic's life, Shane. I know because I lived with one for five years. Sometimes she managed to stay sober for six months and then she'd fall off the wagon. Every single fucking time."

"I'm not so sure about Savannah though. I asked Peyton, and according to her, she'd never seen her cousin under the influence." Stone frowned. "Although, she did mention that the reason Savannah had fallen into bed with Peyton's fiancé five years ago was because she was drunk at the time."

"She what?" Hawk snapped.

"It's not as bad as it sounds. Savannah had no idea he was Peyton's fiancé. She had been on an undercover assignment for a year and Peyton never told her. He was the scumbag for not telling her and jumping into bed with a drunk woman." Stone

33

noticed Hawk's jaw going rigid. To him, this had just added fuel to the fire.

"I'm sorry, Stone but you're not going to convince me. If she was drunk at the time, it could be where her drinking problem began. Whatever the assignment was, it must've been so bad that she could only find relief at the bottom of a liquor bottle."

"We're making assumptions," Shane interjected and looked at Stone. "We identified she had emotional demons from the first day she set foot on the island. I still maintain she's hiding from or being chased by something. My gut tells me it's not alcohol addiction."

"I agree." Stone paused to ponder how to move forward with the situation. He and Peyton had just found each other, and he'd hate to cause her cousin heartache, especially if it could potentially harm their own newfound love.

"You're a Dominant, Hawk, and a powerful one at that. You care about the submissives you scene with, and although you have a strict hand with the trainees, we chose you as the Training Master because of your intuitive nature and your vision of what each trainee has to offer. You see the bigger picture in every situation." Stone hesitated a nanosecond. "This is the first time I've seen you concentrate on petty details. That in itself should tell you something."

"Stone is right," Shane said. "It's in our nature as Doms to protect and care. We can't just cast her out, Hawk. Not before we've at least given her a chance to explain herself."

Hawk sighed and slouched low in the chair. He leaned his head on the backrest and closed his eyes. He knew they were right, but he couldn't get past the disappointment of finding Savannah drunk in a public place. It had immediately placed her out of his reach because of the promise he'd made to himself after Vee's death. One he would never break. He ran a hand over his eyes.

"Very well. We'll talk with her but not today. I need to cool down first." He got up and headed for the door. His body was still strung as tight as a wire. "I'm going to find a masochist who can handle my whip."

Shane turned to Stone once the door closed behind him. "He's more disappointed than angry."

"Yes, and it's because he's attracted to Savannah. I think, in her, he saw the kind of woman who he could move forward with, put the past behind him and finally find happiness." Stone sighed and steepled his fingers together over his stomach. "God, why does life have to be so full of obstacles?"

"It's what makes the world go around," Shane said with a grin. "And Savannah? Have you come to a conclusion about her?"

"I'm with you on this one, Shane. My gut tells me there's more than meets the eye." He smiled briefly. "I have a feeling Hawk is the only Master she'll open up to."

"That, I totally concur with." Shane frowned. "Timing couldn't be worse though. You and Hawk have to be in Hawaii next month to shoot your death scene."

"I thought you said it'll only be in five months? Hawk is going to be pissed. It took hours of convincing to get him to agree to even do the two days' worth of filming."

"I know but I thought the quicker you shoot that scene, the sooner you can move on. Besides, we all owe it to ourselves and our fans to end the characters properly. I know neither of you thought you'd still be acting eighteen years after the first movie, but be honest, Stone, it wasn't all bad. It brought us as family so much closer and we had some pretty good times on set."

"I understand your reasoning but neither of us can afford to go away for a week. Not until we have the DHS servers secured with our technology. I don't deny anything you said, Shane but as we told you a month ago, we've lost the passion for acting. You and Kane have acted most of your adult lives but even you have silently been withdrawing from the limelight."

"Yeah, we both want a more settled life. I'm too old to start a family but I'll be damned if I grow old alone."

"You're not that old. Many men have children at your age."

"Maybe so, but I want a mature woman, not one twenty years younger than me. There's not many of them who would want a baby at that age." He sighed but smiled. "Let's just finish this one movie in the right way."

"Don't worry about it, Shane. I'll get him there."

The United States Penitentiary, Florence High, in Fremont County near Florence, Colorado

"Prisoner 588254, you have a visitor." The loud growl echoed through the Chow Hall just as the inmates sat down for lunch.

"Prisoner 588254! Get your fucking ass over here," the irate guard shouted over the rumble of voices in the dining hall.

"Hey, asshole, are you deaf?"

Decker Cooper shrugged off the hand on his arm. "What?" he barked and glowered at the inmate to his left. He had hoped to be placed at Florence ADX along with Gary Sullivan. At least there he wouldn't have to be surrounded by a bunch of idiots and murderers. He'd be seconded in his cell, twenty-three hours a day. Something he'd prefer over being pestered by these inmates.

"The guard is calling you." The man snorted. "You better get off your uppity throne, fucker. You might've been a hotshot FBI shithead outside, but in here, you're just one of us." He leaned closer. "And we don't fucking like snobs."

Decker was about to get up when he received a vicious fist to the back of his head from the guard. He jumped up and turned on him with a furious growl.

"Yes? Do you have a problem, *FBI Deputy Director* number 588254?" he snarled sarcastically and then guffawed at his own humor.

"No," Decker snapped. "I just didn't hear you calling me over the noise."

The guard pressed his nose into Decker's face. "You better learn to listen, fucktard, or you're going to wish you died alongside your Mexican friend." He stood aside. "Walk."

"Giving the *Deputy Director* privileges again?" a voice shouted from the back.

"Yeah! Fucking shithead!" Another voice sounded along with a plastic tray that hit Decker against the back of his head. He fumed but didn't react. Instead, he sped up. The judge had refused to budge on the request of Decker's legal team to be placed in the neighboring ADX penitentiary where he wouldn't be exposed to inmates. 'It was time to show the world that federal officials weren't above the law,' had been his response. It had been almost a month, and to date, his attorney hadn't been able to make any progress with his appeal.

Decker faced open ridicule and hatred daily. He slept with one eye open every night, waiting on that sharpened object to be plunged into his back. As an FBI official who had played an integral role in many inmates' arrests, he was hated on principle. He might have had power out there in the normal world; here, his life was worth zilch. If they didn't get him out of there soon, he was going to die.

Decker was surprised to see his mother, Dora, when he walked into the secure visitors' room. He sat down and picked up the phone receiver.

"What are you doing here, Mother? I told you to stay away," he snapped without preamble.

"And a good day to you too," Dora returned in an acerbic tone.

Her entire demeanor was one of disgust as she stared at her only son. She'd had such high hopes for him, but he'd thrown it all out of the window, and for what? A promise of gold at the end of another man's rainbow.

"I don't have the strength for your reproach. I'm already in a fucking shithole. I don't need you to add to it." He shifted in the chair. "If that's the reason for your visit, it was a wasted trip." He got up. "I think it'll be better if you leave."

"Aren't you going to ask me how your son is doing?" Dora snapped. She snickered when he sat back down and glared at her.

"What game are you playing, Mother? I don't have time for shit. Say what you came to say."

Dora straightened with her nose tilted regally. She had worked hard to stake her claim as a woman of high class in the society of Washington DC. Something she refused to give up because her son had become greedy.

"I'm tired of playing nanny to your brat. When is his slut mother picking him up?"

Decker's eyes narrowed dangerously. Dora sat back as she regarded him carefully. It was a side to him she'd never seen. It was then that she realized she actually didn't know him that well at all. They'd drifted apart the past eight to ten years and she could never understand why. Now she knew. It was when he'd given in to the lure of power and money. It didn't make sense though. Her family was old money and he'd inherited millions from his father eight years ago. There had been no need to lower himself and mix with the scum of the earth for more.

"My brat? What about your grandson, Mother?"

"Oh, please. You want him in your life even less than I do."

"I never said that," Decker denied with tight lips.

"You didn't have to say it. The fact that I didn't know about his existence until a week ago says it all. Did you honestly think I'd be thrilled to suddenly be burdened with a ten-month-old baby? Did you even think, just for one moment, why you have no siblings?" she asked snidely. "I never wanted children, but I conceded to have you for your father's sake. I've never yearned for another baby or for that matter, to play the devoted grandmother. I'm sick and tired of changing diapers and playing mother to your slut's child."

"How do you know she's a slut? You have yet to ask me her name," Decker said to avoid responding to his mother's accusations.

"If she was anyone noteworthy, she would never have allowed you to take a small baby from her or leave him with you and not bother to check up on him. No, Decker, I'm no fool." She squinted at him when she noticed his left eye twitch. A tell of his since he was a young boy that he was hiding something. "This has something to do with why you're in jail, doesn't it? You're hedging, and you always do that when you're hiding something ... for fuck's sake! Don't tell me you stole the brat! Is that it? That's why his mother hasn't checked up on him. How fucking stupid can you be? You made me an accessory to kidnapping!" Dora was visibly upset and banged her fist on the table in front of her.

"Calm down, goddammit. Do you want to alert the guards?" Decker looked around. He relaxed when no one paid them any attention. Visiting times for family and friends were limited to one Saturday a month. No one was allowed in without special permission. With his mother's contacts in the judicial system, he had no doubt she'd called in a favor from one of the judges.

"I'm not going to end up in jail for your stupidity, Decker. I want that brat out of my house."

"He's not going anywhere. I need you to take care of him, Mother. There's no other way. He can't go back to his mother. He's my son and he's going to grow up in that house." He leaned closer to the thick glass separating them. "Or did you forget who owns the mausoleum you live in?"

"I knew you'd throw that in my face someday." Dora bristled. She'd been furious when her husband's will had been read to find out he'd left the house in L.A. and the one in Washington DC to their son, stating that they were too big for her now that she was alone. That she should buy a condo. What crock and bull. Her, live in a condo! Over her dead body.

"Mother, I need you to promise me you'll take care of him." He looked around cautiously and lowered his voice. "I need him with you. I have no intention of rotting in this shithole for the next thirty-five years." Decker's voice deepened.

He had been in shock when the sentence had been given. He'd be eighty-years old by the time he walked out of there. An old decrepit man. Yes, he'd conspired to assassinate the president of the United States, but the role he'd played had been minor compared to Gary Sullivan. He got a life sentence, but Decker had no intention of accepting his fate without a fight. If he couldn't get free legally, he had to find an alternative way.

"You take care of him, Mother. He's my ticket out of here. The only chance I have."

"Where is his mother, Decker? I don't want trouble when she comes knocking on my door," Dora hedged. She had hoped to hand over the boy soon, and now it appeared she'd be stuck with him for a long time.

"You don't have to worry about her. She believes both my parents are dead and won't come looking for him at the house. I made sure no one will ever find out about you or any of my properties, so you have nothing to be concerned about."

"Very well, but I'm not spending any more time playing the devoted granny. I'm appointing a live-in nanny and you, my son, are going to pay."

"Do what you wish. I don't intend to be here much longer and then I'll personally take care of him." Decker got up. "If that's the only reason you came, you'll have to excuse me. You interrupted my lunch and I'm hungry."

Dora didn't respond as she watched him walk away. She had an uneasy feeling about the baby. She might not have wanted a child, but once Decker was born, her maternal instincts had taken over and she'd loved him at first sight. If someone had taken him from her at such a young age, she would've moved heaven and earth to find him.

"You're a fool if you think your son's mother is any different, Decker. Mark my words, she's going to come looking for him."

Chapter Three

"Oh, gaawd," Savannah whimpered as she tried to force open her eyes. The bright sunlight shining through the wide window almost blinded her with the searing pain that slashed through her brain. Her eyelids fluttered closed.

The aching in her skull ebbed and flowed like a cold tide, yet the throbbing pain remained constant. With another pitiful moan, she understood why it was called a hangover, for it felt like the blackest of clouds were hovering over her head with no intention of clearing. Her throat felt like sandpaper. It hurt to move.

"Never again," she swore as she curled under the duvet and closed her eyes. It was like the flu, only self-inflicted, which meant she'd receive no sympathy from anyone. Not that she deserved any. It might be best to stay out of everyone's way and just sleep it off.

She forced her mind blank and drifted off to sleep only to be woken minutes later by a grating voice, drifting toward her from a distance. She huddled deeper under the duvet, which, with an annoyed huff, was wrestled from her grasp and flung to the floor.

"I said, get up, sub ST."

This time there was no mistaking the harsh order. It invaded the final remnants of sleep.

"Final warning, sub. Get. Up!"

Savannah opened her eyes and struggled to push upright against the headboard. She needed a moment to shed the sleep from her brain, the grogginess of drunken stupor to dissipate, to allow the visions of the night to give way to the day, to move from that which was a dream to something more fixed and real.

She blinked up at the man towering over her, squinting as the sun's rays through the window hurt her eyes, too bright to see the luminescent colors in the room like the backlit images of cinema screens;

she tried to adjust, but the irritated man was fast losing the last of his patience.

"Master Hawk?" Savannah cringed as her eyes clashed with his, scorching, fuming, and dangerous. Gone was the caring warmth, the color of dove feathers, with a hue so softly gray they could've been pencil drawn. Now, they reminded her of ashes and smoke blowing in the wind from a fire that burned everything to the ground. They were intense, raging from the heat that searing deep within his soul. He obviously still harbored the same anger towards her as when he'd yanked her from the bar.

Her breath hitched in her throat as her eyes moved over his gorgeous physique. His hands were planted low on his hips—hips that were clad in a pair of black running shorts with Nike sneakers on his feet and ... *oh my* ... a gloriously naked chest, muscles rippling as he spread his feet apart.

"Staying in bed all day isn't going to help. If you're still not sober after sixteen hours of sleep, then—"

"Sixteen hours? Oh lord, I slept for that long?" Her gaze drifted to the large window. The sun was already mid-sky. Her grumbling stomach attested to the fact that she hadn't eaten anything since breakfast the previous day and it was lunchtime already.

Sleep had been the escape mechanism she had to use once Danton had escorted her to the room that she shared with three other trainees. To take a hot shower and fall into bed and sleep—the only place where she could feel safe, where life was perfect in the realm of dreams. Where she didn't have to face Hawk's fury ... and his disappointment.

"Yes, and it's time to clear your mind. The Masters wish to speak with you." His voice lowered. "Get up, sub ST."

Savannah sat rooted in the bed, unable to move in the face of his anger that swirled in the darkening hue of blue streaks through the gray. It was mesmerizing and left her floundering with the emotions that always flooded her mind when he was near. The memory that of all the trainees, she was the only one he hadn't scened with and had sex with at the end of it, felled her to the ground. It hurt to think that although she desired him with every cell in her body, he was completely oblivious to her existence.

Except when she needed to be punished or reprimanded, then he would award her his attention. But during training sessions, he allocated one of the assistant training Doms to her.

"You don't like me, do you?" She cleared her throat as the words croaked from her dry mouth. His lips flattened within the surround of the neatly trimmed, short beard that accentuated his square jaw and high cheekbones. He ran his hand through his tousled hair that was longish on top and short at the sides. A look that always made her hands itch to do the same.

Why did he have to be so attractive? If he was ugly, I might not be bothered that he ignores me all the time. She bemoaned her fate silently.

His head tilted slightly, and he stared at her over a nose that she'd always thought had been broken a time or two.

His heavy eyebrows drew together as his eyes slitted. "Whether I do or don't, isn't important. Your actions and accepting accountability for them are."

"Why? I know I came here under false pretenses, but I tried to right the wrongs I did. What is it about me that you hate so much?"

"Hate indicates feelings and emotions are involved, sub ST. Both of which, I can assure you, isn't the case. You came here to be trained as a slave." He snorted. "I know that was a lie and yet here you still are. After you helped us to eliminate the threat you brought to our doors, you begged to stay and finish your training. Now I can't help but wonder why. What else do you have up your sleeve?"

"Nothing! I have no other ulterior motives, I swear. All I want is to ... to find myself again," she ended in a soft whisper.

"By pretending to be a sexual slave?" he chipped acerbically. He hated pretense, especially within the BDSM community and he never made a secret of it. If there was one thing that Savannah was not, it was a slave. "Until you're honest with yourself about that, you're still lying, sub ST. To yourself and to all of us."

"Okay! I'm not a sexual slave but I *am* a submissive and that's what I want. There! I said it. Are you happy now?"

His eyes darkened dangerously.

She dragged in a deep breath. "I'm sorry, Master Hawk, I didn't mean to sound disrespectful." She gestured helplessly in the air. "I love it here. For the first time in a very long while, I feel like I found ... home."

"Home? You? The successful career woman who is a department head at data system analytics for the FBI? You seriously want me to believe you're going to give that up and live here for a year and a half for a pittance of the salary you earn there?"

"After what happened, I realized how corrupt the decision makers in the Bureau can be. I'm not ... I don't have the same passion for my job I used to. I haven't for a very long time. I have to face reality and move on." She lifted brooding hazel eyes to his. "This place, Castle Sin, made me feel like a human being again. I need to stay, Master Hawk, please ... I ... what are you doing?" She tried to shake loose her foot, but his grip was too strong as he pushed her feet into a pair of Puma running shoes which he'd found under the bed.

"Wait! Let go," she cried and bore back against his grasp as he pulled her from the bed and dragged her by the hand after him, heading for the door. "Stop! Master Hawk, where are we going?"

"Your head needs to be clear before you face the firing squad of Masters. We're going jogging."

Savannah was sidelined by the sudden shift in topic and the rapid change in his attitude. She hated that he had the ability to completely unsettle her.

All the damn time! And the demon man didn't even have to try. It just comes naturally. I am so screwed. Why did I beg to stay here? She moaned as she felt the heavy weight of her breasts bounce. She grabbed ahold of them. *Shit … I'm not wearing a bra!*

"Jogging? I can't go jogging like this! I'm not even wearing a …" she huffed as she glanced at her ample breasts bobbing up and down as they descended the stairs.

Doesn't the dratted man realize my boobs are going to slap me in the face if I go running without a sports bra?

He stopped once they were outside. His hawkish gaze trailed over her body. A devilish smile quirked his lips.

"You're wearing shorts and a crop top, sub ST. Perfect attire for a brisk jog."

Hawk couldn't help but admire the annoyed blush that bloomed over her heart-shaped face, coloring her cheeks a healthy rosy glow. Or the way her eyes turned from hazel to almost green as she stamped her foot on the ground. A movement that drew his gaze to her breasts, jiggling in reaction. His smile broadened. It was one of her attributes he loved. Her breasts were large but not overly so. They were perfectly round and firm in a healthy C cup by his estimation, the ideal size to fit in his big hands. From memory of seeing her naked during training and in the members' dungeons, he knew her breasts were graced with large coral tipped nipples that when aroused, tightened into tight little stones ... like they did at this moment. That was why he was a breast man. All shapes and sizes, they were such delightful tells of a woman's desires and needs.

Her full pouty lips pursed as she shifted her long legs, which with the sleeping shorts, appeared to go on forever. The streaks of the sun played gaily over her skin that glowed with the healthy shine of marble. The silky weight of her tousled dark blonde tresses tumbled over her shoulders to mid-back.

There was no denying it, Savannah Thorne was a beautiful woman and her perfectly curved body packed a mean punch to his testosterone.

Throwing caution to the wind, Savannah slammed her fists against her waist and glowered at him. She gestured toward her heaving breasts, doing her best to ignore her nipples that stood pointed at him like bullets ready to fire.

"I'm not exactly a minion that's tiny all over, Master Hawk. Jogging with these ... er ..."

"Bountiful tits," he offered with a straight face.

Her stare grazed him with reproach. "I just can't jog without proper support," she ended with her nose tilted regally.

Then he did that thing. She bit back an aroused moan. That eyebrow thing all the damn Masters did with such finesse and yet seductiveness that it left every single woman on the island drooling. His one brow crawled high on his forehead; his nose scrunched as he honored her with a slow, wicked smile.

"Then you shouldn't have overslept, isn't that so, sub ST? You should know by now, trainees who are tardy, suffer the consequences."

She was still stuttering indignantly when he stepped closer and clipped a silver chain into the O-ring of the thin red leather collar she was given to wear on the first day of arrival, which they weren't allowed to remove. He attached the other end of the chain to his wrist.

"Try to keep up, Sub ST. It would be a shame to see those pretty knees scraped and bloodied on this gravel road."

The chain tightened as Hawk began to jog, forcing Savannah to follow him, albeit muttering indignantly about him being inconsiderate. Since he kept a steady pace, she was glad she had continued to run daily to keep fit, otherwise she wouldn't be able to keep up with him.

She ran lightly on the balls of her feet and soon lost herself in the steady rhythm of their shoes hitting the gravel. It didn't take long for her to be slick with sweat, courtesy of the gallons of whiskey she'd imbibed the day before.

Damn Dom, he's forcing me to sweat out the booze, she realized belatedly.

She began to pant as he sped up. Her breasts bounced with every step she took until eventually she grabbed onto them and pressed them tight against her chest. It didn't make for a very even gait and soon the chain began to tighten between her and Hawk.

Irrespective of her discomfort, the breezy run made her feel rejuvenated. She loved the way the sunlight tinted the sky various shades of blue and the lush greenery surrounding them offered a sense of peace.

"Let go of your tits, sub ST, and run properly. You're holding me up."

Hawk's gruff voice yanked her back to the present. She glared at him and blatantly ignored his instruction. It was damn uncomfortable to run with her boobs bouncing all over the place. He stopped so suddenly that she ran smack into him; she stumbled backward.

He turned with a thunderous frown. "I told you to let go of your tits."

"Look, Hawk Sinclair, you might be almighty and powerful in the dungeon and order me around, but this is our free space." She pointed in the air around them. "*You* told us that on the first day. You don't get to bark orders out here and expect me to jump at it." She stamped her foot and planted her fists on her hips. His eyes inadvertently drifted to her enticingly bouncing bosom. "Besides, my tits are huge, and I can't run like this. They're too heavy," she said exasperated, her cheeks blood red as his eyes dropped to her breasts for the umpteenth time since he'd hauled her out of bed.

"They're perfect." His words surprised her as he regarded her critically. His gaze was hot on her heaving chest as he took a step closer, "I agree, your tits need a little assistance." With those words, he yanked down the tank top and her boobs popped out, shouting their joy at the unexpected freedom by tightening into hard nubs.

"You can't ..." She all but swallowed her tongue but before she could voice her protest, he turned to set off again.

"Make no mistake, Savannah, no matter where we are, I'll always Dominate you, don't ever forget that," he clipped darkly. "Keep up, and keep your hands from your tits," he warned gruffly.

Savannah bit her lip to keep back the snarky retort that sprang to her lips. She hadn't missed the dark warning in his eyes and decided to be safe rather than sorry. Besides, she was still basking in hearing her name roll off his lips with such ease. She did her best to comply with his command but as they started descending a hill, she had no choice but to grab onto them again.

He stopped immediately, indicating that he'd deliberately been running to the side of her to keep her in his peripheral vision. He awarded her a sharp look, reminding her of a hawk circling his prey just before he went in for the kill.

"What did I tell you to do?"

"I tried!" she protested. "But running downhill, they're ..." she bumped her fist against her chin, "you know!

"No, I don't know," he uttered in dark voice while at the same time struggling to curb his smile. "Come to think of it. I believe you're a tad overdressed for your exercise regime this morning." He fisted his hand at the front of the crop top and, with one hard movement, tore it in two.

Savannah gaped at the torn garment fluttering to the ground. She grabbed onto his hands as he tried to push her shorts over her hips.

"No! I can't ... *no*! Don't you dare, Hawk Sinclair," she shrieked in a thin voice as he stopped trying to struggle with her to get them off. Once again, he fisted his hands around a piece of her clothing.

He wiggled his eyebrows at her and while she was doing her best to stop her ovaries from bursting out in song and dance at the naughty boy look on his face, he yanked hard and ripped them ... *he freaking ripped them* ... from her hips. They too fluttered to the ground.

He stood back and looked at her with twitching lips.

She felt his eyes on her naked body that left a shiver to tingle in the wake of his gaze. She bit back a moan when her nipples became erect under his stare. She pressed her thighs together to force the tremor in her loins to stop. She was helpless against the lust he awakened in her. It embarrassed her that all it took was one sweltering look. She kept her gaze lowered, refusing to give in to the desire to peek at him and see if her nakedness affected him.

"Better. Much better."

Savannah tore her gaze from the tatters of her sleepwear on the ground. She pointed at the pieces of material. "Th-that's littering."

He chuckled. "Then I guess you'll have to remember to pick it up on the way back, now won't you?"

"Me? You're the one who … damn it, Sinclair! Slow down!" she complained as he started jogging again, at a much brisker pace than before.

Savannah clamped her lips together—just in case he sped up more if she dared say another word. She managed to keep up until he swerved off the road onto a lush piece of grass under the canopy of palm trees hugging the edge of a cliff. Her legs gave way, and she went down, falling onto her stomach and skidded along on the grass a step or two further with Hawk yanking on the chain before he realized she was off her feet. By the time he stopped and turned she was sitting back on her heels. Suddenly, he was facing a spitting tigress.

"You *asshole*! You could've torn all the skin from my body!" Her stomach rolled from exertion and her chest heaved up and down as she struggled to normalize her breathing.

Hawk stayed his concerned movement and rush back to her in the face of her anger. He stared at her with appreciation and pride at the fierceness flashing from her eyes. Finally, she showed some spunk, lots of it and was clearly not intimidated by him. That offered the biggest challenge yet. It was at that moment the decision was made. Savannah Thorne was going nowhere. At least not until he'd coaxed the wild brat inside her to come out and play. And gorge on her body to rid himself of the raging lust and hunger for her that refused to recede.

He did a thorough visual exam of her body, relieved to see only a slight reddening over her breasts and stomach.

"It appears you have too thick a skin to be of any concern." His face turned thunderous as his brows drew together. "What the devil is the matter with you, woman? Why didn't you call out?"

"Typical! Now it's my fault that you're inconsiderate and didn't shorten your strides for me to keep up. I'll have you know, you … you brute, this is all—"

Savannah almost swallowed her tongue as he swooped closer, as quickly as a hawk diving to catch his prey. It was no more than a blur and then he was there. He hooked his finger under the collar around her throat and pulled. She scrambled to her feet as he walked her backwards. She flicked a glance sideways, aware of the approaching cliff behind her.

"Are you sassing me, sub ST?"

"Er … no, Master Hawk, merely strongly disagreeing—"

"Because if you did, it would be rather unwise under the circumstances."

"Oh," she gasped as he pressed her against the smooth surface of a large palm tree. She went on her toes as he tightened his hold on the collar. "W-what circumstances?"

"You naked and staring at me with those come fuck me eyes. Not to—"

"That's a lie! I'm not … my eyes aren't—"

"—mention that enticing bouquet of your arousal teasing my nostrils," he continued unperturbed as he wedged his hips between her legs and lifted her so that his hard cock rested flush against her throbbing pussy.

This time Savannah didn't bother to deny his claim. The wetness of her spread open labia attested to the truth of his words and pressed so intimately against her, she had no doubt he could feel it, even through the thin material of his running shorts. She couldn't tear her eyes from his as he caressed the side of her throat.

Hawk's sharp gaze took note of the furiously pulsing vein he found there. His lazy gaze did a slow gander over the red streaks covering the top of her breasts. He leaned closer, placing soft kisses over the burned path, followed by enticing licks that caused a surprising but arousing sting to stab at her loins.

"Master—"

"Ah, so now I'm Master, am I?" he murmured against her skin, dragging the flat of his tongue with excruciating slowness over her nipples. His eyes darkened as he watched them turn into hard little stones. He lifted eyes the color of polished silver to stare at her. His voice grated deep, "What happened to just Hawk?" he demanded, stumped by the memory of how sweet his name had sounded on her lips.

"Hawk, what are you doing? I thought we ... oh ... were jogging." Savannah breathlessly tried to reason with him, no matter that it was against her own desire and need to surrender to his fervent seduction of her senses. Her legs were rubbery from the blissful feeling of his hard body pressed so intimately to hers, molding them together.

God, I need him inside me. The raw cry echoed inside her mind. She didn't question the urge to feel his hardness take possession of her. Right now, in this moment, out in the open, under the trees with the sound of the crashing surf far below them.

"We did ... until you decided to seduce me," he rasped against her cheek. His smile was evident against her skin when her loud gasp floated into the atmosphere as he dragged his tongue toward her ear. Her moans escalated as he dipped the hard point sensually in and out, in the blatant imitation of sex.

"B-believe me, Sinclair, when ... hmmm ... when I seduce you, you'll know," she croaked as his lips latched onto her earlobe and he sucked it, hard and with long seductive tugs that she could feel in the answering pulse between her legs.

"Ah, remember to let me know when that happens ..." he hesitated and then delivered the punchline in his dark Dom voice, "Savannah."

"Oh god, you don't play fair," she moaned as her libido latched onto her name floating from his lips like the smooth, decadent taste of dark chocolate late at night.

She arched her back as his lips trailed over her shoulder, with hot puffs of breath heating her skin.

"Ooh," she agonized through her trembling lips. She could swear she felt her skin sizzle where his mouth caressed the silky texture between her breasts. His touch turned scorching as it moved closer to the aching tips of her breasts.

"Ahh ... lord, that feels good," the raw cry of ecstasy burst from her when he sucked her nipple inside the wet recess of his mouth.

He lifted his head to appreciate the feverish look in her eyes. Regret washed over him.

What the fuck are you doing, Sinclair? You know she's not for you.

Hawk had deliberately limited the personal contact he had with Savannah from the first day she'd arrived. He always allocated one of his assistant training Doms to attend to her and although he kept an eye on her in the members' dungeons, he had never scened with her or used her for demonstrations. The only time he'd given in to her seductive pull was during her and Peyton's dip and sip punishment, which in retrospect, had been the biggest mistake he'd ever made. Since then, he couldn't get the taste and feel of her silky skin from his mind.

Savannah instinctively felt his withdrawal and conceded to the force of lust he'd awakened inside her to grind her hips against his loins. She curved her back, blatantly offering her breasts for more. Her eyelids fluttered.

"Please," she begged softly and moaned like a lost kitten as he couldn't resist and nibbled on the succulent morsels on display. Raw need pierced her loins, her lower body throbbed incessantly with arousal.

She moved restlessly against him and then wrapped a leg around his waist to draw him closer, moaning as he ruthlessly pressed her back against the wide tree trunk.

"Never demand, Savannah," he warned hoarsely. "Ask or beg, but never, whether by voice or act, demand."

"Then I'm begging, Hawk. Please take me. I want you to fuck me, now," she purred with raw need shining in her eyes.

His large hand wrapped around her throat, and he squeezed as a warning to keep her eyes on him.

"I don't have a condom with me but we're both clean. I won't take the chance at a surprise pregnancy, so I won't spill my jizz inside you, but I'll be damned if I waste my cum."

His eyes glowed like molten silver. Savannah was too far gone to wonder what he meant. She swallowed hard against the hold he maintained around her throat.

"Just fuck me, please Master Hawk."

She gasped as he took back a short step and she felt the cool breeze brush her spread open pussy, her one leg still halfway around his body. He pushed down his shorts as he stared at her puffy labia, leaking with her milky substance.

"So, fucking hot and ready for me," he grunted as he lifted her leg and shifted to press the head of his big cock against her slit. She tossed back her head as the bulbous tip of his cock separated her moist folds.

"Yes!" she cried as the passion that had been simmering between them, boiled over. Her leg tightened around his waist, he dragged the other leg higher, and his hand reciprocated in a dire warning. She licked her lips as the pressure around her throat increased, threatening to cut off her oxygen flow.

"No demands, sub," he warned, his eyes scorching into hers. She reluctantly relaxed her leg.

"I'm sorry, but please, I can't … I need you. Please, Hawk."

"Don't close those pretty eyes, sub. I want to see every emotion, every sensation you feel."

He pushed in deeper, watching her eyes flare as she felt the size of him, the huge girth forcing the walls of her vagina to stretch to accommodate him. She panted as he snapped his hips once, sharply, embedding himself to the hilt inside her.

"Gaawd," she whimpered, never having felt such heat and fullness stretch her to the extreme.

"Indeed," he murmured, his eyes darkening to a light charcoal color. "Now, little subbie, I'm going to pin you against this tree. When I'm done, every imprint of the trunk is going to be carved into your skin. You'll feel it each time you sit down or lie on your back or take a shower and remember my cock pounding this tight little cunt of yours. And then … can you guess?" he demanded as he rotated his hips, rubbing his shaft erotically inside her.

Savannah couldn't even think, let alone respond. She was disoriented and lightheaded by the sensations that he loosened inside her.

"N-no," she whimpered as he pressed his cock deeper.

"You'll crave the feel of my pulsing heat inside you, every day from now on." He pressed his lips against hers, biting her lower lip sharply, exulting in her painful cry. "And I'll deny you the privilege. This is all you'll ever get from me."

"Oh, my god," she gasped as he pulled out to thrust back into her. Hard and deliberate. His hand tightened in warning and her eyes snapped open to gaze into his as he began to pound her.

Her husky whimpers spurred him on to drive into her with powerful thrusts, ending in a hard, rolling motion of his crotch against her clitoris.

Savannah panted, assailed by a myriad of sensations of the like she'd never experienced. She felt her muscles gather, fed by the insurmountable pressure that built inside her. She tried to take a deep breath, but as unstoppable as the waves upon the sand, the orgasm rolled over her. Spasm after spasm shook her body. Her cry carried to the ocean as she slumped weakly against the tree,

"Such a naughty sub," he growled but she was deaf to the hidden threat or the realization that she'd broken the golden rule of climaxing without permission. All that mattered was the pleasure that ran roughshod over her, leaving her numb and energized at the same time.

Hawk's hold on her throat and leg tightened as he powered into her, doing just as he'd promised, pinning her to the tree, imprinting the map of the bark into her back. His groan sounded carnal at every spasmodic motion around his cock. Sweat gathered on his brow. He reached for the swollen nub between her legs and pinched it.

Savannah squealed as she clutched at his shoulders, biting her lips as she exulted in the primal roaring order bursting from his lips," Come, Savannah. Now." Her body shuddered in immediate obedience as yet another orgasm threatened to rip her loins apart.

"Yes, that's what I wanted from you ... complete and utter submission," he growled as his hips snapped faster, harder in quick jabs as he raced toward his own orgasm.

Savannah felt his body solidify and she moaned low in her throat, craving the feel of his hot ejaculate deep inside her. Her cry of loss echoed over them as Hawk pulled out, took hold of his cock and with his body shuddering, his semen spurted forth to splash all over her stomach, her mound, and thighs, coating her skin with his hot cum. He collapsed against her, releasing her leg, and loosening his grip around her throat. His labored breathing matched hers, but his gaze didn't waver from hers, watching every nuance, every realization flash in her eyes. She was just as stumped about their copulation as he was.

Fuck, fuck, fuck! Now you've gone and dunnit, Sinclair. How the hell are you gonna stay away from her after this?

Linzi Basset

74

Chapter Four

"Follow me. The Masters are waiting for us." Hawk's no-nonsense voice echoed through the double volume entrance hall.

Savannah obstinately dug in her heels and bore back against the hard hand clamped around her elbow.

"I'm naked and covered in ..." Her cheeks glowed as she gestured to his dried semen all over the lower parts of her body.

Hawk turned and with deliberation trailed his eyes over her nakedness before he looked at her. There was no mistaking the satisfied gleam in his expression, and to Savannah's shock, the glow of possessiveness in their depths.

"So you are," he rasped. His eyebrow shot into a question mark. "Is that a problem, sub ST?"

Savannah heard the warning in his voice, but it wasn't needed. The years as a submissive before she came to the island had taught her it would be a slap in a Dom's face to complain about wearing the proof of the pleasure he took from her body.

"Of course not, Master Hawk."

He grunted and this time, she meekly followed him, still struggling to come to terms with what she'd seen in his eyes. She couldn't help but wonder if she'd been mistaken. Hawk Sinclair never wore his feelings on his sleeve.

"Are they going to ban me from the island?" she asked in a small voice as they approached the heavy, beautifully carved double doors of the conference room. This was the first time she would set foot inside it, and it scared the bejesus out of her. This was the Masters' domain, where all the hard and tough decisions about the club and submissives were made.

"That remains to be seen." His voice sounded rough. He glanced at her, noticing how pale she'd gone. It was evident from how tight her hands were fisted that she didn't want to leave. "We don't tolerate gross insubordination, especially when it comes to rules. We don't have the time to babysit alcoholics."

"But I'm not! I swear I never drink. This was just ... I needed ... I ... God, this is such a mess."

"Spare your breath for them. Believe me, you're going to need it," Hawk said as he shouldered open the door and dragged her inside. He led her to a large leather ottoman that stood on a raised platform to the side of the massive boardroom where his six cousins and Danton Hill were already seated.

"On the ottoman, please, sub ST, in the Nadu position."

Savannah dutifully obeyed. She sat on her heels with her legs spread wide apart, her back straight and her hands resting on her thighs, palms facing upwards. She lowered her eyes, aware of how her hands trembled. It was with difficulty that she suppressed the desire to curl them into fists. She had never felt as exposed and vulnerable as she did at that moment, like a little mouse scurrying away from a hawk circling in the sky searching for morsels of food.

Her fate was in the hands of the eight men watching her silently. Tears burned behind her eyes as she swallowed with difficulty, courtesy of the lump forming in her throat. This place, Castle Sin, and the tranquility of The Seven Keys Island, had become her sanctuary, her saving grace. It was the thin thread that held her frayed nerves together, that gave her hope that she might survive this ordeal. One that Decker Cooper, or DC as he was known in his position as former Deputy Director at the FBI, as well as a very short-term lover, had forced on her.

When he'd been found guilty and sentenced to prison, Savannah had believed it was over, that everything would return to normal. But she'd been wrong, so very wrong.

"Well, that's a blatant message if ever I saw one," Stone said in a dry voice, laced in amusement as he noticed the dried semen covering the kneeling woman's private parts.

It was an unspoken rule that once a cousin had marked a submissive with his sperm and left it in such a blatant manner for all to witness, that sub was off limits to others. Outside of the training dungeons of course.

"Yeah, and rather surprising, considering who we're talking about," Kane, second oldest of the cousins concurred.

"Hm ... or maybe like his spiritual totem, he might be looking at a bigger picture." Shane, the resident psychologist cousin regarded the younger man. "I just need to figure out what that is."

"Maybe we should just attend to the matter at hand and stop wasting time on petty and irrelevant details?" Hawk's voice slashed through the room with razor-edged precision. He brushed his hand over his naked chest, having arrived in the same attire he went jogging in. He was irritated at himself. He should've realized what meaning his cousins would put on Savannah's condition. He vehemently refused to consider the little voice taunting him that maybe it had been deliberate, albeit an unconscious decision to present her to them in her current state.

"Of course," Stone said dryly. He cleared his throat and looked at Savannah. "Sub ST, you're aware that you broke two key rules of Castle Sin?"

"Yes, Master Eagle."

"For clarity's sake, please confirm what they are."

Savannah's gaze was still lowered but she didn't need to look at Stone to know that all signs of amusement were gone. The man who addressed her now was the Master Dom, the king of the castle. The one who controlled every submissive on the island with an iron hand.

"I left the island during working hours in The Royal Dungeon and without informing anyone and then I ... I got drunk." The last words were uttered so softly the men had to strain to hear. It was evident that guilt weighed heavily on her shoulders.

"I find it strange that a woman who never drinks a glass of wine during dinner or as much as sips on a cocktail in the members' dungeons, felt the urge to break laws and become completely inebriated. Did something happen with one of the members we should know about?"

"No, Master Eagle. All the members always treat us with respect."

"Then what spurred your actions, sub ST?" Stone's voice darkened in warning, a sign that he wouldn't tolerate lies.

Savannah knew Stone Sinclair placed a high value on honesty, so much so that he'd banned, Peyton, who was now his permanent sub, from the island and Castle Sin not so long ago when she'd lied to him about her triggers. He had the sense of an eagle and instinctively identified lies.

"I ... please, Master Eagle, I can't talk about it," she whispered, her face grew pasty.

Stone leaned forward with his elbows on the desk. "Is it your mother? Has Vera suffered a setback?" He frowned at the possibility. He'd grown quite fond of her since they'd rescued her a month ago. The bastards who had tried to blow up their underground security company on the island, Be Secure Enterprises, had used her as leverage to force Savannah and Peyton to do their bidding. In the process, she'd suffered severe beatings that almost killed her.

"No, she's much better." She dared to glance at him and smiled. "She'll be released from the hospital this weekend."

"If not Vera, then what? Understand this, sub ST, unless you can provide us with a legitimate reason for your gross insubordination and discarding of strict rules that are there for your safety and protection, your training will end abruptly, and you'll leave the island immediately." Stone's voice brooked no resistance.

Savannah felt the tenuous hold she had over her frayed emotions slowly crumbling at the thought of leaving. Of not completing the training that had to date been her saving grace. That had forced her to look into herself, to find the woman who had been hiding behind a facade of suppressed needs and desires. Most importantly, it had taught her to climb out of the cloak of fear that had enveloped her for the past five years. Fear that had been the result of allowing others to manipulate her into situations she'd been ill equipped to deal with.

If she lost their guidance now, she'd fall back into the dark hole that had slowly been swallowing her, dragging her into such a deep well of despair and disgust, she had difficulty functioning on a day-to-day basis.

Her body began to shudder uncontrollably. She looked up, her desolate gaze searched for the one man, who had unbeknownst to him, been able to make her feel again, to show her there were emotions inside her that were worth pursuing. That not all men used and abused women for their own selfish purposes, no matter how much supporting justification they believed their actions had. His gaze was brooding as he watched her, waiting for her to continue with a slight frown between his brows.

"Master H-Hawk, may I please speak with you alone? I can't ... not ... just you, please. I ..." A dry sob tore through her chest, her hands fisted on her thighs, but she didn't look away. "I *need* to talk about it but only to you ... I'm sorry, Master Eagle," she whispered as she glanced briefly at him before her gaze shot back to Hawk.

"That isn't how this works, sub ST," Hawk said sharply. "This forum is here to assist you and—"

"No! I can't. Please, I beg you. I need your help. I can't do this alone anymore. I ha-have t-to ..." Raw gasps broke from her lips. She wrapped her arms around her waist as she struggled to breathe. Tears ran over her cheeks as despair washed over her and the dam finally burst. Her eyes pleaded with him. "Please! He ... he took my b-baby," she gasped through the sobs that wracked her body. She began to rock back and forth. The admission she never wanted to make, especially not under these circumstances, tumbled uncontrollably from her lips. "You have to h-help me, Hawk. He's got ... m-my son. He's got my s-son and I have n-no way of get-ting him b-back. He's got my baby ... he's got my baby ... he's got my baby," she sobbed in a mantra as she crumbled into a pitiful bundle on the ottoman.

"Hawk, you better deal with this. She obviously trusts you and needs to talk. I'm going to find Peyton. I don't believe she even knows her cousin had a baby." Stone got up and the rest of the men followed his example. He shrugged out of his shirt and with gentleness he was known for during aftercare, quickly put it on Savannah. He glanced at Hawk who stood watching with a closed expression on his face. "She doesn't need to be naked, Hawk, her soul is already stripped bare."

"I know that, Stone," Hawk said as he moved closer to the ottoman, castigating himself for forcing her in there without clothes. His chest rippled as he tenderly picked her up and carried her to the sofa in front of the wall of windows overlooking the Waterfall of Sin.

"My gut tells me that fucktard, Decker Cooper, has something to do with this and if he does, we better get to the bottom of it and quickly." Stone said as they trailed toward the door. "Parker, I want everything you can find about DC, and you better dig deep. Family, friends, financials, every fucking thing. Get into the dark web and deep web. I've got no doubt he managed to hide details of his life from the world," Stone said to his brother, the resident IT Guru, as they walked out.

Hawk ignored his cousins and the door closing behind them as he sat down with Savannah on his lap. He held her against his chest and stroked her hair. His eyes had darkened to the tumultuous swirl of thunder clouds as he stared at the falling water in the distance.

"You have to h-help me, Hawk. He's got ... m-my son. He's got my s-son and I have n-no way of get-ting him b-back."

Savannah's voice in his mind kept repeating on a loop. He had believed once she'd admitted to being blackmailed that she would be truthful when filling out the new submissive employment application form. It seems he was wrong. That form clearly stipulated she had no children.

A son ... she had a baby boy. Why the thought slammed so hard against his chest, he didn't want to dissect. He might come to a conclusion he wasn't ready for.

His arms tightened as her body shuddered with broken sobs that wracked through her. It was as if she had no control over the tears and her inability to shut them off concerned him. He pushed her upright and cupped her cheeks. He brushed the tears away with his thumbs. It was ineffective as fresh ones kept running down her cheeks.

"There now, Savannah," he said soothingly, his voice even but deep and commanding. "Enough crying. You need to tell me what's going on."

"I'm sorry," she hiccupped. "I didn't mean to br-break down like this."

"I'm surprised you held out for so long under the circumstances."

"I didn't know ... not until yesterday," she said. Her voice sounded raw—a melody of despair.

"I think you better start at the beginning, Savannah." Hawk pushed her onto the sofa and got up. He needed distance between them so that his mind could be sharp and clear. Her closeness had the irritating ability to cloud his train of thought. "You said he has your baby. Just how old is your son?"

Savannah folded her legs under her and wrapped Stone's shirt tightly around her body. She felt bereft without Hawk's warmth surrounding her. She chewed on the inside of her cheek. It still stunned her that she fell apart in front of all the Masters, not to mention that she'd blurted out the one thing she'd kept from the entire world, her own family included … to keep his existence a secret, to keep him safe.

But he isn't safe, Savannah. He's not!

"Luke is ten months old. H-he turned ten months yesterday."

"So, that's why you got drunk? To celebrate your baby boy's ten months of life? Ten months, Savannah, which means you left him when he was six months! What the fuck are you still doing here if you have a small child waiting for you?"

Hawk was incapable of curbing the anger that boiled to rage inside him. He would give anything to be able to turn back time so that he could have the honor of holding his child in his arms, just once. It was incomprehensible that a mother didn't have the same desire to be close to her own flesh and blood. That the mother was Savannah, destroyed all faith he had in her.

"It's not what you think," she said, feeling miserable.

"I can understand at first you came here to save your mother's life because they threatened her, but that's over. They're behind bars, and yet, here you still are, begging not to be banned from Castle Sin while your child is out there without his mother!"

"Is it that easy to believe the worst of me, Hawk? Do you honestly think so little of me that I wouldn't move Heaven and Earth to be with my son?"

"Can you blame me, Savannah? You've been lying from the moment you set foot on The Seven Keys Island."

"You know why! I had no choice."

His gray eyes shot daggers at her, piercing through skin and bone to stab at her heart.

"But you did once it was over, and you *still* chose to lie. Let me remind you, Ms. Thorne, question two-point-four of the *new* application form you completed less than a month ago. Do you remember your answer to the question of children?"

Savannah went paler if that was even possible. A shudder shook her frame.

"No one knows about Luke, Hawk, not Peyton or even my mother," she said whisper soft. Her bottom lip trembled as she battled to keep the tears at bay. "I kept his existence quiet for a reason. I didn't trust him, and I firmly believed he didn't know either."

"Him being?"

"His father."

"Do I have to drag everything out of you?" Hawk was rapidly reaching the end of his patience.

Savannah clenched her hands. She needed help and it didn't matter that he might lose respect for her, she'd have to tell him the entire sordid tale. It was the only way. She had to find Luke and she couldn't do it on her own.

"I always believed he looked out for me. That he went out of his way to protect me and keep me safe, but I was wrong. I only realized it after ... after the affair ended. All he was after was getting me in bed. I had become an obsession of his because I had resisted his charms for seven years. I still don't know why I gave in. I've asked myself that question so many times."

She shrugged; her gaze locked on the waterfall in the distance.

"I guess I was at a particularly low point emotionally at the time ... the anniversary of a particularly horrid day in my life and it ended in me sleeping with him. It was a brief affair. Three weeks of him gorging himself." She snorted. "There's no other word for it. It wasn't making love; it wasn't even sex ... it was all about his deviant pleasures. I suppose the moment he had his fill; he could tick off another notch on his bedpost of conquests."

She stared out to the vast ocean, allowing the memories to filter through her mind, unaware of the silent man watching her impassively. Deep inside he struggled to keep his emotions in check, to remain impartial to her story and most of all, to her, the woman.

"After that, he ignored me, except to force me into situations at work I was completely ill-equipped to handle, just like he'd done six years ago. When I realized I was pregnant ... I was horrified. I believed he'd used a condom every time but knowing now how cruel and uncaring he is, he probably didn't. My first reaction was to get an abortion."

She swallowed hard as the memories assailed her. The devastation and emptiness she'd felt rushed through her mind.

"I couldn't, of course. No matter that the baby's father was a bastard, it was a piece of me." A brief smile lit her face. "I've always wanted children and once the initial shock was over, I realized I was ecstatic over the prospect." Her gaze turned smoky as her voice became hoarse. "I suppose it was instinct, but I didn't tell him or my mother, purely to protect her. I didn't carry big and when I started to show, I took a long leave of absence. He granted it eagerly; I suppose to get me out of the way so he could move on to his next victim ... a young intern that started working there. I guess he worried I might tell her what a bastard he was. I told everyone I was going on a safari in Africa, but instead went to a small town in Tennessee and gave birth there."

"How old was Luke when you went back to work?"

"He'd just turned a month old. I didn't want to go back but I needed money to support him and pay for the full-time nanny. We returned to Washington DC, but I set Luke and Nancy, his nanny, up in a little house in Harrisonburg, Shenandoah Valley in Virginia. I stayed there every weekend. I started looking for another job immediately. I knew I had to get out of the FBI. I was a systems analyst, but I was forced into undercover operations doing things that had nothing to do with my job. Up until six years ago, it had been fun, challenging, and I loved my job. Then he started sending me on all these assignments and I realized I was being used. I knew it wouldn't help to complain to anyone. He was too powerful and liked by everyone."

"Six years and you only started looking for another job a couple of months ago?"

"I kept hoping things would change. I'm not big on moving around in my career and I was good at my job, but by the time I went back, they were already deep into the scheme to assassinate the president. I got pulled into it before I could leave. I suppose he suspected I wanted to leave and that's why I was such an easy target. Stupid! I was so fucking naive!"

"Do I need to guess who he is?"

"No, because I'm sure you already know." She sighed heavily. "It's Decker Cooper."

"Now I have the background. What happened to upset you so much yesterday?"

"I firmly believed Decker didn't know about Luke but according to him, he'd known from the day I returned to work. I have no idea how, but he even found out about the house in Harrisonburg. The lease wasn't in my name. I used an assumed name, but I guess with all the FBI resources it was child's play for him to get past all the precautions I took to keep Luke safe and out of his grasp."

"He threatened Luke and that's why you agreed to be a part of their scheme?"

Savannah lifted tortured eyes to his. Her blonde hair tumbled over her shoulder as she shook her head. "No, he only told me that he knew about Luke the morning they sent me that video beating up my mom." Tears began to flow again. "They were obviously becoming desperate to get into the DHS systems and as long as your NanoT protected their files they were helpless."

"And naive if they believed blowing up our servers meant they'd have access to the DHS data and files. That's what remote network systems are for. Something one would think a clever man like Decker Cooper would realize."

"I don't think common sense was at play anymore. They were obviously under threat from Miguel Muerta and his syndicate for results." Her shoulders slumped. "Peyton had just left the room when he phoned again. I could hear Luke's excited squeals in the background. My heart stopped beating when I realized he was there, right there in the room with my little boy. I have never been so scared in my life. The warning was clear. Either we get our asses in gear and find what they wanted, or I'd never see Luke again. Before I could plead with him, he ended the call. I can't even begin to tell you how stressed I was with worry. We were all cooped up in the bunker after the explosion and I couldn't make a call. I didn't know if he'd escaped and perhaps gotten to Luke. The first thing I did once everything was over, and I could get to my phone, was to get hold of Nancy. She told me they were safe, that apart from threatening her to stay put, they had left them alone."

She smiled wryly. Her hands fluttered in the air. "I was ready to pack up and go home when Decker phoned me from jail. He told me … h-he told me that I should never have kept his son from him. That he'd make sure he grew up knowing his father." Her tears had dried up, but the despair was raw in her voice. "He sent me pictures of Luke and Nancy playing in a garden, a huge garden that I didn't know. He said Luke was home and that if I wanted to see him again, I'd stay on The Seven Keys Island. That when the time was right, he would contact me again." She looked out the window. "I guess I became complacent over the past month because I'd still been able to speak to Nancy. She claimed that they'd been on an outing to a botanical garden in the area the day Decker had phoned me. I'm not sure who was lying. Decker that he'd taken Luke or Nancy that she and Luke were being held hostage."

"And I guess yesterday he phoned you?"

"I don't know what he wants or the game he's playing, Hawk. All I know is that I couldn't get hold of Nancy for the past week. I even phoned the neighbors in Harrisonville. They s-said a big black SUV arrived three weeks ago and that they saw Nancy and Luke leave with them. I've been going out of my mind since then. Decker phoned me yesterday and told me things have changed and Nancy had been let go. That Luke was where he belonged ... for now. That I might see him someday if I don't disappoint him again."

"That's it?"

"Yes. I stayed here after the missile because I believed his threats. Now I know he never had Nancy and Luke at the time. I kept asking her if they were safe and she assured me they were, but I shouldn't have believed her. I should've known Decker had abducted them like they'd done with my mother and threatened her to keep silent. It had been another manipulative way to keep me here. I should've left immediately! I should've gone to check for myself! If I had, I might have gotten to them before he did. God, Hawk, I can't lose my son. I just can't!"

Hawk studied her for long moments. He wasn't unmoved by her plight. No man would be when a child was involved.

"Is there anything else I should know, Savannah? More lies?"

"No, I swear, I told you everything."

"Very well. I want you to take a shower and have breakfast."

"I'm not hungry."

"Are you disobeying an order I just gave you, sub ST?"

The switch from concerned man to powerful Dom was so sudden, Savannah could do no more than stare. She straightened unconsciously and placed her palms facing up on her thighs, a sign of her submission.

"I apologize, Master Hawk, but I really don't think I'll be able to eat anything."

"Yes, you will. Your body took a knock yesterday and needs sustenance to recover." His brows drew together. He asked the one question that had been bothering him since he'd found her in the bar. "Do you always get drunk when you're upset?"

"No, as a matter of fact, I don't like drinking. I'll have the odd cocktail but that's it. I've only been drunk twice in my life and neither time ended well."

Hawk went on his haunches in front of her. He took her hands and rubbed them between his.

"If there's one thing I don't have any time for in my life it's alcohol, Savannah. Don't let me ever catch you drunk again. If anything happens to trigger the need to drown your sorrows, come to me, we'll work through them together, but don't ever go searching for absolution at the bottom of a liquor bottle. Is that clear?"

"Yes, Master Hawk."

He pulled her from the sofa and brushed the last of the tears from her face. "Good girl. Now, do as you were told."

Hawk watched her go; his expression pensive. He couldn't rid himself of a niggling in the back of his mind that there was still something she wasn't telling him.

It was a sixth sense he'd lived with all his life that never failed him. It was enough to warn him that Savannah Thorne wasn't the woman for him.

Chapter Five

"I must say, having all of you around the table discussing Be Secure business feels good," Stone said as he looked at the seven men around the table.

"Yeah, I think being involved in the entire operation to end the coalition formed to assassinate the president between the secretary of defense, deputy director of the FBI, and a Mexican crime lord was rather exciting," Kane said. "It made me realize why you, Hawk, Parker, and Ace are so passionate about leaving acting and concentrating full-time on the business."

"It's exhilarating to be part of something new. The NanoTechnology development I assisted Parker with clinched it for me too. I know I still have many years of acting in me but quite frankly, I find this a hell of a lot more satisfying than finishing a movie," Zeke said.

"I, for one, can't wait to say adieu to acting once and for all." Hawk leaned back in his chair. He had a brooding look in his eyes, which everyone knew had to do with Savannah Thorne. They had all noticed the added attention he'd given her since the day she arrived. It had been a lot more than concern over a trainee that they initially didn't believe was ready to be a slave. Combined with the fact that he kept watch over her like a hawk, but he never personally attended to her during training, or scened with or used her for any demonstration in the members' dungeons.

"It won't be long before we all close the final curtain on our respective acting careers," Shane said. "So, what's up, Stone?"

"We have two urgent items on the agenda. Savannah's son as well as a case the Secretary of State, Sheila Madden, requested our assistance with."

Stone took the steaming latte his PA handed to him. "Thank you, Alexa." He waited until she finished serving the rest of the team their beverages.

They were gathered in the boardroom of Be Secure Enterprises on the second level below ground on The Seven Keys Island.

"Should I request the chef to serve your lunch here, Stone?" Alexa Silver glanced at the large clock against the wall. "It's already twelve-thirty."

"Yes, please. We'll be busy for a couple of hours." Stone looked at the men around the table. "Any objections?" He nodded at her as his six cousins and Danton affirmed quietly. Danton's expertise came from his years as a field captain in the Navy SEALs and he'd proven to be an invaluable asset to their team.

"Madam Secretary contacted me this morning. It seems there has been another attempt to breach the FBI's database." Stone quickly opened the notes he'd saved on his iPad during the phone call.

"What's new? Every government institution has thousands of hacking attempts on a weekly basis," Parker said. He tapped an instruction on his iPad. "And we've not detected any attempts that were a threat to the DHS, FBI, or CIA we couldn't trace and eliminate permanently." He scrolled through the recent system reports. "The only one that looked suspicious is an email with a hidden add-on sent from Assistant Attorney General, Larry Holt for civil rights at the Department of Justice, to the acting Deputy Director of the FBI, Samuel Lomax." Parker glanced at Stone. "He was next in line for the position and was appointed immediately after Decker Cooper was incarcerated."

"I have to admit, I found it strange that the attorney general vetoed implementing our NanoTechnology to safeguard their data when DHS came on board," Zeke said.

"The president and joint chiefs of staff are busy compiling a bill to be passed that our kind of technology or something similar and/or more advanced be incorporated in every federal division across the States," Hawk said around a sip of latte.

"Which poses the question, why they don't use their own cyber division to develop something themselves," Ace said.

"The NanoT we designed is different than anything out there as far as nanoelectronics are concerned. We combined computer engineering and molecular science within a software program. Zeke and I worked on it for years before we presented it to Stone and Hawk. It's impossible to detect in its compacted microprogram system format which also means it's near impossible to copy the technology," Parker explained. "The programmers at the cyber divisions are good, but they don't have the skills to develop NanoT close to ours."

"It's not the kind of combined qualification and skillset many programmers out there have. We're spread wide and scarce," Zeke winked at Ace.

"Lucky for us." Ace smiled at the younger men in acknowledgment of their achievements.

"From what Madam Secretary says, the president and the joint chiefs of staff have lost confidence in their ability to properly control and deflect cyber threats. She hinted that there's a mind shift happening in the White House and that the federal cyber divisions might be dissolved." Stone shrugged. "I got the impression that they're contemplating appointing us to become their Ghost Cyber Division, operating offsite and undetected."

"Do we want to solely be working for the federal government, though?" Danton knew how Stone and Hawk loved the challenges of dealing with a variety of security protocols.

"If it comes to that, we'll expand the company. It's an opportunity we'd be stupid to say no to, but

I'm definitely not going to risk our future on one client, especially one as volatile and dependent on who runs the country or the different divisions."

"Yes, our main goal will still be to gain big international corporate companies that require full security protocols," Hawk said.

"We're digressing. Let's get back to the matter at hand," Stone said, bringing the meeting to order. "The email Parker mentioned is the concern. Is it possible for you to pull it up on screen, Parker?"

"Yep, there you go." He linked the wall-mounted television screen to his iPad.

"As you can see, the email from Holt is feedback on a sting operation conducted around the same time FBI Deputy Director DC was locked up. We already confirmed the authenticity of it. It involved human trafficking of women intended as sex slaves for Russia," Stone scrolled through his notes.

"It looks rather cut and dry. Very specific and to the point," Kane said as he read the email on the large screen.

"Yes, but the attachment contains details of the ten women rescued from the holding house. It's accessible with a passcode that only those involved with the case have access to. Unfortunately, because DOJ's files and systems don't have our technology, that document is hackable." Stone nodded at Parker who opened the attachment. "It places the women in danger, and they've had to put them in protective custody."

"You mentioned an add-on, Parker. What kind?" Ace leaned his elbows on the table as he scrutinized the list.

Parker typed in a couple of commands and scrolled through the string of grammatical rules. He pointed with a green laser at a line on the monitor.

"Whoever created the add-on incorporated their own signature C#, a programming language for supporting concepts of object-oriented programming. It's one of the most powerful programming languages for the .NET framework. It's more like C++ than Java."

"Yes, it's also part of the basis we used to kick start the NanoT programs but that's where the comparison ends," Zeke interjected.

"English please," Shane said as he stared at the rows of numbers and letters that had no meaning whatsoever.

"Just give us the lowdown, Parker. None of us are going to understand programming jargon," Stone said.

"This command here is what drew my attention. Zeke and I created a reverse strain to identify what its purpose is. It's not an add-on, it's a mirror domain."

"In other words, someone is privy to all of Larry Holt's emails. Or do you mean a mirror domain of the entire DOJ system?" Hawk finished his latte and steepled his fingers together.

"That's what we assume it is," Parker said. "I've got the team working on it as we speak. Because our system doesn't operate at DOJ, it means we have to hack into their system to track the mirror domain. It's going to take longer but we'll get there."

"Do we have permission to hack into their system?" Ace asked with a concerned frown.

"Directly from President James Grayson. The attorney general was informed but no one else at DOJ knows of our involvement," Hawk said.

"What's the danger of a mirror domain?" Kane looked from Parker to Zeke. He was highly impressed with their skillset.

"As a mirror, it can be used in two ways. One is to have insight into all incoming and outgoing communication. Secondly, to gain access to the server and files of the recipient's mail through the keystrokes of users on their network. In short, they potentially have access to every operator on the database, their files, and clouds they use to save files. Which is what they did in this instance and why it raised the alarm when they tried to access a secure folder at the FBI."

"What did they attempt to hack?" Ace asked.

"A file in DC's private cloud that he linked to the FBI's server. It's called ... hold on, lemme find it." Parker searched the data with his fingers flying over the small iPad screen. "Ah, yes, Blue Bayou."

"Why does that have such a familiar ring to it?" Stone pondered aloud.

"The Blue Bayou was one of the covert projects we assisted the FBI with five years ago," Hawk recalled aloud. "If memory serves me correctly, it was in relation to a sting operation to dissolve a human trafficking ring involving a Russian syndicate who used a local syndicate to supply female sex slaves."

"What role did BSE play in a sting operation?" Kane slouched in his chair, but his gaze was alive and sharp.

"Because of the sensitivity involved around the pending court case against the local syndicate after the women were rescued, we were asked to create an entire new and traceable life history for each of them," Parker said.

"Isn't that the job of the DOJ witness protection program?" Shane asked.

"They created the new identities but due to time constraints, needed help with building background history so the women could be incorporated into their new lives as quickly as possible," Hawk explained as he searched his memory for more information.

"I do recall there were concerns for their safety," Stone said. "There were rumors that the Russian syndicate had sent soldiers to find and return the slaves. Their testimonies could potentially have meant a crackdown on their operation in Russia if the two governments joined forces. The DOJ didn't want to delay the process in fear of the women's safety being compromised. They were highly traumatized by the experience. They were treated abominably, kept like animals in cages, whipped and starved into submission. We worked closely with the DOJ and FBI's team at the time to make their transition as painless as possible."

"It can't be coincidence that someone is attempting to get into the Blue Bayou folder at the same time another sting operation recovered sex slaves meant for a Russian syndicate." Ace looked at Stone. "Do you think it's the same syndicate?"

"From what I remember, the local syndicate involved at the time was cracked open and all the major players got jail time. They're not up for parole for another fifteen years," Stone said. His gaze sharpened in thought. "However, I suspect it's the same syndicate on the Russian side, especially as the information they're after is of the first group of sex slaves freed from their grasp."

"Yes, but why bother now, after five years?" Hawk said.

"That's a concern. This new sting saved the women before they were deported to Russia, right?" Ace started a search on his tablet. "How could they know to search DC's cloud specifically? It makes more sense that they would target DOJ, seeing as that's the office for victim assistance. Surely their human trafficking prosecution unit, within the Civil Rights Division is responsible for keeping such information on file and not the FBI that only played a supporting role."

"You're right, Ace. There's no reason for Decker Cooper to have a copy of that file," Stone mused as he stared at the large screen.

"Are you thinking what I'm thinking?" Hawk's voice was coated with dark anger.

"Decker Cooper somehow played a key role in the human trafficking and not in saving the women from the bastards' clutches. He must've been involved on a high level of supplying sex slaves to the syndicate." Stone got up and paced in front of the wall of windows, blind to the beauty of the ocean surrounding the island. He glanced at Parker. "I want access to the Blue Bayou file, Parker. I'd prefer not to have to go and visit the bastard in jail to ask for the passcode. See if you can crack it open. There must be something of value in that folder."

"Or someone," Hawk said.

"I'll get on it personally but just looking at it from the surface, it's not the usual kind of passcode. I have a suspicion it might be a voice-activated passcode."

"If it is, Hawk and I'll take a trip to Colorado."

"Give me a couple of days. There might be a way I can use our NanoT to bypass it," Parker said.

"Keep me up to date with your progress, please. Let's move on to the next point on the agenda. Hawk, please fill everyone in about the discussion you had with Savannah this morning."

"Thanks, Stone." Hawk briefly explained the situation around Savannah and her little boy. He ended with, "She has no idea where Luke is or what happened to his nanny, Nancy." He glanced at Parker. "I know you haven't had much time, but have you managed to uncover anything about Cooper?"

"Not as of yet. Getting into the deep and dark web takes more time. Deep web content is never part of a surface layer. Anything that's hidden in deep web content isn't accessible using a traditional search engine. We need to search for source files and access it that way. The dark web is largely linked to illegal activities and there's a security risk, so we can't rush into it."

"I understand, but while you're searching, link up to the history of the live GeoSat system and see if you can trace any movement at the coordinates of the house in Harrisonville that Savannah rented as far back as a month prior to DC's capture. I'm hoping for a lucky break."

"I'll try, Hawk, but finding live feeds that far back is at times near impossible."

"Impossible is a word that's not in my—"

"Vocabulary, yeah, Hawk, we know," Zeke interjected with a wry smile.

"One thing I'm struggling to understand is why DC is adamant that Savannah stays on the island. Did she mention anything?"

"No, and she was so unraveled, I didn't want to push. To be honest, I didn't think to ask at the time. I only considered it afterwards."

"I'd like to talk with her," Stone said after a short silence. "I also insist that she starts daily counseling sessions with Shane."

"Agreed. Just say when and I'll arrange it."

"Thanks, Hawk. Unfortunately, there's not much we can do until the boys find something we can use, except approach the bastard in jail. I'm wary of doing that, at least until we know where Luke is. It might end badly for Savannah and her son if he retaliates when he realizes she discussed it with us."

"You're right," Danton said. "Unless we have that little boy safe and back with his mother, we can't afford DC to get a hint of our involvement."

"I'll get on the GeoSat while Parker works on cracking that passcode." Zeke looked at Hawk. "Don't worry, cuz, one way or the other, we'll find something we can work with. It's a little baby. We'll find him."

A knock on the door was followed by Alexis and three sous' chefs from the kitchen arriving with their lunch. The aroma of rosemary and garlic permeated the air.

"Lemme guess. Chef Gustav's rump steaks marinated in rosemary and garlic butter sauce?" Kane drooled as the plate landed in front of him.

"Yes, he says you're big men and need to be fed a healthy dose of fat and protein," one of the chefs related with a smile.

"Gmphf, not to mention the mountain of fries on each plate. I suppose he has a reason for feeding them loads of carbs too?"

Alexis was known for healthy eating and didn't hide her disgust for the way the Masters at times indulged in steak and fries. She huffed as she placed a large plate of freshly baked rolls in the middle of the desk. "And these on top of that. Good lord, you're all prime examples of how to clog your arteries."

"That's why he added this humongous bowl of salad for balance, little snip. Now scoot, you're souring the experience of what should be a scrumptious meal," Shane mumbled around a bite of medium rare meat.

"Ugh," Alexis shook her shoulders with her lips pursed in a pretty pout as she watched him spear another piece of meat into his mouth. "I hope you realize the dangers of red meat, Master Fox, especially for someone of your ... er ... advanced years."

She slowly retreated towards the door as she watched his jaw slow until he stopped chewing. His eyes did a deliberate foray up and down her body.

"It seems I need to address a certain submissive's attitude in the dungeon." His eyes narrowed as she groped for the door behind her. "You can run, little snip, but you can't hide. Not on this island, and sure as hell not from me. It'll be wise to oil up your hide. It's going to need it."

The last words were uttered to a door slamming shut behind Alexis as she finally got her legs to obey and run. His irritated gaze raked over the seven men guffawing between bites of food.

"Well, you better eat up, Shane. A man of your *advanced* years might need added sustenance to keep up with someone as feisty as Alexa."

"Fuck off, Kane. You're only a couple of months younger than me."

"Yeah, but at least no woman has ever felt the need to point it out to me."

"Probably because they're scared you might have a heart attack and die at their feet," Shane grumbled as he glanced towards the closed door. "Advanced years, my ass."

Linzi Basset

Chapter Six

"Would you rather go home, Savannah? Under the circumstances, we'll understand if you prefer to be with your mother."

She stiffened under Stone's intense regard. He always unsettled her when he looked at her like that. It was as if he could see inside her soul, dissect every thought and home in on every lie she'd ever told. To the one secret she still carried, locked away so deep she made herself believe it had never happened. It was the only way she could attempt to forget the first time she'd given in to Decker Cooper's insistence and gone undercover to assist with an operation. But the nightmares hadn't stopped. Every year they recurred on the same day ... the day she'd realized she was in too deep and was completely incapable of dealing with the situation he'd forced her into.

"Savannah?" Stone's deep voice yanked her back to the present.

Her blonde curls tumbled over her shoulders as she shook her head. "No, I don't want to leave, Master Eagle. Castle Sin is the one place where I feel safe."

"There's one thing I'm concerned about. Did DC give you any indication of why he wanted you to remain on the island, the first time he contacted you from prison?"

"No. I kept thinking he would phone and make demands, but he never did, and I still don't know." She lifted troubled eyes to Stone. "I'm not a person in power, Master Eagle. Not at the FBI or in the local community. I sure as hell can't achieve anything here anymore. Surely, he has to realize you're all aware of my involvement?"

"Does he know who we are in real life? Our real names?" The seven cousins were known to the world as the Rothman cousins, the name that shot them to stardom in a series of Marvel movies over the past eighteen years. Only a selected few people knew their real identities.

Savannah blinked. "Yes, he does. He had me study the entire dossier he'd compiled on Castle Sin, The Seven Keys Island, and its owners. He knows your surname is Sinclair."

"Which means he also knows that Hawk's father is Xavier Sinclair, the chief judge of the Supreme Court of the United States."

She gaped at him. "I can't remember seeing that in the dossier."

"He might've shown you only what he wanted you to know." Stone's expression was impassive.

"And knowing that he probably plans on using me to convince Hawk to get his father to ... to what? Have his sentence overthrown and released from jail?"

"Uncle Xavier might be the highest-ranking officer of the federal judiciary, but that's not how the legal system works, and he'll never be pressured into doing it."

"And if I fail to do what he demands and get him out of jail, if that's his intention, my son—"

"No, don't think like that, Savannah. We have the skills and technology to uncover things buried

119

in cyberspace that no one else can. We *will* find Luke."

Stone leaned back against the chair. She sat across from him in his study in his private apartment on the second floor of Castle Sin. He had wanted Peyton near should she have an emotional breakdown.

"You indicated on your application that you'd been in the BDSM lifestyle for two years before you came to Castle Sin. As you know, Shane and I had our reservations about you wanting to become a slave. You had a reserved look that made us believe you weren't truthful about your desires to be trained. Tell me now, Savannah. Did you have prior BDSM submissive experience?"

She didn't look away from his searching gaze. "Yes, I did. I joined an exclusive BDSM club in Washington DC and completed their two-month sub training course. I'd been a member there for almost three years by the time I came here."

"Did you join of your own accord or did DC force you into it to prepare you for coming here?"

"I joined because I needed something to help me deal with emotional demons at the time. I believed I was beginning to cope when DC approached me. I think it was *because* he found out I was in the BDSM lifestyle that he chose me."

"I'm glad to hear it was something you chose to do. It's the one thing that concerned me about your continued stay here. We don't want anyone here who isn't fully committed to the lifestyle and the training we offer."

"I am committed, Master Eagle. Until I find Luke, please don't send me away."

"If you stay, you'll have to continue with the training. We can't afford that the other trainees believe you're receiving preferential treatment."

"I wouldn't have it any other way, Master Eagle." She shifted in the chair. "Nor do I want any preferential treatment. I'm not a porcelain doll. I know I'm emotional at present, but the training has helped me focus these past couple of months."

"Very well." Stone got up and walked around the desk. He pulled Savannah to her feet and surprised her when he wrapped his arms around her and hugged her against his chest.

The warmth of his body and the strength of his arms holding her so protectively gave her a sense of belonging. For the first time in a very long while, she felt completely safe, compelling her to relax against him. She even dared to circle his waist and returned the hug.

"At Castle Sin, we care for all our trainees and submissives, Savannah." He pinched her chin between his fingers and forced her gaze to his. "Because of Peyton, you're more special to me than any of the others. In the future, come and talk to me or any of us. We're the Masters of the Castle but we're not ogres. We'll always listen and act accordingly."

"Yes, Master Eagle, and thank you."

His lips brushed briefly over hers before he stepped back. "Master Hawk is doing bondage training today." He glanced at his watch. "If you hurry, you'll still be in time before he starts."

Stone watched her hurry away. A brooding look washed over his face. He hated any kind of abuse and Decker Cooper seemed to have slowly whittled away at Savannah emotionally.

"And just who is the woman you just hugged and kissed?"

The chilled voice coming from the interleading door into the great open room of his apartment brought a smile to his face. He loved that Peyton was jealous, but she should have known by now it would do her no good.

He turned around. She stood in the doorway, one hand planted on her shapely hip and the other braced against the door jamb. Her sandal covered toe rat-a-tatted on the wooden floor.

"Is it my imagination or did you just use an accusing tone with me, Petals?" Stone had given her the submissive name to honor the softest part of her body hidden between her legs.

Peyton's eyes dropped subserviently as she pushed away from the door. The straightening of her shoulders was a clear indication that she wasn't intimidated in the least by his Dom visage.

Brave little subby but not very clever to poke at the king of the castle. A wicked smile formed around his lips at the thought in his mind.

"You know how I feel about a response to a question, Petals. Or do I need to repeat it?"

"Oh, heavens no, because we all know how you respond to doing *that!*"

Ah, my little love is highly irritated.

"Hmm ... and yet I still don't hear an answer." The words grated over his vocal cords as he walked toward her. Her head snapped up. Her amethyst eyes shot sparks of violet fire at him.

"Well, tough titties. You're not getting a fucking answer," she all but growled and with that, she spun on her heel and stomped away.

Definitely irritated.

Stone watched her swaying hips for an appreciative moment before he fetched an object from the drawer in his desk and followed her towards the open-plan kitchen. She was rummaging through the fridge when he approached, mumbling nonstop.

"Who the devil does he think he is? To bring another woman into *our* home and have the audacity to ... oww!"

She jumped back as two hard slaps cracked on her buttocks. She rubbed the abused cheeks as she glared at him and quickly retreated as he started crowding her.

"Don't you give me that look, Stone Sinclair," she wheezed through thin lips as she bumped into the counter. She tried to ward him off but her hands pushing at his hard chest was a feeble effort at best.

"What look?"

"That big bad Dom look. This isn't the dungeon and—"

"You're under a complete misconception if you believe my Domination is limited to the dungeon, my pet. I will always be the dominant party in our relationship and sexually the undisputed one."

"Oh, so that gives you the right to ... to *kerfuffle* with another woman right under my nose in OUR home?"

His smile was one of pure pleasure. "I like the sound of our home on your lips, baby."

Peyton's heart flipped inside her chest as his lips found the sweet spot where her neck and shoulder met.

"Do not try and distract me, Sinclair. I'm angry with you."

"And completely disrespectful in the process." He leaned back and granted her a stern look. "Do you honestly think I'm going to let that pass?"

"Look, I'm not going to ... oh, *hell* no! Let go of my dress, you ... you fiend! I'm not getting ... umphf," she mumbled as he wrestled the sundress over her head and threw it to the floor. Her panties ripped in two as he easily tore them from her hips.

125

She sputtered in protest when he spun her around and placed her hands on the edge of the counter of the island.

"Keep them there, Petals."

"Now listen here, Sinclair—"

Crack! Crack!

"Freaking hell! Stop that," she shrieked as his hand connected viciously with her ass.

"What did you just call me, sub?"

Peyton cursed herself silently. She was still too slow to catch the sudden shifts from normal to full-on Master and many a time suffered the consequences thereof.

"Master Eagle, I think it's highly unfair to be punished. I merely expressed my upset about a certain situation."

"No, Petals, you immediately accused and made assumptions. To top it off, when I addressed your attitude, you were grossly disrespectful."

"I was upset and—"

"Enough. You know why you're about to be punished. I don't want to hear another word. Move your feet until your back is straight and your ass pushes out. Good, spread your legs."

Peyton knew when to shut up and obey. Unfortunately, this time, by her estimation, she'd gone past the sensible mark. She'd gotten to know Stone well enough over the past couple of weeks to realize he wasn't going to let her off easy. She shuffled into position and squealed when she felt him squeeze a blob of lube against her anus. Her head whipped around to glare at him over her shoulder.

"Face forward, sub."

His no-nonsense tone warned her not to push him any further. She bit her lip and stared out the window to the calm ocean far below. Her moan sounded more like a growl as Stone worked what felt like a humongous butt plug inside her ass.

"There ... such a pretty purple-colored stone between these delectable cheeks." His large hands cupped her cheeks and he squeezed. "Almost the exact color of your eyes."

He enjoyed her moans while he squeezed the soft globes with one hand while the other probed and turned the butt plug.

"I have a little conundrum, Petals. I'm not wearing a belt."

Her breath hitched in her throat. "It would look kinda silly to wear a belt with running shorts, yes, Master Eagle."

Crack! Crack!

He rewarded her sassy response with two more strikes across both cheeks.

"Using my hand isn't going to work, seeing as your continued cheekiness is begging for something with a lot more sting. Hmm, let me see. A wooden spoon? No, too thin. It'll break with the second strike. Ah! This will do perfectly. Face forward," he warned sternly when she attempted to see what he intended using as a strap to punish her.

"The only movement I wish to see is your hips doing a dance with every strike. You do not close your legs and you do not move forward. Is that clear?"

"Yes, Master."

"Twenty-five strikes should do it. Don't bother to count, Petals, you won't be able to catch a breath in between each one."

Crack! Crack! Crack! Crack!

"Holy freaking shiiit!" Peyton screamed as the first ones connected with a vengeance. She went on her toes and cursed when Stone added insult to injury by rubbing the welts the large and wet dishcloth made that he'd found lying in the sink. One that she'd just washed and was about to hang out to dry when she'd seen him get up and hug the woman.

"Ah, yes, just the reaction I was hoping for. Breathe and lean into each strike, my pet. They're going to become a lot worse."

Peyton's screams and cries married in the great open room with the cracks against her ass and thighs. This time there was no soothing or arousing caresses in between. He landed one strike after the other, tormenting her frayed mind that struggled to comprehend the conflicting sensations that inundated her body.

"Fuckity fuck-fuck!" she wailed and went onto her toes as the next four strikes landed with acute accuracy right against the jeweled head of the butt plug. The vibration it caused deep inside her flared to life a lust so profound, Peyton stood helpless in its grasp.

"Last five. Remember what I said, Petals. Do not close your legs."

"Ah freaking hellll!"

Crack! Crack! Crack! Crack! Crack!

Her raw screams were the final conduit that broke through and awakened the beast inside Stone as he aimed the final strikes at her pussy and clit. He threw the dishcloth in the sink and just as her legs gave in, he thrust his cock balls deep inside her with such force that her upper body lifted on top of the counter.

"Gawwd, Master Eagle! I can't … too much! You forgot about the butt plug," she cried as she clawed at the counter, trying to move forward to find some relief; the pressure of both orifices filled so unexpectedly, was too much for the cogs in her brain to comprehend. A hard hand on her hips held her in place.

"What makes you think I forgot, my pet?" he rasped in her ear. "Do you have something to say to me, Petals?"

Peyton struggled to breathe as her entire body shook from the rush of pheromones that coursed through her veins and centered in her loins. The demanding throb of her pussy combined with Stone's hard cock inside her robbed her of the ability to think.

He reached around her waist and pinched and pulled hard on a nipple.

"Ouch! Dammit! Give me a moment to catch my breath," she said and dragged in desperate puffs. "I'm sorry for being disrespectful." Another hard pinch. "And that I made assumptions."

"Good girl," he praised as he pulled back his cock with deliberate slowness, awakening every nerve ending inside her vagina on its path. Then he began to rock into her, leisurely grinding thrusts that pushed and released the butt plug deeper with every forward plunge.

A rush of heat swept from her loins up her chest and suffused her cheeks. The sound of her haggard breathing was music to the devilish beast that deliberately didn't offer her the wild ride she was after, if her dancing hips were any indication.

"But I had more than enough justification," Peyton snipped once more.

"Ah, Petals, Petals, Petals, you never fail to surprise me. You took your punishment so well; I had every intention of allowing you to climax." A snap of his hips drove his cock hard against her cervix; her moan morphed into a desperate wail as he rolled his hips to grind against the immovable butt plug. "But now you've just clinched your fate. You. Do. Not. Come. Is that clear?"

"No, you can't … ahh!" she screamed as he slapped her clit, hard and ruthlessly while he pounded into her, finally giving her what she and his dark beast demanded.

"You've been warned, baby," he grunted as he sped up. His eyes smoldered as he watched tiny opalescent beads of perspiration appear and situate themselves in a random pattern clinging to the skin along her spine. He drove into her so hard, her ass cheeks separated with each forward thrust. A carnal groan escaped his lips at the sight.

"Master Eagle, please. I need to come," she pleaded on a rich moan that resonated deep within her throat, racing up only to be snuffed in the clench of her jaw as he pinched her nipple in warning.

"No."

Just that. A single word and she knew she was completely screwed. He wouldn't budge. Peyton was faced with a dilemma of her own. Did she obey or did she give in to the screaming demand of her body and let go?

"Ah, fuck it, I'll take more punishment," she whimpered and threw caution to the wind to rock her hips back and forth in tandem with his thrust, reveling in the hungry licks that sparked volcanic heat to lap at her core. She felt the warning pinpricks of her approaching climax in the sting of her clit. She reached back and clawed as his plunging hips, urging him on.

"Yess," she moaned as his fingers found her clit, brushed over it once, twice, and then pinched it between his fingers. His cock swelled that inch more as he ground his hips against her buttocks and pumped in and out with long strokes, reveling in the tightness as he slid against her silky walls. He grunted as she pushed back, submerged in waves of euphoria that rocked her into surrender.

Peyton was overwhelmed by paroxysms of pleasure that dragged her under. Long waves of ecstasy rolled over her as she twitched and jagged in submission to his control as the climax threatened to splinter her in two.

Stone growled, flayed bare and ragged as he ejaculated inside her, pumping and convulsing, squeezing her tightly as he shuddered in its aftermath.

He picked her up and held her protectively in his arms. He buried his face in her fragrant hair and breathed in the familiar scent as he carried her to the bathroom and lowered her feet to the floor in the shower.

Her lucid gaze met his as he brushed back her hair.

"If something bothers you, Peyton, you ask me about it. Never make assumptions and fly off the handle."

"I'm sorry, but I ..."

Her words dwindled away as she swallowed them back. She had never acted this jealous with any of the men in her life and it worried her. Especially since he was the complete opposite. At times, luckily not often, he loved to watch one of his cousins fuck her, exulting in the power he had over her because she could never deny him. In truth, she never minded because he always got her so aroused, she ended up begging to be fucked by whoever he wished. But it made her feel vulnerable. More so, concerned that he didn't have the same depth of love for her as she did for him. She cringed at the thought of having to watch him fuck another sub. Something she knew was bound to happen, seeing as they didn't have an exclusive relationship. He'd warned her, their exclusivity was limited to his cousins and whoever their partners were.

A tender smile played across his face as he untangled her arms from around his neck and looked into her eyes.

"You're so beautiful, baby, and I find you're filling more and more of my heart every day." He kissed her briefly. "I love you, Peyton, don't ever doubt that. I know what you're worried about, but I caution you now, don't ever consider sex as a threat to our relationship. I want kids with you and I'm going to marry you." He smiled tenderly. "The woman you saw me with earlier was Savannah." He noticed her eyes flare. "Yes, I've had sex with her in the past, numerous times and as the Master Dom of this Castle, I probably will again. Know this, you'll always be aware and present no matter who I fuck. No one does to me what you do, baby. You're the one who unlocked my heart and that's what I feel every time we make love."

"I know but I still can't help how I feel," she admitted in a soft lilt.

"It pleases me that you're jealous, my love, and make no mistake, so am I and severely possessive over you. You're mine, freely offered, body and soul as much as I offer myself to you." He ran his finger over her pouty lips. "Mine, Peyton, to decide what, how, where, and when. Don't ever forget that. Only I'll decide and as far as I'm concerned, I'll always discuss it with you in advance, even if it's for a training demonstration. Understand?"

"Yes, honey." Somewhat appeased, she went on her toes and kissed him. Her gasp traveled to the ceiling as he cut open the water and it cascaded over her head and ran in rivulets over her body.

Soon, she forgot about all her concerns and gave herself over to the tender ministrations of the hands and lips of her Master, her lover, and the keeper of her heart.

Chapter Seven

The United States Penitentiary, Florence High, in Fremont County near Florence, Colorado

"Do you know who I am?" The heavy Russian accent drawled ominously in Decker's ear. He stared at the man through the thick glass separating them, who in turn watched him with eyes blacker than tar and as deadly as a striking mamba.

"Yury Kumarin," Decker said through thin lips.

He shifted uncomfortably in the hard, plastic prison chair. The Russian Mafia—or as they were known, *Bratva*, translated to The Brotherhood—was a blanket term for all organized crime across the former Soviet Union. This man was the brother of the most feared of *Pakhans*, Sergei Kumarin, or the Godfather, at the top of their hierarchy. To date, Decker had only had dealings with the second level of the echelon known as the "authorities" from the Contessa Mafia, considered the dominant Russian organized crime group in the United States.

Decker had met Mikhail Orlov, the local leader of the Contessa group, during a sting operation ten years ago in Brooklyn's Brighton Beach. The Russian crime syndicate had established themselves in New York City between 1975 to 1981. It was the success of that operation that had kickstarted his rise in the ranks of the FBI. It was also where Decker had first gotten a taste of the rewards of dirty money.

"Good, then I don't have to waste time on introductions."

Kumarin's presence in the States was unheard of. As far as Decker was aware, neither he nor his brother had ever set foot on U.S. soil. That he did so now and took the chance of discovery by visiting Decker, warned him that something had pissed him off, or rather his brother. The way his black eyes glinted with something akin to violence, made Decker uneasy. *Pakhans* didn't expose themselves to anyone in their organization lower than the echelons and they never became directly involved with the details of their operations. They organized and planned, and the rest had to make sure their instructions were implemented.

"I have to admit it's a surprise to meet you and indeed an honor," Decker quickly added as Kumarin's eyes narrowed.

"I'm not here for small talk. I want to know what you're going to do about the loss of income my brother and I suffered?"

"I'm afraid I'm a little in the dark. I've been in jail for—"

"We didn't receive the consignment we traded for, Cooper. A consignment, need I remind you, that *you* have been paid for in full."

Decker leaned forward in confusion. "What are you talking about? They were loaded on the ship, and I watched it sail out of the harbor in Miami. I took the trip there personally to make sure there were no problems."

"If you had kept your attention on what I paid you for instead of siding with a lowlife Mexican cartel, this wouldn't have happened." Kumarin leaned forward and spat angrily, "The ship was searched before it even left the fucking harbor. Our entire consignment was confiscated and were all placed under protective custody. What are you going to do about it, Decker Cooper?"

Decker was shocked that Kumarin was aware of his involvement with the La-Muerta syndicate. Not that he should've been surprised. The brothers were highly resourceful men and kept their ears to the ground.

"You have to understand that my hands are tied. I'm stuck in prison for the next thirty-five years," he ranted. For the first time since he'd become involved with the Contessa clan, he feared for his life. These men were ruthless. A little matter of being behind bars meant nothing to them. He owed them and they expected him to deliver.

"Your problem, Cooper, not mine. You have a huge debt to pay, or have you forgotten about the little problem of Sergei's escaped whore?"

Decker's face went pasty. He'd hoped to appease the Godfather of the Bratva by ensuring he received healthy and beautiful women to turn into sex slaves over the past five years. It seemed all his efforts had been in vain.

"Yes, he still wants her back. She made an impression on my brother and your time has run out. You better give him what he wants or ..."

Decker spread his hands in a desperate plea, the cogs in his brains swirling to find a quick solution. "Sergei can't hold me accountable for her escape."

Yury pressed his face closer to the window. Decker was hard pressed not to rear back from the promised violence in his gaze. "You've known for five years he wants her back. Imagine my surprise to find out that all this time, she's been right under your nose. Every day, and yet, Sergei is still waiting."

"I don't know what you're talking about," he hedged.

Yury snorted. "Do you honestly think you're our only CI in the FBI, or the government for that matter? We're not idiots, Cooper, and you've made a big mistake to play us for fools." He leaned back in the chair and straightened his tie. "I'll return in five days, and I want a solution or ..." the hesitation was deliberate, "I'll ensure you receive a gentle prodding from one of my soldiers on the inside."

Decker didn't need to ask what he meant. The prison was, like on the outside, filled with gangs fighting for control. The Russian gang, Princes of Thieves, had a corporate entity established in Russian prisons and existed into perpetuity within every prison system, no matter the country. Membership was restrictive, mutually exclusive, and in their case, required a lifetime commitment. Members were marked with a tattoo, the Prince Crown, which conveyed a prisoner's status. When worn on the knees, the crown was a sign of a prisoner who commanded respect. The implied meaning was that he'd never get on his knees in front of anyone. Of all the gangs in the prison, Princes of Thieves was the most feared, even by the guards. It was a known fact that the assassins of the gang carried homemade shivs.

Without another word, Yury got up and with a brief nod and a sharp glance at the guard watching over Decker, he left. It shook Decker to realize that the Bratva had a hold over the guards as well. He was totally and completely fucked.

He only had one trump card to play. He'd had the presence of mind to keep the majority of his cash equity in an account he'd opened under his mother's name in the Cayman Islands, over which he had full power. Of course, she wasn't aware of it, and he intended to keep it that way. He had already identified the guards most viable to corrupt. Luckily for him, he had many friends on the outside that stood ready to assist him. Money talked when it came to criminals—something that over the past ten years, he'd used to his best advantage, not only to firmly entrench himself as a reliable partner within the crime syndicates, but also to fund his rise in the FBI. The director post would've been his in two years' time.

"Fucking bitch cost me my job and the respect I used to have with the Bratva. Mark my words, Savannah Thorne, you're going to pay ... dearly." He muttered under his breath as the guard escorted him back to his cell.

He didn't even notice the cell door clicking closed behind him as he began to pace, his mind already setting his escape plan in play. He'd been conjuring it up since the day he'd arrived but hadn't believed he'd be able to pull it off. Now, Yury Kumarin had given him the incentive to succeed. He didn't have a choice, he had to get out of there. He was too young to rot in prison and definitely too young to die.

"I'm not wasting my time on something as mediocre as a prison break, not in this place, oh, no … I've got an ace in my deck and it's the one card that's infallible to the success of getting out of here." He laughed. "With a clean record, no less."

He rubbed his hands as a familiar feeling of power surged through him. It was wonderful to be able to control people. It didn't matter that he had to use monetary incentives to get them to abide by his demands.

A Cheshire grin splayed around his lips. "But this time, the clincher has nothing to do with money. Oh, yes and I can't wait to gloat and watch everyone bow to the power I'm going to have once I'm out of here." He cackled out a coarse laugh. "Even the FBI is going to come groveling and begging me to accept the position of director. Ah, revenge is going to be sweet, Director Frank Moore. You're about to be dethroned and I'll be taking over … as a free man."

Decker had been furious that the director of the FBI had been the one to lead the investigation into the charges against him. He had been key to the court case being rushed and finalized within less than a week. He could taste the sweetness of revenge on his tongue. For the first time since he'd landed in jail, he smiled with pleasure.

"Soon, I'll be in control of my life again ... and the best thing of all, enjoy the unexpected gift of fatherhood. Yes, my son, I'm going to make sure you grow up knowing your mother threw you away, that you were a burden she didn't want. Yes! It'll be such a pleasure to rub that in as I hand her over to Sergei."

Savannah excused herself directly after dinner, choosing not to participate in the usual chatter with the other trainees and submissives.

The bondage training session had been a trial for her. Perhaps because the dreaded anniversary of the worst day of her life had arrived. She'd broken down again, the moment Danton started to bind her in a tight Shibari harness. He'd cut the ropes immediately, but it was too late, it had unlocked the memories that usually only hounded her dreams. She'd ignored Hawk calling her and ran, locking herself in one of the bathrooms in The King's

Dungeon. The members' dungeons were the last place anyone would look for her as it was unused at this time of day. She'd been able to calm herself and managed to arrive docile and smiling at dinner. The brooding look Hawk gave her warned her he had no intention of letting what happened slide, which was the main reason that prompted her to go to bed early.

She took a long, scalding hot shower, scrubbing her skin like she was trying to rid herself of vermin crawling all over her. Her breathing was erratic by the time she finished and toweled dry her now sensitive skin. She stared at her reflection in the mirror, not surprised to notice that her hazel eyes had darkened to a deep topaz, filled with pools of surrealistic memories. The sigh that drifted into the atmosphere was one of acceptance. The nightmare would be back tonight and there was nothing she could do to stop it.

Savannah was physically and emotionally exhausted. The concern over Luke had drained her of energy, leaving her frazzled and incapable of reaching deep to find the strength that she'd found within herself during the four months of her training at Castle Sin. She felt weak, like a loser. A shudder of disgust rolled over her as a voice she'd banned from her mind whispered like a ghost in the night. It was this man who had stolen her confidence and turned her into a weakling for such a long time.

"You're mine now, little American whore. Say it. Tell me who you belong to!"

She yanked shorts and a t-shirt onto her trembling body and stumbled to her bed in the far corner of the large room. For the first time since she arrived, she wished she had her own room as she fell onto the bed, feeling how the exhaustion swallowed her whole. Her sooty eyelashes fluttered as she allowed oblivion to engulf her, courtesy of the two sleeping tablets she'd taken at dinner. Sleep came over her like cruel shattering waves, more vivid than ever before, as though the intensity of her exhaustion had created a perfect canvas for them. Her legs moved restlessly, her head moved back and forth against the pillow as she fought against the dreaded nightmare that painted her sleep pitch black.

No, no! God please, just let me forget. It's been so long. Why can't I leave it behind me?

Her struggles to fight it off were fruitless, the nightmare closed its claws around her, tossing her restlessly under the sheets. Her mind was flung back into the dreaded memories that always came to her in a dream.

Savannah realized the chatter of her teeth was caused by her body trembling violently. She whimpered as her heart rate increased and pounded the fear against her chest with every beat. As had become the norm over the past week, she awoke to a blanket of darkness so black, it threatened to choke her.

She moved her arms; a raw sob slipped from her lips at the familiar clanking of chains. Her befuddled mind remembered that they were cuffed above her head. Her breaths trembled from her chest as she peered into the darkness surrounding her. A sliver of light in the distance caused tension to streak like a painful knife through her stomach.

"God, please help me. Let him not come tonight. I beg you; I can't take any more!"

Her voice sounded foreign to her ears, croaking and raw. A slight noise penetrated her numb mind and she yanked, terrorized, against the bindings. In the blackened void, the taste of copper blood pervaded her mouth, accompanied by a tart bouquet in her nostrils that battered at her sanity. She could feel her skin buckling into gooseflesh from the chill of the room. She started to tremble violently. She'd forgotten what clothes felt like against her skin, here, where she'd been chained spread eagle and naked for the past ten days.

"He lied to me. The fucking bastard lied to me. How could he send me to a place like this?"

She could detect the desperation in her voice and immediately shunned the accusation against Deputy Director, Decker Cooper at the FBI, and her boss. He couldn't have known. She'd not been part of the group of women intended as sex slaves for the Russian mafia. She'd been a planted undercover agent as a trafficking coordinator. She'd fought against him when he'd first approached her. She was a data systems analyst, a damn good one, not a field agent, and definitely not equipped to deal with situations such as human trafficking. Eventually, he'd cut through all her protests, and she'd agreed.

Her job was to hand over the women and ensure the Bratva was satisfied with their consignment. Once the deal was finalized, she had to contact Decker and give the go ahead. It had sounded so easy, cut, and dried, like nothing could go wrong.

She'd done her part and waited, confident that the Russian FSB would arrive en force and close the operation.

They never came. Yury Kumarin did, the brother of the feared leader of the Bratva, Sergei. She cringed as the memory of his words when he'd walked into the luxurious room she'd been given for the period of her stay.

"So, you're the American whore who believes she could rat us out to the FSB. Bad mistake, slut. We have eyes and ears everywhere."

"I ... don't know what you're talking about," she hedged. Her head cracked against the headboard as he slapped her viciously.

"Don't hold me for a fool," he sneered. "Lucky for you, my brother has set his mind on you as his whore. Get naked, bitch. You're going to serve the most powerful man in the universe from now on." He laughed. "With every orifice you have."

"Over my dead body," she snapped.

"Unfortunately, that's not an option." He pushed his face closer. "My brother has this notion that you must come to him willingly, spreading those

thighs and offering your juicy cunt, begging him to fuck you. So, are you going to him willingly?"

She spat into his face. He laughed with glee, staring at her with a cruel smile. "It seems I am going to have my fun after all."

And that's how the cruel torture had begun. Every evening, on the stroke of midnight, he arrived in the dungeon under the mausoleum of a house he and his brother lived in. He'd started slow, the beatings light but when she refused to give in, they steadily became crueler. He'd gone from his leather belt to a leather flogger.

Then the flames ... oh god, she trembled just at the thought of the pain he'd enjoyed watching on her face when he'd scorched the soles of her feet.

Savannah feared what came next. She'd been praying and hoping that Decker would realize something was wrong and send someone to save her. As two days turned into four and became ten, she'd finally given up hope.

She blinked at the sliver of light that had widened into a beam from afar to narrow like a rapier aiming directly at her. The silence in her ears echoed like the crashing of waves along with the drumming of her heartbeat. She bit back a sob of despair as the haunting echo of approaching footsteps broke through her frayed senses. The large silhouette of the bastard, Yury, pierced the stream of light, a threatening shadow that prowled closer.

No matter how hard she tried, Savannah couldn't stop hyperventilating. Fear and terror threatened to strangle her as he flicked on the lights, and she noticed the whip he held in his hand. It had serrated edges and she could swear she saw the lights reflect off pieces of metal along its length.

In desperation, she began to struggle and writhe to untangle her frayed mind from the horror she could only imagine was about to unfold.

"Ah, I see you're excited about our play toy today."

He flicked his wrist and the loud crack next to Savannah's cheek made her mind reel with adrenalized terror and corroded her voice to a muffled whimper. She struggled to open her mouth and beg for mercy, but nothing would come out.

"There's such beauty in a woman's fear," Yury said against her ear. Her skin shriveled under the rough caress of his hand fondling her breasts. "Personally, I won't mind if you hold out for another

152

week. The fun is only going to get better from now on." His dissonant voice was occluded and nasal as he suckled her ear with a vulgar tongue.

Savannah screamed as he ran his cruel hands painfully over her body, poking and pulling at the soft contours of her shivering form. Tears ran unrestrained over her cheeks. The fear of rape crippled her.

"Yes, slut, he wants you willing, but he didn't put any restrictions on how I got you to submit." He ignored her pleas and plunged two fingers inside her pussy and pumped so savagely that she shuddered and twitched in pain. The fingers of his other hand dug cruelly into her cheek as he forced her to look at him. She knew it was useless and that it fed his demoniac pleasure, but she continued to scream her denial.

"No," he cackled a laugh. "I'm not after fucking your cunt but I'll enjoy watching you thrash as I fulfill my bloodlust."

Savannah's body was bathed in a thin sheen of cold sweat. The sheets were tangled and twisted around her limbs, as she thrashed in her sleep. Her heart pounded against her chest as she whimpered like a small child. She was caught in the horror that she'd been trying to run away from.

She could feel the sharp edges of what she could see up close were small razors attached to the edge of the long whip as he dragged it over her stomach.

"Please," she begged in a broken sob.

"Hm, maybe you're right. A few strikes with my normal whip first will heat up your skin beautifully for the Devil's tongue."

She shook her head as she watched him swap the whip with another. There was no warning strike, the sound of the crack echoed through her mind as the tail wrapped around her hip and kissed her stomach with the snap of a volcano erupting over her skin.

Her mind crashed. The pain from the cruel strikes drove her insane with fear as he continued. Everything dimmed around her. The only thing that registered was the pain. Her skin ached and burned from small cuts caused by some of the harsher lashes. She was going into shock from the agony of the brutal whipping.

"Such a beautiful canvas your silky skin is."
His breath was warm against her cheek. "I'm going
to have so much fun watching it rip to shreds."

"N-no more. I g-give in. I'll g-go to him."

"Willingly? You won't deny him anything, no
matter his demands?"

"Y-yes," she sobbed, her body wracked with
pain.

"Know this, slut. If you're lying to me, I'll show
you no mercy." He handed the whip to the man who
had been standing in the doorway. "Take her to the
surgeon. Make sure she's ready to serve her master
in two days."

A crack of thunder startled Savannah out of
her abysmal nightmare. Her cheeks were wet, and
her body was bathed in a cold sweat. She kicked free
from the sheets twisted around her limbs, feeling
claustrophobic. She trembled so much; she
imagined the bed rattling in effect. She looked
around. The room was bathed in the bluish
illumination of the moon.

Her three roommates were fast asleep,
completely unaware of the horrors she had just re-
lived. A forlorn sob escaped her lips as she struggled

to overcome the remnants of the nightmare still clinging to her mind. A nightmare that was the end of her physical torture but the beginning of the emotional demons of what she'd been forced to do thereafter that would haunt her for eternity.

Chapter Eight

It was a relief that Hawk and the rest of the Masters of Castle Sin were absent the following two days. They'd left to meet with Marvel movie producers in Miami to sign off on the script of the final Space Riders movie. Savannah had been surprised to learn that the seven cousins had the final say, but apparently it had been a condition of the contract they'd signed for the Marvel series.

Savannah used the time to calm her frazzled mind and return to her normal self after the harrowing, recurring nightmare. She knew better than to rush the process, but she had learned over time how to lock away the memories as soon as she awoke. It was the emotional battering her mind was subjected to during the night that took longer to settle. She had also very effectively managed to avoid her cousin since she had blurted out the news about Luke.

"Savvy, hold up!" Peyton's shout echoed in the stillness of the midday air.

Savannah had gone for a run, which usually helped to soothe her mind. Her steps slowed and she stopped next to a clump of palm trees. She sat down on the carved wooden bench and waited for her to catch up. The time had come to open up about Luke and her stupidity in becoming involved with Decker.

Peyton plonked down next to her, gasping for breath. "You really should learn what it means to jog for relaxation, Savvy. I have been running full speed to catch up with you." She waved a hand in the air. "We are on a remote island for heaven's sake. At the speed you're going, you'll circle its entire circumference in less than an hour."

Savannah laughed. "Exaggerating as usual. It takes over two hours with the dune buggy at speed." She gazed out to sea. "It's such a gorgeous place. I don't know if I'd ever be able to adapt to living in the city again."

Peyton sighed and tilted her chin to breathe in the fresh ocean air. "Ditto on that. It's amazing, isn't it? Me, loving to live on an island surrounded by sand and sea." Her smile was melancholy. "I'd been such a fool not to continue with therapy. I knew when I stopped that the fear was still cemented deep inside me."

"Many people who were caught in the Phuket tsunami are still suffering emotionally, Peyton. Don't beat yourself up over it. Besides, the therapy with Shane is working, isn't it? Not to mention Stone's patience in taking you into the surf every weekend."

"I've been blessed to have them in my life." She smiled. "I'm not sure if Stone is going to have enough patience to break through that fear of getting into the ocean. I feel like a scared toddler every time we go near the water."

"The fact that you're willing to try is half the battle won and I know you can do it."

"I've come to realize that love cures many things, especially emotional insecurities."

Silence descended over them, filled with the camaraderie they always used to share when they were younger. Savannah dragged in a deep breath and then she began to talk in a quiet voice. "His name is Luke and he just turned ten months old. He's the mirror image of me as a baby, which is a relief. I would've hated if he looked like … *him*."

Peyton didn't say anything, allowing Savannah to sift through her emotions as the tale of her torrid affair with her boss fell from her lips.

"Decker Cooper, right?" she asked as she stopped talking.

"Yes, DC, as everyone calls him at the Bureau."

Peyton tapped her fingers on her knee. "I know who he is, and I saw a picture of him once in a newspaper article. He's rather attractive if memory serves me correctly."

"Yes, he is but he knows he attracts women, which is why I was never interested in all the years we worked together. I didn't want to take the chance of an office affair souring my work environment." She sighed heavily. "I was stupid to give in, but he caught me at a relatively dark time and once the affair began, he completely overpowered me. Luckily, I came to my senses and ended it within a couple of weeks. He didn't make me feel wanted or needed." She swallowed hard. "I always felt like a …

tramp after we had sex. Like I was nothing but a vessel to ease his lust. I just wish I'd ended it sooner."

"Are you sorry you had Luke?"

"No! I didn't mean for that reason. I meant that the way he treated me, pushed me back into a well of self-disgust and it completely destroyed the self-esteem I'd worked so hard to rebuild. I'll never be sorry I decided to keep Luke. I love him so much and now ... he's gone, and I have no idea where he is."

"I don't understand. Self-esteem? You've always been the strongest, most confident woman I've known. What else aren't you telling me, Savvy?"

"I ... it's something I don't want to talk about. It's in the past and I prefer it stays there."

Peyton regarded her with a thoughtful look. "It has something to do with that assignment in Russia. That's why you got drunk the first night you were back and ended up sleeping with my fiancé."

"I'll always regret that. If I had known who he was, I would never—"

"It's in the past. Explained, accepted, and forgiven. It's you I'm worried about, Savvy. I know you as well as I know myself. There's more than Luke's disappearance haunting you."

Peyton squeezed her hand at the canvas of tortured despair Savannah's face became.

"I'm here if you need to talk. I'll never judge you, Savvy. Life is unpredictable and an undercover op is never guaranteed to run smoothly. I know. I've been there many times as an investigative journalist. Don't let past fuck ups you had no control over, destroy your future happiness. More than that, if there's anything in your past that could be a trigger in the dungeon, I sincerely hope you listed it as a hard limit. I learned my lesson the hard way and I'd hate for you to make the same mistake."

"Peyton, I know you're trying to help, but I'm fine."

"I heard what happened with the bondage training. I'm not judging you and I'm not pressuring you to tell me something you're not ready to. All I'm saying is, know your limits." She hugged Savannah fiercely. "Stone and Hawk won't stop looking for Luke, Savvy. They'll find him. You have to believe that."

"I'm trying, but every day that goes by … the not knowing is killing me. When I could speak to

Nancy and hear his excited chatter when he heard my voice over the phone, I believed that Decker had used the threats just to punish me for turning him over. How was I supposed to know he'd get to Luke from jail? What if he had Nancy killed? And Luke? How do I know if he's still alive? I never realized just how cruel that man is."

"Let's not tempt fate by making assumptions or thinking the worst, Savvy. Aunt Vera? Does she know about Luke?"

"No. I don't know why but I guess instinct warned me to keep his existence quiet. I was scared Decker might talk to her and she'd say something about Luke. You know how badly she wants to be a grandmother and she'd be the proudest ever, gushing to everyone. If he had known, God knows what he would've made me, or my mother do in the sick games he played."

"They'll find him, Savannah. I believe it with all my heart."

"It's the only hope I'm clinging to now, Peyton."

"Sub ST, Master Hawk requested that you join him in the torture chamber in The Dungeon of Sin."

"Do you know why?" Savannah asked the coordinator hesitantly. He never sought her out in any of the member dungeons, although she was always aware of his presence close by. It had set her mind at ease that he was there to look over her. A silly notion, admittedly, because as the Training Master, he did the same for all the trainees.

"I believe he's about to do a Shibari demonstration."

Savannah felt like she had just thrown a bucket of ice water over her. She should've known he wouldn't let the incident with Danton slide. Master Hawk had the innate ability to uncover a sub's deepest secrets without effort. To use her fears and boundaries to loosen the demons inside her. She'd seen him do it numerous times and had stood in awe of his skill. She also remembered how emotionally drained the subs were afterward. Happy, but bared to the bone. Much like she was the other day. She still had no idea why she blathered everything to him. She nibbled on her nail. Not one of the subs had fallen back into their old habits of denial once he'd released them from the chains that held them bound. If only she had the guts to tell him about all her demons, maybe then she'd be freed from the hateful nightmares.

"I can't be one of them. I can't tell him what I've done. I can't stand to see the disgust in his eyes when he—"

"Is there a problem, sub ST?"

Savannah started at the deep voice of Dom Evans, one of the assistant training Doms, next to her. "No, Sir."

"Then I suggest you hustle. Master Hawk's mood has been volatile since his return, to say the least. Making him wait isn't going to end well for you."

She rushed toward the dungeon, but her feet felt like they were encased in lead. Heavy bondage was listed as a soft limit on her application, which meant the Masters would push her boundaries. Chained always made her run, but she hadn't expected to experience the same kind of debilitating fear when Danton had bound that harness tightly around her. And when he'd continued to truss her up to elevate her, she'd lost it. The entire time she'd been in the BDSM lifestyle, bondage had been limited to handcuffs. She'd been put in the stocks with Peyton once for punishment, and that had pushed her limit, but with her cousin next to her, she'd managed to breathe through it.

Fucking hell, Savannah, how naive are you? You knew as a trainee; full rope bondage was bound to happen.

Peyton's warning earlier that day rang in her head. Like her cousin, Savannah believed she'd cope with something that could trigger fear.

It's not too late. Tell him before you flip out again.

It was an excellent suggestion but one she immediately shot down. She wasn't ready. Maybe she'd never be.

Her heart rate zoomed as she walked through the tall, heavily carved doors depicting three lovers in a lascivious position, into the Dungeon of Sin. The familiar sounds and smells of sex and pain engulfed her. Each of the three member dungeons offered similar activities but different kinds of kink. This one was all about lurid and unexpurgated lusts.

Her heels clicked on the tiled floor as she walked down the left hallway. Master Hawk was pacing the entrance alcove in front of the torture chamber. Her steps slowed, suddenly finding it difficult to breathe. Who wouldn't, when faced with the devastatingly powerful and sexy frame of such a powerful Dom.

She couldn't help it; her eyes devoured him, unable to look away. It had been like this from day one, the visceral reaction she had to him, something she'd never experienced with anyone before.

The unexpectedness of his blazing eyes clashing with hers, stole her breath and she had to heave in air to fill her lungs. The intensity of his gaze robbed her of any coherent thought; it was a mixture of concern, of understanding and lust. The warning flash she detected made her realize she should be in the present position and lower her gaze. She quickly did. Her entire body sizzled once she managed to break the intense eye-fuck and then spiked with sparks of heat as he sauntered forward.

"Did you get lost, sub?"

"No, Master Hawk. I apologize for making you wait," she said before he could demand an apology.

Sometimes it was better to be upfront about tardiness.

"Hmm," he grunted. "Follow me."

His deep tenor demanded obedience, which she did without thought. She felt every eye in the massive chamber on them as she trailed after him. It wasn't difficult to keep her focus on the rippling broadness of his back. His entire persona demanded attention from everyone.

He stopped next to a padded torture table with side bars to hook a sub's knees over and iron loops with cuffs at the ready on the four ends.

Savannah glanced toward the opposite corner of the room where the roping section was. Numerous Doms were in the process of performing either Shibari or Kinbaku, both ancient Japanese binding techniques.

"I thought ... Janice said you're going to do a Shibari demonstration."

"I requested Master Bear to take over."

"But—"

"Enough talking. Strip, sub ST." He looked at the black stilettos on her feet. "Except for those."

"What? Why?" Savannah gaped at him. This was a first, since he'd never scened with her before, not during training and definitely not in the members' dungeons.

His eyebrows did that arch thing again, only this time it was laced with a dark warning. It carried enough heat to awaken the bold brat inside her. Her chin tilted and with her eyes on his, she snapped open the front fastenings of the tight red corset she wore and pushed the matching satin mini skirt over her hips with her other hand. She caught it with the toe of her shoe and flicked it directly at Hawk. He caught it deftly as she pushed the narrow straps of the top off her shoulders. She didn't dare throw it at him too, especially as he openly ogled her bouncing tits. His perusal continued lower and when it ended at the red thong hugging her hips, he glanced up at her. The blast of heat from those glowing gray eyes scoffed at her boldness. She felt ridiculed at the realization that he'd seen it for what it was—an act, a failed attempt at bravery. Like his namesake, Hawk had no such troubles. There was no pretense in his bold gaze.

Hell no, there so isn't.

He owned the moment, as bold as his namesake and without reservation or fabrication. Hawk's laser eyes did the impossible. It burned and froze her in place with that one look. Two conflicting sensations at the same time.

How the devil did these Masters do it?

"If I'm not mistaken, you seem to be begging for an attitude adjustment, sub ST."

"No, Master Hawk," she puffed quickly and shuffled into the present position once more. Her cheeks bloomed a becoming rosy tint as she detected the red miniskirt he dangled between his fingers, his brows pulled into a question mark.

"Ehm … I … that wasn't intentional," she lilted, biting her lip to keep the smile at bay. He looked almost adorable with the red piece of satin he twirled around a finger.

"It wasn't?"

"Indeed, Master Hawk." One hand came to the front and fluttered in the air. "A mere … er … slip of my ankle, so to speak."

"I see." He released the skirt. It arrowed through the air toward Savannah. She caught it with a flurry of hands. Her eyes narrowed at the smile of satisfaction on his face with his gaze zooming in on the jiggling movement of her ample breasts.

"You're a pervert, Master Hawk." Her voice was coated with acerbic reproach.

"Is it perversion to appreciate such natural beauty, my pet?"

He encroached on her space, coming chest-to-chest with her. His smile widened at what she realized was an agonized gasp from her lips as his hardness brushed against her nipples. The two traitors acknowledged his closeness by tightening into hard little stones.

"They're too big," she hissed as he moved his chest back and forth, tormenting her further.

He leaned back and stared at her chest, surprised at the reddish glows that covered her skin.

"Hm, personally," he murmured as he cupped them in his large hands, brushing his thumbs over the distended tips. "I believe they're the perfect size. Almost like they were made to fit ... my hands."

Savannah didn't know what to think or how to react to this side of the, up until now, aloof Master. Especially in light of the fact that she'd expected to be trussed up in ropes by now.

"I'm confused. If you asked Master Bear to do the Shibari demonstration, what am I doing here?"

she blathered in an effort to force her wayward emotions under control.

This man could all too easily crawl into her heart, just as he already had under her skin ... and into her loins ... not to mention keeping her ovaries jumping to attention whenever he was in the vicinity. It was overwhelming ... to have his sole attention on her. Now she understood why the trainees literally sank to their knees during a scene when he attended to them.

He circled her, inflaming every inch of her skin with a scorching look. An insolent finger traced the curve of her soft buttocks, the slope of her breast, and even patted the hidden nub between her legs.

Savannah felt the rush of emotions that ran the spectrum from arousal to awe to exasperation. He seemed unperturbed, keeping mum, and continued to tease and torment her.

"Well, did the cat catch your tongue or am I supposed to hazard a guess?" she snipped, desperate for some distance from the digit that felt like it was loaded with a ten-thousand-volt charge.

One moment he was circling her at arm's length and the next, he stepped close to her again.

Dangerous. Stealthy. Deadly. He had the ability to sneak up behind a sub and she'd never know he was there until it was too late. Like now. She had no warning until he spoke against her ear in a deep timbre that rolled over her like warm honey.

"Definitely begging for an attitude adjustment."

"No, I just don't particularly like being the mouse in this game."

"Ah, so finally I meet the real Savannah Thorne. I've been wondering when she was going to come out and play."

Savannah stubbornly pressed her lips together, annoyed at his remark and then she realized how true his assessment was. She had been a meek, frail submissive from arrival. Her true nature had been suppressed since her return from Russia. It had been so long that she'd forgotten how volatile she used to be. Cheeky, bratty, and downright defiant. It was enlightening, enervating, and filled her with hope.

That he was the man to finally unlock her true self didn't register at that moment; all she knew was that she loved bantering with him, challenging him … until he—

Until he what? Fucked me again?

No, he told you it won't happen again, so don't count your lucky stars just yet.

The chuckle from deep within his chest cloaked her in its seductive cords. A ripple of pleasure trailed down her spine.

"Your reaction to the ropes in the training session told me you have a trigger you withheld on your application form." The hesitation was brief, filling the space with a dour warning. "Care to enlighten me about it?"

Savannah heaved in a deep breath. Her chin lowered in defeat. She was going to disappoint him … again.

"I'm waiting, sub."

"Master Hawk, please don't ask me to. I don't want to lie to you, not again but I'm not … I'm not ready to talk about it."

She held her breath, hating that he stood behind her and she couldn't see his expression or guess what he was thinking—if he even believed her. The loss of his heat as he took a step back was enough to cause her knees to buckle. It took a mammoth effort to remain on her feet.

"You have a problem with bondage, but it's not a hard limit for you. Therefore, it leads me to believe that you find it difficult to trust the Dom you're with to read the signs of your distress," The words floated over her skin to soothe her rattled senses. "On your back on the table, please, sub ST."

She scrambled onto the table without hesitation. He'd given her a reprieve and she'd reward him with eager submission.

When Savannah looked at him, her breath caught at the gleam in his eyes, at the wicked smile quirking his lips as he dangled a long red scarf from his fingertips.

Seriously? A scarf?

"I hate to be the one to point out the obvious to you, Master Hawk, but that's not a rope, so what are you intending to do with it?"

"Teach you."

His wrist flicked and she watched in fascination as the end of the soft material floated across her skin in a snake-like curve from her neck to her mons. The sensation sparked her nerves to life.

"T-Teach me?" she stammered. Her tongue did a foray over her suddenly dry lips.

"Ahu."

His attention was on her chest as he guided the scarf around her breasts, tantalizingly first the one then the other until her nipples hardened. Next, he tormented her thighs, trailing it up and down their length.

"Yes, sub ST. Teach you to trust that I'll use bondage only to enhance your sexual experience, not to restrict your freedom or to hurt you." The scarf pooled at the apex of her thighs. "Spread your legs."

Her hesitation was brief but when his eyes lifted to hers, her thighs parted as if those globes shining like polished silver, waved a magic wand and said, *abracadabra.*

"Beautiful, little one," he praised and teased her labia with swats from the scarf that were as light as butterfly wings.

Good lord! Her breath wheezed from her throat at the sensation. It might as well be a flick of his flogger; it was that effective.

Her hips moved restlessly as he continued the breezy caress. The soft moan escaped uncontrolled from her lips as did the arch of her back and her eyes fluttered closed, unconsciously begging for more.

"Savannah."

The unexpected gruffness and the sound of her name zipped her eyes opened and she looked at him. His expression didn't give anything away, but the heat that exuded from his body, threatened to burn her to a cinder.

The scarf fluttered over her pussy.

"Hmm ... I can smell your enticing bouquet, little one. Does that mean you want my fingers inside you?"

"Yes," she whispered immediately, her eyes not wavering from his.

His smile was brief, almost a painful twist of his lips.

"And my mouth, little one? Do you want my mouth there too?"

"God, yes!" she begged feverishly.

"Then who am I to deny you?" His words rolled in a dark promise over her. "Lift your arms above your head."

Contrary to her wariness for bondage, she didn't hesitate. It shook her. Why didn't she? Was it because it was him, the powerful Master Hawk, who with the lightest of touch set her on fire?

"There is such beauty in submission," he purred. He wrapped the scarf around her one arm and slowly tugged it upward to circle her wrist. He secured her hands together and then looped it through the steel loops at the top of the table.

Savannah dragged in a deep breath as she lost his touch. She yanked on the bindings and just like that, the dreaded rush of panic assailed her.

"Easy, little one," his voice wrapped its soothing syllables around her tortured soul and his fingertips trailed over the inside of her arm in a lazy sensual caress. "Breathe, Savannah, and keep your eyes open. Watch me, all the time."

He leaned over her. "Do you trust me, my pet?"

"Yes, Master Hawk, I do." It wasn't a question that needed consideration. She did trust him, unconditionally.

"Then let me show you the pleasures of bondage, little one."

He pulled another scarf from the back of his pants. She bit her lip as he dragged the material over both her breasts. She realized it was a silk scarf, aimed at more tormenting of her senses.

"Such a lovely reaction needs to be rewarded," he said with a smile curling the corners of his mouth as her nipples peaked.

"Oh lord," she squealed as he leaned in and sucked her nipples, teasing little sucks alternating with hard, deep tugs that made her toes curl.

Before she could gather her wits, he straightened and twisted the scarf and slipped it under her back. She followed his quick movements as he crisscrossed the silky material above her one breast and below the other and knotted it in the valley of her cleavage. Her eyes widened as he pulled the roped scarf taut beneath her between her shoulder blades.

Her mesmerized gaze took in the tempting offering of her large breasts, which with the added pressure of the breast binding, looked even firmer and bigger.

"Master Hawk," she gasped as he once again lowered his mouth to her nipple. He sucked. Vigorously. Then softly. He completely shattered her equilibrium with the conflicting sensations when he opened his mouth wider to pull more of her succulent flesh inside his mouth.

A sharp nip on the taut nub stilled her as she started to thrash under him. The heel of his hand on the top of her mound forced her hips down. Her desire soared.

Why aren't I scared?

Savannah realized her hands were relaxed, as was her whole body. She was at a loss as to why the feeling of being bound increased her desire. All the times she'd attempted it at the BDSM clubs, she'd safe-worded the moment the ropes were in place. Was it because he used scarfs?

No, she immediately negated the thought. It was the way he was in control of the situation, of her. Every touch ratcheted her need sky-high.

"Oh ... mmm," she moaned as he positioned himself at the edge of the table between her thighs and trailed kisses in a straight line over her belly button, her lower abdomen, stopping at the edge of the red thong. He pulled it away from her body and released it. Her surprised shriek of pain didn't faze him.

"What does the word strip mean. sub?"

"Oh, I ... must've forgotten, Master Hawk."

"Hm," he grunted and with an efficient tear, ripped the piece of satin from her hips. "Let's just make it easier in the future, shall we? No more panties for you, is that understood?"

"Never?" she asked with bated breath as he brushed his palm over her labia.

"Never." He glanced up at her. "How many times have the Masters feasted on this decadent cunt of yours?" His eyes smoldered with an emotion Savannah couldn't decipher.

"I ... er, didn't keep count, Master Hawk." She stared at him and decided to take the plunge. "But I've often wondered why you always chose not to."

"I choose to now," was the only response he offered. He nudged her thighs open wider with his shoulders as he sat down on the small round chair at the end of the table. "And I intend to make up for what I've lost out on."

He ran the pads of his thumbs up the inside of her labia and opened her like a flower.

"Please," she whimpered as he inhaled before he blew his hot breath on her very needy and wet folds. She had never been this desperate to feel a man's lips and tongue on and inside her girlie bits.

Her hips twitched as he licked her. Delicate, little taps with his tongue, until she wanted to scream at him. Just when she was about to combust, he flattened his tongue and dragged it up her slit, up and down, over, and over. He reveled in the throaty moans and cries falling from her lips. With the tip of his tongue, he drew circles around her clit. Tiny, barely there circles before he flicked his tongue in a tantalizing warning at her entrance before he jammed it inside her pussy completely.

"Oh lord, oh lord!"

Her raw cry echoed around them, her back arched in pleasure, her toes curled in her shoes, and she had to force her hips to stay still and not grind her pussy into his face. That would end in disaster. She'd learned the lesson very quickly. The Master was always in charge, dare to demand more and the cruel reminder would be in the form of withholding orgasms.

She was floating on a cloud of euphoria, her loins throbbed with such pressure, she could barely breathe.

"Master Hawk, please ... I need to come," she begged in a throaty whimper, lost in the strength of his shoulders pushing her thighs further apart and the velvety seduction of his tongue.

"I'd like you to hold out a little longer, little one. I'd like to enjoy your silky and tasty cunt more."

She moaned and cried as he alternated tender licks and brutal sucks, drawing on every bit of liquid he found there. She felt like she was being devoured, eaten like a starved man who couldn't stop feasting on a tasty meal. Her hips jerked as he flicked her clit with a firm tongue.

A carnal moan broke from her lips. Heat engulfed her as he sucked on the tender nub and pushed two thick fingers deep inside her to tap on the bundle of nerves on the inside wall of her vagina. The dual attack pushed her to teeter on the edge. She bit her lip, forcing the climax back, wanting to offer him all he was after. Her legs trembled. She clenched her fists in desperation.

"Gaaawd, I can't ...," she wailed. She'd gone past the go mark, long ago. The pulsing need hovered, waiting to tumble over.

"Give it to me, my pet," he growled against her sensitive flesh. "Now!" Then he sucked her clit hard, alternating with sharp bites as his fingers gently stroked the ganglia inside her. The conflict of relentlessness and gentleness sent her off like a rocket.

She thrashed, she twisted and jagged under the force of his mouth. The scarf around her wrists tightened but all it did was reinforce the urgent pulsing of blood in her veins in the same rhythm as the spasms in her pussy.

Her back arched in a bow as a raw scream splintered over the other sounds around them. He increased the hard sucks, he bit the sensitive nub and shook his head, intensifying the spasms that rolled with ruthless intensity through her.

Her body trembled at the loss when he eased back, stroking her inner thighs, placing tender kisses on the soft skin above her mound.

Savannah felt the shudders slowdown in her body and for the first time, she had the overwhelming urge to curl into a ball and cry. It stumped her, the way he could make her burn hot and fast, purely because he took the time to find her fuse, to show her how good it could be if she offered him her complete trust. She moaned as his hands traveled up her sides to caress the skin below the scarf crisscrossing her breasts. Her eyes flickered open. She'd completely forgotten about the breast binding or her hands that were still tied.

"That was beautiful, little one." He dragged a hard, open mouthed kiss down to her collarbone, the move so possessively erotic she shivered at the thought that he'd left a mark there. The glow of satisfaction in his eyes when he lifted his head, confirmed her suspicion.

"You're a beautiful woman, Savannah, but you're breathtaking when you unravel from my touch."

Savannah was still struggling at the possessiveness of his actions to respond and relaxed as he reached up and untied her.

He checked her wrists for marks and rubbed her palms.

"Okay, little one? No pain or feeling panicked?"

"No, Master Hawk, none whatsoever."

"Next time, we'll use a rope," he said once he'd removed the breast binding and assisted her from the table.

Wonderful. Would I be so lucky as to be fucked at the end? She couldn't help the thought, especially as her loins throbbed and her pussy pulsed in demand of his hard cock taking possession of it.

Hawk tipped back her chin and stared at her for long moments.

"No, Savannah. I gave in to your lure once. It won't happen again."

She gaped at him. She knew she hadn't said the words aloud. How the devil did he know her thoughts?

"Why? You fuck the other trainees and subs in here all the time."

"They're different."

"I don't understand."

He outlined her face with his fingertips, his expression enigmatic. He offered her a smile of regret.

"You're going to leave once you find your son, and if I give into the need inside me to take you … I won't allow you to."

Savannah was still trying to grasp the meaning of what he'd said when Hawk took the stairs to his private apartment.

Chapter Nine

"I think I may know where baby Luke is."

Stone and Hawk looked up at the excited exclamation from Parker as he stormed into Stone's office. They were discussing strategies to be activated the moment they had information about Luke, Decker Cooper, and the Blue Bayou file. They always used the BSE offices underground when they discussed business.

"Did you find them on the GeoSat system?" Hawk asked.

"We did and managed to follow the SUV they were abducted in but only up to the outskirts of Washington DC. We tried to pick them up on the traffic cams but there must've been some kind of disruption in that area at the time, seeing as there was no footage for a couple of days."

"Fuck. I'd hoped to strike it lucky." The frustration was rife in Hawk's voice.

"I did, however, find some very interesting information on the previous and very corrupt Deputy Director of the FBI hidden in the deep web, not to mention what we're uncovering in the dark web."

"Well? Spit it out, Parker." Hawk's voice grated with impatience. Since the scene with Savannah in The Dungeon of Sin, two nights before, he'd spent his time at BSE, leaving his assistant training Doms to continue with the submissives training. He never disclosed his emotions, not visually and sure as hell not verbally. He still struggled to understand why he'd admitted something so personal to her that he'd not even acknowledged to himself.

The moment he'd said it, the truth of it had slammed so hard at his chest that he'd felt the chambers inside opening to the lure of being loved and loving someone—no, not someone—her. He'd forced his mind blank and stomped to his apartment to castigate his stupidity. Now she'd have expectations. He'd stood on the balcony outside his bedroom, staring out to sea for hours without finding a solution to what he knew was the one reason there was no happily ever-after for him with Savannah Thorne.

Her baby boy, Luke. The moment they were reunited, she had no reason to stay and would leave. That clinched it for Hawk. The quicker they found him, the sooner she would leave, and he could go on with his life ... uncomplicated and organized.

And lonely, Sinclair. Don't forget lonely.

Hawk pushed the dreary thought to the back of his mind. He forced his attention to Parker who displayed numerous pictures and documentation on the large monitor on the one wall of Stone's office.

"Decker Cooper is an exceedingly wealthy man. He inherited the biggest chunk of his father's estate. Do either of you recall the Property Developer, Anthony Cooper?"

"That was his father?" Stone tapped his pen on the desk. "He died a couple of years ago if I recall correctly, about the same time DC was appointed as DD at the FBI."

"Correct, a month after to be exact. Many said it was his father's influence and money that got him the job. Even though DC had been a top agent in the

FBI, he wasn't the next in line. There were many unhappy people at the time."

"But he proved them wrong. Apart from the fact that we now know he was corrupt, he achieved a lot in the years in that position." Hawk stared at the photograph of DC. "I can't recall that I'd ever seen any articles about his mother. Did she also die in the accident that killed his father?"

"No, and this is where it becomes interesting. I had to do some serious digging to find her, but she is alive and well. Her name was changed immediately after her husband's death from Fiona Cooper to Dora Brooks." Parker watched them expectantly.

"Dora Brooks? The self-appointed high society dame of Washington DC? The same one who has been seen numerous times rubbing shoulders with congressmen and politicians?" Hawk straightened. "Why would she have changed her name?"

"I can't find any legitimate reason, but if you compare photos of her before she arrived in DC to after," Parker pulled up the two pictures side by side, "it looks like a completely different woman."

"Fucking hell," Hawk leaned forward with his elbows on the desk. "Are you sure that's the same woman?"

"That's what our research indicates, but I'll confirm using a facial comparison program."

"And where is she now?"

"I can't find an address for her. All her bank statements are delivered electronically. There's no vehicle registered in her name, the address on her driver's license is an empty warehouse in Arlington that has been up for sale for years." Parker looked between the two men. "The red flag in all this isn't that she'd changed her name. It's the fact that DC's personnel file at the FBI indicates that his mother is deceased."

"Why would he want everyone to believe that?" Hawk looked at Stone. "DC must've had a reason for wanting to keep her out of the picture."

"Could be that his shady dealings might endanger her life and it was the only way he could think of to keep her safe," Stone said.

"I think you might be right." Hawk leaned back in his chair as he perused the file Parker had handed them containing all the information on

Decker he could find so far. "So, where do you think we'll find Luke?"

"My gut instinct tells me Luke is with Dora Brooks. Now, we just have to find her." Parker closed the documents. "I've got the team running facial recognition through the entire Washington DC area. I'm hoping to catch her somewhere on the street or at an ATM and see if we can use the GeoSat and traffic cams to follow her to her house."

"Well, she loves the limelight, so chances are you'll catch a lucky break." Stone nodded at Parker. "Good work, little bro. Put as many of your team on that as you need. We need to find that little boy and fast."

"One more thing. Like Ace suggested the other day, it seemed strange that the hackers tried to get into DC's Blue Bayou file. We're still verifying certain links, but I can prove without a doubt that Decker Cooper had been involved in human trafficking for the past seven years, more specifically with the Russian Bratva. He's been working closely with the Contessa group, a Russian crime syndicate in Brooklyn's Brighton Beach for the past eight years. He's the one who supplied all the women meant for the Bratva in Russia who they then set up in whore houses as sex slaves. I've got data of all his movements, of the money he received, of the paper trail he left when he tried to scrap all information of the women from the system." Parker leaned forward. "And get this. The women who were saved five years ago? He took the credit for finding them and cracking open the human trafficking ring who shipped them off."

"And no one questioned it? How the hell did he claim to have done that? It was a combined effort between the DOJ, DHS, and the FBI."

"Yes, based on a call made to the FBI from a woman begging to be saved. She even gave them accurate directions to where the women had been kept prisoner. DC claimed it was his undercover agent that had gone along as a coordinator to keep the women calm en route and ensure they were kept safe during the journey there. Somehow, she ended up as one of the slaves."

"Hold on. Those women said they were holed up there for almost a year. Are you saying he never bothered to find out what had happened to his undercover agent?" Hawk frowned as he stared at Parker.

"Oh, no, he claimed he was in contact with her constantly. She had taken her order one level further and swapped places with one of the women so that they could crack open the entire operation."

"Which never happened. Something about information and dockets being lost and they couldn't pinpoint anything on the leaders, Sergei, and Yury Kumarin," Stone said.

"And the undercover agent? What happened to her?" Hawk asked.

"I can't find anything so far. There's some deleted data which we're working on recovering. It might be in there. I suppose it was necessary to keep her identity a secret. If the Bratva found out she was FBI and working undercover for the man who is their supplier, both their lives would be worthless."

"And this latest group of women? Was DC involved there as well?" Stone stared at the information Parker scrolled through on screen.

"Hell, yes. That's why he was in Miami when the missile hit our island. The women were shipped from a small port there, and I found traffic cam footage placing him at the docks at the time the ship sailed." Parker grinned. "I think Deputy Director Decker Cooper is in big shit. He was paid upfront for the women. The Bratva won't be happy, especially as it's the second group of slaves they've lost, and this last group hadn't made them a penny yet."

"Which means DC has a big fat target on his back. The Princes of Thieves is the Russian gang in the prisons. Fuck!" Hawk jumped up and paced the room. "If they kill him, Stone and we're unable to locate his mother in time, she might disappear with Luke in fear of being charged with aiding a kidnapping."

"Let's hope that doesn't happen. I have a suspicion I know the trump card he plans to play to get out of prison, Hawk, and the reason why he wanted Savannah to stay on The Seven Keys Island."

"I'm listening."

Stone briefly told him about the theory he and Savannah had discussed. Hawk didn't say anything at first. He stared out over the ocean with a pensive expression on his face.

"I'll talk to my dad. He'll have to find a way to get him out of that prison."

"No, we can't do that. It might ruin Uncle Xavier's career." Stone got up and walked up to Hawk. "Look, I know you're concerned, we all are, but we have to think logically about this. We can't give in to unlawful practices to a bastard like him."

Hawk turned. "I am thinking logically, Stone. If Parker and his team can find Dora Brooks, we need to get Luke immediately. I believe he's correct in his assumption that Luke's with her. Once we have the boy, we inform Madam Secretary of his scheme. When he's released, the DHS keep track of his movements until they catch him red-handed with the Bratva leaders. Think about it, Stone. It's the one chance DHS and DOJ will have to end one of the largest human trafficking schemes in the U.S., and if there's enough evidence, crack down on the Bratva and Contessa group as well. I sure as hell believe the Russian Government will do everything they can to end the reign of the Kumarin family."

"You do have a point." Stone stared at him pensively. "If she agrees, there has to be no chance that he escapes. Even if it means we have to personally be involved in the field operation. We better discuss this with the entire team. Parker, can you arrange a meeting in thirty minutes?"

"On it."

"One moment, Parker," Hawk interjected. "You said Cooper inherited millions from his father.

Was it only money or did he leave him any property?"

"I know where you're going with this. We already sent a team to DC's house in The Palisades in Washington. There's no one there but his housekeeper. But I'll see if I can find details on the exact content of his father's will."

"What are you thinking, Hawk?"

"He went to a lot of trouble to keep his mother's identity secret. I don't believe for one second he doesn't have her settled in a place where he can keep an eye on her, or for that matter, control every move she makes. It's the only reason I believe he'd leave Luke with her. He knows no one can link the two of them together."

"As soon as we crack the last of the dark web folders, we might have the final pieces of the puzzle on Decker Cooper." Parker gathered his laptop and headed to the door. "See you in thirty."

Hawk was back in the position in front of the window. He couldn't shake the feeling that Savannah was involved in the release of the sex slaves five years ago. He remembered Stone mentioning she got drunk after she returned from an undercover operation and if he recalled correctly, it was five years ago.

His mind shied away from the possibility that she had been the undercover agent DC claimed had swapped places with one of the women. The timing fit and he didn't believe in coincidences. Her voice echoed in his mind.

"Master Hawk, please don't ask me to. I don't want to lie to you, not again, but I'm not ... I'm not ready to talk about it."

It hadn't been his imagination. He'd heard the despair in her voice but the note of disgust that laced each syllable had been undeniable.

Savannah Thorne wasn't who he had believed her to be. He frowned. Or was he too quick to grasp at straws and believed the worst of her in an attempt to keep her at bay? She was a data systems analyst; it would've been unethical and against FBI policies to send her on such an operation. She wasn't trained to handle field situations, definitely not something involving human trafficking. His mind drifted back to the conversation they had the day she told him about Luke.

"After that, he ignored me, except to force me into situations at work I was completely ill-equipped to handle, just like he'd done six years ago.

That confirmed his suspicions. His hands fisted as the visions of what she must've gone through flashed through his mind. Decker Cooper was a bastard, and he'd gotten to where he was through lies, deceit, and downright corruption. The fact that he showed no remorse for what a terrible ordeal it must've been for Savannah—to be forced into sex slavery for a year—clinched his fate as far as Hawk was concerned.

Maybe he was wrong, and it was nothing but coincidence.

Don't rush your judgment, Sinclair. You're making assumptions.

If Savannah was the woman Cooper referred to, she had more than enough evidence to go to the Director of the FBI and report him. It didn't make sense that she wouldn't have. His brows drew together in a fierce frown.

Or is she lying to me? What if she's still a part of the entire scheme? For all I know she's in love with Decker Cooper and is a willing participant in some sick game he orchestrated to take revenge on us for putting him in jail.

He ran his hand over his eyes, tired beyond measure. He hadn't slept for two days, too worked up over his reaction to Savannah Thorne.

Fuck! Am I making another mistake? Am I trusting her too quickly?

His mouth in a grim line, he followed Stone to the boardroom one level lower for the meeting with the rest of the team. He had to talk to her and find out the truth. She might be no more than a game piece in a fucked-up scheme Decker Cooper masterminded.

The United States Penitentiary, Florence High, in Fremont County near Florence, Colorado.

A gush of pain jolted throughout Decker's body. His stomach ached, his arms lost tension and his legs began to weaken. He stumbled back, clutching his stomach.

Fucking bastard! He said I had five days.

He should've known better. Yury Kumarin didn't suffer fools easily and he had a point to prove which was why Decker was being roughed up by Alexei Petrov, the leader of the Princes of Thieves gang. And he knew why. It was to punish him for not sending the bitch Savannah Thorne back to Sergei Kumarin.

How the fuck had they found out about Savannah? She had been there under a different name, Lucy Simms. I kept her real identity locked tight. There is no way they could've found out … except if someone in the Bureau ratted me out. Fuck!

"Ugh!" The fist came out of nowhere and caught him against his temple. He went down like a log. His tongue was soaked in the taste of blood. His cried out in pain as a hard sneaker kicked him in the knee followed by another in his gut.

"Get up, fuckface."

Two men grabbed Decker under his arms and dragged him to his feet. He was fucked. He could fight but he stood no chance against the giant Russian. His muscles bulged as he stepped forward.

Decker refused to be intimidated. He lurched toward him and fisted his shirt in his hand. The attempt to wrestle the huge man to the ground was pitiful, which his roaring laugh of mirth attested to.

"You don't have what it takes to fight me, American," Alexei sneered as he jabbed Decker in the ribs. "The Boss wanted me to remind you what happens to bastards who betray them or stab them in the back. He said you have three days left. If you don't give him the answer he wants, I'll come for you with my shiv."

He grabbed Decker by the hair and with a mighty heave, brought his face down sharply onto his bent knee. Blood flowed from his broken nose as he staggered backwards. One of the Russian's cohorts tripped Decker and he fell to the ground.

Bruised and winded, with his face throbbing agonizingly he struggled to push himself upright. His head pounded from the cackling laughter of the inmates cheering the Russian.

"Well, do you have anything to say, American?"

"Tell your boss, he'll get the answer he's looking for," Decker managed in a hoarse whisper, blood running from his nose to fill his mouth.

It was time to play his trump card, his plan A, the easiest way out and his first choice of escape.

Decker always prepared a backup plan and it had taken two days to get a plan B in place. He couldn't act before everything was set in stone. It was how he operated. He smirked. Nothing would go wrong. By the time Yury Kumarin came back, he'd be ready to leave this hellhole.

Savannah Thorne had no idea what he had in store for her and if she didn't play along ... he wouldn't hesitate to use her brat to force her to compliance.

Decker Cooper felt nothing for the little boy. He'd been annoyed when he'd found out Savannah had a baby. He had never questioned the child's parentage. He'd known it was his. Although she'd joined a BDSM club, she wasn't the kind of woman to sleep around, especially after what she'd been through. Their affair had been short, but he knew she hadn't been involved with anyone else. He'd been keeping tabs on her since the day she'd returned from Russia—closely. He'd played his cards close to his chest. Consoled her and assured her of his attempts to find her. He couldn't afford anyone finding out he'd sent her to Russia. It would've ended his career.

Luckily, she was too emotionally unsettled to doubt his sincerity. He couldn't afford the chance that she'd rat him out. Not that she knew about his involvement with the Bratva or the Contessa group, but the story she would tell would be entirely different than the one he told the Director, and it would raise suspicion immediately. If his plan worked, he needed to reestablish his relationship with FBI Director Frank Moore and couldn't afford Savannah filling his head with stories. He had every intention of stepping back into his old job ... for a while at least.

Mother was right, I don't want the fucking brat, but he'll do to keep the bitch in line. He cracked out a laugh. *And once I've handed her over to Sergei, I'll sell him on the black market to the highest bidder.* He snorted. *It'll be perfect. The sex slave mother and her sex slave brat.*

Chapter Ten

Hawk perused the group of trainees as they sat down at the ten desks in his training dungeon. A variety of twitters exploded through the vast space when they noticed a large dildo in front of each of them. Some were excited, others a little reserved, and a couple appeared frazzled.

With certain subject sessions, they combined two of the training groups for expediency. Today, his and Kane's groups were there to hone their skills to give the perfect blowjob.

Hawk's eyes skimmed over Savannah where she sat in the third row. Her lips were pursed in a displeased pout. As a man who loved a mind-blowing blowjob and a good throat fuck, he hoped it wasn't indicative of her aversion to a big pulsating cock nudging her lips apart. He had been imagining her full pucker wrapped around his dick since the day she'd arrived and swept her tongue over her lips in a nervous gesture.

Clap. Clap. Clap

The rhythmic sound of the crop snapping against his black jeans went unnoticed by the chattering women. They tentatively touched and examined the dildos that very closely represented a man's cock, all purple and veiny. His bicep rippled and bulged as he pushed the tips of his fingers into the front pocket of the jeans. The crop dangled from his fingers of the other.

Clap. Clap. Clap.

His eyes narrowed as he waited, his patience slowly withering under the continued disrespect of the group of trainees. The white t-shirt hugged his muscled chest like a second skin, showcasing the washboard stomach underneath to mouthwatering perfection. It was the one thing all seven cousins took pride in: taking care of their bodies. They spent at least two hours in the gym on the ground floor every day.

Kane and the eight assistant training Doms, stood along opposite walls, watching. No one uttered a word. If any of the trainees looked up, they would've noticed the curt glint in the expression of Master Hawk's eyes as his gaze touched on each of the trainees who seemed to have forgotten the golden rule. Never disregard the Training Master, no matter where you are or what you're doing. They continued to banter and giggle amongst themselves with no care to his presence or that of the other Doms. His silent but chilling reproach traveled through the room. It didn't take long for the trainees, one by one, to catch his bristling gaze. Their eyes lowered respectfully as their chatter died away. They all realized the glint in his eyes promised retribution.

Clap. Clap. Clap.

"It seems we have a problem this afternoon." His voice cut through the atmosphere like a sharp knife. He didn't elaborate, he didn't need to. The women all realized they'd overstepped and waited for their punishment with bated breath. Master Hawk was the strictest of all the Masters and when he dished out punishment, they knew it was deserved and that he wouldn't hold back.

"We have a lot to cover this afternoon, therefore your punishment will wait until after dinner." He looked from one to the other. "If one of you is absent from dinner, the rest will receive double punishment. Is that understood?"

"Yes, Master Hawk." A chorus responded to his dour warning.

"By show of hands, how many of you have performed oral sex on a man?" He immediately slipped into the role of educator.

Of the twenty women, roughly half of them raised their hands, Savannah being one of them.

"Who wants to but are too scared because you don't know how?"

Six women raised their hands. He studied the three women left.

"How many hates the thought of orally pleasing a man?"

Three hands lifted.

"Very well. Oral sex for all genders is the same as any sexual act. It's a preference. As a trainee to potentially be accepted as an employee submissive at Castle Sin, you're all required to acquire the skill of performing blowjobs. You're here because you wish to be the best submissive you can be. If it's an act you refuse to partake in, you won't pass the final evaluation."

He allowed his words to sink in before he continued. The three women shifted uncomfortably but remained seated.

"Giving control to a Dom in the act of oral sex, is a complete power shift. Make no mistake, oral sex, giving head, blowjobs, sucking dick, or throat fuck, call it what you wish, it's all about submission. Those of you who are good at cock sucking already know that taking a hard, throbbing dick into your mouth is about pleasing the Dom and serving his needs. That's it. Nothing more, nothing less. This is the one sexual act where a man will always be superior. The moment his shaft disappears inside your mouth, he exults in the surge of power over you."

Hawk wasn't surprised to notice the trainees blushing as his words brought the carnal act to visual imagining.

"Today, we're going to give you the knowledge and the tools of what it takes to please a man orally. This is the time to embrace your inner cock-sucking slut. Remember, it's you who give him the power. If you listen and follow my advice and use the submission a man takes from you while you give him head, it'll be the best fucking blowjob he'll ever have."

"Master Hawk?" Rose Lovett, who had arrived with Peyton's group of trainees, raised her hand.

"Yes, sub RL."

"I'm one of the older trainees here," she smiled as the others agreed playfully, "and I've given my fair share of head. I've always thought I'm quite good at it, but I often wonder, how do I really know if the Dom is enjoying it?"

"Yes! I mean when we're on the receiving end, we thrash and moan and go all sex crazy, but men just stand there, watching their big, hot erection disappear into your mouth and throat," Cora Dunnings, another newbie, said with glowing cheeks.

"A Dom has the self-control to keep his emotions to himself, no matter how much enjoyment he receives. Just remember, we can tell if you don't enjoy gnawing at our knobs."

Hawk smiled as the group giggled, watching him with animated expressions. All except Savannah, whose gaze had been on her hands the entire time. It toggled at the protective Dom inside him. It was obvious that she was distressed. This might be the perfect time to push her to open up to him. To trust him enough to let him help her drive out her demons once and for all.

"So, if you don't like giving head, you better be an excellent faker. How do you know, sub RL? We might not always moan but if a Dom enjoys a BJ, you can be sure to hear raw grunts. We sure as hell can't fake weak knees and believe me, if your ministrations end in an explosive ejaculation, you'll know you did a great job. Women might be able to fake an orgasm; we can't, so that kind of pleasure comes from the real deal."

"And that's what you're going to teach us?" sub CD lilted eagerly.

"I can teach you the tricks of the trade, sub CD, but you must have the desire to give a BJ like a salacious wanton. Brazen and like a hussy. Carefree like a tart. If you want to give great head and be awarded by the uncontrolled reaction from your man, suck that dick like a dirty, nasty slut."

"I think I can do that," a trainee at the back interjected.

"Hell, me too!" a few more shouted.

"Settle down," Hawk's deep voice grated over their noisy chatter which ended abruptly at his command.

"Before we go into specific techniques, we need to evaluate your current skills. I want each of you to show me how you give head using the dildo in front of you. Yes, subs, those of you who have never done it as well."

Savannah stared at the rubber cock with dull eyes. She struggled to keep down the bile that threatened to rise in her throat. The moment she'd seen the dildos on the desks, she'd known what the training session was going to be. Over the past five years, it was the one thing she'd had as a hard limit; she refused to put a man's dick inside her mouth. She cursed herself for not adding it to her limit list here as well.

Hawk's voice droned in the background, but she didn't hear a word, her mind was filled with unwanted visuals of a time where sucking cock had been a daily ritual. A degrading, painful, and hateful reminder that she was no more than fuckholes for the debasing pleasure of the biggest criminal in Russia. One who enjoyed reminding her day in and day out that she was his willing, cheap whore, a cock sucking slut with only one purpose in life. To swallow his cum and to take every drop of his filthy semen he deposited inside her orifices. She heard her breathing wheeze between her lips remembering what he'd made her do when a single drop fell from her lips or slipped from her pussy once he'd gorged himself inside her.

"Is there a problem, sub ST?"

The mellifluous tone of Hawk's voice reached deep inside Savannah and plucked at a needy chord that vibrated through her core. Her breathing settled and a calmness washed over her. She forced her eyelids to rise, and their gazes clashed. It was the first time she'd seen him since the scene in The Dungeon of Sin.

His raised eyebrows reminded her he expected a response, and her gaze dropped to the dildo in front of her. She licked her lips, words of encouragement raced through her mind as she leaned forward. She had to do this. She realized during the bondage scene that Hawk held the key to release her from all the demons chasing her. He had the magic touch to guide her through it all. She needed him, she knew that, but she couldn't tell him what had happened to her six years ago. What had turned her into the shell of the woman she used to be for the year of her captivity and kept her hostage still. Tears formed in her eyes as she opened her mouth. She'd be incapable of watching the disgust in his eyes when he realized just who and what she really was.

"Make it good this time, Lucy, and make it last. If you don't, my entire brigade is going to queue outside this door, and you'll take all their cocks down your throat. Your belly will be so full of their cum, I won't have to feed you for a week."

Savannah whimpered at the voice slamming against her mind. She closed her eyes and felt the tremor deep inside her body. It hadn't been an idle threat. She'd learned in the first month with Sergei Kumarin that his cruelty knew no bounds. How she hated every time he'd taunted her because she'd been forced to become a willing participant in her own debasement.

"Sub ST, I asked you a question." Hawk's tenor vibrated closer.

She forced down the knot forming in her throat. "I ... er, have a ... my throat is a little sore, Master Hawk," she said lamely, her eyes glued on the dildo.

She felt his presence before she saw his jean clad legs appear in front of the desk. Her lip disappeared between her teeth when he didn't say a word, but she could feel his eyes on her, questioning, demanding. It took all the strength she had to remain seated and not run out of the training dungeon.

"I see." He didn't turn away and she had no doubt he noticed her trembling hands clasped on her lap. "Dom Evans, please take sub ST to the sickbay. Stay until Doc Sanders is finished examining her. I want a full report from him."

"That's not necessary. It's probably just signs of a cold," she protested and then whimpered as he pinched her chin between his fingers and forced her gaze to his. His eyes turned molten silver at the tormented expression he detected there. His lips flattened into a grim line.

"What have I told you about lies, sub ST?" His voice was dangerously soft, meant only for her ears.

"I'm not—"

"You have two options. Either you give that dildo head or you follow Dom Evans to the sickbay." His fingers tightened painfully. "Know this, if Doc Sanders confirms my suspicion, you *will* suffer the consequences. Choose. Now."

"I'll stay." She choked on the words and couldn't get out the required Master Hawk.

He allowed it to pass. His fingers loosened around her chin as he took a step back.

And remained.

Waiting.

Watching.

Just fucking do it, Savannah. It's a rubber dick for fuck's sake. You have the control. Do only as much as needed to appease him.

The little pep talk didn't help to soothe her frazzled mind, but she forced herself to lean in and wrap her lips around the head of the dildo. At first touch her gag reflex immediately protested, her stomach churned as the hateful voice once again taunted her with an unwanted memory.

"Deeper, my little slut. I want to feel your tight throat clench around my cock. Ahh, yes, I taught you well. My own willing fuckhole whore. Suck, Lucy, and swallow my load like it's the last meal you'll ever

have. Fuck! Just like that ... such a nasty little slut you are."

This time the reminder was too much of what she'd been forced to become. With a dry sob on her lips, she jumped up and ran for the door.

"Take over, please, Master Kane," Hawk barked roughly as he set off after her, his expression grim, castigating himself for pushing her.

"No more running, sub ST," he growled as he caught her in the large reception hall of the Castle. Without any effort, he picked her up and in one move turned and lifted her over his shoulder.

"No! Put me down, you bastard! Let me go!" she shrieked, her fists connecting with his strong back as she struggled to free herself.

Crack! Crack! Crack!

Hawk responded with three hard slaps on her upended buttocks as he ascended the stairs to his private apartment.

"Oww!" her cry was one of suppressed anger and self-reproach. Anger that this time she'd failed to keep Sergei Kumarin from her mind and self-reproach that she'd disappointed Master Hawk once again.

"Behave, Savannah."

217

She was so overwrought she didn't notice where he was going, nor did she realize he had carried her into his private apartment when he lowered her feet onto the plush carpet of the luxurious great open room. Her mind had slipped back into the past—to a time where she'd prayed for death rather than to pretend she was willing and enjoyed the time she was forced to spend in Sergei's home. She fell to her knees and shuffled backwards, one hand holding Hawk off, her eyes wild.

"No, please, I beg you, not again."

Hawk was shocked at the fear, the utter helplessness that shone in her eyes—eyes that were fixated on his face but didn't recognize *him*. He'd known she had demons; he'd never realized to what extent they haunted her.

He took a step closer and reached for her.

"Noo!" she screamed and scrambled onto the sofa, hugging herself as she sat on her knees, shivering, and bearing back as far from him as she could.

Hawk froze, watching her with concerned eyes while his heart finally opened its chambers and embraced the frail woman as her continued whimpering threatened to bring him to his knees.

All thoughts of her being a willing participant in Decker Cooper's scheme burned to ashes as he stared into her eyes. He knew he had to reach through the haze of the past demons that blinded her and controlled her every thought in this moment.

His voice darkened. "Enough. Savannah, look at me."

"Let me go. I beg you. I just want to go home," she pleaded in a broken voice.

"Sub ST, look at me."

This time the deep thunder of his Dom voice penetrated her hazed-over mind. She blinked and cringed back into the sofa as she noticed the big man hovering in front of her. He took a step closer. Her eyes didn't waver from his.

"Savannah, it's me, Hawk. Take my hand, little one." His voice softened but the demand and power reached out to her and toggled loose the submissive who needed him, the Master, to care and protect her while it infused the soul of the woman who had already lost her heart to him.

"H-Hawk?"

"Yes, baby, it's me." His voice smoothed out, carried a medicinal healing that reached out to her.

Her hand touched his, she briefly closed her eyes as the warmth of his skin infiltrated the cold fear in her mind. He carefully sat down next to her, cognizant of her trembling form, not wanting to spook her.

"What happened?" She looked around and noticed her surroundings for the first time. Even though she was confused, she was enraptured by the big open space that her darting eyes took in. The delicately carved dining room table and chairs, a gorgeous chandelier in the center hanging from the roof that flowed into a kitchen with the stark contrast of dark wood cupboards to the otherwise shining silver appliances and white marble counters. Finally, the sitting room with its plush white and camel-colored sofas, chairs, and Persian carpet. Colorful paintings and scatter cushions completed the picture. It was inviting and she felt like she'd arrived ... home.

"Where are we?"

"My private apartment."

Her eyes darted back to his. "Why did you bring me here?" she asked in a trembling voice. Snippets of her actions from the past ten minutes flashed before her eyes. She tugged on her hand, desperate to leave, to get away from the darkening eyes that swirled with the tumultuous ferocity of a tornado cloud.

Hawk released her hand only to cup her cheeks and held her gaze captive with eyes that offered warmth, understanding and an emotion she couldn't decipher. Her heartbeat increased rapidly.

"Shh, little one. You're not going anywhere. At least not until you—"

"NO! I'm not ... I have nothing to tell. Please, I beg you, Hawk ... please don't make me," she sobbed brokenly.

It hadn't been his objective to force her to talk, but now that she'd confirmed his suspicion that she'd gone through something harrowing, he had no intention of allowing her to suffer by herself anymore. He'd take care of her. Help her when she needed a strong shoulder to lean on and be there when the demons crowded her in her sleep at night.

"Do you trust me, Savannah?"

"Yes, Hawk, with everything in me, I do," she said without hesitation.

"Then trust me now. I wish to be there for you. We're going to work through each and every demon of yours as and when they force their way to the surface. Will you allow me to help you, little one?"

221

"Yes, God yes!" She clung to his arms as he brushed the last remnants of tears from her eyes.

"Then there's no time like the present," he continued in an even voice. "It's obvious there are bad memories around giving head. You're a very passionate woman and it's something I believe is in your nature to derive extreme enjoyment from offering to a man."

"No, you're wrong! I hate it. I never want to ... to—"

"Lock those memories away, sub ST," he barked. "We're now in a scene. What do I expect from my sub from this point forward?"

"Ehm ..." Savannah licked her lips, desperately searching her mind for the answer while struggling to do as he demanded, to ban those horrid visions from her mind.

"Focus, sub." His voice graveled in a dark command.

The synapses in her brain responded to his all-consuming power. "My mind ... with you and only you in the scene."

"Yes, my pet, with me and nowhere else." He brushed back the silky blonde tresses over her shoulder. "I can't heal you, little one, but I wish to be the one to help you heal yourself. Let me be your meadow, a quiet place to reflect. When those memories assail you, find me inside your mind. I'll be the stillness, there to banish the tornado of your pain to slow down, until it's finally dissolved into shards of nothingness. I'll be your crutch when you stumble, to make you see that you're stronger than you believe, and that you can heal from within if you allow me in. Can you give me that, little one? Here and now, in this moment?"

She looked into his eyes. The words of wisdom her father had shared with her just before he'd passed away and prior to the year in Russia, found its way to the surface.

"Find a man with emotional warmth and you'll see a prince among men. A man who isn't afraid to allow his heart to shine through and you'll know it's the best a man can be, one who loves and holds compassion and kindness as his highest treasures. Then, my precious little girl, you have found a treasure of the Earth. For these values are human values and they're not given without care. It's the qualities that offer freedom, understanding and love of the highest realm. Find that man, Savvy, and you'll be loved as strongly as those storybook princesses.

223

Go out there, my darling and find your prince among men."

Her eyes shimmered like the rare rays of light bouncing off of pebbles on a cloudy day as she stared at him. His voice echoed over and over in her mind. She became lost in Hawk's gaze; warm, compassionate, and beautiful, filled with powerful emotions she prayed wasn't her imagination.

Savannah heard her father's voice urge her on. *"Go out there, my darling, and find your prince among men."* Instinct spurred her on that Hawk Sinclair was the real deal, her *prince among men* who wouldn't hurt her. She boldly took a leap of faith.

"Yes, Master Hawk. I want you to be in my heart, guiding me. In this moment I'm here with you. I am yours, completely."

Chapter Eleven

Hawk stood flayed bare by Savannah's words that flowed through his mind. He was used to submission from women, but it was the first time he got sidelined by emotions of such profound pleasure and exigency lashing at him from deep within his soul that he could only stare at her. What he read in her eyes floored his mind; his heart expanded with the warmth that flooded his entire being, all as a result from that expression of complete trust, of begging to be loved, to be accepted without any reservation.

He forced his emotions under control. This moment was about her, for her, and he intended to give her all the attention she needed to guide her past the block of horror that had made her run out of the training dungeon. His fingers involuntarily found their way to the soft curve of her cheek. "You are so beautiful, little one. At times when you're near, I find it difficult to breathe."

He should've been surprised at the admission, seeing as he always kept his feelings to himself. Then again, no other submissive had ever affected him like this. Not even his late wife, Vee. His hands were gentle as he pulled her against his chest, his thumb tilting her chin upwards. He leisurely traced the curve of her pouty lips, satisfied to notice her tremble. It pleased him that she didn't try to hide her reaction to his touch. He couldn't resist another slow pass, taking great pleasure as another shudder wracked her frame.

He smiled as he noticed her attempting to speak but with satisfaction running through him, he knew at this stage, she couldn't think, period. His powerful Master presence was now in full force, completely taking over her senses and thoughts.

"I've been wanting to kiss these lips again since that morning against the palm tree," he murmured as he leaned in to tease her mouth with his, deliberately gliding his lips over hers, just barely, followed by a heated exchange of mingling breaths. He could feel her trembling with what he had no doubt was heart-pounding, body-tingling anticipation. He knew the effect his kisses had on women. It was a skill he'd perfected over the years. With her, he felt the desire to fill not only her thoughts but every quavering nerve ending on her body.

"Let me in, little one," he rasped against her lips, sweeping his tongue tantalizingly across the seam of her lips. His growl of appreciation followed her mouth blooming open under his like a flower at first touch of the early morning sun. He couldn't hold back, he wanted more and with a salacious lick found his way inside.

"Hmm," he groaned into her mouth at first taste. "Yes." Another lick. "Perfect." A soft suck. Her soft whimper urged his thumbs to feather across her cheeks to gently angle her head and with a carnal moan, he consumed her mouth in a sweltering kiss. He didn't hold back as he poured passion and skill and dire need into the kiss until the barriers of reserve inside her burst open and she returned his fire with blistering sparks of her own.

Hawk felt her fingers fist into his shirt, desperately clutching on to him as she accepted his possessive control. He took her acceptance, it was his, he'd already taken possession of her that day against the palm tree. He'd just been too hardheaded to acknowledge it. He ended the kiss, exulting in the vibration of her body against his.

Her breaths puffed from her lips as she struggled to find oxygen. He teased her lips with his fingers.

"Don't close up on me now, little one. Open, let me in."

She stared at him but opened her lips to allow the tips of his fingers to tease the edge of her teeth, her tongue before he eased two fingers deeper. Her eyes began to haze over, she squeezed them shut as she felt the pressure against the back of her throat. He pulled back slightly.

"No, Savannah. Eyes open. Always look at me. It's me, little one. Master Hawk."

As her eyelids fluttered open, her vision filled with the warmth of his dove gray gaze. She relaxed. Her clenched jaw went slack as he probed his fingers deeper.

"Suck, my pet."

She followed his instructions blindly, sucking, licking, and swirling her tongue around his digits. Freely, enjoying the flashes of heat in his eyes as he pushed deeper and although she gagged, she didn't panic ... too much.

"That's it, little one, accept the pleasure you offer me, the enjoyment that flows through you knowing how you make me feel, how fucking hard you've already got my dick by sucking my fingers."

Surprisingly, his words didn't scare Savannah. Rather, it filled her with hope. Power surged through her as she sucked his fingers deeper, making sure to keep her eyes on him. She concentrated on the feelings that flooded her mind, the shards of heat that pricked at her loins from watching his arousal swirl in darkened shades of metallic blue in his eyes. She had never given a blowjob until Russia, let alone had a man fuck her throat. She had always associated it with pain, debasement and as a result hated it, knowing it would never offer her pleasure. Now, she was taught differently. This was what she hadn't been allowed to experience with Sergei. It had been all about his pleasure and he got off the best if he completely degraded her, made her feel lower than the excrement of a snail.

Crack! Crack!

She whimpered around Hawk's fingers as two sharp slaps on her thighs yanked her mind back to the present.

"No, Savannah," he growled. A slash between his brows turned his expression dark. "Clear your mind. I want you here with me. Fill your thoughts with me, with how you make me feel and how it affects you." He watched her for a moment and then smiled when her hazel eyes glimmered with spots of sparkling green. "Good girl."

Her chest expanded with joy at the praise and her smiling eyes told him as much. She was slowly losing her fear of giving head under his tender ministration.

"Ready for more, my pet?" His gravelly voice soothed the frayed edges of nervousness that threatened to take over when he pulled out his fingers.

"I ..." She relaxed as she found the warmth she sought in his gaze. "Yes, Master Hawk."

"On your knees between my legs."

Her body solidified. Her eyes lost the bright sheen as the first flicker of the wild fear of earlier turned the edges of her iris to a deep topaz.

Hawk realized whoever had traumatized her, had done it in that position. He turned her face to his and kissed her passionately, obliterating the thoughts that hovered on the edge of her consciousness. He brushed his fingers over her delicate eyebrows as he ended the kiss.

"This isn't about punishment, little one. This is for your pleasure as much as mine. And no matter what, I'll never hurt you, even fucking your throat. Always remember, I'm a Dom first and foremost and that means taking care of you. Your pleasure will always be my first priority, except during a punishment, of course. I'll know your fears as much as I can read your needs, your reaction, and your distress.

"You said earlier that pleasing the Dom and serving his needs is what giving head is about. That it's the one sexual act where a man will always be superior." She licked her lips and stared at him earnestly. "That's not what scares me. It's when ... when the man loses control and all that matters is that ... that final race to come." She didn't blink, her body trembled, but she refused to look away. "That's when the pain—"

"No, Savannah. Never. Not in Castle Sin. Not with any of the Doms or Masters here. We do not condone hardcore BDSM. Yes, I'll have all the power, but only because you trust me to offer it to me and not take advantage of it. That's the important difference, little one. Trust and choice. Always trust the man you give such power over you."

He brushed his fingers over the frown drawing her eyebrows together. "Lose those memories, Savannah, and come back to me. Now."

She blinked and smiled tremulously at him. "Yes, Master."

"This might be about my pleasure, but trust me when I tell you, you won't experience fear and never pain." He smiled wryly. "In fact, I daresay, you're going to hold onto my ass and demand I take more."

"I sincerely doubt that, Master Hawk."

Hawk unzipped his cock, watching her all the time. Savannah took note of its eager release from his jeans, already half erect. She'd never given much thought to a man's penis before, but her stomach rolled as he palmed his member in his hand and stroked it with firm movements. It swelled with every rolling motion of his hand. Savannah became sidelined by the drool forming in her mouth at the sight of his cock, all purple, veiny, throbbing, and the satiny skin stretching tighter and tighter by the second.

For the first time, she wondered what he would taste like, how he would react as she took him into the warm recesses of her mouth. At first, she was shocked at the depth of the desire to do what he had said; to give him pleasure and derive as much in the giving of it. But watching the gleam in his eyes as he looked at her, she stopped fighting it. It'd been five years and here stood a man who single handedly was prepared to help her slay her demons. Who was prepared to walk the road of recovery with her. Whatever or however it may turn out in the future for them, now was all that mattered. This moment, this challenge to fully trust in him and offer him full power over her.

The stark glare of arousal in his just-burned-ash-colored eyes, sent a twisted spasm down her back. The unrivaled sense of self-assurance and raw sexuality that exuded from his massive presence unsettled her, but there was no denying how much it excited her at the same time.

"For now, I want you on top of me on your hands and knees, at least until I'm ready to fuck your throat." He frowned as she glanced at him sharply. "Relax, little one, there's no rush. You indicated you've deep throated before, am I right?"

Savannah's hands trembled but she refused to allow the visions to resurface. She'd been forced to become an expert in throat fucking. If only for self-preservation and to ensure Sergei had no reason to repeat the harrowing experience of having his entire staff ram their stinking flesh down her throat. But it had been five years and she was concerned about being able to suppress the gag reflex.

"It's been a number of years, I'm not sure ... I might struggle at first."

Hawk watched for any signs of fear as she straddled him. He tenderly brushed her hair back as she grasped his shoulders. "Perfect, little one. This way I have access to all your juicy bits."

Savannah moved to get on her hands and knees next to him. Hawk chuckled, shaking his head. "For the better enjoyment of what I have in mind, I need those juicy bits to be naked."

With his assistance, she was naked in a few economic moves. She blushed as his appreciative eyes grazed her naked body as she settled on the sofa again.

"So beautiful. It's a wonder I don't explode just by looking at you."

Savannah giggled and slapped her hand over her mouth at the unexpected sound.

"You, of stellar control? I sincerely doubt that, Master," she said with laughing eyes. "But I thank you for the compliment."

Hawk studied her for a moment. She suddenly seemed at ease and relaxed in his presence. He brushed his fingers over her pursed lips.

"Do you need me to guide you, little one?"

Savannah licked her lips, digging deep to find the courage she needed to see this through. It didn't seem such a chore knowing it was his cock she'd be paying homage to. That he was the one she would give the power to. It made her feel less vulnerable, stronger, knowing he gave her the power of choice. A sliver of a smile twitched her lips.

She leaned down and caught his turgid shaft in her hand, wrapping her fingers around the base. She curled her tongue over the smooth, bulbous head, lapping at the viscous drops oozing from the slit. Hawk laid his hand on the back of her head and massaged her scalp, catching her hair in his fist. She stiffened. His hand relaxed.

"Keep your eyes open and on me, my pet."

She moved her lips over the top to suck him into her mouth, running her tongue across the slit. As if savoring her favorite ice cream, she rolled her lips around the tip, lapping at the area where the spongy head connected with the hard shaft.

A soft moan vibrated around his cock in reaction to his finger flicking over her clit until the nub swelled in response. He rubbed the tiny bud, in varying degrees. Soft at first, then hard. Now and then tapping his finger hard against the fleshy protrusion. Savannah jerked, heat filling her veins as her clit throbbed with arousal.

This was different. She shivered. She'd never been aroused during a blowjob. Who was she kidding? The entire year in captivity she'd never been aroused.

"Keep going, sub. No matter what I do."

Savannah hadn't expected to be aroused while giving him head. Judging by the rapid rise in her desire, she had no idea how she'd be able to concentrate while he set out to arouse her with his expertise. With her hand as a guide, she fed his cock deeper into her mouth, sucking as she pushed down. Her mouth stretched wide to accommodate his girth. She kept going until his bulging head nudged the entrance of her throat then started working him up and down, pumping his shaft with her hand.

Hawk pressed two fingers deep into her pussy. Her surprised cry vibrated around his cock as she gagged when she lost concentration the moment he started to plunge them into her pussy.

"You have no idea how the heat of your mouth around me feels. Yes, little one, just like that."

Savannah sucked and pumped his hard cock into her mouth, crying out and moaning around his length the entire time. The sensations he evoked with his fingers shot like wildfire through her veins. Her loins throbbed as the pressure intensified, her clit ... *ooohh fuuck* ... she screamed as he twisted his hand to brush his finger over the throbbing nub while thrusting his fingers rhythmically against its spongy twin on the inside of her pussy.

Her hips danced against his hand as tears began to run down her face from the pressure of Hawk's cock against the back of her throat as she continued to suck on it. Her voice grew hoarse from her inability to release the cries continually cut off in her throat. Spittle streamed from her mouth and clung to her chin. Hawk's hand tightened in her hair, he waited. The moment her breath caught, and her throat tightened, he removed his hand from her soaked pussy. She wailed around his cock as the orgasm that had started to heat her veins receded. He pulled her off him and got up from the sofa.

"I can't hold back much longer. Would you be comfortable on your back on the sofa with your head over the side?

"I think so," she said and got in position with his gentle guidance.

"Beautiful. Spread those gorgeous thighs for me, little one. I still want access to that juicy cunt of yours. Wider, good."

Hawk took his place and folded his hand behind her nape. "Listen to me, Savannah. If at any point you feel threatened or can't breathe, pinch my legs. Do you understand? "

"Yes, Master." She wrapped her hands around his thighs and held on.

"Good girl. Now, open wide, push out your tongue and relax your jaw. Do not tense your throat. Stay relaxed," he coached as he pushed his hard shaft all the way to the back of her throat, then kept pushing. He reached out and brushed his fingers over her clit. She jerked as she gagged in reaction to his unexpected touch.

"Relax, little one, we'll take it slow."

Savannah clawed at his legs as saliva dripped from her mouth. A hard slap on her clitoris caught her attention. She breathed harshly through her nose, concentrating to relax her throat.

"That's better, my pet. Now keep it like that. Here we go; all the way in this time."

He pushed deeper while simultaneously tapping his fingers on her clit. She moaned as she felt her throat close against the intrusion. Another slap on her clitoris forced her to relax which she managed with deep breaths through her nose. Hawk grunted as his cock settled all the way down her throat. He didn't move, savoring the tightness until her throat started to convulse. Savannah thrashed, desperate to draw oxygen into her lungs. He pulled back to allow her to breathe then he started to fuck her throat. Long, even strokes. Slow at first to savor her tightness then a little faster, watching her hips dance against his hand as he pressed his fingers inside her very wet pussy.

Hawk growled as he plunged into her throat, pinching her clit while he thrust faster, releasing a carnal growl as her pussy tightened. A gush of heated juices coated his fingers, splattering against the back of the sofa.

Savannah's body jerked, and her hips soared higher; her scream garbled as she climaxed. She was helpless as a flux of heat incinerated her at the same time Hawk ejaculated down her throat. His ropy excretions slithered from his thrusting cock.

She felt as if she was tumbling into the depths of the sea. She coughed and gasped for breath as Hawk pulled his cock from her mouth, lifting her to sit up. His breathing sounded haggard in her ears as he cradled her in his arms.

Savannah was limp, completely sidelined by the experience. She'd always hated a man fucking her throat. It had made her feel like the whore Sergei called her. With Hawk, it was the complete opposite, and she knew it was because he gave as much as he took. It made her feel enervating and powerful. Her muscles felt like rubber and her skin tingled all over. With a drawn-out sigh, her eyes flickered closed.

Hawk tenderly wiped her body with a cloth, all the while whispering words of praise into her ears. He wrapped her in a blanket, picked her up and carried her to his bed.

"Is she okay?" Stone asked Hawk as he walked into BSE operations hub fifteen minutes later after he'd taken a cold shower. He had a hard climax, but his body was still tense. He knew what he needed was to bury himself deep inside her pussy, to feel the pulse of her heartbeat in the satiny folds gripping his cock to find the release he needed.

"I see news travels fast," he graveled.

"We're all concerned about Savannah, Hawk. She managed to crawl into all our hearts over the past couple of months." Stone chuckled at the sharp glare Hawk shot in his direction. "I never thought I'd see the day when you became so possessive over a woman, but I can't say that I'm not happy for you."

Hawk's face turned impassive. He forced his thoughts blank. It was too soon to attach emotions to what he felt. He had no intention of rushing into anything. He made a mistake once, and he wasn't going to repeat the experience by confusing an all-consuming lust for a woman with something like love. Love happened to him once, or so he thought. He'd learned it wasn't meant to be.

Not for him.

Not then.

Not now.

Maybe never again.

"Don't confuse a desire to help her overcome emotional demons with anything else." He ignored the snorting of Stone and Kane, who had joined them as he'd responded. He shrugged. "I'm not denying I want her, so yeah, add lust to the equation. Fuck, I'm hard whenever she's close and I'm selfish in that. I want all her sexual energy focused on me, so stay the fuck away from her. If anyone is going to fuck that tight little cunt of hers when she's horny, it's gonna be me."

"Hm, I wonder how she feels about it. Who says she doesn't want one of us to fuck her on the odd occasion? Or," Kane stared at him with narrowed eyes, "is there something you're not telling us?"

Hawk contemplated sharing his suspicions with them. It may help if his cousins knew so that they could look for signs of her demons surfacing when she was in a training session with one of them.

"You remember the undercover agent DC claimed swapped places with one of the women in that first group of sex slaves of the Blue Bayou Operation?"

"Yes," Stone straightened and took a sip of his latte. Hawk sat down and waited for Kane who followed his example.

"Do you also remember Peyton telling you that Savannah had gotten completely sloshed after she'd returned from an assignment five years ago?"

Stone and Kane looked at each other. Their eyes flashed as the penny dropped.

"Are you saying Savannah told you she was the undercover agent DC had sent with those women?"

"No, Kane, she didn't tell me, but there are too many things that match for it to be a coincidence. She told me that DC had forced her into assignments she wasn't equipped to deal with, just like six years ago. From certain things that filtered through today, it's clear to me that she'd been exposed to sexual abuse or torture even." Hawk shook his head. "But I don't believe she swapped places with anyone. She's not a field agent and never had any training. She's too clever to get herself into such a position, especially if her sole purpose was to ensure the women were treated well on the trip there and report back to DC on their end destination. I think Cooper lied and there's something about Savannah and that period that even she doesn't know about."

"Parker said earlier he's close to cracking open the Blue Bayou file. I'm hoping it'll give us better insight into the role she played and perhaps confirmation of your suspicions." Stone shifted in his chair. "We need to help her, Hawk. All of us, that's why we opened the training center. Not only to teach them how to tap into their submissive side but to help those who needed to find themselves."

"That's why I gave Evans instructions to move her belongings to my apartment. I want to be there when the demons surface. All of you have to be aware of the possibility of triggers during training. I don't believe she herself knows what'll loosen those memories and visions."

"That we can do. Moving her into your place, you say?" Kane smiled conspiratorially at Stone. "And he claims it's only his horny dick that's affected."

Hawk got up and stretched out lazily. "Stop trying to poke me into admitting something. It's not going to happen. If I were you, old geezer, I'd start looking for a piece of ass to tie yourself to. You're getting way too old and wrinkly to catch one with your looks."

"Insulting me is gonna get you nowhere, young pup. That's the advantage of a mature age. I don't care what people think anymore. As far as getting old is concerned, tell me, Master Hawk, have you ever fucked a woman till she passed out?"

"Can't say that I have." Hawk winked at a grinning Stone. They both knew what was coming ... and it wasn't idle boasting either.

"Then I suggest you don't ditch my ability to find a piece of ass. You know as well as I do, the subs stand in queue when they hear I'm looking for a fuckbuddy for the night."

"Yeah, he's got you on that one, Hawk. He does fuck them until they pass out. Every single time."

"I guess I owe you an apology, Kane, my old man." Hawk ducked and the stapler Kane hurled at him in retaliation, hit the wall next to his head.

"I think I'll make a point of choosing sub ST next time. Just to prove a point," Kane said as he sauntered past Hawk.

"She's free to choose her partners on member dungeon nights, so go for it." Hawk smiled at the snort of disbelief his cousin presented him over his shoulder as he walked away.

Hawk picked up the stapler to hide the black expression he could feel flash over his face from a very astute Stone watching him with an amused expression. The thought of Kane fucking Savannah until she passed out didn't sit well with him.

Not well at all.

Chapter Twelve

"A group punishment, Hawk? This is gonna be interesting," Kane said and settled back in one of the 'throne' wingback chairs, allocated specifically to the seven Masters of Castle Sin.

"Hell yeah, and judging by the fact that all twenty of them are deliciously naked, it can only be worth watching," Ace said as he sat down, chomping away at his second bowl of dessert. He was known for his sweet tooth.

Shane searched the group, his psychologist nature at work. "Is Savannah going to be okay, Hawk? Isn't it too soon after the incident in your training dungeon to expose her to punishment?"

Hawk's gaze had been on Savannah from the moment she'd joined the group on the far side of the Gathering Hall to undress.

"I offered her an out and she refused. Besides, being naked among so many trainees doesn't bother her. It's something she overcame within the first month of her stay here. She's comfortable with all of us as well as the assistant training Doms." Hawk got up. "Better eat up fast, Ace. I daresay all of you are going to enjoy assisting with the punishments."

He sauntered toward the group standing in the Castle Sin present position awaiting their fate. Punishments derived from disobedience or disrespect in one of the Masters' training dungeons were never fun. At least not for the trainees.

"Trainees, you're all aware of the reason for your punishment, correct?" His gravelly voice boomed through the acoustics of the large, spacious room.

"Yes, Master Hawk," they said in a choir response.

"Very well. To ensure everyone present is aware of the reason, sub RL, please tell us why you're being punished."

Rose Lovett's eyes remained lowered, but her voice rang clear and loud to the Masters sitting against the far wall. "We forgot the key rule and disregarded your presence in your training dungeon, Master Hawk. We chatted and joked instead of paying attention to you."

He regarded the row of women facing him with a strict expression. "You're here to be taught the skills of submission. Forgetting the golden rule of the training dungeons is not only disrespectful to me, but it also wastes everyone's time. It will not be tolerated. It's that understood?"

"Yes, Master Hawk." This time, their response was sharp and filled with regret.

Hawk glanced at Danton standing by his side with an iPad in his hands. "Ready?"

"Yeah, and eager to start, Master Hawk."

Hawk chuckled at the enjoyment in his voice which caused the trainees to shuffle uneasily.

"Each of you choose a number from one to four and say it out loud as Dom Danton calls your name. Don't forget that number, subs," he warned and nodded at Danton whose deep voice droned at intervals of numbers being called out by the women until he'd gone through all of them.

"Good. The number you chose, represents the vibrator that you'll wear throughout the punishment. Dom Danton, please enlighten the trainees what their selections are."

Evans approached with a box that Danton reached into and lifted out a rather large anal plug.

"This vibrating beauty is for all the number ones." A couple of trainees moaned regretfully. They already had an inkling what part of their punishment was going to include. Stimulation of all kinds to induce arousal with no chance to satisfy their need to climax.

"Number two gets you this delightful G-spot vibrator, and numbers three, none other than these four, ocean storm vibrating vagina balls. Then ladies, the pièce de résistance is for all the number fours." He held up the toy with a broad smile. "You get this delightful double dong dildo."

Gasps echoed from the trainees who stared at, what Hawk was sure, appeared like monster cocks to them. He actually felt sorry for the women who chose it, seeing as they'd be stimulated by a vibrating cock in both ass and vagina simultaneously.

"Please face the wall, bend over and grab your ankles. Do not move while your vibrating toy is being fitted," Hawk ordered and watched with a satisfied smile as the women immediately turned and took the required position. They knew better than to protest; Hawk was known to slap on additional punishment at the briefest provocation.

He stood with his hands in his jeans pockets as he waited for them to face him again.

"Comfortable, everyone?" He didn't bother to hide the amusement from his voice and chuckled at the disgruntled looks some dared to shoot at him.

"I daresay most of us are too scared to respond, but the truth is, hell no, Master Hawk."

Hawk was delighted that Savannah was the one to sass him. It set his mind at ease that she was relaxed after the private training session in his apartment. More so, that her real cheeky character was slowly blossoming back to life.

"Punishment rarely is, sub ST. Are you perhaps complaining?"

"Oh, no. I wouldn't dare, Master," she grumbled and lowered her eyes as that crawling eyebrow towards his hairline triggered a warm feeling low in her stomach. It was rather irritating that such a small gesture had the ability to spark her arousal, especially in light of the fact that her poor ass was filled with a monster butt plug. She didn't want to think what more the demon Master had in store for them.

"Let's not waste any further time. Seeing as your punishment is curbing the Masters and Doms entertainment for the evening, I've decided to combine the two."

The melody of groans reached the Masters on the far wall and their deep chuckles were promises of intended wickedness that made the women squirm. Whether with trepidation or anticipation was hard to tell.

"Trainees, every second one, please take two steps forward and stand facing the person to your left. Hustle ladies," he snapped when they didn't immediately act. "Good. Remain in the present position while the Doms prepare you for the punishment."

Savannah glared at Dom Danton when he approached her and Rose Lovett, her apparent partner in their punishment. He carried two long pieces, of what she recognized from years of assisting her mother sewing, to be thin, flat elastic bands used in the making of clothes.

"Pay attention in the meantime. Each of you will be fitted with rings of fire nipple clamps. For those who aren't familiar with them, it's a round stainless-steel clamp with four screws that'll be tightened around your nipple. For this punishment, they'll be tight enough to ensure they don't slip off. The elastic bands will be tied to each clamp and the other end stretched out to your partner in front of you and tied to her clamps."

"Freaking hell." Savannah watched as Rose went on her toes, hissing as Danton tightened the screws. Within seconds both were in place, and he hooked the elastic band around the screws and secured it with a tight knot.

"Dom Danton, this hurts like fire," Rose protested, her lips pursed.

"Hence their name, sub RL, besides if they didn't hurt, it wouldn't be punishment, now, would it?" He turned to Savannah. "Ready, my pet?"

"Would it matter if I said no?" she snipped. He chuckled and pinched and pulled her nipples until they hardened.

"Perfect. You know the drill, sub ST, breathe through the pain," he coached as he placed the first one around her nipple and tightened two screws at a time. He watched her the entire time and didn't stop until she flinched and went on her toes, her breath wheezing between her lips.

"Gaawd, I so don't like this," she moaned as he finished by quickly tying the elastic around the screws.

"Good, now I know the pressure you can take." Danton loosened the screws slightly, leaving them at a slight pinch. "There you go. I want each of you to take back three steps."

"Three? Each of us? Dom Danton, this elastic isn't … oww!" Savannah cried out as a hard hand connected with her buttocks. She glared over her shoulder, wincing as her clamped nipples protested at the quick movement.

"Enough back chatting, sub ST. Do as you're told, or you'll be the reason everyone receives additional punishment." Hawk stood so close; he could see the flex of green in her eyes flash her rebellion at him. Her mouth opened but closed immediately as his eyes darkened in warning.

"Yes, Master. Of course, Master." Her head snapped forward and with a bereaved glance at Danton, she and Rose tentatively shuffled back three small steps. The elastic between them began to tighten.

Danton sighed and frowned darkly at them. "I said steps, subs, not a shuffle. Take back two more and make sure they're at least shoulder length ones."

Their whimpers followed the backward movements as the elastic pulled tight and stretched their nipples.

"Good, I see everyone is ready. Balls, please, Doms." Hawk watched the women's expression turn wary as each couple was handed a tennis ball. "This is what you're required to do. You'll throw the ball at each other, overhead only. The elastic isn't allowed to go slack between you, and you may not drop the ball. If you do either, a weight will be added in the center of the elastic bands. You're only allowed eight weights. One punishment means a weight is placed on both sides of the elastic bands between you. If you go past that number, each of you'll receive ten swats with a crop on your ass. The most important thing about this punishment, trainees, is that you're not allowed to climax. If you do, each of you will be punished by one of the Masters over there. You'll walk over to them and call out your number. The Master allocated to that number will decide on the punishment you deserve."

"Master Hawk, may I ask a question?" Savannah's voice sounded pinched.

"Yes, sub ST."

"How long is the punishment going to last."

"An hour. At ten-minute intervals, the screws on the nipple clamps will be loosened for two minutes to allow blood flow to return and then you'll continue for another ten minutes. In other words, trainees. If you reach eight weights before the time is up, you receive your ten swats, the weights are removed, and you start again until the hour is up. The same goes for climaxing."

"In other words, we might be punished a couple of times within that hour?" Rose asked with a thin voice.

"Correct. So, trainees, I suggest you pay attention to how hard and straight you throw that ball." Hawk looked down the line of trainees. "Doms, tighten the clamps so we can begin."

Painful moans echoed through the room as the Doms quickly retightened the screws and stepped back to the side of each couple.

"Trainees, your time starts … now. Begin!"

"Oh lord, Rose!" Savannah squealed as Rose threw the ball and she had to jump to catch it. She landed on her feet. "Freaking hell, that hurts," she moaned. The elastic band had tightened and pulled painfully at their nipples with the jump.

"I'm sorry! I'm not good at ball games," Rose lamented, a pained expression on her face.

"Jeez, Rose, now you tell me! Look at what I do. When you release the ball, flick your wrist down and roll the ball from your fingers. That way it won't go high," Savannah explained as she threw the ball, right into Rose's hands.

They managed fairly well until Danton switched on the vibrators that they had both forgotten about. It was so sudden and such a strong buzz inside their asses, seeing as both had ended up with the anal plugs, that they bent over double. The elastic bands between them went slack.

"First set of weights for you, subbies," Danton said and clipped two ball weights onto the elastics.

"Shit," Savannah hissed as the elastic tightened with the weight bearing it down.

"Throw the ball, sub ST. No resting in between," Hawk rasped from behind her.

She clenched her teeth as the buzz in her ass continued. The last two minutes of the first round weren't as good as the first eight in that their throws went haywire. It wasn't easy to concentrate on keeping the elastic taut, catch and throw a ball with the constant vibration thudding in their asses.

"Time."

"Oh, thank god," Rose moaned as Hawk's voice sounded above the trainees' cries and grunts all around them.

Danton was immediately there to loosen the screws on the clamps and even massaged their areola behind the rings of fire.

"Catch your breaths, subbies. We go again in two minutes," he said with a wink, which both women snorted at as they sat down on their haunches, relieved that the vibrations had stopped as well.

A collective groan sounded from the trainees when Hawk called time and it all started afresh. Over the following thirty minutes, many of the ten couples ended receiving punishment with the crop. More than half of them had already received punishments from the Masters as well.

Cries and moans escalated the closer the end of the hour loomed. Rose and Savannah were no different. They were up to six weights on the elastics. Catching the ball was becoming more and more difficult with the vibrations being changed and increased every couple of seconds. Savannah could feel the slippery stickiness between her thighs from the arousal that threatened to consume her. The constant tugs on her nipples every time she threw or caught the ball combined with the vibrations in her ass had her so on edge, she wanted to scream. Her clit throbbed incessantly, begging for a climax, even her pussy clenched and released with every thud of the anal plug vibrating inside her.

"Gaawd, Dom Danton, how much longer?" she wailed as she had to jump again to catch the ball. Her nipples pinched painfully; her clit felt like it was attached to a live wire. She clamped her thighs together, desperate to contain the lust that surged down south and settled in a demanding throb in her nether region.

"After this rest, two more, subbie, so, get back in place. Master Hawk is about to call time."

This time disaster struck for Savannah and Rose. They were both so aroused, the slightest pull on their nipples elicited raw cries from their lips.

"Ready, Rose?" Savannah bit out through thin lips, her knees locked to try and pinch her clit into behaving.

"Just throw the damn ball," Rose said. "No!" she cried as the ball sailed over her head. She stepped back and jumped at the same time, yanking so hard on the elastic that their nipples stretched to the max. Their painful cries ended in them both on their knees, hugging their waists as the climaxes they'd held back for so long, rolled over them.

"Hmm ... let me guess. You two just had orgasms?" Danton said with a superior glint in his eyes.

"No shit, Sherlock," Savannah said on a puff of breath as she tried to find her composure while Danton slightly loosened the screws of the clamps, giving them relief from the constant arousing pressure.

"Get your booties over to the Masters for your punishment, subbies."

"You don't have to enjoy this so much, you know," Rose snipped as they walked past him.

"Ah, who am I to shun the little pleasures in life? I almost believed the two of you were going to deny me the pleasure of watching the Masters punish you."

Savannah was aware of Hawk's eyes on her as they approached the group of Masters. He leaned his elbows with lazy negligence on the back of Stone's chair, his hooded gaze not giving away any of his thoughts.

"Isn't this a pleasant surprise that the two of you decided to pay us a visit?" Master Bear said with a wide grin. "Numbers, subs."

"We're both number one, Master Bear," Rose said glumly. She did her best to avoid Kane's eyes as he cast a narrowed look at her. Not for the first time, he felt a trickle of familiarity as he stared at her.

"Aren't I the lucky one?" Kane graveled as he noticed the telltale wetness of the women's recent climaxes glistening on their thighs. "It's not going to be fun punishing both of you myself, so I'll elect Master Fox to assist me."

"It'll be my pleasure, Master Bear. What do you have in mind?"

"It'll be a shame to let the effect the rings of fire combined with the elastic stretching their tits go to waste, don't you think?" Kane said with a wicked glint in his eyes.

"I completely concur, Master Bear."

"Oh, for fuck's sake, Golden Oldies, just get on with it," Ace said. "We'd rather watch the punishment than listening to the two of you banter about it for the next ten minutes."

"You said it, cousin," Parker and Zeke interjected in a choir.

Savannah felt her loins tighten as both men unzipped their cocks and with leisurely movements encased their hard lengths with condoms. She had to force her gaze to remain on Master Bear and not dart to Hawk to check his reaction on what she could only gauge was about to happen. Not that she expected him to jump up and stop his cousins. He'd instigated the entire punishment, knowing where it might lead. Why she even wondered annoyed her. Why should he be concerned if someone else fucked her? The way the training was conducted made it clear that there was no preferential treatment of anyone. Her eyes caught Peyton who sat on Stone's lap.

Stone enjoyed watching his cousins fuck Peyton at times, and it was a prime example of how the Sinclair cousins operated. Hawk was most probably no different.

"Sub ST, you're with me, sub RL, go over to Master Fox, please," Kane said in a brisk tone.

Savannah nibbled on the inside of her cheek. She was glad she'd learned in the three years at the BDSM clubs how to deal with voyeurism. This kind of scene didn't bother her, nor did having sex openly with others watching. It took time, but as it hadn't been one of Sergei's favorite pastimes, she didn't have such a hang up over it like she did over being chained and forced to give head.

She took a few steps to stand next to Master Bear's chair as Rose trotted toward Master Fox. Her breath hissed through her lips as the elastic between them went tight and pulled on her nipples. She couldn't help but glance at Hawk, to find his gaze glued on her stretched out nipples. A delighted smile splayed over his lips.

Pervert! Why the devil do I even want him to go all possessive and jealous over me? He made it clear there's no chance more than once already.

"Turn to face each other, subs," Kane ordered. Savannah gasped as his big hands fondled her ass cheeks, squeezing the soft morsels that caused her ovaries to start twerking with expectation. Rose and she were standing over a large coffee table, facing each other, the elastic was already stretched taut.

"Spread your legs, sub ST. Let me see how wet your tight little cunt is."

Savannah blindly followed Master Bear's order, moaning as he pushed his fingers deep inside her, probing the silky heat of her pussy.

"Perfectly hot and ready. Listen carefully, ladies. You'll lower yourselves onto our cocks with your knees spread on either side of our legs. Your backs must be kept straight throughout while you *ride the horn.*" He glanced at Danton. "I'd like you to add four more weights to the elastic, please and then make sure the screws are tightened again."

"Ehm ... Master Bear, may I speak?" Savannah glanced at him over her shoulder.

"I'm listening." The twitch of his lips warned her that he already knew what she was going to say.

"We're wearing anal plugs and ..." Her eyes dropped to his huge cock he palmed in his hand as he encased it in a condom. "Are you going to remove them?" Her voice thinned as his smile broadened.

"Now, why would I want to do that, little dove? No Master interferes with another's punishment." Kane glanced at a grinning Hawk. "Unless you'd like us to remove it, Master Hawk?"

"Why would I curb the pleasure you'll receive fucking a cunt receiving added stimulation from a vibrating cock in the ass, Master Bear? No, sub ST, the butt plugs stay."

"Ah, this is going to be so much fun to watch," Parker said as he slouched lower in his chair.

"Come, sub ST, sit on my cock."

Savannah shuffled back until her legs bumped against his. She spread her legs wide apart and slowly moved into a squat over him. His hands folded around her hips.

"Take the horn and guide him inside, sub ST," Master Bear said.

Guide the horn, imagine that! She scoffed inside her mind. If she wasn't in such a dire situation, she'd have laughed out loud.

She whimpered as she reached between her legs and the elastic tightened but she breathed through it and slowly lowered herself onto Master Bears' huge cock. It wasn't an easy feat with the unyielding anal plug inside her ass. She silently cursed Hawk with every inch she lowered herself. Her breathing was labored once she was fully impaled by Master Bear's pulsing shaft. Her upper body leaned slightly forward as she battled to catch her breath. Her loins clenched as the friction between the rubber plug and the hard cock caused sensations to explode inside her. It urged her to move and dance a wild tango on the inviting hardness.

"Subs, you have permission to come, as often as you'd like until we shoot our loads inside you. Sit upright, both of you. Straighten your back and keep that form, no matter what," Master Bear snapped out the order. They immediately complied and their whimpering cries brought carnal rumbles of appreciation from all the Masters as they watched their nipples stretched out far from their bodies.

"Gaawwd!" Savannah shrieked when Danton added four additional weights and it dragged the elastic down, adding more pressure to their already maxed out tits. She stared at the weights gathered at the center of the elastic and realization struck for the first time. They had to *ride the horns*, which meant they'd be expected to bounce up and down.

Those fucking weights are going to pull our nipples down and keep them stretched the entire time!

Her mind was already frazzled, her body taut and on the verge of tumbling over the edge; all from just feeling the pulsing cock so deep inside her and the painful pressure of her tits stretched out so far.

"One last thing, subs. Master Fox and I want a hard, fast ride. No slacking. If you feel a crack on your ass, you'll know we're not happy and you better speed up. Now ... it's time. Ride the horns!"

Savannah started slow but Master Bear would have none of it and gave her two hard slaps on her ass. She immediately sped up, moaning, and crying out as the heavy weights caused their tits to bounce violently up and down, stretching them even more.

"Oh, my fucking ... HELLL!" she screamed as her body solidified and an orgasm rushed through her so unexpectedly, she was completely sidelined by the strength of it.

"Now, isn't that a beautiful sight," Hawk said as he watched her body twitch and jag in the throes of the orgasm that Kane kept feeding with sharp slaps on her clit.

Kane didn't let up and with his hands around her hips, kept moving her up and down while she struggled to catch her breath. It didn't take long for her body to peak again, and the two women's raw cries slammed against the walls as they came again and again.

"Beautiful, little dove," Master Bear praised Savannah as she attempted to keep bouncing hard and fast, even though her entire body was shuddering while her pussy spasmed uncontrollably around his cock.

Kane nodded at Danton who quickly loosened the screws leaving it with only a slight pressure around their nipples.

"Prepare for the finale, little dove. This time, you're going to fly, higher than you've ever done before," Kane growled in her ear. "Faster, sub ST," he said as he used his hands around her hips to aid her, snapping his hips upward to kiss her cervix with the head of his cock.

"Oh god, oh god, oh god ... Master Bear ... I'm ..."

Kane looked at Shane and nodded. They both reached around the women's waists, rubbing, and pinching their clits until their bodies undulated in wild abundance on top of them, their tits stretched far out.

"Now, Master Fox."

Kane and Shane grasped the women by the shoulders and with a hard tug, yanked them far back, ripping the loosened clamps from their nipples. Their carnal cries merged with the loud cracks of the two Masters slapping their clits as the world splintered apart around them.

Savannah was helpless, the unexpected flash of pain from her nipples supercharged the lust that filled her loins and she got flung to the crest and the next moment yanked right under a rogue wave that clamped around her chest as her body tightened. In that moment, she had no control, every order came from her clenching pussy, violently squeezing every attempt to breathe from her. A hot gush of liquid flushed from her pussy, soaking Kane's pants and splattered onto the floor.

"Fuuck!" she gasped, her back arched in a graceful bow as Kane slapped her clit hard, pinched her nipple and twisted it sharply. She screamed as she squirted again and again as he ruthlessly forced her into a vortex of pleasure that she had no way of warding off. Her mind went blank as another climax clawed at her insides. She struggled to come up for air but this time, the orgasm ripped through her with a violence equal to the tsunami she felt rush through her. She slumped on Kane's chest as he roared and with a hard snap of his hips, ejaculated deep inside her.

"Fucking hell, just look at that. Master Bear did it again. Fucked the sub until she passed out."

Savannah was deaf to the awed exclamation coming from Zeke. She had given over to the tentacles of unconsciousness folding around her even while her body twitched and spasmed in the aftermath.

Chapter Thirteen

Savannah came to as Hawk gently lowered her onto his bed. The large body looming over her in the dark caused her throat to close and she couldn't breathe. She shuffled backwards and cowered against the headboard.

"Easy, little one, it's me, Hawk."

His deep voice flowed through her, reaching all the way into her soul to wrap her in a warm, protective cocoon. His large hand settled low on her stomach as he sat down next to her and switched on the bedside lamp. The room filled with a soft golden glow. She looked around, surprised to find herself once again on his oversized bed. The room enticed her senses just as it had that afternoon when she's

271

woken up alone in the massive bed, her mind filled with visions of their earlier private training session.

The dark wood furniture fit the man, the Hawk, as did the deep rust and green colors the room was decorated in.

"I ... this is your room."

"Very perceptive." His voice droned toward her as he got up and walked into the en suite bathroom.

Savannah felt the blush warm her cheeks at the dry tone in his voice.

So much for pointing out the obvious, Savannah!

The sound of water indicated that he was running a bath and the decadent smell of orchids filling her nostrils told her it was for her. Her eyes widened as she noticed bottles of the same fragrance of perfume that she favored on the dressing table. All three, exactly the same as the ones she'd brought with her. Her gaze moved to the large wingback chairs facing the wall of windows overlooking the ocean far below.

"That's my robe," she whispered as she recognized the slip of soft peach satin negligently draped over the back of one of the chairs.

Her body still zinged from the hard climaxes Master Bear had forced from her, aiding the grogginess in her mind. Her brows creased and pulled her face into a tense frown.

"Why did you have to carry me? I can't remember what ... ohh, my lord," she ended in a soft gasp as flashes of how, once she'd started squirting, she couldn't stop and then passed out.

Passed out! From a climax of all things!

Hawk walked back into the room, amused at her wide eyes visible over her hands covering her mouth in what he could only assume was shock. It didn't take a genius to figure out why.

"Relax, Savannah, it's the one thing we all envy of Master Bear. He has the ability to push a sub to such a level of release they always pass out. You're not the first, and believe me, you won't be the last."

"I squirted! Numerous times, in front of everyone. Just *woosh*! I'm so embarrassed," she wailed and covered her eyes. She dropped her hand to glare at Hawk as he chuckled. "It's not funny. what must everyone think and ... *oh, no*! I have to go and clean it up." She scooted to the edge of the bed but before she could get up, he picked her up.

"Put me down, Sinclair. I must go and clean up the mess I made." The order was ignored as he carried her into the bathroom.

"It's probably already been cleaned up by now, so relax." He shook his head at her shocked look. "It's a big castle, Savannah and we have a large household staff to take care of things like that.

"Not *that!* Good lord, I've never felt something like it before. I didn't realize it was such an intense experience, nor did I know I could squirt for that matter," she ended in an embarrassing mutter.

"And it was a sight to behold. There wasn't one Master or Dom in that room who wasn't hard watching you gush so uncontrollably, or wishing they were the ones on the receiving end."

Her cheeks bloomed red at his words as he lowered her into the tub. "Oh, this is just delicious," she lilted as the hot water soothed her aching muscles. She hadn't realized at the time of squatting over Master Bear how much they'd ached. She peeked at Hawk, surprised at the warm look in his gaze as he stared at her.

"Ehm ... why did you bring me here?"

"I told you this morning, I'll be here for you to chase away your demons. I've had them move all your things in here. You'll be staying in my room for the rest of your training."

"I ... me ... your room ... but—"

"But nothing. This is your room now. At least until you leave. Relax and enjoy the bath." He turned and sauntered to the door. "I'm going to get you a snack. You need sustenance after that session with Master Bear."

"At least until you leave."

His words were like a cold dash of ice rolling over her. For a brief period during tonight's punishment, she'd been able to push her concern for Luke to the back of her mind. She'd forgotten about the bastard Decker Cooper and the hold he had over her. It has been four months since she'd seen her little boy, almost five. A raw sob escaped her lips. He'd been six months old and starting to learn all kinds of cute gestures. She'd never forget the day a week before she'd left when he'd said his first word ... *Mama.* Tears blurred her vision as she recalled how proud he'd been when it had slipped out.

"What if he's forgotten me? Oh, God, I miss him so much."

275

Savannah quickly bathed, doing her best to bring her emotions under control. It didn't help to know that Hawk Sinclair didn't seem at all bothered that she'd leave as soon as they found Luke.

She didn't want to leave. Not now that she'd found the one man who made her heart race. A man who had become, unbeknownst to him, the emotional strength she leaned on, soaking in every bit of power exuding from him.

"I don't want to leave him. He's ... in my heart," she whispered.

Her mood was heavy as she trotted back into the room, wrapped in a fluffy white towel. She prayed to be reunited with Luke soon, but it shattered her heart to know it would also mean she'd never see Hawk again. Castle Sin and The Seven Keys Island was home to the cousins, Hawk's home, and it wasn't a setting or environment for a child.

The familiar sound of her cell phone penetrated. She looked around but didn't see it anywhere. She walked closer to the where the ringing came from and found it inside the bedside table, along with her mini iPad and the books that had been in the room she'd been allocated to until now. It was an unknown number. She stared at it for a moment, a sense of doom clouding her vision.

"Savannah, speaking," she said crisply. Her fingers trembled as the sound of heavy breathing filled her ears.

"You can be glad you answered my call, darling. It wouldn't do to annoy me. Not for you and most definitely not for little Luke."

She dragged in a broken breath as she sank onto the bed. "I thought you said he's your son and that he's going to live with you," she snorted, slowly gaining confidence.

It was the one thing Hawk had taught her early on. To tap into her inner strength, to draw from the driving passion deep inside to succeed, not just as a submissive but as a human being. She did so now. She was sick and tired of this bastard controlling her life. He was nothing but a coward, hiding behind supposed power that he yielded over her like a sword, because she was a woman, vulnerable, and up to now, dependent on her job. No more.

"Don't be snippy with me, Savannah. You have no idea what I'm capable of."

"No, I guess I don't, but Luke is your son, your flesh and blood and I don't believe you're so heartless that you'd hurt a ten-month-old baby. Besides, Decker, you know if you do, you lose all hold you have over me."

"Enough chit-chat. Answer me one question. Do you want your son back?"

"You know I do."

"Then you have one opportunity to do so. One, Savannah, and if you don't, you'll never see him again."

This time the threat wasn't an idle one. She could detect it in the grating quality of his voice.

A movement at the door drew her attention. Hawk watched her as he approached stealthily. He placed the tray he carried on the bed and gestured to his ear as he pointed to the phone. She nodded and activated the speaker on the cell phone.

"What is it you want from me?"

"Freedom."

Savannah barked out a cynical laugh. "You're talking to the wrong person, Decker. I have no means of giving you that."

"You might not, but one of your lover boy Masters on the island can. Why do you think I insisted you stay there?" He snorted. "Sometimes the dice falls off the board, like it did for me a couple of months back, but now, now, my little darling, it's landed on a double six."

"Get to the point."

"It wouldn't be a trial for you, seeing as I believe you and Hawk Sinclair have become all cozy."

Savannah's gaze snapped to Hawk. His brows were drawn together in a dark frown.

"Hawk Sinclair is one of the owners of Castle Sin and the Training Master as you very well know. His relationship with me is in no way any different than with the other women here."

"Keep telling yourself—"

"I said get to the fucking point. What do you want from me?"

"So much fire. Maybe we should rekindle our affair once I'm out."

"Hell will freeze over first." Her voice trembled with emotion.

"Very well. You have two days to convince Hawk Sinclair to get his daddy, the chief judge of the Supreme Court of the United States, Judge Xavier

Sinclair, to arrange my release and to clear me of all charges."

"You're crazy," Savannah croaked as the breath she just took got stuck in her throat. She closed her eyes, dread weighing heavy on her shoulders. Stone's speculation had been spot-on. "I don't have any power to yield over Hawk Sinclair. How do you expect me to get him to do something like that? You're a threat to the President of the United States, for fuck's sake!"

"Well, little darling, you're clever and I'm sure you'll find a way. Besides, if all else fails, use that hot little cunt of yours and put it to work. I'm sure—"

"You're vulgar."

His laughter sounded like an evil demon slaying all that was good in the world. It ended just as quickly as it began. "You have two days. If I don't have an answer by then, expect little Luke's left pinky to be delivered. A small child like that ... he might not even feel it, or what do you think?"

"Hurt my son and I swear I'll ... Decker! Fuck!" she cursed as she realized he had cut the connection.

"Stone was right." Savannah stared sightlessly ahead. "I'm never going to see my son again, not unless by some miracle Parker can find something." Her voice was painted somber with acceptance. She looked at Hawk with sad eyes. "What am I supposed to do now?"

"You're going to eat the cheese and crackers and drink the tea and then you're going to sleep."

Savannah gaped at him. "I'm losing my son and all you want me to do is eat and sleep?"

"You're not losing your son. For now, you need to build up your strength for when he's back home."

"How? Tell me how, Hawk! Just how in the hell do you propose I get him back?" Her voice raised, bordering on hysteria.

"We're going to give the bastard what he wants."

She shook her head. "No, I can't expect you to do that. Your father is the best thing that has ever happened to the judicial system in this country. You can't, Hawk. I won't let you."

"It's not your decision to make." He cupped her cheek, his heart punched hard against his chest as she leaned trustingly into his hand. "Parker and Zeke, along with their team, have been working

281

nonstop looking for clues and they're not going to stop until they find something. I believe they'll find Luke. Hopefully, before that fucktard is released from jail."

Savannah grabbed his hand and looked at him with urgency. "Hawk, it's ludicrous! We can't allow him to get away with what he's done. He *belongs* in jail. There has to be something else we can do." She licked her lips. "I'll never be able to live with myself if your father has to do something illegal for my benefit and he gets caught."

"Leave it to me. Come, let's get something solid in your stomach."

Savannah glared at him as he pushed a piece of cheese inside her mouth when she opened it to protest. Eventually, she gave up as he dogmatically avoided any attempt she made to talk sense into him.

She finished the tea and sat back against the headboard, watching Hawk kick off his heavy boots and slipping on a pair of sneakers. She blinked, her eyelids heavy and she could feel her focus diminishing.

"Where are you going?" she asked, feeling her tongue drag.

"Get some rest, Savannah. I'm going to check in with Parker and Zeke." He helped her to slip under the duvet and pulled it over her, running his fingers over her forehead. "Sleep, baby. Tomorrow isn't going to be any easier," he murmured as he watched her breathing grow heavy as she fell into a chemically induced slumber.

He had no doubt she would realize he'd slipped something into her tea when she woke up in the morning, but he needed her to sleep and not stay up the entire night worrying about Luke. He leaned forward to place a lingering kiss on her pursed lips.

"You're so beautiful, even in your sleep. God knows I want to claim you as mine ... so badly." He sighed heavily. "But it's not meant to be," he muttered as he turned and strode out of the room, heading toward BSE underground bunker where he knew he'd find Parker, Zeke, Ace, and probably, Stone.

To Hawk's surprise, the entire Sinclair clan and Danton were gathered in the Ops Room on the third underground level of Be Secure Enterprises.

"You look angry," Stone said as he joined them at the large brainstorm table in the center of the room.

"Cooper just phoned Savannah. Your suspicion was spot on. He wants her to convince me to speak to Dad to have him exonerated of all charges and released from prison." Hawk took the latte Kane handed him. "Thanks." He took a sip as he stared at the myriad of screens depicting various locations all over Washington DC. "Nothing yet, Parker?"

Parker glanced at him over his shoulder where he and Zeke were pounding away on their keyboards facing the monitors. "I found the nanny's Facebook account. Remember Savannah said Nancy told her they were at a Botanical Gardens the day Cooper phoned and threatened her?"

"Yeah, and?" Hawk spurred him on.

"She posted that photo, along with a couple more." Parker's fingers flew over the keys and six photos flashed onto the large monitor. "Cooper appears on these three. On this one, there's an older woman with him and on this one, she's playing with Luke."

"That's Dora Brooks for sure. I assume you've been able to confirm that's his mother?"

"Yes, I have. I did a facial comparison between Cooper and her. The results indicate an eighty-nine percent familial match. I also did a facial structure scan, using a program I designed a couple of years ago, on a photo of Fiona Cooper before she became Dora Brooks. Her facial features might have changed but her bone structure is an exact match. The woman in that photo is definitely Fiona Cooper, Decker Cooper's mother."

"At least we're getting somewhere," Hawk muttered as he scanned the monitors. "This woman is a known social butterfly. Ever since she appeared on the scene, she's been fucking everywhere there's a premiere, a celebration then suddenly she completely disappeared off the grid? How is that possible?"

"DC isn't an idiot, Hawk. He would know we'd start digging. He must've told her to stay out of the public eye," Stone said.

Hawk grunted with frustration. "I guess you're right.

"I assume you're searching for her via facial recognition?" Ace asked Parker as he scanned the various locations running on the monitors.

"Yes, starting from that day of the photo, but so far, we've not been able to identify that specific garden. If we did, it might be quick but now we're doing a wide—"

"I found her!" Zeke interrupted Parker. Six pairs of eyes turned to him as one. "I've been tracking flight bookings from the various airports with no luck. I expanded the search to private airlines and on a hunch, military airports. It seems she went to visit her son in prison a week ago. Look, there she is. Unlucky for Cooper, she used her connections in the military to bump a ride from the Marine Corps Air Facility in Quantico during a training exercise on the KC-130 Hercules to Colorado. Fortunately for us, the offloading and refueling sequences were filmed as part of their training feedback and voila, there she is, getting off the plane."

"That's fucking brilliant, and it'll be easy as pie to find her on the traffic cams from there. Any chance you know what car she used?" Parker asked, his fingers hovering over the keyboard to start searching.

"Dora Brooks? What do you think? A limousine of course. I traced the plate number to Elite Car Rental in Arlington. I'm already in the company's rental system. All their vehicles have tracking devices ... just give me a couple of moments," Zeke said as he searched Elite Car Rental's database. "Got it, now let's see, what's the date again, Parker?" He located the date file and within seconds he found the log from the Quantico Airbase.

"Got it. She was dropped off at an estate residence in Capitol Hill. I'm sending the address and coordinates to your phones, Stone."

"Yes!" Parker said as he identified the coordinates on screen. "It's definitely the correct address. I just found the details of DC's father's will. He inherited that house," Parker said and brought up a photo of a three-story mansion in one of the most expensive suburbs in Capitol Hill.

"I can't believe someone who's that loaded turned as corrupt as that bastard," Danton grunted in a dark voice.

"Good job, you two." Stone looked at Hawk. "Are you going to tell Savannah?" He headed to the door.

"No, she's out like a light. I slipped a sleeping tablet into her tea. She hasn't been sleeping since Luke disappeared," Hawk said as he followed Stone. "It might be a good idea to ask Peyton to stay in my apartment tonight and be there when she wakes up."

"I'll tell her. Let's get going. We should be there in less than two hours if I push the black lady hard." Stone pushed through the door.

"Based on the aerial views of the property, you should be able to put down the Black Eagle in the backyard. Good luck, bro, and in the meantime, we'll get a drone in the air and do a detailed area scope. I'll hook the live feed to the chopper," Parker said as everyone followed Stone into the elevator.

"Good idea, little cuz, but we'll be there long before the drone does. That chopper of Stone is fast," Shane said as he studied the coordinates received from Zeke on his phone.

"Hey, old timer, it's time you catch up with technology. We've got drones set up in all the states in case we need it. All it takes is to remotely start it and get it in the air. You better hustle, Shane, Stone isn't going to wait on you."

"I'll be the one waiting on them. I don't have sweethearts to kiss goodbye."

"Aww, is my big brother feeling lonely?" Zeke taunted him and then had to duck as a stapler projectiled toward him.

"Geez, what is it with the two oldies and staplers?" Parker snickered as Shane walked out.

Chapter Fourteen

Midnight had come and gone like a rich velvet blanket of black, swallowing up the day, draining the colors to gray and then to nothing at all except for the spattering of stars high in the sky. A brilliant Van Gogh, blurred in the most fantastic way. A crescent moon smiled down; like everything its illuminance touched was pure, void from any evil.

The Black Eagle sat down in stealth mode amid the lush trees and greenery in the back garden of the estate in Capitol Hill, which by now was shades of charcoal and two-dimensional with even the luxurious lawn appearing dull and eerie.

Six pairs of eyes perused the quiet night as the silent hum of the chopper blades whirred overhead. Their arrival was unexpected and as quiet as the wings of an eagle swooping down in search of food.

"According to the heat scanner from the drone, there are only four people on the property. One in the cottage to the south, one on the top floor in the north corner and two on the ground level to the south. We can assume Luke is with a nanny on the ground level. We go in, fast and silent. I want to get the boy and be out of here before anyone wakes up, let alone alert the authorities." Stone glanced at the five men as they put on their night vision goggles. "Shane and Kane, keep an eye on the cottage. It's probably a live-in butler or chef. Hawk and I are going inside to get Luke. Ace, keep guard at the front door, and Danton, keep the chopper running. Anyone detects anything, give us a heads up. We move ... now."

Hawk was already out of the chopper, hunching low as he scanned for movement. The bushes and trees were silhouettes, the blackest of greens. There was no wind, no rustling leaves, all was quiet except for the chirping of crickets.

"Let's move," he said. He ran on the balls of his feet with Stone by his side, moving toward the backdoor without any leaves crunching under their boots.

Stone, Hawk, and Ace had joined the Marine Corps directly after school. During the five years there, they'd started on their degrees, via correspondence studies. By the time they left the Marine Corps, they'd completed the studies and were already in the process of setting up Be Secure Enterprises when Shane approached them for the roles in the Marvel movie. It hadn't been easy to balance the enjoyment of being a movie star with their desire to achieve success and build a business, but with hard work and determination, they succeeded.

"Down," Hawk and Stone hunched behind a large shrub as a soft golden glow from a window to their left broke through the dark night. "Fuck! I'd hoped he'd be asleep when we took him," Hawk said as the sound of a crying baby reached their ears.

"He might fall asleep again. Probably just needs his diaper changed."

"Listen to you. Expert on babies, are you?" Hawk peeked around the leaves, but the window was too high to detect anything.

"You seem to forget the times we had to babysit for Cousin Abby."

"No, but I do recall leaving changing the diapers to you," Hawk said. "Let's hope the nanny doesn't look outside. No one can miss the blackbird on the lawn, especially with the moonlight illuminating it so brightly."

"You're right. Let's move. It'll be better to get inside and keep her quiet than giving her time to alert Dora Brooks."

They approached the mansion built with natural gray stone, now a canvas of hues Mother Nature provided. The paintwork on the trim was brilliant white, flawless, and the path winding to the double oak backdoor was loose pea shingle, which they skirted and kept to the lawn. The windows were mullioned and had an old country look to them.

"We'll have to pick the lock," Hawk said as he eyed the windows. "We won't fit through those."

"Just do it quietly. That light is still on." Stone stood back as Hawk took out his wallet-sized lock pick set.

"It's a pin tumbler lock. Easy enough," he muttered as he inserted a tension wrench into the bottom of the keyhole. He applied slight pressure as he systematically lifted the pin sets with a pick. "Almost there."

"Light's just gone out and crying stopped," Stone said. He tapped his earpiece. "Report back."

"Quiet on the south side," Shane's voice rumbled. "Same in the front," Ace reported. "No movement over here, apart from the light, which I'm sure you saw," Danton said.

"Stay alert. We're almost there."

"Hold on, Stone. I managed to home into the electrical system with the drone. There's an alarm activated inside the house," Parker's voice cracked in his ear.

"Can you remotely deactivate it?" Stone looked at Hawk. "Keep going. We're getting Luke, alarm or not."

"Working on it," Parker said. Seconds that felt like minutes ticked by until he confirmed, "Done. You're safe to go."

Hawk inserted a pick at the top of the lock. With gentle movements, he raked the inside of the plug, simultaneously lifting it up as he pulled back to apply pressure on the pins. The soft click sounded like a gunshot in the silent night. They both froze for a second.

"Let's move." Hawk pushed open the door, relieved when it slid open soundlessly. They had studied the locations of the heat sensors and moved quickly toward the room on the left side of the house. The same one from where the light had just shone. They stood listening against the door for brief moments and with a nod at Stone, Hawk stepped inside.

The night vision goggles turned the room into a luminescent green. He approached the baby crib on silent footsteps. The little boy was lying on his back, sleeping soundly with his face turned to the wall. One arm was flung over his head while his tiny little hand clutched a blue blanket he cuddled against his face. Hawk looked around, relieved that Stone was quietly stuffing clothes and diapers in a suitcase he'd found in the closet. Hawk mimicked drinking in front of his face. Stone extended his search, looking for formula and bottles in the kitchen.

Hawk was enraptured by the perfect little human. His heart ratted like a beating drum as he reached out and traced the tiny hand. It felt like the softest cotton against his rough fingertips. Flashes of pain of what should've been turned him immobile.

Like so many times before, he wondered whether he'd fathered a boy or a girl all those years ago.

"Time to go, Hawk. I've got everything." Stone's hiss yanked him back to the present. "It'll be great if you can pick him up without waking him."

Hawk grunted in response as he reached into the crib and gently lifted the little boy into his arms. Stone covered him with a blanket, and they headed out the door. Within minutes they were in the chopper.

"Did you remember to bring earplugs?" Stone asked as he engaged the main rotors once the entire team was settled inside. "I'll keep the bird in stealth mode, so the noise shouldn't be a problem and I'll fly at a low altitude for as long as possible, but the air pressure might still cause him discomfort."

"Already put them in his ears. I grabbed the bottle from the crib. I read somewhere that if a baby sucks on it, it'll alleviate the discomfort in their ears." Hawk looked at the precious little bundle in his arms. He was startled to find the little boy staring at him with wide eyes, unflinching.

Stone cranked up the torque and within seconds, the big black bird was airborne.

"Easy there, little man. Uncle Stone will get us home safely." A soft squeak escaped Luke's lips, but his gaze didn't falter from Hawk's. He refused to open his lips as Hawk offered him his bottle. Hawk smiled and ran his fingers over the tiny frown on his forehead. His breath got stuck in his throat when Luke's hand curled around his finger. A little gurgle and his eyes fluttered closed. His tiny fingers remained clamped around Hawk's hand all the way back to The Seven Keys Island.

Waking up used to be such a pleasure to the gurgling baby sounds of her little boy from the crib next to her bed. Savannah moved restlessly under the covers. For a fleeting moment she felt whole again, but it evaporated faster than summer rain off the burned earth as reality sunk in. Her sigh trickled with weariness from her lips.

This morning she awoke to the softest of sheets. She could feel the morning light trickle in through the windows. Her mind felt more groggy than usual as she struggled to shed off the remaining glimpses of a dream.

"Mama! Mama!"

Her eyes remained shut as she soaked in the warmth and listened to the gurgling excitement of her little boy. She swallowed back the lump in her throat. If only it wasn't just a dream.

"Mammmma. Mama!"

The familiar sound of his baby voice that sounded so real overwhelmed her all over again as if it were new, fresh, raw. If only she could linger in this blissful ignorance of waking.

Savannah groaned as she became aware of movement next to her, like someone was jumping up and down on the bed. She struggled to force her heavy eyelids to open.

"Hawk?" Not that she imagined for one second he'd be the one doing something that silly, but she was lucid enough to remember that his room was now hers.

"Mama!" The excited shriek so close to her ears penetrated. Her eyes finally obeyed the order from her brain and snapped open to encounter the most precious sight ever. Her little boy stood on his hands and knees, jumping up and down like a little pony in excitement. His mouth was spread open in a wide, toothy smile.

"Luke? Oh, my god! Luke? My baby. You're here!"

He flung himself into her arms as she struggled to push upright. She cuddled his wriggling body against her, murmuring his name over and over as tears fell untethered over her cheeks. She'd never felt joy as she did at this very moment, a happiness so profound she stood bare and helpless in its grasp. Her eyes sought Hawk who stood by the bed, watching silently with a closed expression on his face.

"How? When ... I don't ..." she stuttered as she battled to compose herself. She locked eyes with him and poured every emotion he'd awakened inside her into that one look. "Thank you, Hawk. I'll never be able to repay you for bringing my son back to me."

Luke began to struggle against the tight hold Savannah had on him. She reluctantly loosened her grip and cupped his sweet little face. Her delighted laughter tingled through the room as he copied her and placed his small hands on her cheeks.

"Mama," he said as he patted her cheeks.

"He remembers me." Her eyes lifted again. "I was so scared he might have forgotten."

"He was hesitant at first when I put him on the bed but then he touched and smelled your hair and I think that triggered his memory."

Savannah laughed as Luke grasped her hair and buried his face in the soft tresses like he understood Hawk's words. She couldn't remember that she had ever been this happy.

"He always used to do this, from when he was four months old." She scraped her fingers over the tiny row of teeth as Luke sat back. "He's got so many teeth already. I missed so much," she whispered.

"He's back now, Savannah. That's all that matters."

Luke's face snapped around at the sound of Hawk's voice. He squealed happily and crawled to the edge of the bed. Savannah reached out in fear of him falling off the bed, but he stopped and went on his knees, holding out his hands to the big man regarding him with an inscrutable expression.

"Ack! Ack!" Luke rolled the sound on his tongue, the name too difficult for him to pronounce. He jumped up and down when Hawk didn't move. "Up! Up!"

Savannah could only stare as Hawk picked him up and cuddled him expertly with one arm. He looked so at ease, like it was a daily occurrence to hold a small baby in his arms. It was clear that Luke had already formed a bond with him. It filled her heart with hope when Hawk's gray eyes softened as Luke bounded in his arms, pointing to the door.

"Oh no, little man, no more walking around outside. I think it might be time for your breakfast." He glanced at Savannah. "We brought his formula with and bought some baby cereal. The chef is preparing scrambled eggs for him as well." He smiled briefly. "I'm afraid none of us know much about babies."

"They're not that difficult to understand. They're just little humans," she said, feeling a little bereft that her son preferred to go to Hawk than stay in her arms.

"It's an exciting new place, baby. The fact that he still remembers you is proof that you're the most important person in his life."

Savannah latched onto the endearment. It was the third time he'd used it and the sound of it on his lips made her feel all warm inside, like her heart was about to be swallowed by her soul. She loved him even more for realizing her hurt and fears and not making it off as being silly.

Yes, he's not just in my heart. I love him, with everything inside me.

"I know you're right, but I'm a silly, emotional mother and I just want to hold him in my arms and never let him go."

Hawk smiled gently. "Why don't you get dressed while I show the little man the rest of his home for the next couple of months? Then we'll go to the dining hall together for breakfast."

Before Savannah could gather her scattered mind and ask what he meant by the next couple of months, he was already walking out of the door, his deep voice floating back to her. "Your room is right next to ours."

"Ack," Luke responded with a gurgling laugh.

"Yeah, I know, it's not very little man-like but we'll fix that, don't worry. Uncle Stone makes beautiful baby toys and I bet you he already started carving a rocking horse for you."

"I'll be forever grateful that you found Luke and brought him back to me, but I'm concerned about what Decker will do when his mother tells him Luke disappeared. He'll know he's back with me." Savannah looked around the dining room table where the Sinclair men surrounded her. Peyton was feeding Luke and cooing nonstop.

Savannah had realized the moment they'd set foot inside the Great Dining Hall that she was going to have to fight for attention from her son. And he basked in all the attention, of course.

It soothed her mind, though, to notice that Luke sought her out all the time, like he was checking to see if she was still there.

"He won't," Hawk said and squeezed her hand. "Parker scrambled all the phone lines and temporarily disabled the cell phone towers that service that entire area." He glanced at his watch. "By now, Dora Brooks and her staff have been taken into custody and are being interrogated. The FBI is collaborating with us on this. Rest assured, DC won't find out Luke is safe and sound here with us."

Savannah frowned. "Which means he'd still expect to be released from prison."

"And he will be." Hawk's voice darkened as he glanced at Stone.

"No, Hawk! Why would you do that? He's a dangerous man. I didn't even realize myself just how much until recently," she beseeched him. "Stone, please! You have to listen to me." She turned to him when Hawk's expression remained dogmatic.

"There's more at play here than just Decker Cooper, Savannah. He has connections with the Russian mafia. You might not want to hear this, but he's the one who orchestrated and sold the women into sex slavery to the Bratva over the past eight years."

"What are you saying?" Savannah felt the earth threaten to open and swallow her whole. The implication of what Stone was saying was too far-fetched to believe. If it was true and he had been the one who had sold the women, planting her as a supposed undercover coordinator ... A raw sob broke free.

"What's wrong?" Hawk studied her pale face. His suspicion that she had been sold to the Bratva, albeit under the auspices of an undercover agent was confirmed as she lifted tortured eyes at him. The eye contact was brief as she glanced down and shook her head. Fury exploded inside him. His hands itched to wrap around the bastard's throat and squeeze the last breath out of him.

"It's just … I can't believe he'd be that inhumane."

Her voice was brittle, like the emotions swirling inside her. She was so tired of feeling like this. Of carrying the burden of the harrowing year in Russia alone. She only realized now why Decker hadn't bothered to oversee her recovery or demanded that she go for therapy. Thinking back, she recalled how angry he'd been when he'd seen her among the women who had been rescued. She'd believed it was because she'd been treated as a sex slave too.

How wrong I'd been. How naive and trusting. And to top it off … I fucked him! God! I feel so dirty.

"It's the one chance we have to crack open the entire human trafficking ring he's been involved in. Not just directly to Russia but also to the Russian syndicates here in the States." Hawk rubbed her cold hands. "Don't worry about my dad, baby. He's collaborating with us, the DSH, DOJ, and the FBI. Decker Cooper is going to pay for what he did, I promise you that."

"Mama! Mammma!" Luke's excited voice broke through Savannah's silent grief. She looked around and found him sitting on the floor in the middle of the open conversation area. He slapped his hands on his legs when he saw her looking at him and gurgled a laugh.

"Oh my god! Look at him crawl!" she exclaimed as she watched his little bum wiggle as he headed towards the large archway.

"Geez, the little tyke can motor," Parker said and ran after him. He caught him under the arch and picked him up over his head, pretending to be an airplane, sounds and all.

Luke's delighted shrieks tore through her heart. He sounded so happy, so carefree and all she could think of was how much she hated his father.

Hawk kept the conversation light from that point forward, adamant to lift Savannah's mood. She just got her son back; it wasn't an occasion deserving to be bogged under by bleak thoughts.

Luke started getting cranky. He crawled to Savannah and heaved himself to his feet against her legs. He tugged on her shirt. "Up."

"Ah, just look at those droopy eyes. Is it nap time, mommy's little boy?" Savannah picked him

307

up, and warmth filled her heart as he cuddled against her, burying his face in her hair.

"Mama," he murmured sleepily and just like that, he was fast asleep.

"Parker and Zeke moved the crib from upstairs to your apartment, Hawk," Stone said, his eyes on mother and son. His hand tightened around Peyton's who was just as enamored by her little nephew.

Savannah looked up in surprise. Peyton had taken her on a tour of Stone's home upstairs, including the baby room.

"No, Stone. I can't expect you to do that. That crib was crafted with such love and devotion for your own child one day."

"Which is now my gift to you and little Luke. He deserves a special bed to sleep in. I've been itching to start something, and a new crib might just entice Peyton's lazy eggs to come out of hiding," he said winking at Savannah teasingly.

"*My* lazy eggs? I'll have you know it's those squiggly little dodgers of yours that don't know where to look. Must be because they've been aimlessly swimming around all these years in a vast number of condoms searching in vain for eggs."

"You better have popped the question already, young man. You're not getting this little lady pregnant without a marriage certificate in hand." Shane had always been their conscience and it was the one thing he stood firm by. That not one of them was going to father a child out-of-wedlock.

"Yes, Dad," Stone teased and then had to duck as a spoon catapulted through the air toward his head.

"Geez, old timer, easy with that pitching arm of yours. If it's not staplers, it's cutlery," Zeke interjected in a pretend stern voice.

Amid the bantering and laughter, Luke slept in Savannah's arms. For the first time in years, she felt cocooned within a circle of warmth, love, and companionship. It felt like home ... not just Castle Sin but the entire Sinclair clan made her feel like this was where she belonged.

Linzi Basset

Chapter Fifteen

"There's something I forgot to mention," Hawk said as he watched Savannah and Peyton leave the Great Dining Hall to put Luke to bed.

"Shoot," Stone said as he dragged his gaze from the sensually swaying hips of his sub.

"Savannah mentioned that Decker made remarks about Castle Sin. There's no way he could have insight into what's happening here except if he had someone else on his payroll."

"Peyton mentioned it too when she told me why she was here, but things happened so fast after that, it completely slipped my mind," Stone said.

"Another of the trainees? Or perhaps a sub in our employ?" Kane sat forward as he looked around.

They were alone in the Great Dining Hall. The subs and trainees had left for an early evening of relaxing and watching movies.

"Maybe," Ace said, tapping his fingers on the table. "What about Castle staff? Although I can't recall that we appointed anyone new lately."

"We didn't and I trust the rest implicitly. They've been with us from day one." Stone stretched out his legs. "It must be one of the trainees in either Savannah's first group or the last one that arrived two months ago. We've never had any problems with snoops before."

"I doubt it'll be any of the employed subs. They've been with us for the past two years, including their training period. I'm sure we would've noticed something if any of them started acting out of order." Shane got up and stretched lazily.

"Zeke and I will check the CCTV footage and see if anyone's been snooping around where they're not supposed to. I'll also rescreen their background checks. Now that we know about DC, I can check if any of them had contact with him in the past couple of months."

"Get on it and let us know the moment you find something. In the meantime, keep your eyes open for any untoward actions by anyone." Stone got up. "I'm heading upstairs. It's been a long day and I'm bushed."

"Bushed my ass. You're going to send your lazy *dodgers* on a swimming expedition again," Parker teased laughingly.

"Well, if that wasn't a direct challenge, little bro, I don't know what is, and you know me. I can't resist a sub offering a blatant challenge."

"You just remember what I said earlier, Stone." Shane frowned at him.

"Stop nagging, Shane. I have every intention of marrying Peyton."

"Yeah, sure ... as long as it's before those pink little heels make their appearance."

"I'm heading to bed as well," Hawk said as he followed Stone to the staircase. "I've arranged a meeting with my father tomorrow at noon in DC to discuss the strategy around DC."

"Did everyone agree to our plan to use Decker to draw out the Russian Bratva?"

"Yes. It's the first time such a viable opportunity to crack them open, with solid proof that'll stick has presented itself and get them locked up for good. We'll meet with them as soon as Decker's been released."

"As long as they don't lose sight of the bastard."

"Oh, we won't. Parker gave me one of his micro NanoT trackers. This one is a gem. All you need to do is press it against the skin and it merges with the cells." Hawk held up his hands at Stone's inquiring look. "Don't ask me how the hell he managed to figure that out, but it works. Dad and I are going to meet personally with Decker in prison before he's released and will ensure it's planted. Parker will be able to track him no matter where he goes."

They reached the second level, and each moved toward the staircase leading to their private apartments.

"As long as that bastard, DC, isn't allowed to turn state's witness. If that's their plan, Stone, I'm telling you now, there's no fucking way I'll allow him to walk away scot-free. Worse, to put Savannah and Luke through the hell of him demanding to be a part of that little boy's life. Not that fucking bastard."

"You and I both, Hawk. Be ready at nine. I don't want to have to rush to get there on time."

"I'll be ready."

Hawk took the stairs three at a time. He found Savannah sitting on the bed watching Luke sleep. She looked freshly showered with her long hair tumbling in wild disarray over her shoulders. Her usual night attire of shorts and a crop top hugged her curves like the tender caress of a lover.

"Why are you still awake?" His gravelly voice sounded harsh in the silence of the room.

"I can't stop looking at him. I guess I'm scared if I sleep, he might be gone when I wake up," she admitted in a soft lilt. "I can't believe how much he's grown." A warm smile curved her lips. "He's such a sweet little boy."

"Yeah, he is, and a very lucky one to have a mother who loves him as much as you do." Hawk's chest closed up as he watched the little body turn on his side, one arm once again flung over his head. With difficulty, he dragged his gaze away and looked at her. "You don't have to worry about his safety here, Savannah. You're both safe. We've increased the security around the island with underwater laser beams."

"What you said to Luke this morning," Savannah began hesitantly. She caught her breath as he pulled off his shirt and unzipped his jeans at the same time as he kicked off his sneakers and then stepped out of his pants. He turned to drape the clothes over the wingback chair.

She sucked in a sharp breath as his shirtless torso was exposed to her. It wasn't the first time she'd seen him shirtless, but she still couldn't help but gawk. In the soft glow of the bedside lamps, she was mesmerized by his physique and drool-worthy body. His chiseled chest glowed healthily as he shifted his weight. Her eyes dropped to the perfection of his abs, sculpted in a six-pack that popped, like the male models in a Calvin Klein shoot.

Freaking hell, how am I supposed to concentrate on serious matters with such delicious temptation right in my face.

He glanced at her with an amused twitch to his lips. "I said quite a couple of things to the little man this morning. You'll have to be more specific."

"You … ahem …" She cleared her throat and dragged her eyes from his washboard stomach. The cogs in her brain scrambled wildly to remember what she'd said. "Staying here," she blurted out as the memory flashed through her mind. "You said you're going to show him his home for the next couple of months."

"Ah, yes, that."

"Do I have to drag it out of you, Hawk?" she said exasperated. "What did you mean by the next couple of months?"

"Exactly what it means." His hands landed low on his hips, which of course enticed her eyes to drop to that sinfully v-cut muscle that disappeared under his boxers.

She drooled, literally drooled, for heaven's sake!

"Ehm ..."

Good lord, Savvy! Get a hold over yourself! The man is going to think you're a dimwit.

She closed her eyes and when she opened them, she made sure to stare at Luke, doing her best to avoid the temptation Hawk presented.

"I thought you couldn't wait to get rid of me."

"I don't know what gave you that idea."

"You did," she blurted, and her eyes shot to his. It was a difficult task, but she forced them to remain glued to his face. She wished the dratted man would put on pajamas or at least a robe. Something to cover those bulging muscles and ...

well, the other bulge that turned her ears red and made her ovaries perk up excitedly. "You made it abundantly clear that you weren't interested in having sex with me because I'd be gone as soon as I have Luke back."

"I did say that but that was before I realized the situation you're in. You're not going anywhere. Not now and not in the foreseeable future. At least not until Decker Cooper is no longer a threat."

"I can't become a burden to everyone here either, Hawk."

"You're not a burden." He held up his hand when she opened her mouth again. "No, Savannah, it's not up for debate. You and Luke are staying here, in my apartment, where I can keep you safe." He turned toward the bathroom. "I'm going to take a shower."

She gawked after him and almost swallowed her tongue when she had to rip her eyes from his gorgeous ass, so fast not to be caught drooling, as he spun around and lowered a stern look at her.

"In fact, I believe it would be prudent to sign a Dom/sub agreement between us. That way you'll be under my protection at all times—here, in the dungeons, and everywhere we might go."

"A Dom/sub agreement? Us?"

"Yes." He walked into the bathroom. His voice floated back to her as he turned on the water. "And you'll wear my collar. Every day. I don't want any visiting Dom thinking you are fair game."

"A collar?" she croaked in disbelief as she stared in the direction of the bathroom. "Me and you?" She frowned at his holier-than-thou attitude realizing he had just informed her, imagine that, *informed* her about it.

Her hand stole upward to circle her throat. A smile tore apart the dark cloud that had been strangling her for so long.

"I guess I don't have a say in the matter."

"No, you don't."

She gasped at the deep growl drifting from the bathroom.

How the devil did he hear me?

It didn't matter. All that did was that he had a possessive glint in his eyes when he'd said it. Like he wanted it, not to protect her from Decker Cooper, but because he desired to be her Master.

Just that.

Period.

"What's this I hear about a grandson?"

"Mom?" Savannah whipped around at the familiar sound of her mother's voice who had just entered the bedroom. Tears fell from both sides before they embraced. "You're here. How did you get here?"

"Hawk arranged for me to be brought here directly from the hospital. He and a very nice man, Danton, picked me up in Key West this morning."

"How are you, really? Are you sure you should be out of hospital already?" Savannah still cringed every time she remembered how badly beaten up her mother had been a month ago when Decker and the then secretary of defense had kept her captive to force Savannah to do their bidding. Savannah had spent the first week after everything was over next to her hospital bed, fearing for her life. That she looked fresh and relaxed was a miracle.

"I'm well, my darling." Vera looked around. "Now, young lady, where's my grandson?" She stabbed a finger in the air. "Don't think you're off the hook yet. I want to know why I never knew about ... oh lordy me! Is that him? Little Luke?"

Peyton walked in with Luke in her arms. He babbled animatedly with her in baby language but at Vera's voice, his lips clamped together. He stared at her with the intense curiosity he regarded everyone new person he met.

"Hi, Aunt Vera. I'm so glad you accepted Stone and Hawk's invitation for a visit," Peyton said but realized with a smile that Vera was deaf to her words in lieu of her fascination with the little boy in her arms.

"I'm a grandma," she whispered. "He looks just like you when you were little." She took a step closer. Her smile was brilliant. Luke was immediately captivated by her long blonde hair. He reached out and grasped the tresses in his hands and pressed his face against it. His toothy smile lit up.

"Mama."

Just like that the bond was made. He threw himself into Vera's embrace and hugged her with his short little arms clamped around her neck.

"Oh lordy, I'm going to cry myself dry today," Vera wailed as tears flowed freely over her cheeks again as she hugged the baby body against her. She caught a movement at the door and smiled broadly, "Thank you, Hawk, for this wonderful gift. I'd begun to believe I'd never be a grandmother."

"Mom! I'm only thirty-two," Savannah protested. She noticed that Hawk looked startled for a brief moment. "Don't mind my mother, she's just very happy." She walked closer. "You brought her here? To Castle Sin?" she whispered behind her hand.

"Yes, Savannah. Don't look so shocked. As long as she stays out of the dungeons, she should survive the ordeal." The dratted man didn't bother to keep *his* voice lowered, of course.

"Gmphf, try and keep me out. I've often wondered what goes on inside places like this." She scoffed at Savannah's shocked look. "Don't look at me like that. I'm not a prude. Well, not too much," she conceded at Peyton's raised eyebrows. She remembered clearly that Vera had begged her to convince Savannah to leave the island and the claws of the demon cult. "And you, young lady," she berated Peyton, "know very well why I acted the way I did."

"That's the spirit," Hawk said with an engaging smile.

Savannah tapped her foot on the carpet, regarding the camaraderie that seemed to have blossomed between the two of them with critical eyes.

"You didn't think to discuss this with me before you invited my mother?"

Hawk spared her a brief glance. "You would've said no, so why waste my breath?" He pressed his fingers over her lips. "Shh, enough. Until Decker is no longer a threat, Stone and I believe she'd be safer here. We don't trust him not to follow Gary Sullivan's example to kidnap her again. This time, he'll have no trump cards to play."

"Oh, I didn't think about that," Savannah admitted but continued sourly, unwilling to back down without a fight. Maybe because she was still smarting that after his shower the previous night, he'd gotten into bed and promptly fallen asleep. "That still doesn't give you the right to make decisions about my mother without discussing it with me."

"Shhh." Luke piped up with his little fingers over his lips.

"Oh, hell no!" Savannah said amidst everyone's delighted laughter, of which Hawk's deep rustling chuckle found resonance deep inside her. She stabbed a stiff finger against his chest. "Now see what you've done! You're a bad influence on my son."

"Ack!" Luke shrieked and held out his little arms, jumping up and down in Vera's arms. "Ack." He clapped his hands and raised his voice. "Up!"

"You're getting spoiled, little sir," Savannah said sharply at the display of impatience.

Luke, of course, offered her a toothy grin, slapped his fingers against his lips and with wide eyes, repeated, "Shh."

Hawk took him from Vera, smiling broadly as he made his way toward the door. "You're a fast learner, little man. Can you say Dom Luke?"

"Do ... Do..."

"Hawk Sinclair! Don't you dare teach my son that!" Savannah stamped her foot for effect just as Luke managed to roll his lips around the word.

"Dom. Dommmm," he said, clapping his hands.

"Yeah, you've got it, little man. Let's go for a quick walk. I've got to leave in ten minutes. Say bye to mommy."

Luke waved at the three women watching them leave. Two with wide smiles and one with an expression that was a comical mixture of delight and horror.

"Dom. Dommmm. Dom!" Luke's little voice floated back to them as Hawk walked down the hallway.

"Oh, yes. Hawk is gonna turn him into a mini Dom in no time."

"I'm glad you think it's funny, Peyton. Let's see how you like it when Stone does the same to your sons."

"Oh, hell the hell no!" Peyton said as realization struck. "I'm having girls. That's it. Do you hear me eggies? No boys in the making. Only sweet little girls!"

Vera stared at Savannah with a calculating gleam in her eyes. She couldn't remember that she'd ever seen such hope in her eyes. It might well be time for a little interference. Hawk might be protective over her, but Vera had detected a reservedness in his demeanor. Like he was holding himself back, locked away his emotions and that his heart wasn't involved, no matter how his eyes sharpened when he looked at her.

It was time Savannah found her little piece of heaven and Hawk Sinclair had the key to open the door.

Chapter Sixteen

"Judge Sinclair! I didn't expect you to come here."

Decker was taken aback. A shiver of unease traversed through him. He glanced at the thick steel door with the glass panel, but he could only detect the back of the guard's head standing in front of it. He was alone with the feared Chief Judge, Xavier Sinclair. A man who was kind to the innocent, brutal to the guilty.

The fucking bitch sidelined me!

Savannah had until the next day before he'd planned on phoning her again. The arrival of Judge Sinclair put him on the back foot. Decker didn't like surprises, this kind least of all. He preferred to be in charge, to know what to expect at all times.

Suddenly he floundered, his mind spun as he attempted to compose himself.

"You seem surprised, Prisoner 588254."

The gruff voice promised doomsday and the deliberate dehumanizing effect by not using his name demoralized him. Decker felt like a petulant child awaiting punishment from the principal of the school.

He hated the feeling.

"I ... I guess I ... didn't ..." Decker clamped his lips together. The stuttering response echoed tauntingly back at him. It was the first time in his life that he felt small and vulnerable.

"I'm here, Prisoner 588254 to look the man in the eye who is the biggest coward I have ever come across in my entire career. Actually, let me rephrase that. I'm here to meet the spineless, good for nothing slug who threatens women and an innocent child to make himself feel powerful."

Decker sunk lower in the chair. The clanking of chains mocked the bleakest moment of his lifetime. The cuffs around his wrists and ankles felt like they tightened, threatening to snap his bones. He dragged in a desperate breath. He was already humiliated; he'd be damned if he demeaned himself further by choking on it in view of this man.

"As I thought. Absolutely no backbone when push comes to shove."

Xavier Sinclair got up and looked down on Decker who was taken aback by the size of him. Tall, well-defined, and exuding confidence from every cell in his body.

"You forced my hand, Prisoner 588254." Xavier leaned forward to catch his eyes. "Hear me well. It'll give me the utmost pleasure to be the one to pass your sentence and I have no doubt it'll happen soon. Remember this, Prisoner 588254, I won't waste the state's money by giving you a prison sentence."

Decker started; his stomach lurched at the implied threat. "I am to be fully exonerated of all charges. That was part of the deal," he said in a nasal whine. He cleared his throat, annoyed at how scared he sounded.

Xavier straightened and awarded him a disgusted look over the length of his nose.

"Indeed." He walked toward the door and rapped his knuckles against it. "Your release has been arranged. After you signed the paperwork in the presence of myself and a witness, you'll be free to go."

The door opened. Decker jumped up when he recognized the tall man who walked inside the interrogation room.

"What the fuck is he doing here?"

"Ah, I see you know my son. Hawk is a revered attorney in the U.S." Xavier glanced at Hawk. "Not that he's practicing much at the moment."

"Not the time, Judge Sinclair," Hawk said darkly. It was a regular subject of contention between them. Xavier would love to see his only son following in his footsteps, but Hawk had made it clear he had no desire to become a judge.

Hawk circled the table twice, his eyes shooting daggers at the chained man who had sat back down but twisted in the chair to keep an eye on him the entire time. It was evident that he was even more unsettled by Hawk's presence than that of the Chief Judge.

Xavier took the documents from Hawk and threw them on the table. "Your release papers. I suggest you read it before you sign. I don't want any reason to have to return here."

Decker was so discombobulated that he struggled to read the words. It blurred and he had to blink a couple of times to clear his vision. He couldn't find anything untoward in the document and took the pen Hawk handed to him. He signed the document with a flourish, a self-satisfied grin on his face. Xavier and Hawk followed suit.

"Fucking stop that," Decker sneered as Hawk circled the desk again. "I'm a free man now. Uncuff me so I can leave."

"Not before I say what I came here for." Decker jerked as Hawk suddenly growled next to his ear. His hand clamped around the back of Decker's neck, and he squeezed. "I'm only going to tell you once, so you better listen and make sure you understand what I'm saying."

"Get on with it," he croaked, giving up on trying to get loose from the hand gripping him so hard.

"Stay away from Savannah. If you so much as think about calling her number, I'll know. If you so much as think of threatening her again, I'll know. You got what you wanted. Don't let me find you on the street on the outside, Cooper."

"You can't threaten me like that."

"But you can threaten a woman with her child? Which brings me to the next topic. You better return Savannah's son to her unless you—"

"He's my son! I have every right to him."

"No, you don't. Not until a court of law decrees visitation rights. Taking him from his mother is kidnapping. I've made my intentions clear. Savannah did what you demanded. Give her back her son. Don't say you weren't warned."

"Fuck you, you ... Ahh!"

Crack!

Hawk slammed Decker's head against the steel table. Blood splattered in a dark spray of red against the silver surface as his recently broken nose shattered from the impact. He wailed and covered his face, struggling to stay conscious.

"This is assault. I'll f-fucking press charges."

"Charges of what? I didn't see anything," Xavier said deadpan. "Let's go, Son, the air in here stinks of vermin."

Decker watched them go, his face throbbing and with the blood running into his mouth, the taste of victory was anything but sweet.

"Er ... Mr. Cooper, this is an unexpected surprise." The maître'd struggled to keep his expression civil as he greeted Decker. He was visibly shaken by his arrival, especially in light of the fact that he was supposed to be in prison.

Decker's lips thinned. He should've known the Sinclair bastards wouldn't keep to his stipulations. His exoneration and release from prison hadn't been on any television news report. Not in one newspaper article. As far as the entire U.S. population was concerned, he was still supposed to be behind bars.

"Chief Judge Sinclair has exonerated me. I've been released from jail," he snapped shortly.

"So, there was new evidence?" he pondered out loud. "Strange they didn't report on it."

"I requested it to be kept quiet."

Decker straightened his shoulders. He winced at the sharp pain shooting through his head. He suppressed the desire to check if the splint was still in place around his nose. Hawk Sinclair was going to pay for breaking his nose again. It hadn't even begun to heal from when the bastard in prison had broken it, which meant he'd end up with a crooked nose. If Hawk thought he had the upper hand, he had a surprise coming. Decker didn't have connections in the U.S. Russian Syndicate for nothing. His eyes darkened at the distrustful look from the maitre'd. It irked him to no end, but he wasn't about to stand there and defend himself to a lowly waiter.

"My table?" His voice breezed like a winter storm toward the stiff man watching him with slitted eyes.

"Oh, I'm terribly sorry, sir but your usual table isn't available. I have another in the corner." He pointed to a table hidden behind a large potted plant.

Decker simmered at the blatant snub as there were numerous, more suitable tables but he refused to lower himself and make a scene, knowing they could very well be booked. In fact, the maitre'd was being cordial by not asking him to leave because he didn't have a booking.

He shifted his shoulders, breathing in a calming breath as he ran his hand over the crispness of his suit, tailored to perfection, in a high-end Manhattan tailor's shop where he had all his clothes custom made. It felt good to be wearing breathable clothes again that made him look rich and powerful.

He used to have a standard table available at this restaurant in Dupont Circle in Washington DC. It was usually booked solid two months in advance, and not the kind of place you'd get a table on impulse. With its large, mullioned windows, long embroidered curtains, dark walnut tables, and delicate lilies on each table, live background piano music, and a lounge area with plush leather couches, it shouted rich and famous. The infamous Michelin chef, Harry Durand, drew diners from all over the States for one taste of his decadent meals.

"I'll take it. Thank you," he added as an afterthought.

"Very well." He looked around and snapped his fingers. "Leonard, please escort Mr. Cooper to table six." He nodded at Decker. "Enjoy your meal, sir. Oh, I have to apologize but your standing account was closed when you were ... er ... you know ... and I'm afraid I'll have to ask you to pay for your meal before you leave."

Decker didn't respond but followed Leonard to the table, fuming at the further humiliation he had to suffer at the hands of the Sinclairs. One news report. Just one would've cleared his name and this kind of thing wouldn't have happened.

Leonard handed him the wine list and stood stiffly in his starched white shirt and black bowtie as Decker silently studied it. He barked out his favorite Chardonnay as well as his preferred starter, seared Ahi Tuna, and sat back to study the diners through the leaves of the fern palm tree. The low buzz drifted from all around as each occupant savored their own collective privacy, an intimate haven to be seen but not heard. A couple of regulars glanced his way but looked away immediately, like they'd be hung by the neck for their curious indulgence.

Leonard arrived with his wine and tipped the bottle for a taste test.

"Just pour," Decker snapped as he broke off a piece from the freshly baked bread rolls Leonard had placed on the table and nibbled on it while he waited.

"Your starter will be served in five minutes, sir."

Decker took a sip from the wine and savored the rich, full-bodied, woody taste of oaked Chardonnay in his mouth before he swallowed.

"Heavenly," he sighed as the citrus flavored decadence flowed down his throat. He choked and struggled through a cacophony of coughs as his eyes were caught by a gaze as black as tar. He sat like a statue as he watched Yury Kumarin weave through the tables, with his trusted burly bodyguard close on his heels.

"Do you mind if I join you for dinner, Deputy Director Cooper?" The sneer on his lips discounted the humble tone in his voice. He didn't wait for confirmation but took the chair opposite Decker.

"What the fuck are you doing?" Decker grated through thin lips. "I just got out of prison and was exonerated. I can't be seen with a known associate of the Russian Mob."

"A leader of the Russian Bratva. Get it right. One would think that after all these years you of all people would know exactly who and what I am."

"That's not the fucking point. I can't be seen with you."

Yury rolled his shoulders in negligent rebuttal. "Calm down. I'm not associated with lowly

Mexican cartels, never will be, therefore the reason you were locked up in the first place has nothing to do with me."

"I can't believe you're that naïve, or are you deliberately trying to have me thrown back in jail? As a senior in the Bureau, I have no reason to collude with anyone in a cartel, especially not openly in a public place such as this."

"From what I heard, you haven't been reinstated as of yet."

"Nor will I be if this meeting is made public."

"I thought it important to meet with you here, to make sure you understand that I have eyes on you, no matter where you go. Don't try and fuck with me, Decker Cooper, my thread has been unraveling rapidly. I want to go back to Mother Russia, but Sergei promised me dire consequences if I arrived without his whore." Yury leaned forward. "What is your plan to get her to me?"

"I just got out of jail. Give me time to readjust, goddammit."

Yury barked a laugh. "You don't need to readjust. You were barely in there for a month. Think of it as a vacation gone wrong and move along. Quickly, too. You have ten days. If I don't have, number one: Sergei's little cunt, and number two: compensation for the loss of the last consignment, in the form of replacement whores as well as the profit we should've made by now, you serve no further purpose to the Bratva." Yury got up. He took the glass of wine Decker had put down and emptied it down his throat. "Ten days. Or else ..."

With the words left hanging ominously in the atmosphere, he walked out of the restaurant.

Just like that, the thrill of having a good meal for the first time in a month diminished as Decker's appetite vanished with the man leaving.

"Fuck! I feel like a goddamn piece of salami caught in a sandwich."

On the one side, the conundrum of his own making from the Russian Bratva, and on the other, an equally concerning threat of divine vengeance from the Sinclairs. At this stage, he couldn't differentiate which of them presented the biggest commination. If he didn't give Sergei and Yury Kumarin what they were after, he'd end up as shark bait. If he disregarded Hawk's warning, which he had no doubt wasn't an idle one, he'd end up dead. Either way, the future looked bleak.

"Give her back her son. Don't say you weren't warned."

Hawk Sinclair's voice echoed through his mind. He cursed softly. "Now I've got to fucking deal with the brat as well," he muttered.

"Your starter, sir." Leonard placed the aromatic plate of Ahi Tuna in front of him. "Do you wish to place your order for your main?"

"No, I've lost my appetite."

Leonard retreated, the morose tone more than enough indication to do so. Decker waited until he was gone before he made a call to his mother. It went directly to voicemail. The landline similarly to the answering machine.

"Where the hell are you, mother?"

His mother was impulsive and known to disappear for weeks on end to some exotic location for a luxurious vacation. The way she complained about Luke, he wouldn't be surprised if that was why he couldn't get hold of her. It was her indulgence as she called it. To break away from everyone, switch off her phone and concentrate on her selfish pleasures without interference from anyone. The question was whether she'd taken his son with her.

'You better not be out of town, Mother," he rumbled. "I need that brat ... yes! I'll use him to lure the bitch off the island and once she's out from under the Sinclairs' watchful eyes ... perfect!"

Decker's mind swirled as he started setting a plan in place. Sergei Kumarin would leave him be once he had his hands on Savannah Thorne, aka Lucy Simms, which had been the identity he'd created for her at the time.

"... compensation for the loss of the last consignment, in the form of replacement whores as well as the profit we should've made by now."

Yury's voice inside his mind shattered the belief that he could disappear as soon as he'd handed her over. The Bratva wouldn't stop chasing him until he'd fulfilled all their demands.

"This is such a clusterfuck." He pushed back the plate of uneaten food and finished his third glass of wine. He settled the bill and within minutes was on his way to his house in The Palisades.

He sat down in the study and powered up the laptop he'd just purchased, since the FBI had confiscated all his electronic equipment when he was arrested. All might not be a complete loss. He'd already started compiling a group of women targeted

341

for the next consignment to Russia before he'd landed in jail. He usually spent six months searching for the perfect matches. Women who had no family and struggled to make ends meet. Who wouldn't be missed or raise questions if they disappeared with no more than a note that they were starting over in a new city.

"What the fuck!"

Decker typed in his password to access his private cloud account again, but the same message glared back at him.

Password incorrect.

"It's not fucking incorrect," he snapped as he carefully retyped it, bellowing in anger as he received the same results. Every attempt he tried to reset his password ended in the same results.

Unable to connect.

"Bastards!"

He'd linked his private cloud to his FBI network account for ease of use and to hide certain irregularities from his superiors. The hacker who had set it up for him had assured him the link was secure and would never be detected by the IT division.

"How the hell am I going to get access to that file now? I need that information, or I'm totally screwed!"

He searched the contacts on his phone and dialed the hacker's number. This would cause a delay he couldn't afford. His instructions were short and to the point when the call was answered.

"I'll pay you an additional bonus if you can sort it out within twenty-four hours. I need access to that cloud and quickly."

"Not to worry, Slick. I'll get right on it. Your bonuses are usually worthwhile, so I'll have you up and running in no time."

Decker tried his mother again with no luck. He grabbed his car keys and headed out to Capitol Hill only to arrive at dead man's door. He got the spare key from the cubbyhole in the car and let himself inside. He stomped toward the kitchen.

"Goddammit!" His angry shout echoed in the quiet house as he read the note on the blackboard his mother used to relay messages to the staff.

Gone to Hawaii. Back in three weeks.

A search of the house confirmed that she had taken Luke with her. There were none of his clothes or toys to be found anywhere.

He didn't have the patience to look for her. As far as he knew, she'd never been to Hawaii, so he had no idea where she'd go, except to one of the most expensive resorts on the island.

Another delay he could ill afford.

Chapter Seventeen

"Luke is already asleep, and Vera will be here the entire time watching him. The bracelet I gave him has a NanoT micro tracking chip. He's safe, Savannah, and you, my little pet, need to relax your mind."

"And I suppose that's what you're going to do in The Royal Dungeon tonight. Relax me?"

"Among other things, yes."

"As long as there's no punishment involved."

"You know very well none of the Masters give punishment unless it's earned, so, as long as you're a good little subbie, you have nothing to worry about."

Savannah fiddled with the hem of her top. She glanced uncomfortably toward the kitchen where Vera was busy preparing a cup of tea.

"It feels ... weird going to the dungeon and doing ... *stuff* ... knowing my mother is three floors above me. I don't know how I'll be able to relax, Hawk. Lord help me, what do I do if she decides to pop in to see what's going on in there!"

Hawk chuckled at the horrified expression on her face.

"Relax, baby. Your mother might have expressed a desire to see what Castle Sin is all about but she won't be allowed inside any of the dungeons unless she has passed the BDSM 101 crash course."

"Oh, hell no! You're not going to go anywhere near my mother! I'll die a thousand deaths if you have to see her naked or touch her ... like *that*. No! Just no."

"It won't be me, and in honor of the fact that it's your mother, neither will any of my cousins. Danton will do the training." He studied her with eyes that darkened to a gunmetal shine. "Apart from Kane and Shane, he's about her age." He sighed heavily. "I keep forgetting how much younger you are than me."

"Oh, please. Age isn't a factor in this day and age, and you know it, Hawk, and besides, twelve years doesn't make you ancient."

"It doesn't bother you that I'm closer in age to your mother than you?" His gaze kept hers captive.

"I just said as much, didn't I?" Her eyes did a seductive foray over his drool worthy frame already dressed up in black leathers and a matching open vest. "Besides, with your physique and bad boy attractiveness, you don't look anything near your age."

"Hmm, I'm not sure if I should be pleased or insulted."

Savannah laughed at the disgruntled expression on his face.

"It's baby doll night in The Royal Dungeon, so dress up in a sexy teddy." His eyes moved over her blond hair. "Preferably something in red." He tapped her on the nose. "And barefoot."

"Barefoot? But—"

"Barefoot, sub ST. You have ten minutes. I'll be waiting for you in my study downstairs. Don't be late."

He didn't say it but the 'or else' was there in the stern tones of his voice. She rushed toward their room. The group punishment had been more than enough to last her for a long time. She had no intention of eliciting more anytime soon.

Savannah only thought to wonder about the reason to meet him in his study as she entered it to find Stone slouched in the chair opposite Hawk. She felt her cheeks bloom with color under the collective lustful stares of the two men.

She'd taken Hawk's instructions to heart and selected a lingerie baby doll set. It was a delicate red, sheer see-through material with lace patchwork across her breasts and a matching lace G-string thong.

"You look exceptionally beautiful tonight, sub ST," Stone said.

"Thank you, Master Eagle." She blushed, remembering the salacious encounters she'd had with him in the past. Her cousin's Master was a powerful man in more ways than one. She glanced at Hawk, taken aback at the dark look in his eyes as he glared at her. "Should I wait for you in The Royal Dungeon, Master Hawk?"

"No, Savannah. We're here to formalize the Dom/sub agreement we discussed." He paged through a document in his hands.

"Far be it for me to point out that *we* didn't discuss it, *you* did," she dared to mumble. She stood in the present position and quickly lowered her eyes as his hawkish gaze drifted to her.

"True, I did, and I made the reasons clear." He hesitated. "Do I tear up this contract, Savannah, or are we signing it?"

She shot a brief look at him. It suited her that he'd demanded because then it all came down to him, ordering her into the relationship. Asking her made it real and she didn't know if she was ready for it. Hawk had integrity and strong expectations of trust and honesty from everyone around him and she didn't doubt, more so from his sub. The painful secret that strangled her every day of her life could be her downfall. It was the one thing she'd not be able to tell him.

Not now ... not ever.

"Yes, Master Hawk, it'll be an honor to be in a relationship with you." She gasped as the words floated back to her. Completely unintended and uttered in contradiction to her thoughts. Just like that her good intentions flew out of the window. She was in love with Hawk Sinclair, and more than that, with each passing day it grew stronger. This might

349

be the only chance she'd ever have at happiness, even if it was short-lived. Because she had no doubt that if he ever found out the horrid tale she was hiding from him, he'd walk away for good.

Not because he'd judge her for what happened, but because she couldn't bring herself to trust him enough to bare her soul to him.

"Just to be clear you understand. This isn't a temporary arrangement, Savannah. Yes, I want you close to protect you against Decker Cooper but also to take care of your needs and desires as a submissive ... *my* submissive. In signing this agreement, you do it with the understanding that it's not going to conclude once the danger of DC has passed. My expectation is that it'll grow and flourish into a long-term and permanent relationship."

"I ... are you serious? That's not the impression I got the other night."

She stared at him, flummoxed but struggling to contain the joy that burst to life inside her heart. She searched his expression, but as usual, it was devoid of any emotion. She was disappointed that she couldn't detect even a speck of feeling to give her just a little reassurance that maybe he had started to develop feelings for her too. That this wasn't a relationship purely based on lust and her submission.

"I've had time to think it over and yes, I am serious."

"What about my work?"

"Correct me if I'm wrong, but didn't you tell me you'd already decided you were done with the FBI?" Hawk studied her intently.

"Yes, I did but that doesn't mean I don't want to work at all."

"I've looked at your CV, Savannah, and we could use someone of your skillset at Be Secure Enterprises. Once you're ready to go back to work, it's an option. If you'd rather work somewhere else, I won't stand in your way, as long as you're home every night."

"Where will that be? Will we live here, in the castle?"

"You don't like it here?" Stone asked with raised eyebrows.

"I love it here, Master Eagle, but I have a small son, who is going to grow up and no matter how gorgeous the island is, or Hawk's apartment," she looked beseechingly at Hawk, "it's not the perfect environment for a child. Yes, he might choose a

BDSM lifestyle when he's grown but I can't expose him to it just yet. Young boys are inquisitive. How do I explain it to him if he explores the Castle one day and walks into the dungeon and witnesses a flogging or a whipping?"

"I live here because it's convenient, as the Training Master as well as running BSE. There's no rush in regard to living arrangements, Savannah. Luke is ten months old. If you're looking for excuses, this is a waste of our time. Let's just—"

"I'm not, but I'm a mother and my child's welfare will always come first. If you can't understand that, a relationship between us won't ever work."

"I do understand and it's commendable that you have that outlook and *I* need *you* to understand one thing. Luke's welfare is just as important to me as it is to you, but I won't stand you manipulating me in any way, using Luke as a buffer."

"That's not what I'm doing," she frowned at him, the present position forgotten as she slammed her fists on her hips and tapped her toes on the carpet. "I'll sign your goddamn agreement, Master Hawk, but don't for one moment think I'm going to be a yes Master, no Master, kind of slave at your beck and call twenty-four hours a day. And I insist that we agree to discuss where we'll live as Luke grows bigger."

"That's better. I prefer this Savannah above the pretend one you fall back to at times." Hawk leaned back in his chair and watched her over the length of his nose. The smile that curled his lips promised wicked delights.

Savannah gaped at him. She hated when he blindsided her like this. Here she was all riled up, ready to throw punch after punch and he had the audacity to take the wind out of her sails by praising her. She snapped her mouth shut as Stone leaned closer and tapped his finger against her chin.

He chuckled at the expression on her face before he straightened in the chair and glanced at his watch. "Time's a ticking; Hawk and I've kept my sub waiting long enough. Are you signing or not?"

"Yes, we are," Hawk and Savannah chorused.

Hawk pushed three sets of the contract to Savannah and handed her a pen. "Read this through properly and then initial each page and sign in full on the last one."

The strict command in his voice brooked no resistance and she made sure to read every line in the contract, detailing his expectations, rules and what would constitute a breach of contract from both parties. An entire section was allocated to the use of a safeword, even within their relationship. It was a well-drawn up agreement aimed to protect both parties.

She signed it and handed it back to Hawk.

"Is there anything on your existing limit list you'd like to change or add?" He pushed it across the desk. "Please check it now. You'll notice that I indicated my expectations and needs on certain items. I need to know if you agree to those upfront."

While she studied the list, Hawk and Stone added their signatures.

"I'll leave you to finalize the list. Leave a copy on my desk once you're done so I can add it to my file." Stone got up and sauntered out the door.

"I'm not sure I understand what you mean by using a masochist."

Hawk's gaze caught hers in a snare so strong, she couldn't look away.

"There are times when I have the desire to inflict pain. In a way, it's a technique to reduce tension and anger and I use a whip to achieve it. I've seen you flinch and avoid floggings and completely disappear when there is mention of training in the whipping chamber, therefore I won't expect you to be the submissive assisting me during those times. I've always only used masochists whenever I have the need and I'll continue to do so."

"Apart from reducing tension, do you sometimes do it because you enjoy hurting a sub? And do you become aroused by it?"

"It's not a yes or no answer, Savannah. Yes, I enjoy watching a sub writhe in pain because I know I have the skill to push them past a level where nothing else matters but the pleasure they achieve through it. A masochist needs the addition of pain to become aroused. Do I enjoy inflicting pain for the sole purpose of hurting them? No, I don't, and I'll never use anyone to that extent. And yes, I do become aroused. I almost always reach a Dom high when I whip a masochist."

"Do those whippings end in you fucking them?"

"Yes, it does."

Savannah didn't like the sound of that or that he responded so readily. She had to be a realist because she knew that because of the brutal whippings Yury had exposed her to, it was something she'd never be able to do. She bit her lip. Hawk had watched her getting fucked numerous times and he always seemed to enjoy it, much like Stone with Peyton.

It was disconcerting to acknowledge how much it excited her to see the enjoyment on his face when he watched her fall apart. At the same time, it tore at her insides to think she'd have to watch him do the same thing. In the almost five months she'd been on the island, she'd only seen him fuck a sub in the member's dungeon once. It had been on the night she was supposed to join him for a bondage demonstration. Of course, she knew she couldn't and had hidden in the ladies' room with the excuse that she was nauseous. He'd used someone else by the time she made her appearance an hour later. She'd been miserable as she'd watched him walk over to where Stone and Peyton were in a scene. She couldn't look away as he'd fucked Peyton with a longing that she still remembered.

Talk about double standards, Savvy. This is the BDSM lifestyle they live. You'll either have to accept it or walk away.

"Then I want to be present." Her wayward mind made the conclusion before the thought formed in her brain.

Hawk looked at her with obvious surprise. It was the last thing he'd expected she'd say.

"You're not going to demand that I stop it altogether or rather fuck you than the sub I whipped?"

"I have no right to demand such a thing from you, especially if you're as skilled as you say. Nor can I expect you to fuck me, while the sub has become aroused through the whipping and deserves to achieve the fulfillment she obviously craves from the experience." She cleared her throat. "I might not like it, but I'll accept it."

Respect for her inched up a notch. "Anything else?"

"I don't mind ménages and multiple partners as long as it doesn't include women. I'm not homophobic at all but I do not wish to be caressed, aroused, or fucked by a female."

"Granted."

She looked around the room, fidgeting with the paper in her hand.

"What is it, Savannah?"

She couldn't look at him, not with the darkest of memories assailing her at that moment.

"If you ever force me to do anything with another Dom or Master, after I said no, I'll walk away."

"No is a meaningless word in here, sub ST, you should know that by now. There's only one thing that'll prevent or end any action from me or anyone in here. I deliberately added an entire section on it in our contract."

"The Castle safeword."

"Yes, which is?"

"King."

"The moment you utter that word, I'll listen or stop whatever we're doing. Don't ever forget that and don't ever be scared to use it. Is that clear?"

"Yes, Master Hawk."

He pinched her chin between his fingers and forced her to look into his eyes. His searching gaze made her fear that he could read every thought in her mind like a movie trailer.

"I hope you'll come to trust me enough to one day tell me about those demons eating away at your soul."

"I ... please don't—"

"Because if you can't, I'm not sure there's a long-term future for us."

He dropped her chin, gathered the signed documents, and placed them in a folder in his drawer.

"From this moment onward, you're no longer a trainee but, like Peyton, there are certain training sessions you'll be expected to attend. Think about a club name for yourself as we walk. I'm going to need it by the time we reach The Royal Dungeon."

He took her hand and strode toward the door, giving her no choice but to jog to keep up with him. She did her best to curb the pain and devastation his words had caused like a sword had sliced through her heart.

Why was it so difficult to trust that he'd understand? She trusted him with her body, lord knew with her heart, and above all, with Luke. How did she get past the block in her mind that kept telling her otherwise? She had never spoken to anyone about that year. Not even with the therapist the Bureau had demanded she see. Decker had tried but she'd clammed up even with him. It had been too painful and degrading to rehash everything she'd willingly participated in.

It didn't matter that it had been for her own survival. In the end, *she* had been too weak to resist and had given in. To this day she couldn't get over the disgust she felt for herself. It didn't bear thinking that he would be able to.

"Have you decided on your club name?" Hawk asked as they walked through the massive double doors into The Royal Dungeon. These doors had a beautifully carved couple in a loving embrace. The details were so intricate, it looked like real people molded into the wood.

"Maybe I can just continue using the name I have been at the clubs I attended?"

"Which is?"

"Scarlett." She felt her cheeks heat up as he regarded her stoically.

"Does the name have any significance to you?"

Savannah flinched. No one had ever asked her that, but she should've known Hawk was too astute not to make some kind of connection. She'd deliberately chosen the name as a brand to remind herself of the stigma of her weakness to withstand Yury that had turned her into a willing whore.

"I ... ehm, just liked the name," she said with lowered eyes.

"Eyes," he snapped and watched her heave in a deep breath before she looked up at him. For a moment he didn't talk, noticing the same torturous expression paint a canvas of self-castigation over her face. His sigh formed a bridge of acceptance that she soaked up with a flash of relief she couldn't hide.

"I don't like it." He took her chin between his fingers and turned her head this way and that. "Hmm ... Tulip. I believe that'll be more fitting."

"Tulip? You see me as a bright and happy flower?"

"A tulip is a jewel among flowers, Savannah, and described as the perfect flower to mark the beginning of a new and colorful year. This is your new beginning, our time, Tulip. With me as my sub. I'm going to make it my mission to destroy all the scarlet letters in your mind until only the glorious petals of happiness and acceptance flows through you."

"Hawk, I wish I could ... I wish I had the strength to ... to—"

"Shh," his fingers caressed her lips as he silenced her. "Tonight, we concentrate on the future. No thoughts of past mistakes, demon, or memories to darken the celebration of our new commitment to each other. Can you give me that for this night, Tulip?"

"Yes, Master Hawk, for this night and all the others to come."

"That's the spirit, Tulip." His eyes warmed her soul. "You have more strength inside you than you realize, little one. That's what you need to tap into, that which has brought you to Castle Sin."

"I didn't have much choice. You know DC—"

"No," he cut her protest short and cupped her cheeks between his palms. He brushed his thumbs over her lips. "I see you as a jewel, Tulip. *My* jewel because of who you are when you're with me and how you shine from within when you look at Luke. At how fiercely you protect and love your son. I admire your survival instincts. One thing I'm going to teach you is that it took courage to give in to that bastard's demands. *You* are the strong one, *he* was the weakling. You gave of yourself, you compromised your morals, your integrity to protect those you love while he cowered behind threats."

Savannah stared at him as his words buried themselves deep within her, crawling through the crevices of disgust that had rooted itself through every compartment of her mind.

"Come, it's time for the ceremony."

He tugged her along with him to the large Royal Chamber where the majority of activities and scenes took place. He headed toward the raised platform in the center of the room.

"What ceremony?" she whispered as she pressed against him, aware of the people turning to watch them. Even the couples in scenes stopped and looked at them.

"The collaring ceremony." He smiled at her wide-eyed expression.

In the other clubs, a couple only performed a public collaring ceremony to announce their upcoming marriage as a Dom/sub couple.

"Don't look so surprised, Tulip. Now that I've made the commitment to us, I aim to do it properly and ensure everyone here knows who you belong to."

Hawk brushed his thumb slowly along the curve of her lower lip, his eyes the deep shade of rolling clouds just before a storm. He treasured the shudder that followed in its wake and took great pleasure in treating her to another leisurely pass. Satisfaction flashed in his eyes at the effect he had over her as she trembled from his touch again.

"I hope you're ready for me, Tulip, because I promise you, from this point forward, I'm going to unleash the full power of my lust onto you."

Her ovaries broke out in a quick step samba at his words, discombobulating her thoughts as her mind simultaneously stumbled over the possibility of a future that promised happiness and love. She was still struggling to compute the sudden shift in her destiny when he fastened his mouth to hers in a whisper of heated breath. He kissed her slowly at first but soon the heat and the unexpurgated passion he poured into the caress bowled her over. She exulted in the sensual way his hot, wet, demanding tongue warred with hers. Her moan came in the wake of his fist clamping a tuft of her hair, angling her head exactly how he wanted it.

"Ahem ... are you ready, Master Hawk?" Stone cleared his throat loudly and elaborately behind them.

Hawk refused to be rushed and ended the kiss leisurely with a hot lick over her lips, now swollen from his fervent possession of her mouth.

"Yes," he said as he turned to face Stone, circling his arm around her waist and dragged her along with him. "Now, I'm ready."

God, I'm so screwed, she wailed in her mind. *How does he do this to me?* The sound of his husky voice sent frissons of desire all through her, buzzing like she had just been zapped by a bolt of lightning.

"In view of all present Master Hawk pledges his Domination to ..." He glanced at Hawk, who offered Savannah's club name softly. He smiled and continued. "Submissive Tulip, in a Dom/sub relationship." Stone turned to Savannah. "Do you, Tulip, accept Master Hawk as your Dominant, to care and protect you from this point forward? Do you undertake to be honest with him at all times, trust him with your body, that he knows what it needs, and to communicate your fears and desires to him? What is your pledge to these questions, sub Tulip?"

Savannah was shaken at how badly she desired more than a submissive pledge. The words that resembled wedding vows strengthened the roots Hawk had planted inside her soul earlier with his words of encouragement. To tap into her inner strength, to find the courage to face the demons and embrace what the future held. Her eyes sought out the man who had so brazenly stepped into her heart.

She was compelled by everything about his physical charisma. There was always a fire dancing in his eyes, and it was there all the time. She knew now it burned for her, even when he wasn't looking directly at her, she could feel it all the way in her soul. His full lips flattened into a thin line and a strong muscle popped in his jaw as he returned her intense regard. As always, she stood helpless against his magnetism that pulled her in. She reached out to brush back a section of hair that fell across his forehead.

Her smile was the opening of her personal heaven to him. A sign of her willingness to delve into the depths of her tortured past and allow him inside.

"Master Eagle, I hereby pledge my complete submission to Master Hawk. I offer my body freely into his care and protection, knowing he would know what I need at all times. I offer him my trust, honesty ..." her voice cracked on the word, but she bore on without flinching, "and commitment. I accept Master Hawk as my Dominant."

"Master Hawk, how do you pledge to sub Tulip?"

Hawk took a step to face Savannah. His smile was tender, warm, and offered her so much more than she could have hoped for. She found it difficult to accept how fast things were moving, how his entire attitude had softened toward her. His finger pressed against the frown drawing her brows together.

"No, Tulip. Trust in me, little one, that's all I ask."

That brief touch, his innate ability to read what was in her mind was like magic that dissolved the doubts forming inside her at birth.

"I do, my Master."

Her breath caught in her throat as he removed the red leather collar and replaced it with a piece of jewelry that felt cool in contrast to his warm fingertips. As she looked at him and noticed the possessive glimmer in his eyes, the unabashed admiration as he looked at the collar he locked behind her nape, she was inundated by the heat that infiltrated her skin wherever the piece of jewelry touched.

"With this collar, I pledge to honor the submission you freely offer to me. To care for and protect you and give your body what it needs to unleash the fiery woman inside you. I offer you my trust, honesty, and understanding." His voice lowered for her ears only. "I offer you me, Savannah Thorne."

Then he kissed her once more. This time it was a promise, a tease, and she completely lost herself in the moment, in him. He cupped her chin in his hand and looked deep into her eyes.

"Every inch of you is beautiful. Trust in me that I don't wish to change you, Tulip, only enhance the woman I know is already there."

"Master Hawk ... I don't know what to say, how to express what I feel at this moment."

"Say nothing, Tulip, just ... feel." He fisted a tuft of her hair and drew her against him for a long, deep, wet kiss.

Savannah felt her body shake as he pulled back. His smile was an echo of the satisfaction of witnessing her reaction. He leaned in for another kiss. A lazy one that made her toes curl. It was a sensual exploration, a promise of what was to come. The low rumble came from deep within him as he cranked up the intensity ... and turned her weak-kneed, threatening to slide into a big puddle on the floor.

"I give you, Master Hawk and his sub Tulip."

Neither heard the deep rasp of Stone's voice nor noticed the excited applause. Not while sealing the explosive emotions that racked through their collective bodies.

"Be warned, little one. You're mine now. Mine, and I'll never let you go."

Chapter Eighteen

"And now, ladies and gentlemen, the final part of the collaring ceremony. You are to witness the complete trust a submissive offers her Master," Stone said and snapped his fingers.

Savannah's eyes widened as the lights dimmed, leaving only the center stage lit by a spotlight.

She grasped Hawk's hand, forcing the flash of insecurity down.

"Master Hawk? What's happening?"

"Relax and trust me, little one." He cupped her chin and brushed his lips over hers.

A rhapsody of exhilaration caroused through her entire body like the sizzling sparks of an electrical current. Savannah glanced up and was snared by the dark and enigmatic look that gleamed with love and passion. Her skin tightened and she felt goosebumps rising everywhere. They were standing next to an examination bed.

Hawk's eyes ran down her body with obvious appreciation.

Savannah's gaze traveled over his naked chest. He'd removed his shoes and shirt and was only wearing his leathers. He looked dangerous and droolingly sexy. Her hands lifted and she reached toward him.

"Savannah," he barked in warning, and she froze, her hands hanging between them. They were on show, and he expected proper decorum from her.

"Please, may I touch you?"

Hawk dragged a tortured breath into his lungs as he shook his head. If she touched him now, his mind would be filled with visions of fucking her. Imagining the soft, velvety muscles of her pussy grab hold of his length and lose focus, which he couldn't afford. Forcing back a low grunt, he planted a quick peck on her lips.

"Not yet, Tulip. We need to start the scene. Get rid of that teddy and then get on the bed. On your back, please."

Dutifully, she undressed and climbed on the bed with his assistance, settling on her back, glancing at him questioningly.

"I still don't know what we're going to be doing."

Offering her a tender smile, he secured her wrist cuffs to the O-rings welded at the top of the bed above her head. Moving to the bottom of the bed, he spread her legs to secure her ankles in a similar fashion.

Savannah forced her breathing to remain slow and even, relaxed as his soothing voice kept her connected to him. Whatever Hawk planned; she trusted him. Somehow, she knew they were on the verge of exploring something that was going to put her trust, devotion, and acceptance of her needs and desires, to the ultimate test.

Savannah was stumped that she didn't experience a twinge of fear in mind; all she felt was excitement coursing through her veins. A sensation she sensed Hawk was engulfed in as well. Savannah knew in her heart that he knew what she craved and would never hurt her. He offered her mutual respect and above all, control. It was the one thing that humbled her. That he wanted her to have control over everything he did to her.

His fingers moved in fluttering caresses over her stomach, her hips, all the way to her ankles and back, leaving her skin to tingle in the wake of his touch.

"I can't resist to need to taste you," he grunted as he ran his tongue over her collarbone, placing a tender kiss in the center of her throat. Savannah arched into his touch. His hands continued their lazy exploration of her body. She was on the verge of combusting as he placed small kisses along her jaw, ending in a sensual lick below her earlobe.

Hawk smiled. He'd found that sweet spot and loved how she moaned in a husky, catlike mewl.

"Masters, Doms, and subs, welcome to a scene that will make you squirm in your seat, heat your insides, and arouse every inch of your body. Master Hawk is going to perform a hot and cold wax scene with his sub, ending with a strapping. The ultimate test of trust in submission." Stone's voice droned over the soft hum of voices.

Applause sounded, followed by excited twitters all around. Savannah stiffened.

Hot wax. No, not that, I can't ...

Fear speared through her. She flashed a panicked look at Hawk's frowning countenance.

"What's the matter, Tulip?" He'd immediately picked up on her withdrawal.

"I can't do this." She gave the cuffs a panicked yank. "Please untie me."

Hawk laid his hand on her heaving stomach and leaned over her, filling her vision with his eyes—the only thing she needed to focus on. His touch, the warmth she needed to surround her.

"Savannah, this is me, Hawk. You know I would never hurt you. Talk to me, baby. Why are you scared?"

"I ... before ... please, I can't do this."

"He burned you? With candle wax?"

Hawk had examined every inch of her skin during training in the dungeon. He hadn't seen any burn scars anywhere.

"No ... he used a f-flame ... on the soles of my feet." She shook her head to shake off the vision and took a deep breath. "It was excruciating. Even though this is just wax, I can't do it, please, my Master."

"Baby, listen to me. This is nothing like that." He kissed her and noticed the fear lingering in her eyes. "God I'm going to fucking rip him apart," he sneered. "This is an erotic scene, Savannah. You know my rule and that I'll always take care of you, little one, even here and now, while I use the wax. You've given me your trust to know that I'll never push you more than what you can take. Now, I ask that you give me the trust to offer this to you. I promise you, Tulip, I'm going to blow your mind."

Savannah sighed and relaxed her body as she looked into his glowing, emotive silver-gray eyes. She trusted Hawk. Implicitly. She nodded and smiled.

"I'm sure you will, my Master."

"Do I have your promise, Tulip?"

"I promise I'll use my safeword if this becomes too much."

"And if you get scared?"

"I will say King."

"Good girl." Hawk looked up at Stone and nodded.

"Without any further ado, I now hand you over to Master Hawk and his sub, Tulip."

Savannah watched as Stone handed the receiver unit to Hawk. He hooked it in his leathers and settled the mouthpiece in place. He smiled at her.

"Relax, little one. Seeing as it's our collaring ceremony and there's a big audience, it's imperative they understand what I do and how it affects both of us throughout the scene. Think of it as a demonstration at the same time. Teaching is what we do," he assured her gently.

"I understand, Master," she lilted with a smile.

He brushed his fingers over her lips. "Good girl." He looked at the audience. "The human skin is susceptible to burn easily, so you always need to use wax with extreme care. No Dom would ever wish to burn such luxurious skin as this." Hawk ran his fingers over her nipples, which pebbled to hard little stones immediately. Her breathing increased, but his soothing touch calmed her immediately.

"The first thing to remember is to ensure the candle isn't too close to your sub's body. The aim is to allow the wax to drip gently from a distance. That way, it cools a little before splashing on the skin.

Waxing is very much a visual scene and therefore I won't be explaining what I do. I invite you to watch and soak in the ambiance of the scene, the sensations, and emotions such a highly erotic scene evokes. Always remember with any erotic scene, the importance of touch and arousal. Now, I'm going to give all my attention to my lovely sub."

Hawk moved the mouthpiece out of the way but didn't remove it completely. It was important that the audience experienced the emotions as it escalated during the scene.

"How are you feeling, baby?"

"I'm a little shivery, my Master."

"Do you trust me, Tulip?"

"With my life, my Master."

He stepped to the trolley next to the bed and lit a broad red candle. A sweet smell of roses tickled Savannah's nostrils. It made her heart beat faster as he moved back to her.

"You are so beautiful, little one," he whispered as he left a slow trial of kisses down her body.

Like always with Hawk, her fear dissipated as the excitement inside her grew. She was blindsided as a sudden longing to be pushed to her ultimate limit broke to the surface. She'd been scared for so long and longed to be free from all the chains that bound her to a very painful past. Her eyes caught his and she knew instinctively that was why he had chosen this specific scene—to push her ultimate boundary. She acknowledged that Hawk was the only man, capable of offering her the release she craved. It was more than physical. She needed the emotional release she knew was imminent.

She shivered as his tender kisses moved over the concave of her waist, over her belly, his tongue caressing her skin as he traveled downward. He deliberately avoided kissing her hot pussy, which made her want to scream with the frustration that had already morphed to desire. The hot juices slithering from between her labia was proof of the sheer excitement she had no control over. Hawk placed hot kisses on her thighs, lingering between her legs. She could feel his smile as her moans turned feral when his hot breath scorched her pussy. He had the innate ability to tease the deeper reserve of her sexuality and left her in helpless surrender of the aroused hunger inside her. A soft moan escaped her lips as his tongue, hot and wet, caressed the back of her knee. A gravely moan ended in a violent jerk of her body.

"Hmm, little one, the perfect sweet spot."

Savannah looked at him where he stood at the foot of the bed just enjoying her abundant beauty.

Lord, how I love this man.

Savannah was overwhelmed by the feelings for Hawk that consumed her and filled her entire being. She had never thought she'd ever be able to experience such unwavering trust for any person, let alone a Dominant who she had given complete control over her body. But she couldn't deny she did, and it was entwined with a deep passion and desire to please him.

Her mind spun as Hawk moved up her body, caressing her with a mixture of infinite tenderness and roughness that sparked a flash of heat to surge through her and settle in a low throb in her loins.

He cupped her cheeks and stared deeply into her eyes. His voice was earnest and stern. "I'm keeping you to your promise, Tulip. This is an intense scene and involves a level of discomfort. There's a thin line between erotic pain and true pain. You will stop me the moment you feel even a little uncomfortable, understood?"

"I will, my Master."

Her trust in him shone in her eyes and he couldn't resist leaning down to caress her lips, his tongue chasing hers. Savannah felt the warmth and moisture gather in her pussy as her body became engulfed in passionate heat.

Music started playing in the background, the Heavy Metal sound of Def Leppard's 'Pour Some Sugar On Me' filled the atmosphere, the melody fit the mood to perfection.

Savannah blinked as the lights went dark. She glanced around in wonder. Candles were placed all around the bed, on the floor and on little tables, giving the scene an ambiance of romance. She licked her lips as her stomach rumbled, realizing what it meant.

Her eyes were glued onto Hawk as he stepped closer. Her eyes widened just before he placed the blindfold over her eyes and tied it behind her head.

"My Master, no. I prefer to see."

"I need you to be relaxed and to concentrate only on the sensations and feelings. I don't want you to tense up and watch. Trust me, Tulip."

Savannah pushed the fear to the back of her mind as he caressed her cheek and traced her lips.

His hand circled her throat, gently caressing the soft skin. His fingers tightened slightly.

"Remember that you belong to me, Savannah. Tonight, I have complete control."

"I trust you, Master Hawk."

Savannah was lost in helpless excitement as he caressed her breasts while leaving small bites and kisses on her neck. His tender touch turned rougher. His fingers closed around her nipples, and he tugged, softly at first, then he firmly pulled and twisted. She cried out as sensations curled and wrapped around her core like a heated cocoon.

Hawk retrieved a long length of red rope from the tray.

"Yes, little one, that's the sensations I want you to experience," he said as he noticed her tremble in the wake of the edge of the soft rope he ran between her breasts. She relaxed into his touch.

"Easy, baby," he gentled her as he bound her breasts with quick efficient movements.

Savannah breathed in as she felt the same amazing pressure she had when he'd bound her with sashes. Her nipples were tight and tingled and throbbed with every breath she took, with every beat of her heart.

"Not too tight, is it Tulip?" He circled one budding nipple.

She delivered the "no" in a breathless moan.

Hawk retrieved a small bowl of ice, a feather, and another red candle from the tray. He placed the bowl and feather between her legs and then lit the candle.

"You're so beautiful, baby."

He teased her nipples until they turned into hard pebbles. He lifted the candle over one of her bound breasts and tilted it.

"Oh, my god," Savannah gasped as hot wax spilled over a tender nipple. "Lord!" she breathed as the chill of an ice cube soothed the sting before it fully penetrated her mind. She was still trying to comprehend the contrasting sensations when she felt the soft tease of a feather brush around her nipple and areola.

He tipped the candle twice more over the same nipple, cooling it immediately with ice and awarded her reaction with the gentleness of the feather. Savannah's moan was one of sheer ecstasy as the hot wax hardened and she felt it pull at her skin. Her moans were now constant as her back arched high, silently begging for more as he offered the same treatment to its twin.

"Master, this is ... oh," she groaned as he continued. He crisscrossed drops of wax over her stomach, cooling each splash of hot wax with the ice and followed with the feather. He trailed a line of red wax on the top of her one leg to her knee and back up the other. The faithful ice and feather trailing in its path.

Savannah writhed and moaned in her bonds, her mind in a whirlpool from the erotic mixture of pleasure and pain that quivered through her body. Hawk's fingers tapped her denuded pussy and her breath puffed from her lips, disappearing into thin air.

"Breathe, Tulip," he chuckled as he ran his finger through the sleekness of her glistening slit, smiling at her wet excitement.

"It seems you have lost your fear, little one. Are you enjoying it, Tulip?" he asked as he twirled his fingers inside her sweet pussy.

"Oh, Lord, Master Hawk, you have an expert touch," Savannah replied between soft, husky moans.

Hawk rubbed her clit until she mewled and thrashed, helpless in the hold of unexpurgated lust. A crimson bloom flushed her cheeks. Being encased in darkness intensified all her senses and she was helpless against the effect the varied sensations had on her. The throb that pulsed through her swollen loins became suffused with heat that threatened to push her over the edge when he tipped the candle. Hot wax spilled onto her outer labia.

"Fuck," she gasped for breath and pressed her hips into the unmoving bed, trying to escape the heat searing her skin. She yanked at her bonds, writhing from the unexpected heat.

"Easy, Tulip." His low timber soothed the panic before it took seed as he instantly cooled the heat with ice, brushing the softness of the feather immediately after. With a sigh, she gave in to the sensation consuming her as rivers of cold, melted water seeped into the folds of her pussy.

She was unprepared as this time, he tipped the candle just where the slit of her pussy began. Her excitement catapulted to dizzying heights, anticipating where he was going next. She realized she was holding her breath eagerly.

Hawk stood back, admiring her bronzed body covered in the red wax.

"Red is definitely your color, Tulip," he praised. His smile turned feral as she squirmed in helpless exaltation at the pleasure she had just experienced. "You have permission to climax, my pet but only once."

Before Savannah could wrap her mind around his words, the world around her tilted as he tipped the candle and hot wax seared her clitoris.

"Beautiful." His soft chuckle reached her ears as he brushed the ice over her throbbing piece of flesh. She thrashed; her hips soared high in the air. Another splash, another scream and when the ice touched her throbbing nub, her back arched.

"Gaaawwd," she cried as a climax rippled through her. A slow unfurling wave of pleasure that heated her from the inside, swirling through her veins and bursting to the surface in a blinding flash.

Thrashing in helpless surrender, Savannah battled to ride the exhilarating emotions that overwhelmed her.

Heart, mind, body, and soul.

Moving down to her legs, he rubbed his hands over every inch of her body. Caressing and gently peeling the wax off her skin as he moved up. A harsh moan escaped her lips as he scraped the wax off her clit and her hips jerked upwards violently.

"No, Tulip. You do not come again," his dark voice warned.

Hawk took special care removing the wax coating her breasts, realizing they were sensitive because of the slowed circulation from the binding ropes. Savannah bit her lip as he very gently pried them off. With each pinch of a nipple, little currents of pain pulsed through her body that triggered a throbbing in her clit, with such intensity that Savannah could not withhold a carnal moan.

"Keep your eyes closed, baby. Allow the light to penetrate your eyelids," Hawk coached as he removed her blindfold.

When her eyes flickered open it was to his crooked smile. She winced as she noticed what he held in his hands.

"Oh lord," she gasped, doing her best to suppress her fear of being whipped.

"Relax, Tulip and keep your eyes on me. This is me, Master Hawk," he gentled her fears as he moved back to the foot of the bed, slapping the black leather strap against his thigh. The glide of the soft leather over her skin felt like a caress that dissolved her immediate fears and she relaxed into his gentle touch.

"Good lord."

She couldn't believe that he once again evoked an untethered lust in her. He ran the strap over her stomach and circled her bound breasts, teasing the nubs until they tingled and tightened with painful arousal. Need radiated through her entire body.

Without warning, he snapped his wrist and slapped each nipple eliciting a mingled cry from Savannah as the tingles turned to jolts of painful pleasure. Continuing with light slaps across her breasts, each strike became more zealous, painful. Squirming, Savannah squealed as a mixture of overwhelming pleasure and pain flooded her brain. The sensations pushed her ruthlessly to the edge of her boundaries. Her breathing quickened and her heart raced wildly with each swing of the strap. Hawk kept his eyes on her, reading her responses. She was on the verge of shouting her safeword when he stopped and softly caressed the tips of her blazing nipples with the strap.

He nibbled on her ear and gently kissed the sensitive spot in her neck, drawing a saturated color of an aroused groan to spill from her lips.

"Easy, Tulip. I'm so proud of you. You're adapting to the added pleasure of evocative pain so beautifully. You're exquisite in your uncontrolled arousal, little one."

Savannah basked in his praise and arched her back as the strap slashed against the tender flesh of her stomach, heating and tingling her skin, just short of stinging pain.

"I need you, Master," Savannah whimpered as she felt the increasing heat gather between her legs.

"You are so fucking wet, Tulip," he muttered as he brushed his fingers over her slick pussy, delving inside to twirl them against her soft, velvety walls.

His smile turned carnal as he tapped the strap against her inner thighs. Her hips lifted off the bed.

"Ready, my pet?"

"For what," she puffed, desperate to draw a proper breath.

"For this, baby." His low voice timbered through her as with precise accuracy, the edge of the strap connected with the tip of her swollen and throbbing clit.

"Holy shit!" The primal scream echoed around them as the sudden burning pain of the lash penetrated her mind. The cogs in her brain were still scrambling to pull her equilibrium back together when Hawk leaned over and slowly licked the throbbing nub, obliterating her control. She was engulfed by overwhelming pleasure of his tactile affections.

"Come for me, Tulip. Now, my pet, come." **The lust that clutched at his loins portrayed itself in the raw carnality of his voice.**

Savannah couldn't breathe—her mind was in total disarray, unable to unscramble the myriad of sensations that flooded her.

"Master Hawk ... I'm ... please." Her plea turned into a scream as her body tightened. Warm liquid gushed from her loins and pooled under her body. Her hips jerked as she thrashed on the bed in a desperate attempt to draw a breath, helpless against the paroxysms that rocked her as long waves of ecstasy rolled over her.

"Easy, Tulip," he soothed as he took off the ankle cuffs and rubbed the tender skin. He lifted her foot and placed tender kisses on her instep.

Good lord! For someone who didn't even know she could squirt, I sure as hell make a habit of it now.

Savannah sighed as he moved his hands up her body to slowly loosen the rope binding her breasts. A small gasp was testimony of the sweet mixture of pleasure and pain that throbbed through her breasts and nipples at the rush of blood as her circulation returned to normal.

"I've been looking forward to this moment since we walked into the dungeon, little one." Hawk pushed her knees apart as he got onto the bed and settled between her legs. He gazed into her eyes, easily gauging her renewed arousal. His smile took her breath away as he leaned in and whispered against her lips, "You're mine now, Savannah Thorne."

Savannah was helpless against the flood of emotions that filled her heart to near explosion as his words found resonance deep inside her soul. In it she heard the ones he didn't utter, the promise of love and happily-ever-after. It filled the void she'd suffered for so long.

"I am yours, my Master, all of me."

"Yes, honey, every delightful inch of you," he growled as he pushed his hard, throbbing cock hilt deep inside her needy pussy.

Hawk thrust slow, setting a delightful deep, grinding rhythm as he glided his cock in and out of her tight, wet sheath.

"You're the perfect match for me, Tulip." His eyes glowed as he lifted her legs and hooked her ankles over his shoulders.

"Good lord," she huffed as she felt him go deeper than ever before. She became mesmerized by the rhythm he set as he began to thrust in quick, hard jabs that left her panting, desperately trying to breathe.

Hawk fisted a tuft of her hair, angling her face to look into her eyes. He pounded her then, so powerfully that Savannah was completely lost in the raw passion that emanated from him into her. He grunted, his hand tightening in her hair to brace himself in the plundering of her body, watching every nuance flash over her face.

It was the ultimate high; an essential pleasure so enormously addictive that it transcended the boundaries of normative sexuality. It was the rogue monster to the big wave surfer. Growling, Hawk buried his head against her throat as pleasure surged through his loins.

"Come, Tulip."

His orgasm was surreal as wave after wave of pleasure rolled over him, tossing him about an ocean of pleasure so intense, it left him floundering helplessly. He plundered her pussy, bottoming out as he felt the spasms ripple around his length as she climaxed. It felt like his balls were connected to a foray of shooting bullets as he ejaculated violently inside her. His roar overpowered Savannah's cry as she was once again flung into an abyss of pleasure.

Untying her wrists, he wrapped her in his arms, starting as applause erupted, having completely forgotten the members had been party to the final conclusion of the ceremony. It was evident that everyone had been affected by the tenderness and passion of the couple.

Savannah wrapped her arms around his waist and hugged him tightly, trembling with exhaustion, but with a sense of satisfaction she had never experienced before. To her, it was the biggest hurdle she'd overcome to date.

"Thank you, my Master. You have truly shown me that there are no boundaries I can't overcome with your guidance. I've never dreamed of trusting someone so completely or reaching the level of pleasure you've taken me to tonight."

"No, Savannah, you don't need to thank me. We both offered each other what we needed."

Hawk wiped her clean and carried her to the reception area of the dungeon. With a broad smile, he looked at the beautiful woman in his arms as he sat down next to Parker. She was already sound asleep.

"Fuck, Hawk, that was an absolutely riveting scene. I would bet we're going to receive a number of requests for an erotic wax training session.

Hawk just smiled and brushed his lips over Savannah's forehead.

Tonight, he'd made progress with her. Soon, her trust in him should be complete.

Chapter Nineteen

"Judge Sinclair, it's good to see you and an honor that you're willing to assist us in this matter," said Secretary of State, Sheila Madden, as she shook Xavier Sinclair's hand.

"Likewise, Madam Secretary."

Stone, Hawk, and his father were meeting with the secretary of state, secretary of Homeland Security, Adrian Duncan and the FBI Director, Frank Moore, at the J. Edgar Hoover Building, the Federal Bureau's head office in DC.

After the greetings concluded, everyone took their seats.

"Cooper was released immediately after you filed the exoneration papers, Judge Sinclair. I know it couldn't have been an easy decision for you, but we appreciate your willingness to work with us on this matter." Frank Moore shifted in his chair, his expression fierce. "I still can't believe I never realized what Cooper was busy with."

"There was no way for you to know, Frank. I realized the same thing about Gary Sullivan. I still find it incomprehensible that the secretary of defense colluded to assassinate the president. Let's just be thankful Stone and Hawk's team managed to put an end to that." Sheila Madden paged through the file in front of her. "I trust your team is monitoring Cooper's movements, Frank? The only reason we agreed to this was to ensure we crack open the entire human trafficking operation. It's the first opportunity we have to find solid proof to finally get rid of Contessa, the Russian Syndicate in the U.S. It'll be a bigger coup if we can assist the FSB in finally getting the leaders of the Bratva behind bars."

"I've got two secret service teams on him twenty-four-seven, Madam Secretary. I want to make damn sure that bastard goes back to where he belongs. This time, to rot in jail," Frank said passionately. To him, it was a personal failure. He'd spent years mentoring and preparing Cooper to take over for him one day. To be repaid by his deceit was a slap in the face.

"As long as all of you realize there's a ten-day holding period on that order. I didn't fully exonerate him. The danger he represents to the country is too much of a high risk to leave him roaming around indefinitely." Xavier Sinclair looked at Stone and Hawk. "I understand your reasons, son, as well as everyone's here to use Decker as bait, but I'll not budge on that timeframe. I suggest you do what needs to be done to push him to act and quickly. I'm retracting that release order nine days from today."

"Cooper is in a corner, Dad. The moment he realizes he can't access his private cloud to get the information he needs to pacify the Bratva, things are going to escalate quickly. The Kumarin brothers aren't known for their patience."

"What do you know that we don't, Hawk?" Adrian Duncan looked between Stone and Hawk. He leaned forward expectantly. He was the kind of man who liked to have his finger on the button the entire time.

"Yury Kumarin, the alleged second in charge of the Bratva, visited Cooper in prison. We're still trying to ascertain how he got permission as it wasn't during scheduled weekend visiting hours."

"It had to have been someone with a high level of authority. The warden at Florence High isn't easily intimidated," Sheila speculated thoughtfully.

"Exactly our thoughts, Madam Secretary," Stone said. "Kumarin also joined Cooper briefly at the restaurant he went to have dinner at last night. He didn't stay long and neither did DC after he left, so we can only assume it was to issue a threat."

"How do you know about that? I haven't even received a report from the team yet." Frank sat upright, his gaze sharp.

"DC is a threat to both the women in our lives, Peyton Jackson and Savannah Thorne, whom I'm sure you know as well, Frank," Hawk said shortly. "We're not going to depend on others to ensure their safety. We have our own methods to keep an eye on him."

"Savannah Thorne? I don't understand. DC told me she resigned and left the country, a week before he was incarcerated."

"He lied. He used her as a game piece in the entire scheme."

"Good lord. Is she okay? Do you have her in a safe place? If, as you say she was a game piece, it means she'd be the first one he'd try to eliminate. Decker would know she has incriminating evidence against him that could have him back in jail even though he believed he was exonerated."

"She is." Hawk didn't elaborate. The fewer people who knew where the two women were, the better.

"You mentioned a threat, Stone." Sheila leaned back in the chair. "Do you believe it has something to do with operation Miami Blue? The recovery of those women from the boat at the coast of Miami?"

"We believe so, yes. Sergei Kumarin can't be happy that a consignment of sex slaves was never delivered. Our intel indicates Cooper had been compensated for their delivery in advance and Yury is here to recoup their losses. It's either replace the women or pay up. Somehow, I don't believe Yury would come out all the way here just to politely ask for a refund, and that's what concerns us. There's something else at play."

The door opened after a brief rap of knuckles and a black clad SWAT commander entered.

"Apologies for the interruption, Director, Madam Secretary. We need to evacuate, stat. We've received a bomb threat. The bomb squad just arrived but we can't take any chances. Please, follow me."

"Why didn't the alarm sound?" Frank asked as they met up with the SWAT team waiting in the hallway.

"No idea, sir. I'm sure it'll be looked into later. For now, we need to get to safety."

Hawk's phone buzzed and he answered on the run. He was on Sheila's heels who was in the lead of the group behind the SWAT commander.

"DC is outside the Hoover building, Hawk, loitering across the street at the front entrance. I've unlocked the backdoor into the server so he could gain access to—"

"Down! Get down!" Hawk shouted as his trained ears—from the years in the Marine Corps as an explosive expert—detected the sharp whine of a remotely activated unit seconds before a bright flash preceded a deafening explosion. It resulted in a superheated blast that rocked them off their feet. Hawk caught Sheila Madden as he went down. He covered her body as a fiery orange ball flicked its massive tongue through the open door to their left, the eager flames licking at the clothes on his back.

"Move! Crawl backward. We have to get out from under the flames." Hawk hunched over her as she blindly followed his instructions, clenching his teeth at the searing heat spreading over his back. He pulled her along as he shuffled as quickly as he could to get out from under the glowing heat. Hard hands closed around his ankles and yanked him the rest of the way. His arm around Sheila's waist carried her along. He could feel her body heave as she coughed violently. Before he could catch his breath, Stone flung his jacket over his back and began to roll him over and over.

"Fuck! Talk to me! Hawk! Stone! What the blazes is going on there?" Parker's concerned cry sounded distant and faint from the cell phone with the crackling of the flames in the background.

Stone took the phone Hawk still clutched in his hand and bit out breathlessly, "Bomb explosion but we're both fine. Hawk is a little toasted, but it doesn't look too bad."

"DC is here. That's why Parker phoned." A cacophony of coughs croaked from Hawk's throat. "Tell him to keep his eye on his personal cloud account. I'd lay my head on a block that's why he's here." Hawk struggled upright. "Jesus ... what do you mean a little toasted?" He glared at Stone. "My fucking back is on ... ugh." Another hoarse cough cut his words short as he leaned against the wall. The excruciating flash of pain that tore from his back to his brain as he struggled to breathe was accompanied by the claws of unconsciousness that dragged him under.

"Hawk! Son!" Xavier's hoarse cry echoed over the phone to Parker and the rest of the team listening from the operation's room at The Seven Keys Island.

Stone ended the call and rushed to Hawk's side. He looked around and noticed the EMTs assisting Sheila Madden who struggled to breathe. Realization struck as he kneeled beside Hawk, listening to the shallow and haggard breaths that wheezed from his chest.

"Oxygen! He needs oxygen! He was caught in the cocoon of carbon monoxide and smoke that formed under the flames. Hurry the fuck up!" Stone yelled at the second team of EMTs that came rushing toward them. Fear of the danger Hawk was in left him shaken.

"His back is also burned," Stone cautioned as they stretched him out. Stone and Xavier watched with concern as the EMT immediately covered Hawk's face with an oxygen mask before they carefully turned him over and cut off his jacket and shirt.

"Is he going to be okay?" Xavier asked as he hunched next to them. The EMTs didn't stop working but one responded in an even voice.

"Madam Secretary and he probably inhaled a full blast of harmful smoke particles and gases which seems to have inflamed their lungs and airways." He looked at Xavier as he continued. "Combustion causes chemicals to form that injure skin and mucous membranes which in turn damages the respiratory tract, causing swelling and airway collapse. From the smell of it, the bomb contained ammonia and sulfur dioxide which are chemical irritants in smoke."

"Are they in danger of carbon monoxide poisoning?" Stone asked.

"It's too soon to tell. For how long were they exposed to the smoke?"

"Minutes, seconds? I don't know. It all happened so fast."

"Then the chances are slim. The fact that you got them out from direct exposure and further inhalation of smoke helped. We're giving them a hundred percent blast of oxygen."

"Then why is he still unconscious?" Xavier asked as he hovered around the EMTs as they lifted Hawk's body onto a stretcher.

"The burns only affected the top layer of his skin but the pain when he leaned against the wall might have caused him to pass out. We've put cooling compresses over it. Don't worry, we'll keep a close eye on him, but his breathing has normalized. Unless there are complications, he'll be fine." The EMT nodded at his partner. "Let's go."

"I'm going with. I want you to take him to John Hopkins Burn Center."

"Then we better get going." The EMTs pushed the stretcher down the hallway with Stone and Xavier on their heels.

"I'll follow in the car and meet you there," Stone said and ran to where he'd parked. He groaned as he jumped into the GMC rental. His knee throbbed painfully, triggering a memory of hitting the wall from the force of the heat blast as he'd dived to get Xavier to safety.

He dug out his phone as it began to buzz and answered as he cranked the engine and pulled away, his voice strained with concern, "Yes."

"Stone, are you okay?" Parker's voice sounded thick.

"Just a busted knee but I'm fine. No one got hurt except for Madam Secretary and Hawk. We're on the way to Hopkins Burn Center. The EMTs assure me Hawk's going to be fine." Stone caught up with the ambulance and switched on the hazard lights. "Tell me about that fucking bastard DC." His voice turned hard, vicious.

"The fucktard waited until the fire trucks arrived. We caught him on the GeoSat. He entered the building from the south side along with a group of firefighters and cut straight up to the server room. It's the only way he could get access to his private cloud account. Some clever hacker must've told him."

"And did he get access?"

"Yes. He downloaded all the files onto a flash drive but don't worry about it. It gave me the opportunity to hack into his cloud account and I cloned it. Lucky for us, he opened the Blue Bayou file. I suppose he wanted to check if it's intact with all the information because he immediately closed it. It gave me the opportunity to gain access to it. I also loaded a Nano Virus on the flash drive. As soon as he accesses it, the virus will corrupt every file he copied. It'll be impossible to recover anything, no matter how good the hacker is."

"Good. That means we can finally find out what's so important in that Blue Bayou file."

"Yes, Zeke and I have already started to work through the folders. We're all heading toward the hospital as we speak. We should have intel by the time we get there."

"It's not necessary for all of you to come here. I'll keep you updated."

"We're coming, Stone. Hawk's family and we want to be there for him."

"And who's protecting the women?"

"Danton's there and he brought in a couple of his old SEAL team buddies. Don't worry, big bro, we've got this."

Hawk struggled to escape the black cloud that kept him floating in limbo. A frown slashed between his brows as noises began to penetrate his mind. The soft beep of machines, the hum of voices in the background, and the beating of his pulse against his temple. His mind swirled in confusion.

Where the fuck am I?

His eyelids fluttered open. Everything was blurry. For a second, he didn't know where he was and why the hell he was lying on his stomach. He never slept like that. His muscles tensed and he groaned sleepily as he attempted to turn onto his back.

"Fuck," he puffed as pain pinched from his back to his brain.

"Careful, Hawk, you have to stay on your stomach for now."

Stone's deep voice infiltrated his scattered thoughts. It was all that was needed for the pieces of the puzzle to fall in place. The explosion, the flames licking at his back, and the battle to breathe.

"Shit," he moaned as he took in his surroundings. "Where am I?"

"The John Hopkins Burn Center," Stone said as he appeared in Hawk's scope of vision.

"What? For being toasted a little? That's a bit extreme, isn't it?" He grimaced as he carefully pushed himself onto his elbows and looked around.

"I wasn't prepared to take any chances," Xavier mumbled by his side.

"Hey, Dad. You okay?"

"Yes, courtesy of your cousin tackling me through a doorway away from the blast wave. How are you feeling?"

"Groggy."

"Any pain?"

Hawk smiled at his father who hovered at his side. "No, Dad. Stop worrying. You know I've got a thick skin." He looked at Stone. "How long was I out?"

"It's morning. The doctors had to sedate you because you kept fighting them when they tried to keep you on your stomach."

"Good, which means I've done the overnight stay and can go home." His gaze landed on the rest of his cousins crowding the end of the bed. "What the hell are you all doing here? Who is protecting the women if you're loitering by my bed? I'm not a fucking invalid and I'm not on my deathbed, for fuck's sake."

None of them took offense. They knew his crassness stemmed from concern for Savannah and Luke. Parker's explanation about Danton and his SEAL buddies made him relax somewhat but not enough to keep him from pushing into a sitting position.

"Goddammit, Son, lie down. This is no time to play Rambo."

"Nor am I going to lie here and count the hours, Dad. Get the doctor, will you, Stone. I want to know the extent of the burns and if my lungs are clear."

"You're such a stubborn son of a bitch, do you know that? It's little wonder I went gray before I was thirty," Xavier grunted irritably as Stone left to find the specialist who he'd seen earlier when he went for coffee.

Roy McCord shook his head as he walked into the room with Stone and found Hawk sitting upright. "I suppose I shouldn't be surprised, based on how you fought us yesterday."

"I'd like to know the extent of the burns," Hawk said without preamble.

"You suffered first degree burns, which means only the top layer of your skin is affected. Luckily, it's not across your entire back, just in patches. The jacket you wore protected you to a certain degree."

"How long will it take to heal?"

"Most of it should heal within three to five days. There's one patch that might take a little longer."

"And my lungs?" He tugged on the tubes of the oxygen cannula he wore.

Roy placed the stethoscope in place and checked his lungs. "Breathe in deeply ... and out. Again." He repeated the process a couple of times on Hawk's chest and back.

"It sounds much better than last night. You were lucky. I still can't believe that everyone walked away without serious injuries."

"The main blast shot outward," Stone said. "We just got hit by the backlash of the heatwave."

"Based on what you just said, Dr. McCord, my injuries are minimal, and I can go home," Hawk pressed Roy for an answer.

"Preferably, I'd like you to stay another twenty-four hours." He smiled at the dogmatic expression on Hawk's face. "I see that's not up for debate. Very well, I'd like to do a chest x-ray first, just to be sure there's no chance of pulmonary complications. As far as your back is concerned, you'll need to try and stay off it until scabs form. Chafing it might cause infection. Keep it covered with the sterile bandage for another day. I'll prescribe a petroleum-based ointment you need to apply two to three times per day. I'll release you, Mr. Sinclair, with the understanding that you come and see me at the first sign of redness or soreness on your wounds."

"Agreed."

"I'll arrange for the x-rays." Roy nodded at everyone and walked out of the room.

"Talk about hard-headed," Xavier muttered.

Stone's phone rang. He smiled as he identified the caller. "Hi baby," he said, feeling warmth flood his chest as he heard Peyton's concerned voice.

"Are you okay? I know Parker said you were, and they wouldn't let me go to you, but I had to find out for myself."

"I'm fine and—"

"No, I need to see. I'm switching to video call ... wait, lemme ... yes. Honey? Where are you?"

Stone shook his head and lifted the phone in front of his face. He smiled goofily. "See? All smiles and just looking at your beautiful face, horny."

"Hm, I guess that means you're okay. And Hawk? How's he doing?"

"Demanding to be released."

"Men are just so hardheaded. Is he close by? Savvy wants to speak with him."

"Yeah, he's right here."

Stone handed the phone to Hawk. He pulled off the oxygen tubes before he took it. He was stumped at the rush of emotion when he looked at her. Concern was rife on her face, and he could swear she'd been crying.

"Hawk? Please tell me you're not badly hurt."

Her voice was the sweetest sound he'd ever heard. The sight of the diamond collar with the topaz colored diamond teardrop lying snugly in the hollow of her throat made him want to reach through the phone and touch her.

His lips twitched in a ghost of a smile. "A little discomfort from the burns but other than that I'm well. The specialist said it should heal in three to five days."

"Please rest and do what they tell you."

"I'll be doing that there. As soon as the x-rays are done, I'm coming home."

"But that's too soon! What if you get an infection? What if your lungs collapse? What if—"

"Savannah, breathe. I'm not going to be irresponsible. The burns are minimal, and my lungs are clear. Stop worrying, little one," he said in a soothing voice, smiling when she relaxed visibly.

"Ack! Ack!"

"Luke! Stop that. Give me back the ... Luke!" Savannah disappeared from the screen as the phone seemed to go airborne.

Hawk chuckled as little hands reached for it and picked it up.

"Ack! Ack!" Luke shrieked as he saw Hawk's face, hopping excitedly up and down on his butt.

"Hey there, little man," Hawk's voice thickened as Luke's mouth split open in a wide smile at the sound of his voice.

"Ack!" He looked at Savannah who appeared in the background and picked him up. He clutched the phone with both hands. "Mama ... Ack," His little lip began to quiver. "Ack ... Up."

Savannah wrestled the phone from his grasp. He started to cry, calling out for *Ack*.

"I'm sorry. I better go. Please be careful on the trip home."

"Yeah, sure." Hawk battled to bring his emotions under control. Just looking at Savannah and Luke made him realize how valuable time and unpredictable life was. Did it really matter that she was hiding something from him? If it was what he suspected, could he blame her? Maybe it was time to grasp what life was throwing at him with both hands before fate stepped in and fucked up his destiny once again.

Xavier studied Hawk as he handed the phone to Stone.

"That baby ... is there something you forgot to tell me, Son?"

Everyone laughed at the look on their uncle's face. Hawk shot his father a dark look. "He's not mine, if that's what you're alluding to," he said curtly.

"He sure is attached to you," Xavier kept prodding.

"You better tell him. He's not gonna stop hounding you until you do," Stone said with a laugh.

Hawk briefly explained who Savannah was and ended with, "And I'm in a Dom/sub relationship with her. A permanent one."

"Well, miracles do happen it seems," Xavier said with a broad smile. "About time you found happiness again, my boy."

Chapter Twenty

"Ah, the taste of success," Decker swirled the whiskey in his glass, listening to the chinking of the ice cubes, breathing in a fragrance that only years in an oak barrel could achieve. The concern about the Kumarin brothers faded, even before the first taste. Just watching the gentle amber vortex was hypnotizing enough to push his worries to the back of his mind—if only for a little while. At the moment, a little self-indulgence was needed.

"The end of all my troubles is near."

But first, there was aged single malt directly from Scotland. It was his one vice, and this time, he intended to make a virtue of it, savor it, not race to the bottom of the bottle like he usually did. When the liquid settled in the glass, he brought it to his lips, allowing the amber fluid to sit in his mouth a while before swallowing. With a sigh of pleasure, he sat back on the sofa and closed his eyes, dwelling only on the flavor.

God it was good.

He listened to the light jazz he'd put on a few minutes earlier, basking in the success of earlier.

He laughed at the memory of how easy it had been to walk into the FBI amid the panic of the explosion, straight up to the server room and gain access to his cloud account and walk out again.

"I need to remember to give Razz a little extra for his detailed instructions to get into the server and my cloud account. Clever bugger."

The nasally sound of his voice reminded him of his broken nose and he tentatively touched it. It was healing too slow for his liking. He hated walking around with the white splint on his face, but it couldn't be helped. At least he wouldn't end up with a crooked nose.

He finished the whiskey in one shot and straightened. He pulled his laptop closer which had powered up while he'd sipped on the booze.

"Time to get the ball rolling. The quicker we can get those girls ready, the sooner I'll have Yury Kumarin off my back."

He inserted the flash drive and pointed the cursor on the Blue Bayou folder. He clicked on it.

"What the fuck!" He frantically clicked on the folder that started to shake. "No! No-no-no!" He watched in horror as the folder opened and every file was tagged as a corrupt file. He clicked on one after the other, swearing nonstop as he received the same message from all of them.

File corrupted. Unable to open file.

Decker stared in defeat at the flashing message. He was fucked. Completely fucked. He permanently deleted the content of his cloud the moment he'd finished downloading everything and checked the Blue Bayou folder. The warning Razz gave him echoed in his mind.

"Be sure you've copied everything before you type in this code, DC, because once you hit enter, it'll permanently delete it. It won't be in a holding folder or hidden drive where I'd be able to recover it. Be sure you want it gone forever. Don't come crying to me later if something goes wrong. I won't be able to help you.

"They knew. The motherfuckers knew I'd try to get access to my cloud. They fucking knew!"

He jumped up and refilled his glass. This time he swallowed the rich liquor in one gulp. His breath wheezed from his throat as the liquid wreaked a burning path down his throat.

"What the fuck am I gonna do now? I can't find a group of ten high class women who won't be missed in such a short time. Jesus, what a clusterfuck."

For the first time, he regretted not keeping hard copies of the information he'd gathered of the women, but he'd believed it would be the safer option to reduce a paper trail. His heart thumped painfully against his chest as the full implication of the dire situation he found himself in drove home. He had nothing to give Yury Kumarin. No women, no Savannah.

"Just when life started looking up again." He paced the living room, his mind scattering about in search of a solution.

"Fuck this. I can at least give him the bitch. All I need to do is find my mother to bring back the boy."

He sat down in front of his laptop and started searching the hotels in Hawaii. After the tenth unsuccessful call, he gave up. It was a waste of time. For all he knew, she wasn't even in Hawaii.

"I'm such an idiot," he said as a slinky smile curved his lips.

Savannah didn't know the boy wasn't with him.

"All I need to do is make her believe he is. It's the perfect solution." He smiled broadly as the plan fell in place. "I'll tell her to fetch the brat as part of the bargain I made for my release. Yes!"

He cackled out an evil laugh as he filled another glass of whiskey.

"I won't even have to exert myself. I'll just make sure Yury is personally there to take her off my hands. It might pacify him to give me some time to find a new group of women."

A smile spread across his face as a feeling of victory bloomed inside his chest. It was like he had won the billion-dollar lottery.

"Just better ... so much better."

"Stone said you managed to get into that Blue Bayou folder, Parker," Hawk said as soon as they were airborne in the private plane Shane had rented to take them home.

"Yeah, we did," Parker said as he glanced at Zeke.

Hawk looked between them. A sense of doom prevailed at the expressions on their faces.

"Well, spit it out."

"Decker Cooper is an even bigger bastard than any of us believed," Zeke sneered.

"Yeah." Parker cleared his voice as he opened his iPad and linked to BSE's cloud drive. "There are a couple of folders and voice clip recordings we're still working on to decode the passwords for, but we can confirm your suspicions about Savannah, Hawk. She had been part of the group of women who left on that boat for Russia, but on the dockets in the folder, she was listed as one of the intended sex slaves, not as a human trafficking coordinator. From all the inscriptions made by DC it's also very clear that he never bothered to search for Savannah in the entire year she was held captive like he'd told the Bureau at the time of their release."

"Why the fuck would he bother, seeing as he sold her to them in the first place?" Hawk leaned forward in the seat to keep his back away from the backrest. "What about Vera and Peyton? How could they just have accepted her disappearance for such a long time without a word?"

"They didn't know. We found roughly fifteen video recordings. There are a couple that are clear and definitely Savannah skyping the two of them. It must've been during the boat trip there. The rest ... they were taken in a dark room. Skype recordings between them and who they believed to be Savannah. You can't see the woman's face, just the outline of her body. It sounds like her voice, but the audio is so bad you can't be sure. He must've had someone stand in for her. The calls were kept short, so they had no reason to doubt it was her and because they believed she was undercover, they accepted not hearing from her too often."

"Fucking bastard thought of everything. I wonder how long he intended to keep it up if she hadn't managed to get the word out and escape." Ace struggled to contain his anger.

"Not all the women have been so lucky. Of the first group that were brought back, four committed suicide over the past five years, or what was believed to have been suicide," Zeke said as he scrolled through his iPad.

"Why do you say that?" Kane asked.

"Remember we had their original information because we assisted in the Blue Bayou operation. All the women, including the ones who were recently saved don't have any family. They're loners but most of them were successful, well-educated and had thriving careers. According to the psychologist reports, they all recovered well and have been leading a normal life, albeit under a new identity. The four who are dead had managerial positions at the companies they worked at, earning big salaries. They had friends and three of the four had gotten married. Does it sound like any of them had suicide tendencies?" Zeke glanced at his cousins.

"And the Blue Bayou file DC had contains the information of their new identities and to where they were relocated?" Shane asked, sipping on a soda.

"Yes." Parker tapped his finger on his iPad. "I could track the times DC opened that folder. He worked on it at least three times a month. He had an individual file for each of the women which he'd created a month after they returned. I'm telling you, Hawk, he's killing them one-by-one to ensure none of them ever talk."

"Having them killed," Hawk spat with disgust. "He's too much of a coward to do it himself."

"Did Savannah receive therapy?" Stone accepted the soda Parker handed to him and cracked it open.

"From what I could find, only a couple of sessions with a professional. It stopped when DC apparently cleared her and declared her fit for work. He made notes of personal sessions *he* had with her, supposedly to rebuild her confidence." Parker snorted. "Fucking asshole."

"What I don't understand is why there were no details of Savannah in the Blue Bayou file or even at the time we were involved. Surely, if she was his undercover agent, her name would've been listed with the other women?" Ace said.

"According to Director Moore, it's because of the fact that she's a federal agent that her real name was kept secret, to ensure she was safe, and her identity wouldn't be compromised. Decker had created a complete background and new persona for her at the time, so no one could associate Lucy Simms with Savannah Thorne. Of course, he didn't do it to protect her, he did it to have her disappear off the face of the earth." Stone looked at Parker. "Anything else?"

"We also found a file with details of fifteen women. We did a quick background check into them. They fit the criteria of the other women DC had sourced in the past and sold to human trafficking. Parker and I believe it's the next group he intended to sell." Zeke closed his iPad. "And that's about all we had time to work through."

"Good job." Stone finished his drink. "Parker, get that file with the list of women to the Secretary of Homeland Security, Adrian Duncan, stat. That's probably why DC needed the folder. Yury Kumarin isn't here on a vacation. He's here to collect."

"Already done. I'm hoping DC didn't keep hard copy information because he'd get jack shit from that flash drive."

"I doubt he does, otherwise he wouldn't have gone to such extreme measures to gain access to his cloud account. That means he's panicking. It makes him dangerous." Hawk frowned. "If Savannah believed she was undercover, the Kumarins won't know here real identity either."

"Except if there's more corrupt officials in the FBI. The only name we can found is Lucy Simms, her own name isn't mentioned anywhere."

"Cooper will do anything to keep the Bratva off his back." Hawk's lips thinned. "It's obvious he did it so that the Bratva couldn't find out she worked for him. That would be detrimental to him because if she had to disappear again, the FBI would've started asking questions and he might have been exposed. So, if he's looking for an out, what better way than giving them the woman who was responsible for losing fifteen sex slaves five years ago, as well as a couple of their whore houses in Russia at the time ..." Hawk's eyes turned dark and glimmered dangerously.

"It means Savannah's life is in danger," Stone said in a quiet voice.

"Hawk!" He caught Savannah as she flung herself into his arms when the seven cousins walked into the Great Dining Hall.

"Fuck," he winced as her arms wrapped around his back. She immediately let go and tried to step back but his hold around her tightened. "Just keep your hands off my back, baby ... for a couple of days at least."

"I'm so sorry. I didn't think." She touched his chest, his arms, his cheeks in what he assumed was to check if he was still in one piece. "How are you feeling?"

"Very weak," he rasped.

"I knew the flight would be too much for you. We need to get you into bed." She attempted to push away from him.

His hands slid up and down her back, caressing the slenderness of her waist. Her skin vibrated from the gruff timbre of his voice when he spoke into her ear. "From the need to feel your lips under mine." His mouth skimmed hot over the side of her neck.

"Hawk ... you need to ... mmm." Her head tilted as his lips glided across hers, imparting softness, and heat. She moaned against his mouth, her hands grasping fists full of his shirt. He didn't rush, rather he reveled in the taste of her lips as his moved with sensual perfection over hers, memorizing the shape of her mouth. His arm around her waist drew her in closer, the other moved up to cradle the back of her head.

She was entirely in his thrall: her body yielding without hesitation and her will with jubilation.

"My memory didn't deceive me. So warm and soft. I missed the taste of you, baby," he murmured, taking his own sweet time.

"Ack!" Luke's shriek echoed shrilly from behind them. He turned and chuckled as he watched the little body squirm violently in Vera's arms to be let down. She sat him on the floor and with his head lowered he crawled with amazing speed toward them. He pulled himself up against Hawk's pants. "Ack ... up." He jumped up and down and squealed happily as Hawk lifted him into his arms.

His throat clogged up as the little arms wrapped around his neck and he held on, murmuring his name over and over.

429

"He missed you," Savannah said. Her eyes misted over as she watched the two men she'd come to love more than life itself.

"Yeah, I missed him too. The little tyke is easy to grow attached to." He returned the fierce hug as no amount of coaxing from Hawk could get Luke to let go of his neck.

I wish you'd grow attached to me as well.

Hawk had only been gone one night but Luke had been impossible and refused to go to sleep, calling for *Ack* the entire time. He'd eventually cried himself to sleep.

Savannah had finally admitted that her life would be senseless without Hawk. Her heart, for one thing, would be in shatters. She smiled tenderly as Luke finally drew back and placed a wet kiss on Hawk's cheek.

I love him. So much.

"Please, let's sit down," Savannah gently prodded Hawk toward the relaxation area in one corner of the room. The entire Sinclair clan, Peyton, and Vera trailed behind them. Savannah tried to take Luke on her lap, but he refused. He couldn't stop touching Hawk. He ruffled his hair until it stood tousled and reminded her of his just woken up look. He tugged on Hawk's short beard and giggled when it tickled his hands. Through it all, Hawk sat as patient as a Sphinx and didn't say a word. She wished she knew what was running through Hawk's mind as he watched the animated little boy.

It wasn't long before she noticed the tension around Hawk's mouth and the pallor of his skin.

"I think it's time to go upstairs. I'm sure you're hungry. I've decided I'm going to cook tonight."

"That's not necessary, baby. Dinner should be ready here soon." Hawk smiled at her.

She stood up. "Do you think I can't cook?"

"I didn't say that," Hawk said carefully and smiled as her toes did their familiar tap-tap on the floor, a sign of her rising irritation.

"Then I'm fixing dinner for us. Besides, it's almost time for Luke's bath. You can relax or take a short nap while I take care of him and dinner."

"I'd rather watch you give him his bath." Hawk got to his feet. The room swayed and he planted his feet firmly, waiting for the world to stop spinning. He hadn't realized how tired he was.

"You're as stubborn as a mule, Hawk Sinclair. You're dead on your feet. You should really take a nap," Savannah berated him as they ascended the stairs. She deliberately walked slow, cognizant of the fact that he was weakened, and that Luke refused to allow her to carry him.

Bath time was Luke's favorite playtime, but Savannah rushed through it. She only relaxed once Hawk finally settled on his side on the sofa in the great open room.

"Parmesan and parsley-crusted salmon with roast potatoes, veggies, and garlic bread sound okay for dinner?" she asked. She couldn't resist, and ran her fingers through Hawk's still tousled hair, gently combing it in place.

"Sounds delicious. Why don't I feed the little man in the meantime? He seems a little cranky."

"Are you sure? You know dinner turns into a game with him."

Hawk reached up and cupped her cheek. He smiled reassuringly. "Stop mothering me, babe. I'm healthy and strong. A little burn isn't going to get me under."

Savannah quickly heated the baby food Vera had cooked and kept in the freezer. She started dinner once she assured herself Luke behaved, which she was surprised to see that he did. He was quieter than usual and didn't demand to play feeding games while Hawk fed him. It was as though he somehow understood Hawk wasn't his usual self.

"Are you going to tell me what happened?" Savannah asked during dinner.

"Do we have to spoil such a lovely meal?" he said as he speared a piece of fish into his mouth. "You really are a wonderful cook. The salmon is the best I've ever tasted."

Savannah wasn't fooled. A sixth sense warned her there was more to the incident than any of the cousins had admitted when they'd told Peyton and her about it. She shivered as a feeling of doom settled over her.

"It was Decker, wasn't it?" Her fork clattered to the plate. "He tried to kill you!"

"How the devil did you come to that conclusion? He had no way of knowing about our meeting, Savannah. Frank Moore didn't even know until we arrived. Don't go chasing ghosts where there are none."

"Hawk Sinclair, don't for one moment think you're fooling me. I'm not an idiot. Tell me! Was it Decker?"

Hawk sighed in defeat. "Yes, but not because he tried to kill Stone and me. He needed a diversion to get into the server room to gain access to his cloud account that's linked to the FBI network."

"Why did he need to do that? Surely, he could access it from anywhere?"

"No, he couldn't." Hawk briefly explained about the attempted hack that led them to a file the hacker tried to open via the FBI network on DC's private cloud. "The security feature we installed on the FBI system, automatically locks any folder or file a hacker attempts to access."

"Then how did he manage to do it from the server?"

"There's always a backdoor the very best of hackers can find. One we covered when we installed the system. When Parker realized what was happening, he disabled the lock on the server to allow him to get into his cloud." He squeezed her hand. "Enough of this. I'm going to get cleaned up, so you can put the ointment on my back before we go to sleep."

"Ack!" Luke immediately sat up where he was quietly playing with his toys when he noticed Hawk walk toward the door. "Up!"

"Oh, no, you don't." Savannah intercepted him as he furiously started crawling after him. "Come here, you little menace. Leave Hawk be for a moment. He needs to—"

"Shhh," Luke said as he placed his hand over her mouth. His bottom lip quivered as he slapped his hand on his knee. "Ack!"

Savannah didn't know if she should laugh or berate him. He was such a clever little boy, and it worried her that he'd become so attached to Hawk in such a short period of time.

What would happen if it didn't work between her and Hawk? Her little boy's heart would be just as broken as hers.

Chapter Twenty-One

"I think it's time to push Decker Cooper, Stone." Hawk paced in front of the window in the Castle Sin boardroom. "It's been three days since the explosion. He must know by now that the flash drive is useless."

"I agree." Danton had joined Hawk and Stone to discuss strategy on how to proceed. "According to the NanoTracker you planted in his neck, he's been holed up in his house in The Palisades, except for dinnertime. He has dinner like clockwork every day at six-thirty at the same restaurant in the DuPont Circle."

"I warned him what would happen if he doesn't return Luke to Savannah. Are we sure he hasn't been able to contact Dora?" Hawk sat down at the table.

"Definitely. Dora Brooks is still in protective holding in the safehouse in Merrifield and guarded twenty-four-seven by a special FBI unit. Frank Moore confirmed that there has been no contact with him. Apparently, she's livid with her son and has given her full cooperation in whatever the FBI needs." Stone leaned his elbows on the table. "I'm not so sure putting pressure on DC in regard to Luke is the way to go. Yes, he doesn't know we've got Luke, but our end goal is to crack down on the entire human trafficking ring."

"I'm with you, but if I don't follow up on my threat, he might realize something is amiss. We need to keep the pressure on him, Stone. People pushed into a corner make mistakes. Yury Kumarin is still in Washington DC, which means he must've given DC an ultimatum as well. I can't just sit and wait any longer. Something needs to happen," Hawk said passionately.

"Maybe he's testing you and deliberately waiting to see if you're going to contact him," Danton speculated. "But, if that's his angle, it raises a red flag and means that either he never had any intention of handing Luke back or he has something else up his sleeve. I'd opt for the latter. I don't trust people like him who are in cahoots with crime syndicates."

"Blackmail? Extortion? The man is loaded. I can't see either of those being his aim." Hawk frowned. "Has Parker and Zeke found anything else in the Blue Bayou file?"

"Nothing that can help us, I'm afraid. There's incriminating evidence that he colluded with the Kumarins, however, they've been very clever in paying him. Always via a cash transfer from an unassociated account in the Caymans." Danton shook his head. "They know how to stay out of jail, and so far, they've walked away every time the Russian Government tried to prosecute them."

"We need to use DC to get to them. Both the Kumarin Bratva as well as the Contessa Group in the U.S." Hawk started pacing again. "So, he's been holed up in his house. Doing what? Is there a way Parker can find out if he's been on the web and what he's doing? For all we know he's trying to source women to sell again."

"That could be, and we might have to be patient and wait until there's another handover. At least that way we can assure we hit both sides. Fast and hard."

"I won't be able to relax for as long as DC is out there, Stone. He's a danger to Savannah and Luke. Yes. it would be the best way to crack open the entire operation, but time is running out on the timeframe my dad put on his exoneration. I don't want that fucktard back in jail. He's got too much money and corrupt connections on the outside to continue his dirty work."

The door opened and Savannah rushed inside. She looked pale as she walked into Hawk's embrace. "He phoned again."

"What did he want?"

"I didn't answer. I thought it would be best if you're present when I do. I might just lose my temper and blurt out that Luke is already home."

"It seems Decker Cooper is ready to make his move, Hawk." Stone pressed the intercom button on the desk. "Alexa, please ask my cousins to join us, stat."

"Will do, Stone."

"I want everyone involved in this," Stone explained as he cut the connection with Alexa.

"I agree. We've always achieved more as a team," Hawk said as he pulled out a chair for Savannah and sat down next to her.

Within minutes all seven Sinclairs were seated around the table.

"I have a feeling he's got an agenda and he's going to give a very tight timeframe," Stone said. "We need to be ready. Parker, is there a way you can hack into his cell phone? And is it possible to listen to his calls and get access to his text messages?"

"Yep, easy as pie. I've already hacked into the only listed number I could find for him, but he hasn't made any calls from it, apart from trying to get hold of Dora Brooks." Parker looked at Savannah. "Is there a caller ID showing when he phones you?"

"No, it just says private number."

"It might be that he's using a burner phone. Best I can do is hack into Savannah's phone and as soon as the call comes through, see if I can use the Signaling System Number seven network interchange service to identify the number and then hack into it."

"Do it. Let's hope it's an additional phone and not a burner so we can listen in to any calls he might make to the Russians."

Parker had just hacked into Savannah's cell phone when it rang.

Hawk squeezed her hand. "Stay calm, baby, and make it clear from the outset that I'm with you. Put it on speaker."

"Savannah, speaking."

"Such a sweet melody in my ear, darling."

"I suggest you drop the shit, you fuck, and get to the point," Hawk grated out through clenched teeth. His hands balled into fists. He'd like nothing better to beat the bastard to a pulp.

"I guess I shouldn't be surprised that you're hanging onto her skirt at all hours. She has quite the tempting—"

"How's the nose?" Hawk's voice took on a chill that signaled the cold anger boiling inside him. Silence followed and he snorted. "Just as I thought. Big mouth now that there's distance between us but you and I know you're nothing but a coward."

"Do you want the fucking brat or not?"

"You took your sweet time about it, Decker. I can't but help to wonder why?" Hawk kept taunting him.

"Because I initially had no intention of giving him back," he snapped, but he couldn't hide the underlying excitement that gave his voice that added pitch.

Hawk looked at Shane for affirmation. He nodded, having identified it too. Shane was an expert in voice intonations and accurately identified the meaning or emotions attached to each one.

"I assume something happened to change your mind?"

"I want my job back at the FBI and if Savannah starts throwing around accusations of kidnapping, it'll never happen, so ... this is your chance. Come and get the brat."

Parker gave a thumbs-up that he'd managed to identify DC's phone number and hacked into it. "I've got your address. We'll be there in three hours."

Decker cracked a short laugh. "What kind of fool do you think I am? I'm not fucking going back to jail for kidnapping. Oh, no, Sinclair. If the little whore wants her boy back, she comes for him. Alone and—"

"Forget it. I'll be the one coming for him."

"Then it's no deal."

"Please Hawk! I want my baby. Let me go," Savannah played her part at Stone's prodding.

"That's more like it," DC said in a gloating voice.

"If you think I'll let her go alone, you're an idiot. I'll be with her," Hawk snapped.

DC was silent for a moment, obviously weighing the odds of his ability to deal with Hawk face-to-face.

"Very well but be warned, Sinclair, if I see any of your cousins lurking close by, I leave … with the boy, and then, Savannah darling, you won't see him again."

"No! It'll only be the two of us, I promise. Please, just give me back my son."

Stone gave Savannah a thumbs-up and smiled.

"Tomorrow, eleven pm at Rukert Terminal One at Lazaretto Point at Port Baltimore in Chesapeake Bay. Don't be late," Decker said and immediately cut the connection.

"I want someone monitoring that cell phone all the time, Parker," Stone said. "It's not a coincidence that he sets up a meeting at a shipping dock. I suspect you were right, Hawk, and he managed to find women to ship out tomorrow. Seeing as we all know he doesn't have Luke; he must have a good reason to want Savannah there."

"Ship out to where?" Savannah asked in a brittle voice.

"Has to be Russia," Danton said.

Hawk rubbed her hands. "Relax, baby. You're not going anywhere. There's no way I'm putting you in danger. Our aim is to catch Decker red-handed in human trafficking. If we can assist the DOJ and the FSB to crack down on the Russians at the same time, it's a bonus."

"Decker isn't stupid, Hawk. If he doesn't see me, he won't expose himself," Savannah said with dull eyes.

"She has a point," Kane said. "He played his hand by demanding Savannah be there personally."

"Granted but I also agree with Hawk that we're not putting Savannah in danger," Stone said sternly. "She's been through enough."

"I might have a solution," Danton said as he sent a photo to Parker. "Pop that up on the screen, Parker." He pointed to the picture of a pretty blond woman on the screen and looked around the table. "This is Carry Rice. She was awarded the Silver Star for her actions during a firefight that took place outside Baghdad in 2005. She left the military ten years ago and started her own security company. She has assisted me on covert ops as one of the team numerous times. She's about Savannah's height, same hair color and with the help of makeup and the dim lighting at the docks ... we should be able to fool DC into thinking it's her."

"No, Danton! We can't take the chance of them capturing her. I'll never forgive myself if she ends up as a sex slave." Savannah had gone pasty, her voice sounded raw, and she couldn't hide her agitation.

"No one is going to end up a sex-slave, baby. Go find Luke. I think it's time for lunch, isn't it?"

"Don't you dare send me away like a naughty child, Sinclair," she snapped at him.

"Savannah, we've been preparing ourselves mentally and physically for this moment for weeks. Decker isn't going to get away with this and neither is anyone else involved in it. We can't afford to be distracted, and if you're there, it'll put all of us in danger and jeopardize our chance of cracking open the trafficking ring." Hawk cupped her cheeks.

"Trust us with this, honey. We know what we're doing."

"I just don't want anyone to get hurt. It's my fault that all of you are involved in this."

"No, Savannah, it's not. We've been approached by the DOJ and DHS because of the security protocol we've installed for them. You're also just an innocent bystander." Stone's voice darkened. "Hawk is right. We can't afford to have you as a distraction when we meet up with DC. What Danton is suggesting is our best way to open the can from the inside. You have a son who needs you, little one, remember that."

"I guess you're right." She got up and leaned in to kiss Hawk lingeringly on the lips. "Just promise me you'll be careful. Decker is more dangerous than he looks."

Hawk brushed his fingers over her cheek. "We're always careful. Go, babe. Luke must be hungry."

As soon as Savannah left, Parker said, "Zeke, see if you can find information about a ship by the name of Seagull, docked where DC wants to meet. He just spoke to someone about delivering the five packages tonight at ten." He looked at Hawk. "Five women?"

"Got it. It's docked at Rukert Terminal Three, Lazaretto Point in Chesapeake Bay. The vessel belongs to Tai Ling, a Chinese trading company that does regular trade with Russia.

Parker's fingers flew over the keyboard. "Right, there's a shipping docket indicating one twenty-foot container to be loaded at Lazaretto Point, destination, the Port of Kaliningrad."

"If memory serves, Kaliningrad is the closest Russian port to Mainland Europe, between Poland and Lithuania on the Baltic coast, correct?" Kane said.

"That's the one," Zeke said.

"It's also the port less used since trade turnover has declined drastically over the past four years there. Might be why they use it for human trafficking. It's easier to pay off port officials," Ace said.

"How fast can you arrange a ship for us, Danton? Not too big but one that can carry enough fuel to get us to Russia and one that won't draw suspicion on the water," Stone said. He looked around the table. "We can leave it all in the hands of the DHS and DOJ, but I want to be prepared if something goes wrong. Like Savannah said, Decker is dangerous, and we'd be foolish to underestimate him." His gaze seared Hawk. "You're not going alone to meet him with Carry. I'm not watching that boat sail away with you trapped on it."

The dock was quiet with the only sound the soft crashing of waves against the concrete walls. Under the moonlit sky the water was dark without the speckles of light that came with a sunny day.

"I fucking hate places like this at night. It makes me think of all those thriller movies where murders and shootings happen," Carry Rice said as she peered through the windscreen of the black SUV.

"You've got that right," Hawk said as he looked around. The darkness around them was broken only by the dim lights scattered at intervals against the warehouse. He was struck by the strange, deserted feeling of the city's atmosphere. He shifted in the seat. The rows of shipping containers looked eerie and offered the perfect hiding place for skunks lurking in readiness. A warning of impending doom trickled the back of his neck, something he never ignored.

"You were right about the Seagull, Zeke. It's still here but looks like a graveyard on board."

"It's set to sail at first light, so the crew must be asleep," Zeke said.

"Or ready and waiting to go as soon as they've got Savannah on board," Hawk bit out. He glanced at Carry. "You've been tagged with the NanoTracker?"

She rubbed a spot on the back of her neck. "Yes, not that I have any idea how it works but at least it offers security."

"Hawk, DC is approaching from the east. Very slowly. He might be on foot," Parker's voice echoed in their ears. The microchip communication devices he'd given them were undetectable and offered another buffer of assurance knowing Parker could hear everything as well.

"How do you know it's him," Carry asked.

"Tagged him before he was released from prison. We've been keeping an eye on him all the time." Hawk straightened as he detected a movement between the first row of containers in front of them. "It's him," he sneered as DC's face was illuminated by one of the building lights for a brief moment as he approached. "What game are you playing, motherfucker?"

Hawk checked his gun and flicked a look sideways. "Got the recording ready?"

She pushed her hand into her jacket pocket. "Yes, and I've practiced enough times. I won't fuck it up."

"Keep by my side and press against me. He needs to believe you're scared and seeking my protection." Hawk chuckled at her expression. She was a ju-jitsu black belt expert and didn't scare easily. "Play the part and don't be brave. I don't want you hurt. If anything happens, you get in this car and go. Is that clear?"

"And leave you alone? I guess Danton hasn't told you much about me. Forget it, buster. We're in this together."

Decker stopped a couple of yards from them. He stood in a relaxed pose with his hands in his pants pockets.

"Do any of you detect any movement?" Hawk looked around.

"Nothing," Stone said in his ear. "Be careful, Hawk. I've got a feeling we're about to be sidelined."

"Ditto on that," Hawk muttered as he reached for the door handle. "Remember, Stone, if I get taken on board the Seagull, you don't come charging in like superheroes. We need to get as close to the Kumarins as possible."

"Just stay alive, Hawk, no matter what." Stone's voice sounded strained.

Hawk pushed open the door. "Here we go."

He walked in front of the SUV and stood waiting. He'd be damned if he made it any easier for Decker Cooper. Carry rushed over to him and pressed against his side.

"Now isn't that too sweet. Scared your new lover is going to get hurt, darling?"

"Go fuck yourself. Where is my son?" Savannah's voice sounded clear in the quiet night as Carry played the recording they'd made the previous night. Her voice was too hoarse and wouldn't have passed as Savannah's even with the excuse of having a cold.

"He's close. I just had to make sure you're alone." He looked around but didn't approach. Hawk felt the trickle of unease against his neck again. His senses went on high alert.

"You're wasting our time. We're not here to chit-chat. Get Luke or we're leaving," Hawk's voice timbered across the distance.

"Don't Hawk, please." Carry placed her hand on his arm, looking up at him and then back at Decker. "You're a bastard, Decker. What do you want?"

"Ah, yes, I tend to forget how clever and sharp you are ... sometimes. This time ... not so much." He cracked an evil laugh. "It's not what I want, *Lucy,*" he taunted. His teeth flashed in the dark night as he smiled. "Sergei Kumarin isn't a happy man. You were such a good and willing little whore for him that even after five years, he wants you back."

Hawk went cold all over. Savannah had confirmed the previous night that she'd been forced into sex slavery but he'd never in a million years considered that she'd serviced the feared Russian mob leader himself. It just added a completely new dimension to the situation. They weren't just in danger. They were fucked, especially if Sergei Kumarin had to get his hands on *Lucy's* new lover.

"Jesus!" Stone's curse echoed in Hawk's ears as he came to the same conclusion. "Get the fuck out of there Hawk. Move! Now."

The excruciating pain against the back of Hawk's head came out of nowhere, the hit undetected by sound or visual. He fought the black shroud that crept rapidly closer.

"Get out of here. Go," he rasped as he sank to his knees, but Carry's surprised gasp indicated she'd been caught too. Hawk shook his head and surged to his feet. He felt a warm liquid, which could only be blood from a wound at the back of his head, trickle down his neck.

"It's payback time, Sinclair. Pity I won't be around to witness them tear you limb from limb." Decker's taunting voice drove Hawk to his feet and drew his footsteps in his direction. Through blurry eyes he saw him turn and took off at a sprint.

"Fuc-king coward," Hawk's steps slowed, his head throbbing painfully.

"Watch out! Hawk, turn and punch," Stone shouted in his ear.

He blindly followed his directive, but the movement was sluggish, deterred by the blinding pain in his head. A masked face blurred in front of him. He grunted as he felt the prick of a needle in his neck. He stumbled and then his legs crumbled as the dark veil of unconsciousness closed around him, with the husky whisper in a heavy accent coming to him from afar.

"Get them on the boat. Quickly. The engines are already running. We sail in five."

Hawk came to in stages, courtesy of the pounding headache that sounded like the constant beating of drums in the background. Flashes of what had brought him there, ran through his mind. He didn't move or open his eyes. He silently took stock of his surroundings. He was lying on a steel floor, it was sweltering hot, and he could feel his shirt sticking to his body. He felt the rolling pitch and cursed softly.

I'm on the ship and already at sea. How long? How fucking long have I been out?

He forced his eyes open. It was dark but not an impenetrable darkness. More a charcoal haze. He blinked and looked around, easily identifying the inside of a shipping container. A soft whimper drew his gaze to the front of the container. Through the remaining blurriness of his vision he detected five women huddled on thin mattresses covered with blankets. They had a dazed look in their eyes, probably from being drugged like he had been. He pushed upright against the side of the container, grunting as his head protested with a searing pain.

He cursed as he found the rest of the container empty.

Where the fuck was Carry?

"Are you ladies hurt?" he asked in a raw croak. His throat was as dry as the desert.

"No, but we have no idea where we are or how we got here."

"Is there any water?" he asked hopefully.

One of the women got up and handed him a bottle. The rattle of chains alerted him to the fact that he was chained but not immobilized. He smelled it and took a tentative sip. It tasted relatively harmless, so he took a few more, just enough to alleviate the dryness in his throat.

"Thank you." He looked around. "Didn't they bring a woman in with me?"

"They did but they took her somewhere this morning."

"Morning? How long have we been on this fucking ship?"

"Five days," one of the women said in a dejected voice.

Hawk was shocked that he'd been out for that long. It didn't take much deduction to realize that they'd kept him sedated. He did a quick calculation. If the ship travelled at twenty-four NMPH and didn't go to port anywhere else, they should reach Russia in another two to three days.

He tried to keep his thoughts in the present and not dwell on the fact that even though he had fully committed to Savannah, she still didn't trust him to believe in her. He'd prodded her on the night before they were to meet Decker to open to him. His mind drifted back to the conversation.

"Hawk, please don't ask me to go back to that time. I've been trying to forget it," Savannah pleaded with him, her eyes lowered.

"But you're not, baby, and that's the problem. I watch you every night struggling with those demons in your dreams. I hold you when you start crying and whimpering in your sleep." He tilted back her chin and stared into her eyes with warm compassion in

his. "I know from what you say during those dreams what you went through."

She shook her head and tears formed in her eyes.

"No! Please, don't tell me that. I don't want you to know. I ... I did things ..."

"No, love, you were forced to do things. Don't you know me well enough to realize I would never judge you? No matter what you did in your past, willing or not. All I want is to help you forget."

She wrung her hands and looked away. "Then you know I ... the assignment Decker sent me on went wrong. I wasn't supposed to be there. I should've stayed behind on the ship, but they ..." She swallowed hard. "I became one of the sex slaves," she ended in a rush.

"Why didn't you go for therapy to help you cope on your return?"

"I did but I couldn't talk about it, not to a stranger, and Decker ... he pushed me to work harder, to go on other assignments to help me forget."

"In which whorehouse did they keep you?"

Savannah clamped closed like an oyster. She shook her head.

"Honey, is there something you're not telling me I should know before I meet with Decker? If I end up going to Russia, I need to be prepared."

"No, nothing." She clipped out the words and with a sob stormed out of the room.

If only she'd told him then they'd have been better prepared. He would never have allowed another innocent woman to become victim to these bastards. Now, he and Carry might be traveling to their death.

The silence in his ear meant that the rest of the team was out of range. Luckily, they'd be able to keep on their tail with the NanoTrackers.

Other than that … he was on his own.

Linzi Basset

Chapter Twenty-Two

"Wake up, American bastard!"

Hawk gasped as the cold water splashed into his face. He lifted glowing eyes that promised retribution to the burly guard who had been taking pleasure in beating and slicing him up since he'd been dragged into an underground basement two days ago.

He lifted another bucket and walked a wide circle around Hawk.

"This one is gonna make ya scream," he growled in broken English as he hurled the lukewarm water at Hawk's back.

Hawk clenched his teeth and his hands balled into fists, but he didn't make a sound. He'd be damned if he gave Goliath, as he'd christened him, the satisfaction of watching him suffer. He forced his body not to jerk as he got doused with salt water. The slithering streams enveloped him like a lover's caress. His raw grunts echoed only in his mind as every cut on his back stung as the salt washed through it.

"Tough fucker, aren't you?" Goliath spat as he stared at Hawk through narrowed eyes, searching for the smallest sign of weakness.

"Better a fucker than a coward like you," Hawk taunted him. He breathed shallowly as swirls of pain mercilessly penetrated the cells that were left open and raw. He pushed through the pain until the initial ache ebbed and he could lose himself in a moment of newfound weightlessness. "But thanks for sterilizing my wounds."

The guard's cheeks blew up as he stuttered in anger. "Shut your trap and stop talking shit."

Hawk's laugh slammed back from the walls to taunt him to puff up further and turn red with anger. It was evident he had no idea if Hawk was telling the truth. He was clearly annoyed that he might have aided in keeping his prisoner from going weak from possible infection.

"Hang in there, Hawk, we're here."

Hawk had never been this happy to hear Stone's voice. He'd begun to wonder if they had lost the tracker signs as well. He had to muster all his strength to hide the joy from his expression.

"Behave yourself, American. My arm is itching to swing the devil's tongue and I will if you show any disrespect against the big man."

He quickly shuffled to stand against the wall as the door leading into the basement slammed open above them. Hawk detected two sets of feet descending the stairs. He'd seen pictures of the Kumarin brothers, but it didn't prepare him for the cruelty that shone from their eyes as they entered the room.

Sergei Kumarin stopped in front of Hawk; his eyes boring into him like he was attempting to see inside his soul.

"So, you're the American bastard who now enjoys the pleasures of my Lucy."

"You wouldn't know about her pleasures. Forcing a woman into submission is an act of a coward." Hawk didn't bother to hide the disgust from his eyes as he looked the imposing man up and down. "You have no idea how to give a woman pleasure."

Hawk jerked back his head, but he had nowhere to go chained as he was and was forced to watch Sergei's fist edging closer to his face. He must've thrown his body weight behind the punch as it connected with his jaw with such force blood pooled inside his mouth. Pain erupted from the point of impact.

Sergei roared in fury as Hawk spat the blood in his mouth directly into his face.

"Still a coward I see. Hitting a chained man. Little wonder your cock is useless to a woman."

"Jesus, Hawk, do you have a death wish? Shut up for god's sake! We need ten more minutes." Stone sounded exasperated as much as concerned.

Hawk bit back the groan of frustration at the delay. He'd summed up Sergei as a man who boasted about his achievements. He hoped he could keep him from burying a knife in his gut until Stone and the team arrived. His expression turned amused as he watched Sergei furiously wipe the bloodied spittle from his face. His brother Yury couldn't keep the mirth from his face either, which infuriated Sergei.

"Get Lucy. I want to show this useless dick just how willing the little whore is to offer her cunt to whoever and however I tell her to." He cackled a laugh and turned on Yury who didn't move. "Get the whore!"

"She's on her way, brother. Igor has gone to fetch her," he said, gesturing to indicate the burly guard had left. "I'm rather surprised that you haven't already gorged yourself on her since she arrived."

"I've waited five years. A few more days won't matter. Besides, I want to teach her and her lover a lesson."

"Would that be me or your partner Decker Cooper who planted a baby in her belly?"

Sergei turned into a statue. Fury exploded in his eyes. He spun to face Yury. "What is this? Why don't I know about this?"

"Two minutes, Hawk. We already got the five women freed and on their way to the ship."

Hawk sighed in relief and then smiled as he watched the brothers face off against each other. "I thought I told you Cooper lied to us all these years. That she works for him."

Sergei sputtered in fury. It was evident Yury hadn't wanted Sergei to get Savannah back. He obviously had his own agenda and Hawk suspected it was a ploy for the position of power.

"You never told me! You knew this all along and you never did anything to get her back. It's your fault the bastard dirtied her womb with his seed." He swung his fist and Yury slammed against the wall. "You did this. My own brother! She's fucking useless to me now."

He swung again but this time Yury swerved out of the way and threw a punch straight into Sergei's gut.

"Calm the fuck down. A cunt is a cunt, no matter if she'd born a child," he growled angrily. They stood facing each other, heaving for breath when the door opened, and Igor pushed Carry inside. She stumbled but stayed on her feet. Her face was bruised and swollen, her clothes bloodied from being beaten up, but when she caught Hawk's eyes, they shot a fiery message at him.

"Go Carry," he shouted and fisted his hands around the chains above him and heaved up his legs. He caught Sergei around the throat and locked his knees in place. "Get the fuck out, Carry," he snapped.

"Hell no. I'm not about to walk away from a real fight," she said and dropped to the floor in a backwards swipe kick that took Igor's feet out from under him.

Hawk tightened his hold on Sergei, finding pleasure in the helpless gurgles sputtering from his lips as his ability to breathe was restricted more and more with every twist of Hawk's knees.

"Gun!" he shouted as he noticed Yury draw a pistol and aim it at Carry who had just shattered Igor's esophagus with a snap kick against his throat. She straightened with raised arms and then all hell broke loose as Stone led the team down the stairs.

A gunshot deafened Hawk in the close confines of the basement. He watched with satisfaction as Yury's body catapulted backwards and slammed into the far wall, his chest blooming red with his blood as he slithered to the floor, dead before he hit the floor.

"Fuck!" Hawk grunted as he felt a searing pain in his leg. Sergei yanked on the knife and pulled it out to slice at him a second time. "Forget it, motherfucker," he sneered and with a quick twist of his body he yanked his legs to left, snapping Sergei's neck. His body spasmed as Hawk released him. He watched dispassionately as his lifeless form fell to the floor. His eyes stared upward with an expression of disbelief etched on his face.

"That was for Savannah, you useless bastard."

"You look like shit," Stone said as he unchained him.

"Yeah, because you took your sweet time to get here." He rubbed his wrists and stood unmoving, forcing his legs to accept his full weight. He looked at Carry who was leaning against Danton.

"You okay, Carry?"

Her eyes met his and she smiled weakly. "I've been better but turning this bastard's throat into butter made up for it." She kicked Igor against the head.

"Are you sure?" Hawk prodded. He studied her intently. "They didn't—"

"No, Hawk, I wasn't raped, thank God for that. They just beat me up to get me to go to the *big man* willingly as his sex toy … like I did in the past," she ended softly. "God, I don't even want to know what they did to Savannah to make her give in." She spat at Yury's body. "They aren't men, they're not even human beings, they're the slime of the lowest fucking slug on earth."

"Yes," Hawk said with a closed expression as he stared at Sergei. "His death was too quick."

"It's over, and now Savannah will finally be able to put it behind her," Shane said as he prodded the wound in Hawk's leg.

"Maybe," Hawk said caustically.

Shane studied him intently. There was an underlying sadness in Hawk's eyes that penetrated through the anger still humming inside him.

"Hawk, you can't blame or judge Savannah for something she had to do for survival," he said softly. They'd all heard the ugly things Sergei had said.

"I'm not." He gratefully accepted Ace's shoulder to ascend the stairs. "But she chose not to trust in me. For that ..." He clamped his lips shut as the picture of an empty future blurred his vision.

"You're losing too much blood." Kane said. "Sit down," he ordered curtly and with quick movements tied his belt above the knife wound and wrapped Hawk's leg tightly with a towel he'd found. "That should hold until we get to the boat."

Hawk didn't say another word and ignored the concerned glances his cousins awarded his way. The trip home was no better. The closer they got to the U.S., the more withdrawn he became.

It hurt, knowing Savannah hadn't trusted in him to believe in her, the woman he had come to love with everything inside him. She filled his heart, his soul, his entire existence.

It hadn't been enough for her.

She couldn't reach out to his heart with hers in full and complete trust in what he offered to her freely, without reservation.

Himself.

That was what he couldn't accept.

For the second time in his life, he felt lost. Only this time, the pain throbbed deep and constant, exacerbated by the echo of the sweetest little voice that kept calling to him over and over.

"Ack! Ack!"

It was mid-morning when they arrived at The Seven Keys Island. without discussing it, they bypassed the Castle and took the elevator down to the second floor of Be Secure Enterprises.

Hawk's wounds were healing well, which had been confirmed by Roy McCord. Stone had insisted that Hawk and Carry go to the hospital before they headed home. Roy had been impressed with the sutures Kane had done on his leg.

"Just take it easy for a couple of weeks, Hawk. Your body took a knock with the fire and now this. Give yourself time to heal properly."

Roy's words echoed in Hawk's mind as he took a long sip of the latte Alexa had handed to him the moment he sat down. She clucked around him like a mother hen, insisting that he lift his leg and rest it on the ottoman. He smiled and let her be.

Yeah, I can let my body heal, Roy, but what about the hole in my heart, the unravelling of my soul, and the emptiness that keeps growing inside me? How the fuck do I heal that?

He sighed and leaned his head against the backrest of the chair. He closed his eyes. He couldn't remember that he'd ever been this tired. It was more than physical or even emotional. He was soul tired.

"Give us the lowdown on the report from the KGB, Parker," Stone said as Alexa finally left the boardroom, satisfied that they were all comfortable and taken care of.

"It was a good thing they agreed to do the sting operation with us, otherwise we would've been in big shit. The Russian government doesn't take kindly to interference from foreigners in their business," Zeke interjected.

"Fuck 'em, we did them a goddamned favor," Parker said fervently. "The FSB would've preferred to have the Kumarins alive to make an example of them and put them away behind bars for the rest of their lives. Fortunately, they were pacified that the soldiers caught that day sang like canaries. It enabled them to crack down on all the whore houses the Kumarin Bratva owned. They're already in the process of assisting the DOJ to return the U.S. women."

"Best of all is that they also cracked down on their drug distribution center and destroyed four drug manufacturing plants," Zeke said. "The four *Avtoritet* or Brigadiers offered solid information on the Contessa Groups in the U.S. in return for a reduced sentence. It'll enable the FBI and DOJ to disable most of them across the country."

"Where is Decker Cooper?" Hawk muttered without opening his eyes.

"Our team has been keeping track of him. He's been keeping a low profile from the reports I've studied on the plane from DC. He's holed up in a mountain cabin in Humphreys Peak in Arizona. I think his plans to get his job back at the FBI has been shot to pieces," Parker said.

"Keep me updated. If he moves, I want to know."

"We only have a lock on him for the next day or two. The NanoTracker dissolves after about twenty-five days."

"Fuck!" Hawk stood up. "I want the coordinates of that cabin."

"Hawk, you heard what Roy said. You—"

"He's not going to walk away from this, Stone. Not this fucking time." He walked toward the door. "And he sure as hell isn't going back to prison," he said as he stomped out and from there headed directly upstairs to his apartment.

His footsteps dragged as he approached the front door. The sound of light jazz floated through the door. He could imagine Savannah sitting on the sofa reading. He closed his eyes briefly and then stepped inside.

"Hawk! Oh my god! You're alive and you're here," Savannah shrieked and ran to him. She stopped short of flinging herself into his arms as the stoic expression on his face registered. Her heart missed a beat. She looked into his eyes and flinched. They were empty, the dullest gray she'd ever seen them. It was as if the light inside his soul had been switched off.

A sob tore from deep within as realization set in.

"So, now you know," she said dully.

Hawk didn't respond. He skirted around her and strode to the bedroom. She couldn't stop her feet from following and when she found him methodically packing his clothes, she wished she hadn't.

"Aren't you going to say anything?"

"What do you expect me to say?"

"Anything. Please don't just leave."

He continued folding his clothes neatly.

"Hawk, please. Say something. Anything. Shout at me, tell me you understand, and if it'll help, that I'm a filthy whore. Please, I beg you, don't walk away from me."

"I never shout, and no, I don't understand, and you're a filthy whore," he said tonelessly as he closed the duffle bag and walked away.

Savannah couldn't stop the tears upon hearing the words from his lips, no matter that she'd put them there. She ran after him and skidded to a halt in front of him, barring his way to the door.

"I wanted to tell you so many times, but my throat closed up every time I tried."

Hawk turned away and stared out of the window. Savannah felt defeated, shattered to the core that he couldn't even look at her.

"I asked you the night before we left if there was something I should know, and you said no."

"I know and I'm sorry. I should've told you."

He turned on her, his nostrils flared as he sneered, "Yes, you should have. Because of your denial I took an innocent woman with me into a hellhole. Wasn't it enough that you suffered through it?"

"Oh god, I'm so sorry."

"It's too late now, Savannah. Don't you think I needed to know you were Sergei Kumarin's whore before we went there? Fuck! I get furious thinking what could've happened to Carry because you kept your mouth shut."

"I couldn't tell you! I love you, Hawk, with everything in me and I was scared and so ... *so* ashamed."

His hands closed around her arms. Shaking her, he bit out through clenched teeth, "Yes, you should be ashamed." The timber of his voice vibrated with suppressed fury. He cursed as the tears began to fall and her face turned red with shame. "You *should* be ashamed Savannah, not because of what he forced you to become but because you didn't trust in me to believe in you." He shook her again. "YOU, this woman in front of me, the one I gave myself to. *That,* Savannah was your pass to freedom from the demons you allow to keep chasing you. Trusting me, allowing me to be there for you. That should've told you I would never judge you, that I found myself inside you ... that I trust and believe in the woman you are when you're with me." He dropped his arms. "But I guess that's not enough for you."

He picked up his bag. "I want you off the island in two days," he said as he walked toward the door.

"Ack! Ack-Ack-Ack-Ack!" Luke shrieked out his name as his little bum wriggled like a turbo motor toward him from his bedroom where he'd been sleeping until Hawk's voice woke him.

Hawk's steps faltered. He closed his eyes but didn't move even though his mind shouted at his feet to go, to get the hell out of there. Then the little boy pulled himself upright against his pants and jumped up and down, excitedly demanding, "Ack ... up-up-up!"

Without any conscious thought the bag hit the floor and Luke was in his arms. He wrapped his little chubby ones around Hawk's neck and held on, saying his name over and over. Hawk hugged him against his chest, his world slowly crashing down around him.

"I'm going to miss you so much, little man."

His voice thickened and he didn't bother to stop the tears that spilled over his cheeks as he untangled Luke's arms from around his neck. He sat him down on the floor and before he could change his mind, he slammed through the door.

Luke stared with expectant eyes at the door, waiting with his little arms spread wide. His bottom lip began to quiver when it remained closed, and his beloved *Ack* didn't return.

"Aaaacck," he wailed as he burst into tears. He leaned his little head forward onto the floor between his hands and sobbed his heart out.

Savannah couldn't move from where she'd sunk to the floor, her body shuddered in tune with Luke's sobs. Eventually she managed to crawl toward him and laid down next to him, cuddling him in the cocoon of her body. He was inconsolable, sobbing out Hawk's name until eventually he quieted and fell asleep.

She didn't move, just held the little precious bundle against her as she battled with the emotions running rife through her.

Regret. Sorrow.

It gnawed at her, accusing her of being a weakling to allow past demons to rule common sense. She wished she could turn back time, to rectify the mistake, to show Hawk how much she loved him and trusted him.

Alas, it was impossible. She would have to live with the remorse etching at her heart. A tear trickled down her cheek as a forlorn sob shuddered through Luke's body. She had caused his pain. Guilt gnawed like a worm at the core of an apple. Her heart was in tatters and so too was her little boy.

And she had no one to blame but herself.

Chapter Twenty-Three

"It's time to go."

Regret washed over Savannah as she listened to the pain in her voice, like the long slow waves rolling onto the beach she stared at from her favorite spot on the edge of the cliff behind Castle Sin. A shiver ran down her spine. Longing to make things right had kept her awake for the past two nights. If only she'd taken a different path.

"It's too late for if only, Savannah. Nothing is going to change and there's no way back, no way to make it right." She blinked tiredly.

She'd lived with emotional demons for five years, but in the face of the remorse that ate away at her, it faded to nothing. None of it mattered anymore. She picked up a pebble and stared at it in envy; hard and lifeless, unable to feel the torments of life.

"Savvy? Are you okay?" Peyton's concerned voice forced her out of the dark well of self-reproach. She glanced at her dully.

"No, I'm not and neither is Luke and it's all my fault." Her gaze moved listlessly to stare out to sea. "I kept hoping he'd come back, so I could tell him how sorry I am, admit how wrong I'd been not to trust that he'd never judge me." She sighed as Peyton sat down next to her on the small bench. She stared at the pebble in her hand. "I guess you heard."

"Savvy, I wish you'd spoken to me. I could've helped you cope. At least be there to show you none of it matters." She squeezed her hand. "It pains me to know you've been suffering on your own for all these years."

"I don't think I'll ever be able to shake off the stigma … the shame of what I've done … the things—"

"Shh, darling, listen to me. You have nothing to be ashamed about and there's no stigma attached to you."

"Yes, there is! I wasn't … I wasn't a sex slave, Peyton. I became Sergei Kumarin's willing whore. A filthy slut who did everything he told me, no matter how vulgar, how humiliating … how painful. I gave him all he asked for and I did it willingly."

"You had no choice," Peyton said with a thick voice. "The guards told Stone how badly Yury Kumarin whipped and tortured you to force you to accept your fate and do it willingly. You gave in because you had a will to live, to survive … and you did. You rose above it all when you managed to escape and freed not just yourself but all those women." Peyton took her hands and stared at her intently. "It's not too late, Savvy. You love him and I have no doubt he loves you too."

Savannah shook her head. "I killed whatever he felt for me by not offering him my trust. That's all he asked of me, Peyton, and I couldn't give it to him because I allowed the shame and stigma that makes me nauseous to this day guide me."

"Everyone makes mistakes in life; takes one misguided step and ends up on the wrong path. It's how you fix them that matters." She cupped Savannah's face and brushed the tears off her cheeks. "Don't give up on Hawk, Savvy. Fight for your future. Fight for your love."

"I'm scared," she admitted the deep fear that he wouldn't listen and chase her away before she opened her mouth.

"Don't you think you've allowed fear to rule your life for long enough, Savvy? Because that's what it is, not the stigma and not the shame. You're scared to open your mind and heal. To allow someone to rescue you from those demons. Because they've become a part of you, and you don't know how to let go. How to live without them inside you. Let Hawk be the one to help you heal. Let go of the fear before it completely destroys your mind and soul. Don't give those bastards more power over you, Savvy. They've held you hostage for long enough. It's time to let go and grasp your future with both hands. It's there, right in front of you. All you have to do is have the courage to seize the power love gives you. To accept the strength Hawk offers you in his desire to carry you on his wings. To care and protect you. Trust in him that he'll never fail you and never let you fall."

Savannah listened to Peyton's words and allowed it to fill her mind, to wrap around the frayed edges of her thoughts. It castigated her for not admitting all of it to herself. Every word Peyton said rang true and she was right. Savannah had lived with the fear inside her for too long. It was time to dig deep and find the courage to fight for Hawk ... for love.

"I don't know where he is, Peyton. How do I make it right if he hides from me?"

"He went home."

Savannah glanced at her in confusion. "What do you mean he went home? I thought this was his home."

"No, he stays here because it's convenient. Hawk's real home is in Key Largo." Peyton smiled and winked at her. "And I know where it is."

Savannah didn't hesitate. She got up and pulled Peyton along with her. "Will you take care of Luke for me?"

"Of course."

"I have to do this right, Peyton, and I know just what to do to prove to him just how much I do trust him." She smiled for the first time in days.

"Now that's the spirit!"

The sand was the gentlest hue of gold, earthen and muted, the humble star of the scene. Hawk loved the serenity of the enclosed private beach in front of his house in Key Largo on Bay Road. His listless gaze took in the driftwood that rolled upon the buoyant waves like tiny rescue boats. This morning there were signs of seaweed in the distance, the flora of these salty waves, as deeply green as any high summer foliage. His gaze moved over the softly rolling dunes, and he listened to the whispers of the tall grass rustling sweetly into the gusting breeze.

He soaked in the peacefulness around him as he felt the breeze through his hair, turning the usual neat strands into a tousled mess.

Hawk sat looking out to sea on the steps leading to the beach from the large wraparound porch of his two-story house, sorting through the angry disappointment in his mind. He'd wasted his time on a trip to the cabin where Decker Cooper had been holed up on Humphreys Peak in Arizona. He wasn't there, and like Parker had warned, they'd lost the NanoTracker signal. It seemed Decker had also gotten rid of the cell phones Parker had hacked into before. Not that it surprised Hawk. Decker wasn't stupid; he'd known he'd be on the Sinclairs and the FBI's radar.

Decker had made a calculation error. A big one when he'd offered Hawk on a platter to the Bratva. They might have killed him, but DC realized too late, he'd still have to deal with the rest of the Sinclair clan and the consequences of that decision.

Now, he was gone. Somewhere out there, walking free. It infuriated Hawk. He wouldn't stop looking for him and he wouldn't rest until he'd paid for what he'd done to Savannah. Until then, he'd have to make sure she was safe.

"Yeah, brilliant asshole. You want to keep her safe, but you chased her off The Seven Keys Island."

He sighed heavily as he listened to his voice. He was bone tired. He had hardly slept on the trip back from Russia, and since his harsh words to Savannah four days ago, he didn't even bother to try. He couldn't, because every time he closed his eyes, he saw the devastation in hers, but the most crippling was the tearful wail of the little boy that had seared through his heart as he'd walked away.

The sound tortured him every second of the day. *"Aaaacck."*

It was in moments like this that regret castrated him, ripped through skin and bone to lash at his conscience. It seeped to the foreground of his mind and demanded to be re-examined again. But he knew no amount of analyzing his feelings and how much her mistrust hurt, was going to turn back the clock. He had to get on with the here and now. She was out of his life by his own demand and no matter how much he wished differently, he knew his decision wouldn't change.

As a Dom, trust was the ultimate bond he required from his submissive as much as he offered it himself. Without it, the foundation a relationship such as theirs was built on would never survive. Love alone wasn't strong enough.

"Love ..." He said the word and listened to it drifting off with the wind. His body turned stiff. He'd only recently given his feelings for Savannah a name. He loved her with such depth it was torture to know it could never be. Pain shot through his chest.

"Time heals all wounds," he said in an attempt to force the emotions from his mind, but deep inside, he knew he was fooling himself. He'd not felt this much pain and loss with the death of his first wife, Vee. It was all consuming and threatened to bring him to his knees, to forget about his strong beliefs. To throw it all to the wind and bring Savannah back.

He exhaled slowly as he discounted the thought. It would never happen. He could never become someone or something different than what he was. A man of integrity who would never rape his values for anyone or anything ... not even love.

He dragged himself back inside. A refreshing shower might help to keep his mind occupied, if only for a short while. He got hijacked on the way by the melodious chime of the doorbell. He stopped and stared indecisively at the door.

"I'm not in the mood for people," he grumbled and headed for the stairs, deciding to ignore whoever it was. He cursed as it chimed again and again.

"I'm fucking coming," he growled as he flung open the door ... and froze.

"What do you want?" The words fell uncontrolled from his lips; harsh, albeit unintended and wrung from the surprise to be faced with the one person he'd expected the least—the woman who had just filled his mind.

Savannah took courage from the fact that he didn't immediately chase her away or close the door in her face. She skirted around him and walked into the grand open space to stand in front of the wall of windows, staring out to the blue ocean. Her mind swirled at the beauty of his home.

"I asked you a question."

She turned to face him. Her eyes brushed over his wind-tousled hair, his neat beard, and his gorgeous body on display in a pair of swimming trunks. Her tongue did a foray over her suddenly dry lips.

"I have so much to say, and I practiced it so many times on the way here and now ... it's gone, my mind is blank." She looked into his eyes. "You do that to me. Strike me mute, with no more than your presence, your physique and the power that exudes from every pore in your body." She brushed her hair back over her shoulder and chewed on her lower lip.

Hawk didn't say anything, just stared at her with the usual stoic mask in place.

"I came here to tell you, you were wrong. I do trust you, Hawk, with everything in me. It's me I don't trust. I've lived with the shame and fear for so long, it became part of me, entrenched itself into my soul and I didn't know how to separate it from the present. How to be *me* without it." She fiddled with her fingers. "Maybe I still don't, but I do know that you managed to crack the shell around my insecurities, coaxed the fear to let go of the emotional demons and find *myself* to start seeping through. It's because of you I've become a stronger person over the past couple of months. I want … I want more of that, Hawk. I need more of that. I need you."

She walked closer to him. She had to dig deep not to reach out and touch him.

"I know I deeply disappointed you. I know how much I hurt you because it's the same pain I feel inside me knowing what I had done. I don't know if you'd ever be able to forgive me for putting your life in danger or for holding back that part of me *you* of all people deserve to have." She looked at him pleadingly. "All I ask is that you give me a chance to prove to you how much I love you and how deep that love has ensconced the trust I have in you."

491

She walked toward the door and said softly, "I'll be waiting for you tonight at ten o'clock in The Dungeon of Sin." She smiled tremulously. "I pray with everything in me that you'll be there." She swallowed back the knot that formed in her throat but pushed ahead. "If you don't come, I'll understand and I'll never bother you again."

It was a long time after the door closed behind Savannah before Hawk moved. He was pensive as he ascended the stairs to take a shower. Seeing her had opened the lock around the feelings for her that he had banned from his mind. Mocked him for the fool he was. Her words echoed through his mind.

"All I ask is that you give me a chance to prove to you how much I love you and how deep that love has ensconced the trust I have in you."

Hawk felt the first stirring of excitement deep inside him. Whatever Savannah intended was likely to blow his mind. He'd be a fool to stay away.

"I'll be waiting for you tonight at ten o'clock in The Dungeon of Sin."

Maybe love *was* all that mattered. He had wanted her trust. Now he should trust in his love for her and believe she was sincere.

"Are you sure about this, Tulip?" Stone asked with a concerned frown.

They had just watched video recordings the FSB had sent that they had found in the Kumarin mansion. He'd never forget the look on Hawk's face as they watched the brutal torture sessions and listened to the demented Yury Kumarin gloat about how he'd reformed the American woman and turned her into a willing whore for his brother. If Yury hadn't been dead already, he would've died a slow and extremely painful death—at the hands of the entire Sinclair clan.

"Yes, Master Eagle. I love him and I need to show him that I don't fear the memories of my past. That I trust him to guide me through the halls of recuperation, of finding the woman I had lost along the way. He is the only one who can."

"It doesn't have to be this way, my pet."

"Yes, Master Eagle, it does. It's the biggest fear I carry from the time I was captured. I need to bury it once and for all." She smiled gently at his obvious concern. "I know he has the need for masochists at times, but I have faith in him, in his love for me, although he has never said the words. I know Master Hawk will never hurt me."

Stone brushed his fingers over her cheek. "You're a very courageous woman, Tulip." He smiled and backed up a step. "Very well, if you're adamant to do this, let's get you ready." He took Peyton's hand and tugged her with him, aware of her concern about what Savannah was about to do. "Come along, Petals. You can assist me by moisturizing her skin."

Between the two of them they had Savannah ready in no time. Stone studied her intently as he straightened. She appeared calm and relaxed. She offered him a sweet smile.

"Stop worrying, Master Eagle. I promise you this is what I want from my Master tonight."

"Hmm ..." He ran a finger over her breasts, watching with a quirk of lips as her nipples budded into tight little stones. "You do realize that you'd not be up to having sex after this, Tulip, so if you had any thoughts of your Master pounding your pussy ..."

Savannah moaned amid the chuckles of the members who gathered in a wide circle around her, eager to witness the scene about to unfold.

Her eyes glimmered. "I've got a thick skin, Master Eagle. If my Master thinks he's not gonna ease my hunger for his rowdy cock, I've got more than one surprise in store for him."

Stone laughed. "I'll be right back." He winked at her. "Don't go anywhere."

The members laughed and Peyton glared at him. "That's not funny, Master Eagle," she chirped in a snooty voice.

"I suggest you don't either, Petals. There's a specific punishment bench over there with your name on it."

He chuckled at the expression on her face as he walked away, whistling a lively tune.

Hawk and the rest of his cousins had just arrived in front of the dungeon as Stone pushed through the heavy doors.

"Ah, there you are."

Hawk narrowed his eyes. His nose scrunched as he looked at his cousins circling him. They all carried similar expressions of expectation.

"It seems I'm the only one in the dark as to what Tulip has planned for tonight."

"Ah yes, well ... she might have planned it but it's your execution we can't wait to witness," Kane said with a grin.

"You're going to be late, Master Hawk. You don't want little Tulip to think you're not coming, do you?" Stone said with one eyebrow crawling higher as he tapped a finger on his watch as he led the way to the whipping chamber. Stone was prepared should it be necessary to convince Hawk to offer Tulip what she needed with this scene. He knew Hawk well enough to know that after the videos he'd just watched, he'd blatantly refuse to accommodate her.

Hawk soaked in the sounds that was true to the Castle Sin Masters as they entered the whipping chamber. It'd been over a month since he'd been inside the dungeon and like always after a long absence, it wrapped around him like the welcome of his own home. He listened to the loud crack of a whip, the lash of a flogger, the cries and screams of subs in various stages of punishment or arousal and the best of it all, the sound and smell of lust and sex.

The group of members who stood milling around in the center of the room drifted apart as they noticed his approach.

Hawk froze and his breath hung in his throat. For a moment, his lungs refused to cooperate. His eyes scorched over her, from her feet up her long, naked legs, rounded hips, and narrow waist. His gaze was riveted on her hardening nipples as it touched on it and then stayed to enjoy the evidence of the effect he had on her.

He drew in a long staggering breath. doing his best not to appear like a gawking adolescent boy.

Savannah was naked with her arms cuffed above her head to the pulley chains hanging from the rafters. Her feet were spread wide apart with a steel spreader bar. His red twelve-foot kangaroo leather whip snaked around her shoulders. The ten-inch handle snugly settled between her breasts, while the finely cut twelve-foot braided tail curled down to the floor. His cock twitched as his gaze drifted higher. Their eyes met, his darkened in awe, hers murky and pleading.

Hawk had no recollection of moving, but the next moment he stood in front of her. He cupped her cheeks and urgently searched for the fear he expected to lurk in the depths of her hazel eyes.

"Savannah? What are you doing?"

"It's time, my Master."

Hawk felt the hard punch of his heartbeat increasing exponentially. His hand itched to wrap around the handle of his whip, but visions of the brutal whipping that had robbed her of the woman she used to be, kept racing through his mind.

"For what, Tulip?" The timbre of his voice lowered as he kept searching her eyes.

"I don't want to be scared anymore. I need to bury the emotional demons darkening my sleep and place limitations on moments like these. It's time to lay to rest the horror that has hounded me for five years."

"There are other ways to do this, Tulip. Come, let's get you out of this." He reached for the cuffs.

"No! I beg you, Hawk, please. I can't live like this anymore, not if I want a fulfilled and happy life with you. Please, my Master, I beg you, help me."

Hawk dragged his thumb over her quivering lips. The fury in his eyes burned like lava erupting. "I saw what he did to you, baby. How he got you to submit to their demands. Let's find another way.

This is enough to give me the trust I needed from you. I don't need more, and I don't want this to be the one thing that might push you right back into that nightmare."

She smiled lovingly at him. "I trust you, Master Hawk, and I know you'll take care of me, that you'll never hurt me. In your hands, this gorgeous whip will drive out the memory of a year I'm desperate to forget. I love you, Hawk, so much it frightens me. I have to do this. I need to prove to you how much your trust in me means and show you the joy of being your chosen one. Please."

"You're trembling." He traced the curve of her shoulder.

"I'm scared shitless, that's no lie but I know if I keep my eyes on you the entire time, watching you, to know it's you yielding the whip, I'll get through this. It has to be now, Master Hawk ... for our future."

"No, Savannah. I don't believe you're ready."

"I have never been more ready. I trust you, my love. I'm prepared for the hurt and the pain, but I also know you'll take care of me. I have faith . . . faith in you and you alone."

Hawk kissed her, his lips fluttering over hers like the wings of a butterfly. His smile was tender.

"No little one, it won't hurt. I'll never hurt you, baby, even with a whip in my hand, I'll never cause you pain."

Hawk covered her lips with his and for long moments he didn't move, just savored her taste, her feel, and drowned in her love. He heaved in a deep breath and stepped back. His eyes caught Stone's gaze.

"Has she been prepared properly?"

"Yes, rubbed down and moisturized."

"Tulip, this is one of those instances where I need to remind you to use your safeword. Tell me what it is."

"King, but I won't be needing it."

Hawk nodded, palmed the handle of the whip from between her breasts. He watched her as he slowly dragged it from around her neck.

"Oh lord," she hissed as the long tail curled and slithered along her skin.

"I love your tits, Tulip. Have I told you that?" He stood close and teased her aroused nipples with the tail of the whip.

"Ehm ... not in so many words, but your eyes tell me every time you leer at them," she gasped as he took another tantalizing pass.

Hawk stepped back, snapped the whip quickly back and with a sharp flick of his wrist brought it down in a light stroke against her inner thigh, a few inches below her labia.

"Ah, lord," she gasped at the sudden shift obliterating her focus. She was caught off guard by the warm pleasure the sting caused to rush through her. Every muscle in her body tensed as the unexpected stimulus ended in a demanding throb of her clitoris.

Hawk kept his eyes on her, watching her intently as he copied the strike on her left thigh.

He circled her while dragging the tail of the whip against her skin until he stood in front of her. He caressed her breasts, gently massaging each with his free hand while rubbing the tail of the whip over the other. Again, the whip stroke snaked around her upper thigh and immediately on the opposite one.

"How do you feel, my pet?"

"Kind of excited, Master Hawk."

He moved behind her and introduced the curve of her back to the leather of the tail. His wrist snapped, planting a moderate blow first on the left, and then the other soft curve of her ass cheeks.

Savannah became lost in the tantalizing warm sting that made her want to lean into each strike. Her back arched as she pushed her buttocks out, sighing as a barely there brush of leather shuddered against her skin.

"Beautiful, Tulip. You have a natural instinctive reaction to the whip," he praised as he watched her give in to the heat coloring her skin. He continued snapping his wrist, giving her a series of blows covering her ass, slowly increasing in strength as her flesh took on a rosy hue.

"I love this color on you, little one."

Hawk stepped against her to tease her nipples between his fingers, trailing his hand down her belly and without warning pushed two fingers inside of her.

"Oh my," she gasped at the unexpectedness of it and felt her pussy flush with heat. His warm breath against her ear teased her nipples to harden more.

"So hot and wet. Do you want me to continue, my pet?"

"Yes. Please, Master."

"Remember to breathe, Tulip. It's going to start to sting a little." He stood behind her, spread his legs and rolled his shoulders, loosening his muscles. His arm pulled back and he swung it forward, snapping his wrist at the last moment. Savannah cried out and arched away from him.

"Shit!"

Hawk looked at Stone who was his mark in front of her. He smiled and nodded, indicating that she wasn't stressed. He continued raining blows over her back and then started circling her. His movements were fluid and graceful, mesmerizing as if the whip was an extension of his arm. The muscles in his arm and back rippled, tightened, and released. He switched the whip to his left hand and continued with flawless precision, watching, and talking to Savannah all the time.

"I can't believe ... ohhh," Savannah cried as another strike landed on the soft part of her stomach. She had lost the ability to distinguish where the pleasure ended, and the pain began. Her clitoris throbbed in time with each crack of the whip.

She whimpered as she felt the warmth of her essence slither down her thighs. She was floating on a cloud of euphoria so profound that her head spun wildly. There was no thought of another hand lashing with cruelty at her body, of pain so blinding she wanted to die.

What she felt and experienced was so much more; she felt tears form in her eyes. It was enlightening, enervating as she finally released the chains that had held her prisoner in a painful past.

The next blow landed on her clit and labia. For a split second there was no reaction as Savannah was too shocked at feeling the sting of the leather on her sex. Her body jerked as she tried to avoid the next strike. She'd never felt the like, not even with the strap during their ceremony. She had no idea how to compute the sensations that ran wildly through her.

"I can't, please, Master, it's too much." She subsided with a whimper, her whole body slumped, and her arms carried all her weight as her legs turned to rubber.

"Easy, baby. Just relax, Tulip," he gentled her as he stepped against her and caressed her back with the tail before snapping it upward between her legs, allowing the end of the whip to crack on her clit.

Savannah's body went rigid against him. Her head moved against his shoulder as she arched her back.

"Fuuuck," she released a high-pitched scream.

Hawk pinched her nipples while landing a slightly harder blow on her swollen labia and throbbing clit.

Her cries echoed in a chorus in the chamber at war with her ragged breathing as he continued to rain sharp, stinging strikes against her clit, each one harder than the last.

"Oh my god, oh my god, oh my god," she whimpered, writhing, and futilely fucking the air in a desperate attempt for that final much needed push to drop into the abyss.

Hawk moved around to face her, alternating a series of strikes between her breasts, clit, and her pussy. The sensations lost all individuality, every single one aimed at one goal—a climax. Totally out of control, the coil inside her snapped, flinging her so high she couldn't breathe as spasm after spasm rolled over her.

When Savannah finally managed to draw a breath and the tilting world around her settled, she felt Hawk's arms holding her from behind. He nuzzled her throat and kissed the side of her neck.

"How do you feel, my love?" He watched her intently, not missing the tiniest flash of emotion or sensation that filled her topaz eyes. The warmth, love, and thank the lord, complete and utter trust glowed in them for all to see.

"Invigorated and ... free. Thank you, my love, for shattering forever the chains of past memories."

She didn't know how or when he'd released her from the chains, but the next moment, she was in his arms, and he carried her wordlessly up the stairs to his apartment.

He placed her on the bed, undressed quickly, and with tender movements rubbed arnica all over her body, paying special attention to her clitoris and pussy.

She caught his hands in hers and tugged until he yielded to settle in the warm cocoon of her thighs. She wrapped her long legs around his waist and canted her hips against his.

"Now, for dessert, Master Hawk," she cooed seductively.

"Oh no, you're too tender and ... fuck," he gritted as her hand folded around his aroused cock and guided it to her heated center.

"I need you inside me, Hawk. I need to feel your heart beating with every thrust of your body inside me. I love you and this is the night I'll never forget."

He stilled and stared into her eyes. Her heart missed a beat at the love and open adoration that glittered in their depths.

"You are my heartbeat, Savannah. The blood that pumps through my veins is fed by my love for you." He kissed her gently. "I gave you me, Savannah, I am yours from now until eternity. Are you mine, love?"

"Always." Her smile brightened the entire room. "I give you me, Hawk Sinclair. I am yours from now until eternity."

He drew back his cock with deliberate slowness, triggering every nerve ending inside her pussy along the way. Her breath wheezed from her throat.

"Wanna know something?" he asked with that naughty boy smile on his face.

"Tell me."

"I'm going to marry you in a church, very soon, with all the bells and whistles, but right here, right now, I take you as mine, my wife, to love and to hold until death do us part."

He thrust back in and watched her splinter apart, overwhelmed by the emotions his words evoked and the lust he always awakened in her with no more than a look.

"Ah, Tulip ... you're in for a wild night, my love. You better hold on."

Savannah held on, all through the night until finally he allowed her to fall asleep in his arms, content and happy. Hawk pulled the sheet over them and closed his eyes.

"Ack! Ack-ack-ack! ACK! Up-up-up!"

The shrill noise penetrated through Hawk's hazy mind. It felt like he'd just fallen asleep.

"Ack! Ack-ack-ack! ACK! Up-up-up!"

Luke's excited voice finally penetrated his subliminal mind. He squinted against the brightness of the sun shining through the window.

Without opening his eyes, he reached out and lifted the wriggling little boy on the bed. He fell onto Hawk's chest and hugged him.

"Ack!" he demanded with a tap against Hawk's cheek.

He forced his eyes open and smiled as the sweet little face came into focus.

"Hey little man." His voice thickened as Luke's face splintered into a wide smile.

"What's the time?" Savannah asked in a groggy voice.

"Almost twelve," Vera shouted from the kitchen. "Sorry to wake you but Luke was impossible. Well, I'll be off and leave you three alone."

"Mama," Luke said and planted a wet kiss on her cheek. He sat up between them and looked from one to the other. He clapped his hands.

"Luk ... Mama ... Ack!" He crowed a giggle as he managed to string the three names together. He jumped up and down.

"Luke, not so—"

"Shh!" Luke pressed his fingers against her lips and then sat on his heels, puffed up his chest and frowned. He pointed at his chest.

"Dommm ... Luk!"

"Oh, sweet lord, save me," Savannah moaned and amid the laughter of the two *Doms*, buried her head under the pillow.

Twenty-four-hours later, deep in the Superstition Mountains in Arizona ...

"No! Let me go. What the fuck do you think you're doing?" Decker Cooper lamented as he fought against the hard hands that forced him into the trunk of the black sedan. His cries were muted as the masked man pushed a stinking oil cloth into his mouth. Decker gagged but bound as he was, he could do nothing. He watched bleakly as the trunk closed and a black void swallowed him inside.

Fear owned him in that moment. He'd known he wouldn't be able to run from them forever. He just didn't think his time would be this short.

The trip was over before he could wrap his mind around the precarious position he found himself in. If only he could talk to the man, offer him money. He had billions and could top any amount the Sinclairs paid to have him killed.

He didn't struggle as he was dragged from the trunk and shoved to the ground. He looked up and turned cold as he encountered not one but two tall men staring down at him. One took a step closer and yanked the rag from his mouth. He coughed and dragged in a deep breath. His stomach turned as he swallowed the oily residue the rag had left in his mouth.

He struggled to his feet.

"You don't have to do this. Whatever you're paid, I'll triple it. We can go to my house right now and I'll do the transfer. Cash, no questions asked."

The men looked at each other and hope surged to life inside Decker until their dark laughter doused it.

"Triple the value of nothing, stays nothing, so it's not much of a deal, I'm afraid."

Decker stumbled back a step. "I don't understand."

He wanted to turn and run, not wishing to know their identities when they reached for the ski masks and pulled them off. Decker's world crashed.

"You?" Decker laughed. "You just made a big mistake to let me see who you are. You can beat me up all you want but you'll be sorry. I'll make sure the world knows all about—"

"I don't think he gets it."

"Nope, he sure doesn't."

Decker looked between them. "What the fuck are you talking about."

"You're responsible for the suffering of all those women. We saw what those bastards did to Savannah Thorne, all because of your greed. You have been judged, Decker Cooper."

"And found guilty on all charges."

"Fuck off. You can't play judge and jury. I don't give a fuck about the repercussions for me. I'm going to talk. Stay the fuck away from me."

"He still doesn't get it."

"Nope, he sure doesn't."

Decker retreated as the two men crowded closer. "Stop talking in fucking riddles."

"It's simple, really, Decker Cooper."

"Yes ... you may have heard this expression before."

Decker screamed as they doused him with a clear liquid. He sputtered and coughed. He heaved in a breath and suddenly he couldn't breathe as the sweet smell of benzene enveloped every sensory nerve in his system.

His world collapsed as reality sank in for the first time as they picked up uncapped gasoline tanks. He tried to move but his legs had gone numb. He began to beg as they swung the open containers in asymmetric arcs.

Fuel coughed and gushed in great torrents as they soaked him amid his muffled screams for mercy.

"NO!"

"Yes, Decker Cooper. Finally, you get it."

"Dead men don't talk."

A flick of light was the only warning as they lit the cloths in the glass bottles of gasoline in their hands.

Decker started to run, screaming as he heard the shattering of glass before he felt it break apart against his back.

WHOOSH!

It took less than ten minutes. His clothing acted like a wick, burning upwards consuming his chest, face, and hair. Superheated air and flames were sucked into his mouth as he fought to breathe. He stared at the men watching impassively.

The last visual to be imprinted in his mind of the two Sinclair cousins he'd least expected to see.

Kane and Shane Sinclair.

He had stopped slapping at the flames while rolling on the ground, praying in a weakening wail for the end to come. As if his prayer was heard, the thin layer of pleura that covered his lungs burst, killing him. The body spasmed once, stilled, and as he puffed out his final breath, the remains glowed like a beacon in the dusky light of sunset.

"Let's go home, Kane," Shane said as he closed the trunk of the rental. "Leave his carcass to the coyotes."

His gaze was contemptuous as he stared at the pitiful corpse on the ground. "Let's just hope they don't choke on the rot of a human disgrace he was."

Kane took one last look at the charred body on the ground. It triggered loose a memory he'd tried to bury so many times before.

"Yeah," he said slowly.

Taking out his wallet, he flipped it open. His fingers trembled as he found the small, faded photograph inside. His vision blurred as tears gathered in his eyes.

"I won't forget, my love. I'll never forget."

The End

Read on for an excerpt from Kane, book 3 in the Castle Sin series.

Excerpt: Kane

CHAPTER ONE

"The answer is no, Cleopatra. I've had my fun and I'm going to bed."

He sighed. He could be a bastard … at times. Something he readily admitted to himself. That in itself wasn't a big deal but there were times that he deliberately fed the dark demons inside his soul.

Then he didn't give a fuck who was on the receiving end of those beasts demanding relief from the emptiness inside his soul—that dark void. A never-ending swirling vortex that consumed everything, left him feeling nothing. Desolate. Sweet fuck all to subside in his hollow soul that crept in the shadows.

Lately, he'd been drawing back from people more and more because its emptiness had become so all-consuming it threatened to drown him.

"But Master Bear, I have so much energy left." Cleopatra slid closer to the brooding man at the bar. She had been left breathless after the devastating scene with him in The Dungeon of Sin, and still now, long since his aftercare had finished, her entire body sizzled. He, on the other hand, had smiled at her, patted her chin, and walked away. Like he hadn't just fucked her until she passed out. Her loins throbbed for more, and tonight, she wasn't allowing him to deny her like he had done with every sub who begged to spend the night with him.

It was a known fact that many of the full-time employed submissives had tried to get under the elusive older Master's skin. He exuded confidence and a high-octane power that acted like a magnet. The fact that he was mountain-man rough and attractive, not to mention he fucked like a stallion, made him even more alluring to women of all ages.

"I can make your bed less lonely, Master Bear. I'd love to repay you for the earth-shattering climax you just gave me," she cooed in his ear as she pressed against his side. Her hand stole over his stomach, inching towards the bulge in his leathers.

"Did I give you permission to touch me, sub?"

Cleopatra froze as his dark voice timbered through her. She glanced at him as she retracted her hand which started to tremble from the glacial look in his eyes. She'd forgotten about his cast in steel rule—never to touch without permission—in her eagerness to prove she'd be the one to win him over. Master Bear was known as one of the easy-going cousins of the seven owners of Castle Sin, an exclusive BDSM club on the privately-owned, The Seven Keys Island, in Key West—until you rubbed him the wrong way.

"I apologize, Master Bear. I never meant to be disrespectful," she murmured with lowered eyes and stood in the Castle Sin present position with her hands behind her back, feet spread apart, and her shoulders straight with tits pushed forward.

Kane Sinclair felt listless. The demonstration he just had with Cleopatra had been intense and ended in an explosive climax. Not that it mattered. He still felt charged. His cock at half-mast was an indication that yet again, he hadn't achieved the mind-blowing climaxes he used to with ...

"Fuck," he cursed the unwanted memory searing through his mind, like a burning ember that just wouldn't die no matter how hard he had tried over the past sixteen years. He turned his gaze to the petite blonde submissive, waiting on his wrath.

"What's your position here at Castle Sin, Cleopatra?" His voice slashed like the cutting edge of a knife through the air. She visibly trembled and licked her lips nervously.

"I'm an employed submissive, Master Bear."

"Yes, and that means you're here to serve whom?"

Her chin lowered an inch more, her voice into a whisper. "The paying members of Castle Sin, Master Bear."

"Then I suggest you go back to The Dungeon of Sin and do just that."

Kane didn't feel anything at the surprise that flashed in her eyes. He didn't appreciate manipulative submissives, those who tried to top from the bottom, like Cleopatra subtly attempted. Sometimes getting old was a fucking nuisance. Every submissive and trainee was careful not to sass him and Shane, the oldest two of the seven Sinclair, aka Rothman, cousins as they were known in Tinsel town as actors. Probably because they had the reputation of dishing out harsh punishments.

That was part of the bullshit listlessness he felt. He loved brats, cheeky subs who weren't scared to push his boundaries, willing to take a chance, no matter the repercussions. That was the kind of challenge he missed. Training the Doms and submissives fulfilled him to an extent but on a personal level, he had yet to hit the mark.

Like Stone and Hawk had with the two cousins, Peyton, and Savannah, whom they'd fallen in love with. Cheeky as they come and challenging their mighty Masters fearlessly.

"Do you mean ... aren't you going to punish me, Master Bear?" Cleopatra asked with a mixture of fear and excitement in her voice.

"No, I'm not, but if you insist, I'll ask Master Fox to take care of it in my stead."

Cleopatra's wary gaze flickered to Shane Sinclair, the oldest of the cousins, who sauntered closer. She retreated a couple of steps. Master Fox was the one Dom she walked circles around. His reputation of wielding two whips simultaneously in both hands was well known.

"That won't be necessary, Master Bear. Thank you for choosing me for the demonstration. I had a lot of fun."

Kane didn't respond. She quickly made herself scarce as Shane reached the bar and slipped onto the barstool next to him. He didn't look at Shane as he sipped on the rich, dark flavor of the single malt McMillan whiskey he'd been nursing for a while.

"Where's your mind at, Kane?" Shane studied him for a moment. He didn't miss the rigid line of his jaw or the impassive expression. "Even during the scene, you made the sub fly, but I got the impression that you weren't in it. Not like you're supposed to be."

"You're right. I shouldn't have done the demonstration." His eyes drifted to the couple to his right. Peyton Jackson, Stone's sub, faced off against him, her foot tapping in frustration as she stabbed a stiff finger against his chest.

Stone's deep rumble reached their ears. "Ah, Petals, I love it when your bratty mouth lands you smack in the middle of punishment."

"I guess I'm tired of floating between subs." Kane shrugged as he turned his attention back to

Shane. "Since Stone and Hawk found their proverbial birds of a feather, I've felt myself searching." He glanced at Shane. "I want what they have, Shane, and not just any permanent sub, the kind of woman they found—cheeky, bratty, and challenging. That's what I'm after." He sighed. "Besides, I can't allow the past to keep haunting me. I'm fucking tired of walking the path alone."

"I've waited over sixteen years to hear you say that." Shane squeezed his shoulder. "Neither of us ..." Shane swallowed visibly as he found his mind floundering into chambers that had been off limits for an equal number of years. "We're too fucking old to compete with these young studs."

"Old, my ass. In case you haven't noticed, we're the only Masters every sub here, no matter their age, tries to lure to their bed for the night."

"There's much to be said for experience." Shane chuckled. "Is that what Cleopatra was after?"

"What else?" Kane swallowed the last of his drink. "You know what's the worst of it, Shane? Of becoming so entrenched with our acting careers, fame, and fortune?" He tapped his finger on the counter, indicating a refill before he looked at Shane. "Being fatherless. I've always wanted children, a daughter, and a son ... for that we're too fucking old. No woman over forty will be willing to have a baby and I'm not interested in younger women ... not as a wife."

"It's the same void I feel. A wife and children." Shane's voice sounded whimsical. He accepted the drink the bartender handed him and took a sip. "You know we only have ourselves to blame. Instead of using the time between movie productions to find someone, we buried ourselves in the war zones accepting covert black ops."

"It was the only way I could cope ... and forget." Kane's eyes filled with sadness. "I suppose it was watching that bastard, Decker Cooper, who caused Savannah so much pain, burn to death that unchained the memories and this feeling of ... I don't know ... need."

"It had to be done. He'd have found a way to avoid jail again and he would've continued tormenting Hawk and Savannah," Shane said silently.

As the oldest cousins of the family, they took protecting and caring for them and their loved ones very seriously. No one had been there for them all those years ago and they'd sworn to keep their family safe. Decker Cooper was the scum of the earth who had enriched himself with human trafficking. It was at his hands that Savannah Thorne, Hawk's sub, had ended up as a sex slave for a year to the feared leader of the Russian Bratva. He had to pay, and they made sure he'd never hurt anyone again. Neither of them felt any remorse for the horrid death they'd bestowed on the man. It had been deserved.

Kane nursed his drink between his hands. "But it was too quick. He should've died a slow torturous death."

"At least he suffered until his dying breath." Shane hesitated briefly, knowing why torching, and watching the bastard burn alive had been haunting Kane. "Have you ever visited her grave?"

For a moment, the question hung heavy between them.

"For what? It's not as if that's where her body is buried. It's an empty fucking coffin, Shane. No. I didn't attend the funeral and I'll never go to the grave." Kane got up. His expression turned somber. "And let's not fool ourselves. We didn't go searching for a woman because we never got over losing the ones we had."

"In my case, I was the fool." Shane got up and caught Kane's eyes with an earnest look. "Narine would never have wanted you to be alone for this long. It's about time, Kane. Way past time."

"I'm done for the night. I'm going to—"

"Oh, hell no. You're coming to the dungeon with me. Who knows, there might be one of the trainees or subs we've overlooked that might be perfect for either of us."

"Who are you trying to fool, Shane? You want to check if Stone's PA is playing tonight." Kane chuckled and forced the tiredness off his shoulders as they walked toward The Dungeon of Sin.

"You can't deny Alexa looks rather scrumptious on a Saint Andrew's Cross." Shane's eyes glimmered. "I have a feeling about that one, Kane. She tickles something inside me that I haven't felt in a long time."

"So, go for it."

"Soon ... for now, I'm enjoying playing cat and mouse too much."

Kane laughed as they entered the Torture Chamber, and he found his eyes searching the room. He was startled when he realized what he was doing.

"Fuck me," he grunted.

"What?" Shane looked around and followed his gaze that was riveted on a scene in the far corner. "Sub RL? What's ... ah! I see," he smiled. "So, you already found what you sought."

"I only just realized that I search for her every time I walk into one of the dungeons. It's like my eyes automatically zoom in on her, like my mind connects with her before I know where she is."

"She's a beautiful woman, and if I recall correctly, mid-forties? Perfect age for you."

"Hmm ... problem is, the moment I walk into a room or approach her, she clamps shut and runs in the opposite direction. She hardly ever looks directly at me. I get the impression she deliberately avoids getting close to me."

"Well, unfortunately for her, as of tomorrow, she won't have a choice. She'll be up close and personal in your training dungeon for a month."

"Perfect timing, I'd say," Kane chuckled. "You find your little mouse, Shane. I'm going to mosey over there and see what the fuss is all about."

Eyes turned to watch Kane as he strolled through the Torture Chamber. A regular occurrence, as the subs were magnetically drawn to the powerful Master who exuded confidence by his mere presence. He was the perfect portrayal of the bear totem, his spiritual animal. Always equanimous, he reflected qualities of emotional strength and fearlessness. Everyone was in awe of the subtle way he projected it to others. He had become a grounding force for many subs over the years as he guided them to find their inner submissive, embrace it, and become the best they could be.

"Just what gave you the right, sub? No wait, you're not a submissive of the club, you're still a trainee, according to the red band on your wrist." The irate voice of a Dom Kane didn't recognize, grated in his ears as he approached. His eyes narrowed as sub RL slammed her fists on her hips and tossed back her hair.

Blatant disrespect, sub RL? You should know better by now.

His gaze followed the luxurious curtain of chestnut tresses tumbling down her back. She was the kind of woman that other females of all ages loved to hate. She was forty-four, if memory served him correctly, but she had the exuberance of youth enhanced by her poise and a sexy strut that exuded confidence. She was tall, probably five-foot-seven, and a little on the plump side but with a perfectly curved body and gorgeously rounded hips that he'd witnessed made many Doms stop in their tracks and stare. He halted a couple of steps behind her, accessing her profile as she turned her head to the Dom scowling at her. His fingers itched to trace the line of her high cheekbones, to feel if her skin was as smooth and silky as it looked in its flawless perfection. Apart from the small laugh lines around her eyes, she didn't show any signs of her age. Her breathtaking beauty was enhanced by the intelligence and confidence she always radiated, which was the conduit of his attraction to her.

Her rosy lips glistened as she licked them once, pursed the fullness into a pout and took a deep breath.

"I might be a trainee here, but I've been a submissive for a long time and I'm not an idiot."

Kane's ears pricked as she openly sassed the angry Dom. Her voice had a scratchy roughness that caused his cock to twitch delightfully. His instincts about Rose Lovett had been spot on. This was the kind of woman he'd been searching for.

"You are indeed if you think I'm going to stand for a sub talking to me like that," the Dom sneered.

"I don't care but I'll not stand by and allow this scene to continue."

"Really?" The Dom turned to the small gathering of people behind him. "Did someone hear this sub use her safeword? No, she didn't and—"

"Because she's in too much pain to even think! Anyone can see that sub is in distress." Rose pointed furiously toward a woman on a spanking bench, crying pitifully. Her naked buttocks were covered in vicious red streaks.

Kane's curse exploded into the atmosphere as his gaze found the target of her stiff finger. All attention centered on him. He rushed forward and with two economic yanks, the sub was loose. He assisted her upright and held her shivering form against his chest.

"I'm sorry, Master Bear, I should've used my safeword, but I couldn't get out a word. I was too shocked and in so much pain." She gulped back a sob. "We agreed on a medium flogging not ... not what he did."

"It's over, Violet. I've got you." His deep voice soothed even the people who had gathered once the spectacle began.

"Master Bear, is it? Well, I demand to punish this trainee for interrupting my scene, not to mention her blatant disrespect toward me."

Kane turned to face the fuming man, his expression stoic as he stared at him. The Dom puffed up his chest and straightened his bulky form as he met Kane's brown eyes that glimmered like sunlight shining through whiskey.

"You don't deserve respect," Rose all but spat in his direction. Her eyes fell to the floor the moment Kane's head turned in her direction.

"We'll discuss this matter in my office." Kane looked around in search of Dom Evans, one of the senior Doms and training managers at Castle Sin Training Academy. He gestured to him. "Dom Evans, please take care of Violet. I'll be back to check on her in a bit."

Kane brushed the tears from her cheeks and smiled encouragingly at her. "Dom Evans will rub some arnica and the Castle's special soothing gel on to give you some relief." He frowned in thought. Violet had been an employed submissive at the

Castle for the past ten months. She was well liked and had five years of experience behind her. "Was anyone present when you discussed the scene, Violet?"

"Yes, Master Bear. I requested Dom Danton to be there, seeing as I don't know this Dom and I felt I needed some reassurance."

"Good girl. Now, go with Dom Evans." Kane turned to the irate man who steamed angrily as he watched Evans pick Violet up and carry her toward the aftercare area. "I don't believe we've met?" The distrust gathered like clouds before a thunderstorm in Kane's eyes as he stared at him unflinchingly.

They were very strict about visitors. Only an exclusive member could request to sponsor a guest. Even then, they were first screened, and a background check ran before permission was given.

"I'm Dom Gunther Locke from Tampa." His nose inched higher to indicate he deemed himself to be a man of importance.

"Who is your sponsor, Dom Gunther?" Kane's voice grated darkly from his lips. He didn't appreciate people riding high on personally induced self-importance.

Kane's hand snaked out to catch Rose's arm as she tried to edge unobtrusively away from the scene. She froze as his fingers wrapped around her elbow. Her surprised gasp floated toward him. It was a musical melody that offered him immense pleasure. Sub RL wasn't as unmoved by his presence as he'd believed. He dragged her against his side.

"Senator Martin," Dom Gunther crowed with another flash of blustering opinionism.

"Shall we go?" Kane started to walk. His hand tightened around Rose's arm as she hung back. He flicked a warning glance over his shoulder. "Is there a problem, sub RL?"

"No, Master Bear. I just don't see why I need to accompany you."

"Then you're in bigger trouble than you could imagine," he rasped.

"Me? Why the devil am I in trouble? I'm not the one who—"

Rose all but swallowed her tongue as he turned on her and she walked slam bang into his hard chest. Her hands spread out to push away from him. Her breathing faltered, her muscles locked, and she couldn't move, no matter how hard her brain screamed at her to.

Damn, he's so warm. How can he be this warm all over?

Kane held out his hand and clicked his fingers. Jenna, a club coordinator, placed a thin chain in his palm. She always served him when he was in attendance at the member dungeons.

"Hands behind your back, sub RL and make sure they stay there." He clipped one end of the chain into the O-ring of the red leather collar all trainees wore. The other end he attached to a loop of his pants. It irritated him that she didn't look at him but kept her gaze centered on his chest. "Keep up, my pet, and I suggest your mouth stay shut unless I specifically ask you question. Is that understood?"

"Yes, *Sir*," Rose snapped to attention, her eyes flared as she clamped her hands behind her.

Crack! Crack!

"Freaking hell ... oww," she wailed as his huge paw connected with her ass. She had no idea how he even managed to reach seeing as he stood facing her.

"What did you call me, sub RL?"

Her cheeks bloomed red, and she couldn't even pretend it had been a slip of the tongue. It had been deliberate. An attempt to ...

What? An attempt to make a complete ass of yourself, Rose? Not to mention a freaking scorching ass as reward!

"I'm sorry! I meant Master Bear," she squealed and stepped out of reach as his hand rose threateningly when she didn't respond quick enough.

"What's the hold-up?" Gunther Locke sneered behind Kane. "I came here to play and—"

Kane took off, ignoring the complaining man, with Rose tagging along behind him, muttering all the way about his inconsideration for not shortening his steps.

"You're ratcheting up the punishments, sub. I suggest you zip your lips and quickly."

Kane stopped next to Stone where he was overseeing a whipping demonstration by one of the assistant training Doms.

"I have a situation with a visiting Dom. Apparently, Senator Martin is his sponsor. Know anything about it?"

Stone's eyes flicked to the man approaching. "Yes, but the condition was that he had to be accompanied by Senator Martin at all times. Do you need me to take care of this?"

"No, I'll handle it. Please ask Senator Martin and Danton to join us in my office." He looked around. "Find out who the Dungeon Monitor on duty in this section is, Stone. If he had been doing his job, this wouldn't have gone as far as it did."

"I agree. I'll take care of it."

Kane continued toward his office, leaving Rose no choice but to jog to keep up with his long strides. He sat down behind the desk and tugged on the chain.

"Down. On your knees next to my chair, please."

Her eyes widened as he pointed to a spot next to him. He noticed that she still managed to keep from looking directly at him when she said in an indignant sputter, "You expect me to sit on the floor like a ... like a ..."

"A well-behaved pet." His voice sounded as smooth as silk. "Yes, sub RL, I do." The wicked smile quirking his lips was in reaction to her delightful brattiness, exactly what he'd been missing from other subs and trainees of Castle Sin.

To Rose, it was anything but a pleasant smile and it promised all kinds of *Dom* retribution. Just thinking of the punishment scenes she'd witnessed from him, made her legs crumble and she plopped onto her knees without any attempt at grace.

"It's a good thing you're in my training dungeon as from tomorrow. It seems you have a lot to learn about decorum and elegance."

She opened her mouth to snap at him, but the timely arrival of Dom Gunther saved her from plunging herself deeper into trouble.

Find the sensational story of Kane and Rose here: https://books2read.com/CS3-Kane

Books by Linzi Basset

Louisiana Daddies
Covert Daddy – Prequel
Black Ops Daddy – Book 1

Grace's Initiation
The Interview – Prequel
S is for Safeword – Book 1

The Guzun Trilogy
Vadim – Book 1
Vanya – Book 2
Arian – Book 3

Decadent Sins Series
Dominant Nature – Book 1
Dominant Desire – Book 2
Dominant Demand – Book 3
Dominant Thrills – Book 4
Dominant Mercy – Book 5

Castle Sin Series
Hunter - Prequel
Stone – Book 1
Hawk – Book 2
Kane – Book 3
Ace – Book 4
Parker – Book 5
Zeke – Book 6
Shane – Book 7

Danton – Book 8
Billy & Mongo – Book 9
Peyton – Book 10

Club Devil's Cove Series
His Devil's Desire – Book 1
His Devil's Heat – Book 2
His Devil's Wish – Book 3
His Devil's Mercy – Book 4
His Devil's Chains – Book 5
His Devil's Fire – Book 6
Her Devil's Kiss – Book 7
His Devil's Rage – Book 8
The Devil's Christmas – Book 9
The Devilish Santa – Book 10

Club Wicked Cove Series
Desperation: Ceejay's Absolution–Book 1
Desperation: Colt's Acquittal – Book 2
Exploration: Nolan's Regret – Book 3
Merciful: Seth's Revenge – Book 4
Claimed: Parnell's Gift – Book 5
Decadent: Kent's Desire – Book 6
Wicked and Fearless – Box Set, Books 1 – 3
Wicked and Deadly – Box Set, Books 4 - 6

Club Alpha Cove Series
His FBI Sub – Book 1
His Ice Baby Sub – Book 2
His Vanilla Sub – Book 3
His Fiery Sub – Book 4
His Sassy Sub – Book 5

Their Bold Sub – Book 6
His Brazen Sub – Book 7
His Defiant Sub – Book 8
His Forever Sub – Book 9
His Cherished Sub – Book 10
For Amy – Their Beloved Sub – Book 11

The Bleeding Souls Trilogy
Kiss the Devil - Prequel

The Stiletto PI Series
Fierce Paxton – Book 1
Fiery Jordan – Book 2

Billionaire Bad Boys Romance
Road Trip
Rogue Cowboy

Dark Desire Novels
Enforcer – Book 1

Their Sub Novella Series
No Option – Book 1
Done For – Book 2
For This – Book 3
Their Sub Series Boxset

Their Command Series
Say Yes – Book 1
Say Please – Book 2
Say Now – Book 3
Their Command Series Boxset

Romance Suspense

The Bride Series
Claimed Bride – Book 1
Captured Bride – Book 2
Chosen Bride – Book 3
Charmed Bride – Book 4

Caught Series
Caught in Between
Caught in His Web

The Tycoon Series
The Tycoon and His Honey Pot
The Tycoon's Blondie
The Tycoon's Mechanic

Standalone Titles
Her Prada Cowboy
Never Leave Me, Baby
Now is Our Time
The Wildcat that Tamed the Tycoon
The Poet's Lover
Sarah: The Life of Me
Axle's Darkness

Naughty Christmas Stories
Her Santa Dom
Master Santa
Snowflake's Spanking

Box sets

A Santa to Love – with Isabel James
Christmas Delights – with Isabel James
Unwrapped Hearts – with Isabel James

Books written as Kimila Taylor
Paranormal Books
Guardian's Spell
Zaluc's Mate
Slade: Blood Moon
Azriel: Rebel Angel

Books Co-Written as Isabel James

Zane Gordon Novels
Truth Untold

The Crow's Nest
A journey of discovery on the White Pearl

Christmas Novellas
Santa's Kiss
Santa's Whip
Mistletoe Bride

Poetry Bundle by Linzi Basset & James Calderaro
Love Unbound - Poems of the Heart

About the Author

"Isn't it a universal truth that it's our singular experiences and passion, for whatever thing or things, which molds us all into the individuals we become? Whether it's hidden in the depths of our soul or exposed for all to see?"

Linzi Basset is a South African born animal rights supporter with a poet's heart, and she is also a bestselling fiction writer of suspense-filled romance erotica books; who as the latter, refuses to be bound to any one sub-genre. She prefers instead to stretch herself as a storyteller which has resulted in her researching and writing historical and even paranormal themed works.

Her initial offering: Club Alpha Cove, a BDSM club suspense series released back in 2015, reached Amazon's Bestseller list, and she has been on those lists ever since. Labelling her as prolific is a gross understatement as just a few short years later she has now been published over fifty times; a total which excludes the other published works of her alter ego: Isabel James who co-authors.

"I write from the inside out. My stories are both inside me and a part of me, so it can be either pleasurable to release them or painful to carve them out. I live every moment of every story I write. So, if you're looking for spicy and suspenseful, I'm your girl ... woman ... writer ... you know what I mean!"

Linzi believes that by telling stories in her own

voice, she can better share with her readers the essence of her being: her passionate nature; her motivations; and her wildest fantasies. She feels every touch as she writes, every kiss, every harsh word uttered, and this to her is the key to a never-ending love of writing.

Ultimately, all books by Linzi Basset are about passion. To her, passion is the driving force of all emotion; whether it be lust, desire, hate, trust, or love. This is the underlying message contained in her books. Her advice: "Believe in the passions driving your desires; live them; enjoy them; and allow them to bring you happiness."

Stalk Linzi Basset

If you'd like to look me up, please follow any of these links.

While you're enjoying some of my articles, interviews, and poems on my website, why not subscribe to my Newsletter and be the first to know about new releases and win free books? You will also receive a free eBook copy of The Interview and The Poet's Lover.

Go to my website,

www.linzibassetauthor.com, and while you're

there, subscribe to her newsletter:

https://www.linzibassetauthor.com/subscribe

Find all my social links and follow me here:
https://linktr.ee/LinziBasset

Don't forget to join my fan group, Linzi's Reading Nook, for loads of fun!

Don't be shy, pay me a visit, anytime!

Made in United States
Orlando, FL
01 August 2023

35667788R00328